4/20

A FIBER FIB

She struck a model's pose, there in the doorway, showing off a jacket made from indigo fabric as dark and lucent as a midnight sky—Granny's signature dye color and one that's very difficult to achieve consistently. The jacket narrowed slightly at Nicki's waist, then flared with a short peplum. It was beautiful, though it would need taking in a bit to fit her perfectly . . .

"Do you mind if I . . ."

"Touch it? Of course not," Nicki said. "Wipe your fingers first, though, would you?"

"Nicki!" Debbie sounded scandalized. "Kath knows more about handling textiles than any of us. She's a professional whatchamacallit."

Being a polite, as well as professional, textile preservationist, I didn't laugh at Debbie's flub of my credentials or bridle at Nicki's precaution. I smiled at both, carefully wiped my hands on a clean napkin, and touched the jacket at the sleeve and shoulder. Granny's dyed and woven raw silk. I felt like petting it. I must have sighed.

"Oh, I know what you mean," Nicki said. "I was so touched when Ivy gave it to me."

"She did?" For a second, everything in the room stopped. Sound ceased. Movements froze. There was nothing but my hands on the jacket and Nicki's smile after telling me my grandmother had given it to her. I didn't know what had happened. And I didn't know how. But I knew, absolutely, that Nicki was lying . . .

LAST WOOL
and
TESTAMENT

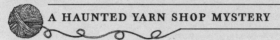

A HAUNTED YARN SHOP MYSTERY

Molly MacRae

AN OBSIDIAN MYSTERY

OBSIDIAN
Published by New American Library, a division of
Penguin Group (USA) Inc., 375 Hudson Street,
New York, New York 10014, USA
Penguin Group (Canada), 90 Eglinton Avenue East, Suite 700, Toronto,
Ontario M4P 2Y3, Canada (a division of Pearson Penguin Canada Inc.)
Penguin Books Ltd., 80 Strand, London WC2R 0RL, England
Penguin Ireland, 25 St. Stephen's Green, Dublin 2,
Ireland (a division of Penguin Books Ltd.)
Penguin Group (Australia), 250 Camberwell Road, Camberwell, Victoria 3124,
Australia (a division of Pearson Australia Group Pty. Ltd.)
Penguin Books India Pvt. Ltd., 11 Community Centre, Panchsheel Park,
New Delhi - 110 017, India
Penguin Group (NZ), 67 Apollo Drive, Rosedale, Auckland 0632,
New Zealand (a division of Pearson New Zealand Ltd.)
Penguin Books (South Africa) (Pty.) Ltd., 24 Sturdee Avenue,
Rosebank, Johannesburg 2196, South Africa

Penguin Books Ltd., Registered Offices:
80 Strand, London WC2R 0RL, England

First published by Obsidian, an imprint of New American Library,
a division of Penguin Group (USA) Inc.

First Printing, September 2012
10 9 8 7 6 5 4 3 2

PUBLISHER'S NOTE
This is a work of fiction. Names, characters, places, and incidents either are the
product of the author's imagination or are used fictitiously, and any resemblance to
actual persons, living or dead, business establishments, events, or locales is entirely
coincidental.
    The publisher does not have any control over and does not assume any responsi-
bility for author or third-party Web sites or their content.

ALWAYS LEARNING   PEARSON

For Mom and Dad,
who gave my life warp, weft, and words.

Jane Canby MacRae
James Lawrence Woodward MacRae

ACKNOWLEDGMENTS

This book wouldn't be here without the amazing kindness one finds in the mystery-writing community. Thanks especially to Linda Landrigan, Cynthia Manson, and Sandra Harding for opportunities and encouragement. Thanks to Janice Harrington, Betsy Hearne, and Sarah Wisseman. I'm grateful for your sharp eyes and good ears, but your friendship means even more. Thanks also to the people, buildings, streets, and history of Jonesborough and Johnson City, Tennessee. You've shaped my writing world and don't seem to mind my detours and embellishments. Thank you to the members of the Champaign Urbana Spinners & Weavers Guild, who let me sit among them taking notes. And thank you to my friends at the Champaign Public Library, who will find themselves in these pages, some more blatantly than others. Your generosity exemplifies the beauty of those who work to put books in people's hands. And thank you always to my Mike.

LAST WOOL
and
TESTAMENT

Chapter 1

It wasn't how I'd planned to spend my thirty-ninth birth-day, driving like a crazed woman from Richmond, Vir-ginia, to a cemetery in the mountains of east Tennessee. But I straightened the curves and flattened the verdant hills along I-81 through the Shenandoah Valley with sac-rilegious fervor, willing both my car and myself not to break down. Tears and taking a hand off the wheel long enough to hunt for Kleenex at that speed would be disas-trous.

I stopped for gas outside Abingdon, not waiting for the receipt to print before burning back up the entrance ramp.

Over the state line, a blur of miles into Tennessee and a few switchbacks from my destination, it looked as though I'd get there in time, when what to my wondering eyes should appear but flashing red lights in the rearview mirror? Then my ears caught the wailing siren that went with the lights and my record of never in my life having received a speeding ticket was toast. I pulled over, shut the engine off, rested my forehead on the steering wheel, and waited.

"Ma'am."

I tried to dredge up a calming image or some Zen-ish phrase that might help me get through the next however-many-minutes this was going to take and back on the road without falling apart. Nothing in particular came to mind.

The officer knocked on the window. "Ma'am?"

"Oh, sorry." He couldn't hear me. I lowered the window. "Sorry, sorry. I've never done this before. I'm so sorry."

"Well, ma'am, it looks to me like you've got the speeding part of it down as good as any expert. What I need for you to do now is hand me your license and then keep your hands where I can see them."

"It's in my purse," I said, pointing to my bag on the passenger seat. "In my wallet. May I get it out?"

He gave a curt nod and I very slowly, very carefully reached over.

He coughed and I jumped.

"There's a remarkable difference between sudden moves and glacial ones," he offered.

"Oh, right." I handed over my wallet, then didn't know what to do with my hands so he could see them and my license at the same time. I noticed my hands were shaking, though, and wished I could sit on them to still them. I tried to read the name over his pocket, but between his height and my jitters I wasn't able to make it out.

"Officer, I'm sorry . . ."

"Deputy. It's Deputy Cole Dunbar." Deputy Dunbar would have been intimidating even without the height. There was a lot of muscle on his frame and nothing soft about him. Not the stereotypical paunch of a middle-aged lawman, no brush of a moustache to take the edge off the set lips. There might have been smile lines at the corners of his eyes, but his face appeared to be as starched as his khaki and brown uniform.

"Deputy Dunbar, I'm very sorry I was driving over the speed limit . . ."

"Twenty miles per hour over the speed limit."

"Oh my God. Really?" My God, I'd been driving like

an idiot. "Um, Deputy Dunbar, I don't know if it makes any difference, but I'm on my way to my grandmother's funeral, and I'm running late and I really need to be there because she's all I had left. Ivy McClellan. Did you know her?" Now I was babbling like an idiot but I couldn't stop. "She owned the Weaver's Cat, down on Main Street, in Blue Plum. The little shop at one end of the row house there, with the yarn and wool and weaving and all? Ivy McClellan. She was my grandmother."

Some of the starch left Dunbar's face. I wasn't sure the flash of recognition in his eyes improved anything, but maybe invoking Granny's name had eased the situation. Maybe his wife or mother or a teenaged daughter was one of Granny's devoted customers. Maybe he was. Maybe I'd be lucky and he'd tear up at her memory, then tear up the ticket he was scribbling and give me an escort to the cemetery.

"You're Crazy Ivy's granddaughter?"

"What?" Seems I was wrong about easing the situation.

"If nothing else, by your size, I can see the resemblance. Little bitty red-haired thing like you shouldn't be going so fast." He glanced at my license again. "Ms. Rutledge, is it? You slow down, Ms. Rutledge, or you'll end up in the cemetery sleeping next to Crazy Ivy. Hey, now, are you feeling all right?"

Little bitty thing like me might have been growling and ready to bite. I closed my eyes and took a deep breath. "Her name was Ivy McClellan. She was a kind, caring, generous woman and a wonderful human being."

"And some folks called her Crazy Ivy. Didn't you know that? Well, you're from way up north there in Illinois, so maybe you didn't."

Actually, I did, but I didn't think a sheriff's deputy ought to be calling her that on the day we buried her. "I spent plenty of summers here with her and never saw or heard anything from anyone but love and respect for her."

"And I'm sure plenty of people will miss her and are sorry she's passed on," he said. "I just think it was mighty convenient for her that she did."

"I beg your pardon?"

"Her death. Convenient. As in good timing."

With those jaw-dropping statements, he handed me the ticket along with my license. Then he stood, chest puffed out, hands on hips, waiting for me to continue sedately on my way, duly chastised and contrite.

Being pulled over by an insulting, insensitive oaf of a sheriff's deputy wasn't in my happy birthday plans, either. I sat for another moment, memorizing his face in my side mirror, promising myself that never would I or any of my children, should I have any, ever consider procreating with the likes of, or a close relative to, Cole Dunbar.

I started the car, wishing it could backfire and belch black smoke on command. As Deputy Clod disappeared behind me, the fresh green Tennessee mountain air flowed through my open window, providing aromatherapy of the simplest kind. Grief washed over me again, replacing anger. I followed the road down through a wooded hollow, across the single-lane bridge over Little Buncombe Creek, and around the last bends of cracked and faded asphalt climbing Embree Hill. The final stretch passed in another blur, this one not due to excessive speed.

Then there were the wrought-iron gates, standing open like welcoming arms. I hesitated, wiped my eyes. Now that I could make out the burial party in the distance, farther up the hill, urgency took over again. Not checking to see whether Clod loomed behind me, I scattered gravel with a final burst of speed up the cemetery's winding drive.

I left the car door hanging open and ran to join the others, knowing I was late, hoping they'd waited. I got there in time to see my grandmother's ashes lowered into the grave. Pressing one hand to the stitch in my side, I held the other to my mouth and finally let the tears come.

No, it wasn't the way I'd planned to spend my thirty-ninth birthday. Then again, it wasn't the way Granny had planned to spend it, either.

Chapter 2

Granny might not have planned *when* she'd go, which was a month after her own birthday. Eighty was a fine age, by any standard, to still be competently in charge of one's own business and living alone, but it wasn't the ninety or one hundred Granny had hoped to see. Nor had she anticipated *how* she would go—walloped to the floor by a massive heart attack. She'd been feeling puny, as she called it, and the doctors concluded she'd had a sneaky, silent heart attack that left her feeling out of sorts but otherwise unaware of the damage or danger.

But Ivy McClellan was an organizer and she knew exactly *what* she wanted to happen after her death. She left instructions with her lawyer, the funeral home, her longtime store manager, and me, her only living close relative. The gist of those instructions: cremation, no funeral, minimal burial service, and no plastic flowers, *ever*, on her grave.

Her plans were meticulous and complete, so when I was walloped to the floor myself, by the phone call telling me she was suddenly and unexpectedly gone, I was able to get my feet back under me by burying myself for a few more days in the textile evaluation I was doing for a small museum in Richmond before charging down to Blue Plum.

I'd meant to be up by five thirty, on the road by six.

That didn't happen, and between the late start, construction delays, and the very annoying stop for speeding, I missed most of Granny's minimal burial service. I heard the final words, spoken after the ashes were lowered, through sobs I muffled with a wad of Kleenex. After the conclusion, and after pulling myself mostly back together, I saw what a nice-size crowd had made the trip out from town to this pretty hillside to see Granny off.

She'd told me she chose this cemetery, Oak Grove, because of the view. She hadn't liked the cemetery closer to town. That one was convenient, but it ran along the highway like a bedraggled bit of rickrack, squeezed between the new jail and the county nursing home, neither one a joyful prospect for eternal contemplation. In Granny's estimation, Oak Grove was more like it. From this hill, with its scattering of sheltering trees, you could see the classic setup of the mountains. Ridge behind ridge behind ridge, like an appliquéd quilt, each layer of hills a deeper color, from jade to emerald to cyan to amethyst, the last disappearing into an indigo so black you could imagine infinity.

"Kath, honey, you held yourself together real well." Ardis Buchanan brought me back from that infinity with her forgiving lie. Then she drew me into her honeysuckle embrace.

I murmured something even I couldn't quite hear. Ardis was a foot taller than I and her hugs were all-encompassing. She was Granny's store manager and had worked at the Weaver's Cat for as long as I could remember. Granny nimble and spry, Ardis solid, steady, and always smelling of honeysuckle.

At the point where I might have had to gasp for air, Ardis let me go, then whispered, "I know she didn't want any fuss, but some of us are having a little wake down at the shop after we leave here, and we need you there."

"Why the sotto voce?" I whispered back. "Are you

afraid she's listening and will find out you're already bucking her instructions?"

"I'm afraid the Spiveys will hear and crash the party." Ardis tipped her head toward three women who had the funeral director cornered behind an ornate pink granite headstone. Neil Taylor nodded to whatever they were saying, his solemn face polite. Only his crossed arms hinted at impatience, or maybe resignation.

"The twins and who else?" I recognized Shirley and Mercy. They were well past sixty, with married names decades old, but in Blue Plum they were still, and always would be, the Spivey twins. They were also Granny's cousins, once or twice removed. Or, as Granny often said, the further removed, the better, bless their hearts.

"The third one is Angela," Ardis said. I must have looked blank. "Mercy's daughter."

"Really?" Angela looked to be about my age, but she wasn't familiar to me. "Did I know the twins had children?"

"Possibly not," Ardis said. "You know Ivy wasn't one to spread bad news."

"Ardis."

"What? I'm not speaking ill of the dead. Actually, I think there might be hope for Angela. Used to be, you could call her Mercy Junior, but after she married she got herself a little tattoo. I don't know if she's ever officially told her mama, but if she bends over it's hard to miss."

"Tattoo of what?"

"I'm not entirely sure. That's an area of Angie I've never wanted to stare at. But here, now, I'll let you go. Other people are waiting."

"Thanks, Ardis." I gave her another quick hug that felt like home. "Can we talk later?" I was remembering my encounter with Deputy Dunbar. I'd decided to be charitable and not blame him for slamming the brakes on my mad dash to the cemetery. He was only doing his duty. But I wasn't about to forget his bizarre remarks about the timing of Granny's death, or his attitude toward her. Ardis would know, if anyone did, where that came from.

"We'll talk at the shop, hon. And it looks like later might be sooner."

She was right. The breeze was picking up, dark clouds moving in. The farthest ridges were blacker yet, wilder and foreboding.

"Kath?"

I took another look at the sky, then refocused on the person in front of me. Nicki Keplinger stood there, dabbing her eyes.

"You look so sweet, Kath." Nicki was another of Granny's employees. She'd been at the shop a couple of years. She was in her late twenties, my height but boyishly slim. According to Granny, she was also bright and dynamic, with a good grasp of e-tail possibilities. I didn't know her as well as I knew Ardis, but Granny sang praise of her ambitions for the business. She grabbed my hand now and pressed it between both of hers, bending her head toward mine so we were nose to nose and looking into each other's eyes. Hers were red from crying, as mine must certainly have been. Her dark hair swung forward and brushed my cheeks, making me more claustrophobic than Ardis' enveloping hug.

"Ivy and her gifts will be sorely missed," she said, "but all anyone will ever have to do is look at you and they'll think they're seeing her all over again, you favor her so much. Except for your age, of course, because she was your grandmother and you're younger. Though I believe you are older than I am, aren't you?"

"Nicki?" I took a half step back, wondering where her level head had disappeared to.

She clapped her hands over her mouth and burst into tears. Debbie Keith and I watched Ardis lead her away.

Debbie rounded out Granny's staff, working part-time at the shop and more than full-time raising sheep on her farm, out in the county, along the Little Buck River. She was only a couple of years older than Nicki, but always struck me as closer to my own age. Granny said they both brought energy to the store and complemented each other. Nicki was her sprite—all fizz and imagination. Debbie was her young earth mother—grounded and full of common sense. "Nicki hasn't been herself since she found Ivy," Debbie said.

"Nicki found her? Oh, poor thing."

"Truly awful. It's given her nightmares. I don't think she's ever lost anyone close that way before." Debbie had. I'd forgotten. Granny told me she'd lost her husband three or four years before, after only three years of marriage. Maybe that was one of the reasons Debbie seemed older.

She gazed after Ardis and Nicki, looking wretched, and shook her head. Then she sighed and nodded as if confirming that assessment of nightmares and death. I didn't feel capable of adding anything more eloquent. She gave me a quick hug and then followed Ardis to her car.

"People like to hug on us," Granny had told me once. "Something comes over them when emotions run high and short women are present, and unless you have the heart to nip it in the bud, you might as well get used to it." Granny tolerated hugs, generally, and she would have been proud of me that day. I exchanged them with people I knew somewhat from distant summers, and others I'd met during more sporadic visits in recent years, and with many more I'd rather have met with Granny standing beside me.

"Kath?" The woman holding her arms out to me now looked like one of those elegant, silver-haired models in ads for expensive retirement communities. "I'm Ruth Wood. Your grandmother bragged to me about your studies and career every chance she got. Congratulations on all you've accomplished."

"Ruth, yes, of course. The Homeplace, right?"

She nodded. "Ivy was so proud of you. I'm sorry it took this occasion for me to finally meet you."

"Did you know she called you 'the Elusive Ruth'"?

A laugh bubbled up from somewhere in Ruth. She looked as though she might be able to keep it down, but it spilled over and she gave in to it. "Oh," she finally said, "it breaks my heart. Ivy was one of my favorite people. But look at you—you don't need to be comforting me. I do have a message for you, though, from my husband. He was Ivy's lawyer."

"Handsome Homer?"

She laughed again. "Ivy was always right. Yes, well, 'Handsome' was horrified when he realized he needed to be in Knoxville today and couldn't be here."

"Granny wouldn't have minded."

"But he did. Anyway, he wanted you to know he expects to be back in time for your appointment tomorrow morning. And *I'd* like you to know that if you need anything, anything at all, while you're here, you can just call me." She took a business card from her purse and handed it to me. "The number for the Homeplace will reach me during the day. The cell will reach me anytime."

"You're very kind. Thank you, Ruth."

She shook her head. "She was a dear. I'm going to miss her."

As I tucked her card into a pocket, thunder rolled across the hills and the first fat drops of rain began to fall. Ruth touched my shoulder, looked at the sky, and ran to her car. There were people I hadn't greeted yet, including the Spivey trio. That was probably no loss, but I wanted to thank Neil Taylor, the funeral director. His faithful attention to Granny's instructions had eased my burden.

Another roll of thunder, and the rain came down in earnest. A few people waved before sprinting. I caught Neil Taylor's eye. He shooed me along and I obeyed. The car seat was already wet when I leapt inside, thanks to my earlier negligence in leaving the door open. I was about to pull away when Mr. Taylor materialized out of the rain and rapped on the window.

"You're getting soaked," I shouted, lowering the window a few inches and squinting against the rain pelting in.

"I won't melt. I have something for you." He leaned in close and quickly passed me an envelope wrapped in plastic. "From your grandmother."

"Thank you. Thank you for everything."

"She was one in a million. Don't let anyone tell you different."

"I won't." Wait a second. Why would they? But before I could ask him, he disappeared into the downpour.

I raised the window and looked at the package in my hand, recognizing Granny's forethought in the plastic wrapping. It was a cheery orange. Probably a rain wrapper she'd recycled from the *Blue Plum Bugle*. She liked to say if you could see the top of Banner Mountain that meant it would be raining soon. And if you couldn't see the top, then it already was.

From what I could see through the wrap, there wasn't anything special about the envelope. Just standard legal size. Several sentences in Granny's neat script stretched across the front. I shook the worst of the rain from the plastic and then unwrapped it, being careful of stray drips.

Kath, Dearie, don't open this envelope just yet. Find some time when you can be alone this evening. Fix yourself a cup of cocoa. You might as well add a nip, while you're at it. Then make yourself comfortable, read this letter, and remember, always, I am your loving Granny.

Cocoa with a nip? An interesting suggestion—and I didn't think she meant adding a dose of chili pepper to the drink. Was she telling me I'd require a little something supportive while reading and digesting the contents of this letter? The orange plastic caught my eye from where I'd dropped it on the floor. It didn't look quite as cheery now. More like orange for caution.

Ardis could probably shed some light on Deputy Dunbar's remarks, but this letter? I read Granny's instructions again. *Find some time when you can be alone this evening.* Hmm.

I tucked the envelope in my purse and headed into Blue Plum for the clandestine wake at the Weaver's Cat.

Every time I returned to Blue Plum as an adult, I was struck by how small everything looked. The Victorian houses with their curlicues of gingerbread and deep front lawns, the redbrick storefronts lining Main Street downtown, the three-story courthouse, and the soaring church spires all loomed large in my childhood memories. In reality, the town sat toward the "quaint" end of the municipal scale. It was a tidily stitched sampler rather than a blanket of mass-produced yardage. On the other hand, the Weaver's Cat, Granny's pet, seemed to expand every time I turned around.

Main Street was awash with the rain. I waited behind an idling bus while a gaggle of die-hard tourists hopped off, ducked their heads, and darted into the beckoning shops. Only the Weaver's Cat was dark that afternoon. A few shoppers stood on the porch, obviously wishing they were inside the store. The colors and textures displayed in the windows and the enticing glimpses of more skeins and fibers farther in lured even the most resolute. Anyone with the least fiber fetish had to work very hard not to salivate when stepping over the threshold. Finding the door locked must have been painful.

I turned the corner and found a parking space in the lot across the side street. The Cat occupied one of the attached houses in the only row house in town. A doctor from Philadelphia, with an itch to construct, built the row in the 1850s, using bricks made on-site in the backyard. The three houses could have been called One, Two, and Three, or A, B, and C, or something more fanciful such as Lilac, Lily, and Loosestrife, but instead were dubbed Left House, Middle House, and Right House. My grandparents received Left House as a wedding present a hundred years or so after Dr. Thompson built it, and Granny turned the backyard into her garden.

"Come on in before you wash away." Ardis was watching for me and opened the back door. "We've got food."

"Bless you." I hadn't taken the time for breakfast, hadn't stopped for lunch. "In the kitchen?"

"No, on through and upstairs." Ardis led me through the kitchen, which doubled as a classroom, and up the steep back stairs.

People who were focused on the utility of big-box stores might see the Weaver's Cat as an inefficient enigma. But anyone who ever imagined turning an old house, with all its rooms and nooks, into a shop full of quirks and charm, finds perfect and comfortable sense there. The shop started in a small way, more like a kitten, taking up a cozy corner of Granny's front parlor. Over the years, as her interests meandered and grew, the shop spread and spilled over into one room after another. After my mother left home and my grandfather died, Granny let the Cat stretch and take over the house completely. She bought another little house over on Lavender Street and happily walked home there each night to sleep.

"We're borrowing TGIF's space." Ardis puffed over her shoulder. "We didn't want people seeing lights on downstairs. They can wait to shop one more day and we'll open again tomorrow, like Ivy wanted. Whew. Can you believe she was still running up and down these stairs?"

We stopped at the top for Ardis to catch her breath. She probably hadn't run up or down the stairs in a decade but was happy to plow her steady way in either direction whenever it was called for. She often said her two regrets about growing older were thinning hair and a thickening waist. Neither seemed to bother her overmuch.

"Who all is here?" I asked.

Ardis smiled. "Wait'll you see. It was Debbie's idea."

She crossed the landing to one of the rear bedrooms, now taken over by TGIF—Thank Goodness It's Fiber—an eclectic group of fiber and needlework artists that Granny started way back when. They taught classes, donated their creations to the hospital gift shop, and helped organize the annual Blue Plum Fiber Festival. Some of the older members gave the impression they'd taken up residence in the overstuffed chairs dotted around the shop. Two or three or four of them were always there, working away at the latest projects and gossip.

"Here she is," Ardis announced to the room but blocking the doorway and my view of the gathering.

By the murmured exclamations, I guessed the room was full of people. There were hurried shuffles of feet and scrapes of chairs. I detected the ever-present scent of wool laced with promising whiffs of coffee, just-baked bread, and melted chocolate. Someone whispered; someone else shushed. My stomach growled. Then Ardis stepped aside for the big reveal.

A dozen or so women faced the door. Faced me. Their eyes shining, reflecting their warmth and love. And something else. Anticipation?

A small movement to the right drew my attention. Debbie leaned down and lifted the hem of her long embroidered skirt. And then I knew what they were waiting for. With a catch in my breath, I looked from one to the other, all the way around the room. Every one of them wore or held something knitted or stitched or woven from Granny's threads and yarns—sweaters, hats, scarves. Ardis had joined them, pulling on a deep-rose-colored ruana. One member held a basket overflowing with a rainbow of skeins; another had draped herself in a tablecloth large enough to be a tent. When she caught my eye she did a twirl. And Debbie's lifted hem exposed a pair of ridiculous, glorious puce, raspberry, and tangerine argyle socks. The room was alive with Granny and I couldn't help laughing.

"We were afraid you'd cry," Debbie said.

"I can do that, too."

"But let's not, at least for now," said Ardis. "Come on over here and see what a feast we have."

The women parted and Ardis ushered me to the back of the room, where four mismatched Welsh cupboards lined the wall, providing storage for TGIF's various materials. The dresser tops were clear of the usual disarray of spindles, niddy-noddies, and whatnot. Instead, each was covered with a pretty lace or embroidered dresser scarf and each offered its own tempting contribution to the wake. On the first sat the bread I'd smelled from the hallway—three round, crusty loaves, raisins peeking from their split tops. The loaves smelled even better at close range. A plate of creamy herbed goat cheese sat on the second dresser. On the third were two flat, round cakes glinting with caramelized sugar and studded with chunks of dark chocolate. I held my hands over them, felt the warmth rising. Obviously straight from the oven. A coffee urn and two glass pitchers of juice or punch sat on the last dresser.

It all looked like heaven. Except maybe the stuff in the pitchers, which appeared to be thick, almost opaque, and was an eyebrow-raising shade of pinkish, reddish, I-wasn't-sure-what-color. I hated to prejudge it, but it looked either way too fruity and sweet or too spiked for an empty stomach.

"I hope you don't mind, but we didn't want to do the casserole thing," Ardis said as we filled plates.

"Oh, please. Granny was so not casseroles. This is perfect."

Debbie stood by the last dresser, handing full cups and glasses to people.

"Just coffee, thanks, Debbie."

"No, no, try this." She handed me a glass of the red stuff.

"Fruit punch?" I asked, trying to look happy about it.

"Don't worry. It's safe," she said with a wink.

Ardis and I juggled our plates and drinks over to one of the room's oak worktables. We joined the formerly-tablecloth-draped TGIF member, who introduced herself as Thea Green. She looked familiar, but I couldn't place her until she said she was from the library.

"It's the Queen Latifah look that throws people," she said.

"That and the voice," Ardis said.

"What can I say? I'm a loud librarian. I've thought about pushing a cart of books around with me as a visual aid, but then they'd be handing me overdue books when I'm in the checkout line at the grocery store. And expect me to make change."

"Oh, gosh, I'd better look to see if Granny has any books out."

"All taken care of," Thea said. "She had a couple of mysteries out. Maybe a Peter Lovesey and the latest *Murder, She Wrote*. I'll keep them renewed until you turn them in."

"Thank you."

Looking around the room, I realized Nicki wasn't there. Over the sounds of contented munching, I asked Ardis how Nicki was doing.

"She was in shock. Well, we all still are," Ardis said, "but, for Nicki, being the one to find her, well, you can imagine."

I didn't want to, but I could.

"I know, I know." Ardis patted my hand. "It's going to take time, honey. And don't worry about Nicki. She's coping and she's full of bubble. She loved Ivy and she loves a party, too, so we might see her yet. Now, tell me, did you notice the theme of the food?"

I roused myself from my imagination and looked at the food in front of me. "Mmm, besides delicious?" I looked at the hunk of bread I'd smeared with goat cheese, popped it in my mouth, chewed, savored, swallowed. "Rosemary? Wait a second." I took another bite of cake. The caramelized sugar gave the top a wonderful crunch; the chocolate was still semimelted. "Is there rosemary in everything?"

Ardis nodded. "For remembrance. That was Debbie's idea, too."

Debbie, watching from across the room, smiled and toasted me with her glass of red drink.

"Rosemary and raisins in the bread, rosemary in the goat cheese, and rosemary and chocolate in the cake, which is something I've never heard of but definitely want the recipe for," I said. "But what is this?" I held my glass of as-yet-untasted punch to the light. It was actually gorgeous. "Okay, I'll swallow." I did and it was, indeed, thick. And tart with lemon . . .

"It's rosemary-infused watermelon lemonade," Debbie said, joining us. "Ivy's latest addiction."

"Wow." I completely understood that addiction.

"And let me tell you, it's not easy finding good watermelon this time of year." She'd anticipated my reaction to the concoction and brought one of the pitchers over with her. She poured me another glass.

Below, the kitchen door banged and a voice called, "Hello, all!" Light footsteps ran up the stairs and Nicki appeared.

"Hello, all. Here I am. It's stopped raining and I saw a double rainbow over Banner Mountain. That has to be good luck, don't you think? It made me feel better, anyway. Even if Ivy did step over one of them, its twin will bring some part of her back again. I think I kind of believe that could happen, too. Isn't that funny? Oh, Debbie, I'm sorry I wasn't here in time for your surprise. It was such a cute idea, too. Look, Kath, here's my part of the tribute to Ivy."

I didn't remember what Nicki wore at the cemetery, but it wasn't what she had on now. She struck a model's pose, there in the doorway, showing off a jacket made from indigo fabric as dark and lucent as a midnight sky— Granny's signature dye color and one that's very difficult to achieve consistently. The jacket narrowed slightly at Nicki's waist, then flared with a short peplum. It was beautiful, though it would need taking in a bit to fit her perfectly.

I couldn't be sure without seeing it closer, but from where I sat, the fabric looked like raw silk. The buttons, nearly matching the fabric's color, were unobtrusive, allowing the texture, cut, and drape to take center stage. I was by no means a clotheshorse, but I felt drawn to that jacket like a silk moth to mulberry.

"That's absolutely beautiful," I said, wondering if I sounded as jealous as I felt.

"Oh, do you think so? Thanks, Kath. That means so much to me. Hang on a tick. I'll get a plate and I'll be right over."

"She's bubbling, for the time being, anyway," I said quietly to Ardis.

Nicki came back with minuscule portions of everything and sat next to me.

"Do you mind if I . . ."

"Touch it? Of course not," Nicki said. "Wipe your fingers first, though, would you?"

"Nicki!" Debbie sounded scandalized. "Kath knows more about handling textiles than any of us. She's a professional whatchamacallit."

Being a polite, as well as professional, textile preservationist, I didn't laugh at Debbie's flub of my credentials or bridle at Nicki's precaution. I smiled at both, carefully wiped my hands on a clean napkin, and touched the jacket at the sleeve and shoulder. Granny's dyed and woven raw silk. I felt like petting it. I must have sighed.

"Oh, I know what you mean," Nicki said. "I was so touched when Ivy gave it to me."

"She did?" For a second, everything in the room stopped. Sound ceased. Movements froze. There was nothing but my hands on the jacket and Nicki's smile after telling me my grandmother had given it to her. I didn't know what had happened. And I didn't know how. But I knew, absolutely, that Nicki was lying.

Chapter 3

I left soon after Nicki joined us, claiming a headache and fatigue. The truth was, I couldn't stand being near Nicki while she wore that jacket. How weird was that? I chalked my reaction up to my own shock over Granny's death, forgave myself, and made plans with Ardis to meet the next day to discuss the future of the Weaver's Cat, now that the weaver was gone.

"I'll see you in the morning, then," Ardis said.

"It might be closer to lunch. I don't know how long it'll take with the lawyer."

"Whenever you get here is fine."

She'd pressed me to take some of the food with me, but I'd lost my appetite. The headache and fatigue were true enough, and I got in the car, as happy to head for Granny's little house on Lavender Street as she had always been at the end of a day. The house and the business were both mine now. I'd known since my mother died that Granny planned to leave everything to me. I'd just thought I would have a few more years before I had to deal with it all. At the next stop sign I rubbed my temples, wondering what my options were, realistically.

I had spent many of my childhood summers with Granny in Blue Plum, just as I told Deputy Dunbar. And I'd spent countless hours behind the sales counter, playing at keeping store, a nuisance more than a help, most likely. I loved the Weaver's Cat and I loved Blue Plum and even though I eventually took the academic rather than the business route, Granny quite easily passed her love of fibers along to me, too. I studied and worked hard to become the expert I was and I had my own successful career as a textile preservation specialist at the state museum, "up north there in Illinois," as Dunbar put it.

Thinking of Deputy Dunbar made my headache worse. I couldn't believe I'd forgotten to ask Ardis what he could have meant about Granny's death being "convenient." And where did he get off calling her Crazy Ivy? Where had that stupid name come from, anyway?

I pulled into the driveway on Lavender Street, glad to be home, even without Granny there. Glad, that is, until I saw the Spivey twins sitting on the porch swing. One of them waved. The other held up a casserole dish and smiled. I killed the engine and groaned once, in private, before getting out.

"We wondered where you were," the twin with the casserole called as I grabbed my suitcase from the trunk.

"Took you a while to get here from the cemetery," said the other.

"Casserole's about thawed out by now."

"Was that your car in the lot over on Depot?"

They weren't dressed alike, thank goodness, so I knew that as soon as I figured out which was Shirley and which was Mercy, I'd feel on firmer footing.

"We thought we'd do our duty and drop this by," the one with the casserole said.

"That's awfully kind of you, Sh—"

"Mercy."

"Mercy, of course. Thank you."

"No, I mean Mercy has something to tell you. I'm Shirley," the casserole bearer said.

"Oh. Well, thank you, Shirley. Thank you both." I held my hand out to take the casserole but Shirley held on to it. And then, unfortunately, my good manners went into overdrive. "Would you like to come in? I don't know what there is to offer, but I'm sure there's coffee and I'd love to make you a cup."

They smiled and nodded and I dug for the keys, which weren't in my hand anymore. While my manners had been inviting the Spiveys in for coffee, my better judgment had dropped the keys back in my purse and buried them, trying to save me. The Spiveys smiled and waited.

"Ah, here we go." I dragged the wayward things out and fumbled my duplicate of the house key into the lock. To no avail. Confused, I looked to be sure I had the right one. Yes, the one with the cat key fob. Just like Granny's. The cat on the fob was the cat from the store's logo. I tried again. And again. Felt like swearing.

"Huh," Shirley said. "Isn't that something? Ours didn't work, either."

"What?" I turned and looked at her. "Since when do you have a key to the house?" My manners were suddenly scarce.

"Since Ivy asked me to feed the cat," Mercy said.

"She did?" That seemed so unlikely. "When?"

"The last time she went to Atlanta for a trade show of some sort." The way she said "trade show" made it sound as though Granny had traipsed down the road to a flea market.

"The last time she went to Atlanta for that show was three or four years ago." That news failed to perturb either of them, but it gave me a sharp jab. I hadn't given a thought to Granny's cat, Maggie. "Oh my gosh, who's been feeding her since . . . Who's been taking care of poor Maggie?" I put my ear to the door, didn't hear any yowls.

"No one asked us to." Mercy looked put out.

"Take a look in the window," Shirley suggested help-fully.

I brushed past her, cupped my hands to the glass, tried to see through the sheers drawn across the front window. No frantic Maggie peering back at me. No little tabby huddled and mourning under Granny's loom in the corner. "Someone from the shop must have her," I said, kicking myself for not thinking about her sooner.

"Probably for the best," Shirley said. "That cat never liked you, anyway."

That was sadly true, if somewhat rude of her to point out. I looked at the key and the door again. "What's going on here?"

"That's what I was about to find out when you drove up," Mercy said. "I'll call Angie." She pulled a phone from her purse, pulled her glasses to the end of her nose to see the phone more clearly, pressed buttons. Then she smiled, saying, "Hey, Angel," turned her back, and walked to the end of the porch.

Shirley and I eyed each other. I wanted to ask her why calling Angie would solve anything but, for whatever perverse reason, didn't feel like showing my ignorance. Instead, I tried to see some of Granny in this removed cousin of hers.

It didn't work. There was certainly nothing of Granny in the pastel polyester stretch outfit Shirley wore. The thought of that fabric touching my skin made me itch. Granny was the kind of old lady who could and did wear blue jeans and a T-shirt and made them look good.

"Why don't you add some color to your hair?" Shirley asked, eyeing the top of my head. "Brighten it up some. Red like yours fades so as you get older."

That was another difference. The twins had several inches on me, so they would have towered over Granny.

They also had several doses of sour to Granny's sweet. And beadier eyes.

Mercy returned then, her beady eyes screwed up with annoyance.

"If that doesn't beat all," she said. "Max had the locks changed."

I decided to forget about looking ignorant. "Who's Max?"

"He told Angie," Mercy said, ignoring my question and studying the door's hardware, "that someone got in here." She took hold of the knob and gave it a violent shake.

"You could probably get in through this window easier than anything else." Shirley, still holding the casserole, attempted to raise the window.

"Who is Max?"

They slewed around to stare at me. I might have shouted that question.

"And where might I find him?" I asked more politely when I had their attention. I had a few questions for a man who changed locks on my doors. Or if the house had been broken into, maybe I owed him thanks.

"Oh, didn't we tell you that to begin with?" Mercy looked unconvincingly nonplussed. "Well, we just found out ourselves last week. Ivy didn't own this house. Max does. Of course, he only just found that out, too, when he inherited it. But it's a rental, and for some reason Ivy wasn't paying the rent. So Max found new tenants, and you'll have to clear Ivy's things out. By the first. That'd be next Wednesday."

"That'd be a week from yesterday. We thought we'd lend a hand," said Shirley.

"Except, according to Angie, Max is off visiting kin in Kentucky and didn't leave the new keys. Although I believe he did leave you this. I found it in the mailbox." Mercy handed me an envelope with my name, the Lavender Street address, and no return address. "It's probably a bill for the rent she owed," she said. "Why don't you go ahead and open it, see what it says?"

I jammed it in my purse, snapped the purse shut, and started to open my mouth. Mercy opened hers first.

"Angie's husband," she said. "That's who Max is." Then she turned back to the door. "I do believe we can get this open, anyway, if we work at it."

Fifteen minutes later, after I'd declined their offers of help and watched them mutter their way back down the front walk with the casserole, which had begun to smell unpleasantly of tuna, and after I'd started breathing normally again, I pulled Max's envelope out of my purse and ripped it open.

Inside, on a sheet from a generic receipt pad, was *$1,200—Ivy owed* written on one line, and on the lines below it, *Now you owe. I'll be in touch.* No doubt the spare approach was small-town and laid-back, but it was the poorest excuse for a piece of business correspondence I'd ever seen. Not itemized, unsigned, and no contact information—so I couldn't even call him and be irate with him for going off to Kentucky with the only keys. But maybe he'd thought that through and saved himself an earful by not including his number. That only made me want to call him and be more than irate. Instead I jammed the letter back in my purse, letting my fingers take a bit of comfort as they brushed Granny's letter. Then I called Granny's lawyer.

Except I got his answering machine because, of course, he wasn't in and it was that kind of day. Then I remembered Granny's good friend Ruth. Ruth, who was Handsome Homer the lawyer's wife, and had told me to call if I needed anything. I could have called Ardis, but I remembered Ardis had her hands full with an elderly father disappearing into Alzheimer's. She didn't need me whining on her sofa bed. Besides, what I needed now was legal assistance, and calling Ruth put me one step closer to getting it.

"I don't think there's anything we can do about getting you into the house tonight," Ruth said. "If they're right about ownership, and without keys, well . . ."

I could hear the head shake in her words, and she must have heard the exhaustion in my sigh. She was suddenly brisk, decisive.

"How long are you in town?"

"Two weeks. I put in for some vacation time."

"Not personal or compassionate leave?" She sounded surprised. "Sorry—I'm being nosy. Occupational hazard of being a site director."

"That's okay. Illinois is in worse shape than usual and our budget's been cut off at the knees."

"Then my idea is even better. You don't need to be spending money staying in a motel or B and B. You know where the Homeplace is?"

"Follow Buffalo Road out past the old school and turn left?"

She laughed. "Except they pulled the old school down, so it's like that joke, look for where the school isn't and turn left when you don't see it. There's a Quickie Mart there on the corner now, so look for that. And you'll see the signs. Can't miss them. If you get there first, wait for me. The gate will be locked."

I lugged my suitcase back to the car, looked sadly at the little house, and went to find out what Ruth's idea was. I hadn't even asked. But the sun was on its way down and my spirits had already sunk. I'd lost Granny and now the house on Lavender Street? How could that be? I shook my head as I started the car. As long as Ruth's plan involved a bed and a pillow to cry under, I was all for it.

As I passed the shop, going back down Main, I

reminded myself to call Ardis and find out if she knew anything about Maggie. So what if Maggie didn't like me; she came from a long line of cats that hadn't. Cats gravitated to Granny. She was a cat magnet. They took one look at me, sneered, and stalked off. Or bit me if I tried to pet them. It was something I didn't understand, but it didn't mean I didn't like them or didn't want one to sit on my lap someday and purr.

A sign for the Holston Homeplace Living History Farm popped up as soon as I turned onto Buffalo Road. People in Blue Plum were fond of saying the Homeplace was their own miniature version of Williamsburg, except that it was a farm instead of a city and it represented the early nineteenth century instead of the late eighteenth. There were costumed guides, though, and farm animals. Tourists and Holston family members from all over the country and the world flocked to visit.

Ruth waved when she saw me turning in. She swung the gate open and motioned for me to park on the far side of the caretaker's cottage, which sat just inside the entrance. I got out of my car and followed her along a flagstone path.

"What do you think?" she asked over her shoulder. "Perfect solution?"

"Are you serious?" The path led us around to the front of the cottage.

"Why not? We'd be doing each other a favor. We're between caretakers for the time being. It's clean, furnished. The kitchen's not gourmet but the appliances work. The bathroom is small but not claustrophobic. I like having someone out here. It's yours, free and clear, as long as you need it."

I opened my mouth. She didn't give me a chance.

"You'll want to look at it, of course. Here's the key. Kath, I think you should do it." Brisk and decisive.

She took the key back from my motionless fingers,

unlocked the door, and went inside. I stood a moment longer, looking at the place. Not much, but not bad. It was an unpretentious, unadorned clapboard rectangle, with a half story under the eaves and a room with a shed roof off the back. Pretty cute, in its workaday, antebellum simplicity. The front door sat dead center, with a small garden planted on either side of it, running along the stone foundation. And right there, where a hand could brush it going through the front door, was a clump of sweet-smelling lavender.

Ruth raised a front window. "What do you think? Yes?"

It was a place to put my head on a pillow. At least until the mess over Granny's house got straightened out. "Yes."

"Good. I thought so. I brought linens."

I followed her to her car, deciding it was very nice having someone in charge. Then the Spiveys strayed through my mind, bringing an involuntary shudder along with them, and I amended my thoughts. It was nice having someone competent and pleasant in charge.

"Towels, sheets, pillow in here." Ruth pulled a duffel from her trunk and handed it to me. "And blanket," she said, lifting out a brown shopping bag. "Actually"—she hesitated and her face softened—"it's a coverlet Ivy wove. I thought it would be appropriate." She took the coverlet from the bag and draped it around my shoulders.

She must have said something more then, but I didn't catch it. I'd lifted a corner of Granny's soft blue and white coverlet to my cheek and nothing else seemed to matter at that point, or to compute.

"Kath?" Ruth touched my hand.

"Oh, sorry." I gave my head a shake to clear it.

"Never mind. It'll keep. Two more things for you, though. A key for the gate. And this." She handed me a plastic grocery bag with something square and heavy in the bottom. "For dinner or the freezer. I hope you like tuna?"

The rooms in the cottage, two down, one up, with the kitchen in the tacked-on room at the back, were as plain as the exterior. Their charm came in their proportions and the eccentric angles where floors and walls, walls and ceilings met. The door and window frames had never known a plumb line. The place was clean, though, as Ruth had said, and simply and adequately furnished. The kitchen lacked cupboard space but made up for that with a walk-in pantry. The pantry door was cattywampus, I discovered, and swung open unless latched with the hook and eye that was conveniently fitted to door and jamb. The tuna casserole Ruth had handed me fit perfectly in the freezer.

I lugged my suitcase up the steep, narrow stairs to the half story where the bedroom and bathroom were squeezed under the eaves. I made up the bed with Ruth's linens, spreading Granny's coverlet on top. Then I wrinkled my nose and opened the windows at the gable ends to let the breeze slip in and out, taking the stale, closed-up air with it.

It was so tempting to fall into bed then and there. Granny's coverlet called to me the way her lap had to any cat within earshot. I didn't, though. I stroked the coverlet one more time, went back downstairs, and took her letter from my purse. *Find some time when you can be alone this evening,* it said on the envelope. *Fix yourself a cup of cocoa.* I was alone, true, but the cupboards were bare. Luckily, the Quickie Mart was just an evening stroll away. I tucked the letter in my purse once again and plucked a sprig of lavender on my way out the front door.

The Homeplace encompassed several dozen acres of fields and forest on the western edge of Blue Plum. Although housing tracts and roads surrounded the site, the woods bordering the property let me pretend I was alone in the mountains. I stretched my arms, breathing in the deep green scent of moss and pines, felt their peace seep into me. A mockingbird sang from the top of a tall tree and another answered.

The air inside the Quickie Mart was permeated with old doughnut grease and steamed hot dogs, but the store surprised me by carrying more than mundane instant cocoa. I picked up a quart of milk and opted for a packet of Dark Chocolate Amaretto Amoré from the pseudo-gourmet selection. I remembered Granny's recommendation for adding a nip to the cocoa, but after the surreal day I'd had, imitation amaretto was probably all the nip I needed.

Speaking of nip, the sun had disappeared faster than I'd expected, taking light and warmth with it. I shivered on the half mile walk back to the cottage, picking up the pace, eager to be inside with my hands around a steaming mug. If I'd remembered how quickly night came in the mountains, I might have worn a jacket or left a light on.

Or maybe I had left one on. Stress of the day, no doubt, forgetting to douse the kitchen light after I'd explored my new digs. Its glow spilled from the window, welcoming me, looking safe and homey. Glad to see I'd at least remembered to lock the front door, I let myself in and tried to find the wall switch for the light in the parlor. I couldn't find it, gave up, started for the kitchen, and heard a noise. I froze.

Silence.

I was imagining things. Stress of the day. Old house, odd sounds.

And yet . . .

I took another step and the board under my foot creaked. Immediately there was a corresponding creak in the kitchen followed by a sound softer than a thump, a thump that almost wasn't there. A door pulled carefully to?

There were three doors in the kitchen of the quaint,

now slightly creepy, cottage—the interior doorway I was approaching, which was only a frame and lacked an actual door, an exterior door leading to the side yard, which I hadn't opened or unlocked as yet, and the cattywampus pantry door with its hook and eye. I dared another few steps and peeked around the corner to the left and then the right. Side door closed, chain slotted. Pantry door closed, hook not in eye. That was not possible. According to my experiments, without the hook in the eye, the door would have swung open and banged into the counter and cupboard.

Another slow creak. Definitely from the pantry. Could someone be inside, holding the door shut? By now I was sure I heard someone in there holding his breath.

Leave immediately and call 911; I knew that was what I should do. But the person in the pantry already knew I was there, and running out into a dark, unfamiliar yard, not knowing who *else* might be waiting out there, was nuts. What I did do was probably equally nuts.

I gauged the distance from my current position to the pantry. Quietly, quickly, I put the milk, cocoa, and my purse on the floor. Took my phone out of my purse. Took three deep breaths. Pressed 9-1-1, and rocketed across the kitchen to latch the pantry door.

"Hah!"

"Hey!" came the startled cry from inside the pantry.

"Save it, bud," I shouted, and shoved the kitchen table against the door for insurance. Then I realized I'd dropped the phone. Oops. I scrambled after it. It had skittered into the corner and was still alive, but it was also still searching for a signal. Stupid thing.

Pantry Guy threw himself at the door.

"Don't you dare!" I shouted. "I've got a gun!" I don't lie well, but he gave me the benefit of it.

"Hey, hey, hey, now. There's no need for that. No need for guns. Let's be reasonable. Look, I'll even tell you my name. How about I do that, okay? I'm Joe. You can call me Joe." He had a nice voice, but he also sounded like a good bet for *The World's Dumbest Criminals*. "Now, I don't know who *you* are," he continued, slow and friendly, "or what you're doing here."

"I'll tell you who I am," I interrupted. "I'm the one standing out here who just got through to 911."

"Shit."

Help arrived at my door in the guise of Deputy Cole Dunbar. I felt like echoing Pantry Guy's expletive.

"Ms. Rutledge, isn't it?" Dunbar greeted me. "Well, now, ma'am, I don't know what you're doing here." Oddly enough, he was parroting Pantry Guy, too. "According to the dispatcher, you've reported an intruder?"

Funny how easily he made me feel like I was the one intruding. I attempted to explain the situation without sounding defensive and as subjectively as I could. I might have gloated some, though, when I told him that Pantry Guy had identified himself as "Joe." I knew a useful clue when I heard one. Dunbar's starched face hadn't relaxed any since our traffic-stop introduction, but with a minor shift near the left side of his mouth and a tightening around the eyes he managed to convey that he was more annoyed than impressed with that piece of information.

"And you say you have him locked in the pantry?" He eyed the pantry door and my kitchen table barricade and said "Mm-hmm," which I interpreted as mumble code for "Pfft! Women."

He moved the table aside and unhooked the door. I stood behind the table, ready to run if things got rough. The door swung open and . . . nothing. The pantry was empty. In the wall opposite the door an open window let in the cool night air.

"Mm-hmm."

I thanked Dunbar for coming out, feeling as though

I should also apologize for not memorizing window placements in my new abode. I didn't apologize, though. His "mm-hmms" didn't deserve it.

"So, um, do I need to do anything to follow up?" I asked. "Sign a statement or something? I probably ought to call Ruth Wood, anyway, and let her know."

"I wouldn't bother," Dunbar said.

"What? Why not?"

He rocked on his heels and considered that, then came to an irritating conclusion.

"Well, nothing much happened, did it? A guy got in, but nothing's broken or missing. You weren't assaulted." He stopped rocking and looked at me. "You weren't assaulted, were you?"

"No."

"And can you describe 'Joe'?"

"No."

He shrugged.

"Are you saying I made this up? That I invented Joe?"

"No, I'm not. I'm just saying, I looked around the rest of the farm before coming over here and I didn't see anything unusual. But I think you should make sure your doors and windows are securely locked after I leave."

"I will. Wait a second. You checked the rest of the site *before* you came here?"

"Well, you did tell the dispatcher that you had the intruder secured in the pantry, Ms. Rutledge."

"Yeah, I did. I was doing your job for you. Locking up the bad guy."

"And look how well that worked out."

I stared at Deputy Officer Clod Dunbar. This was my second less-than-satisfactory police experience with him. In one day. One very stressful day. He owed me. I breathed in, out, in, centered myself as I imagined someone who meditates might. I put on my professional demeanor.

"Deputy Dunbar, can you explain to me your remark

of earlier today? The remark I refer to is the one in which you said my grandmother's death was convenient for her. 'As in good timing,' I believe you added. Would you care to elaborate on that incredibly insensitive statement?"

"Oh, well, please excuse me, then, Ms. Rutledge." The starch melted into raised eyebrows and a sarcastic smile and he held a hand out as though presenting the kitchen, the cottage, to me as proof of something.

"What?"

"I mean, excuse me for offending your sensitive nature."

"What is that supposed to mean?"

For answer, he walked into the other room and jabbed his thumb toward the stairs. "I'm just saying."

"You're just saying what?"

"I'm saying it takes a certain lack of a sensitive nature, and some kind of nerve, to sleep in the bed where a man was found murdered."

Chapter 4

"Mur-mur-mur-mur—" I snapped my mouth shut to keep the rest of my shock contained.

"Yeah," Dunbar said, "you heard me right." He over-enunciated the next word in case I was still having trouble with the concept. "*Murdered.* Old Em was murdered up there in his bed." He jabbed his index finger toward the ceiling, then stared at me.

Never having looked at myself in a mirror immediately after hearing I was in a murdered man's house and planning to sleep in his deathbed, I could only guess at the expression he saw on my face.

"You don't have the slightest idea what I'm talking about, do you?" he said. "Well, hell." He took off his Smokey the Bear hat, ran his hand over the memory of hair, and continued spitting soft expletives, shaking his head as each one popped out. He looked and sounded genuinely upset, and I briefly thought he was commiserating with me over my own day and its slide downhill from rancid to rotten. But then he screwed his mouth sideways so that he looked like a dyspeptic Elvis, except without the hair, and I realized he wasn't feeling sorry, he was being pissy.

He stalked over to a recliner in the corner of the room and dumped himself in it, dislodging a poof of air and one last guttural curse from the back of his throat before muttering "I am so freakin' tired" and subsiding. His eyelids slid to half-mast.

To give him his due, he did look exhausted, as though the knife pleats in his uniform had been the only thing keeping him upright. Maybe he'd been up since way before dawn saving the world from speedy women. But I'd been up just as long and was way over my quota of lousy for any single day and he'd just taken the only comfortable-looking chair in the room. Sure, there was a halfway decent–looking sofa and I could dump myself just as dramatically as he did, but it was the principle of the thing. Instead I waited for him to fill me in on this latest jarring turn of events. He gave me one last squint and closed his eyes.

"Deputy Dunbar?" I tried to sound respectful, empathetic even.

Nothing.

"Deputy Dunbar, would you please tell me what's going on?"

Nothing.

"Some elaboration? An explanation, please?"

Silence.

"Hey, Dunbar, do you have a badge number I can report?"

If at that point he'd started snoring, I would have kicked him in the shin. But either my words or something in my tone got him back on his feet, even if I pretty obviously hadn't endeared myself to him any further. I drew myself up as tall as five-three in low-heeled boots allows and planted myself in front of him.

"Deputy, you are right. I don't have the slightest idea what you're talking about. So fill me in. It's been a long, trying, emotional day, and now I want answers so I can decide what to do." Granny would have tut-tutted because I didn't say "please" that time, but by then I didn't care.

"Well, it's like this, little Miss Kath—"

"Oh, no, no, no. Wait. It's not like that at all, Deputy Dunbar. I am not "little Miss" anything." I gave him a look I've used with good effect on junior curators who mishandle fragile textiles.

Dunbar only rolled his eyes. "Beg pardon, Ms. Rutledge. The facts are these. Emmett Cobb, caretaker here at the Holston Homeplace Living History Farm and resident of this house, was found dead two weeks ago. Upstairs. In his bed. Poisoned."

I suddenly felt like coughing, maybe even gagging as I imagined toxic, noxious vapors swirling in eddies around us. "Wow. Okay, that's awful." I cleared my throat, swallowed. "Um, what kind of poison was it?"

"I forget the name. It was in something he drank, though. Not a real quick exit."

"That's horrible."

"Yeah, very messy. High retch factor involved, if you know what I mean. Can't imagine anybody wanting to sleep up there after what I saw."

We looked at each other, noses wrinkled, then tilted our heads back and looked at the ceiling, he now frowning and grim, me trying not to picture what he'd seen up there. Out of the corner of my eye I saw a shiver run through him. For an absurd second I was tempted to reach around his back and tap his shoulder and yell "Boo." But that was a gun in his holster.

"But you caught the, the . . ."

"Bad guy? No, we did not. Bad guy, one. Cops, zip. Old Em, zipped up and six feet under." He grinned nastily at my reaction to his scorecard.

And, me being me, I reacted again. "Deputy Dunbar, what do you call it when a policeman talks to a civilian? Is there a term for that?"

"Huh?"

"You know, with a doctor it's called bedside manner. Is there an equivalent term for cops talking to regular people? Roadside manner, maybe? Or how about badge-side manner?"

"I don't get it. What are you talking about?"

"I'm talking about whatever it is you don't have. Whatever it's called, you need to sign up for a refresher course in it, maybe see if you can get some kind of continuing education credit for brushing up. I've only met you twice and the first time we probably didn't even exchange a hundred words. Yet each time we've met, you've managed to be insensitive, sneering, and downright rude. Why? Is this how you always are? Or is it a problem you have with women? Or is it just a problem you have with me? And if that's the case, then what is that problem? You don't even know me. You know what? I'm like you; I don't get it." My voice might have risen a tad toward shrill.

Deputy Clod clapped his hat back on his head. "I'll tell you a story, Ms. Rutledge. A couple of weeks ago, I sat out there in the kitchen with Emmett Cobb. We played a little friendly poker. I had a beer and Em had his usual glass of sweet tea because he wasn't much of a drinker. In fact, Em wasn't much of anything but an old guy. And then, next thing I know, not two days later, Em winds up dead. Dead in a way I wouldn't wish on a dog or that dog's worst enemy. And now here you are moving into Em's house. Well, excuse me if I'm a little worked up. You asked if we've caught the murderer. You asked if I knew your grandmother. You can draw whatever lines or conclusions you like between those two statements. I'll be happy to wait while you do that, and in the meantime I'll call a motel for you."

The phrase "well, shut my mouth" shot through my mind, ricocheting back and forth along that line he expected me to draw. But why was he being so coy about it?

"This line you want me to draw, Deputy, is it the official line?" I demanded. I've always thought "shut my mouth" was a silly phrase, anyway. "You think my grand-mother poisoned that old guy, don't you? But is she any-one else's suspect, or is she just *your* suspect? You decided that sweet, innocent old lady, who never had an evil thought in her life, who only ever charmed and helped everyone she ever met, you decided she was guilty. And I'll bet you badgered her, too, didn't you? What possible reason would she have to kill that man? If I find out you were giving my eighty-year-old grandmother the third degree and caused her blood pressure to spike so she had a heart attack—"

A curious change came over Deputy Clod while I waxed hysterical. A line of sweat beads broke out on his forehead. He wiped away several of them as they slid down his nose. His feet shifted, as though they itched to be somewhere else, and his eyes, though they kept return-ing to my face, spent more time darting glances into the corners of the room.

"It's entirely possible you're right, Ms. Rutledge," he said, managing to sound stiff as a prig and uneasy as a long-tailed cat at the same time, "and I do apologize. But if you'll gather your belongings now, I'll be happy to call that motel for you and we can both get out of here." He pulled a handkerchief from a back pocket and wiped sweat from his eyes.

I couldn't help staring at him. He must have sensed my lack of hop-to-it from behind the mopping handker-chief, though, because he made hurry-up motions at me with his other hand. And that got all over my perversity buttons.

"There's no need to call a motel." I walked over to the recliner and sat down, crossing my legs and casually swinging my foot. The chair was every bit as comfortable as it looked. I fit right into Em's accustomed hollow. The whole room was warm and homey from that perspective.

"You can't think you're going to stay here," he said.

"Because of the retch factor?"

"Hell, yes, that and—"

"And nothing. Deputy Dunbar, the director of this site invited me to stay as long as I need to. Indeed, as long as I like. And frankly, I wouldn't leave now if the place was haunted."

Chapter 5

The first thing I did after *Oaf*ficer Dunbar left was call Ruth Wood to let her know about the intruder and to ask why she hadn't mentioned the reason this charming cottage was available for unaware out-of-town guests. I was relieved, though, when her voice mail kicked in. Ruth had done me a favor, albeit a tainted one, and I didn't want to risk derailing again and end up yelling at her. My rant at Clod Dunbar to the contrary, confrontations weren't ordinarily my thing. It was time for me and my rancid, rotten day to wind down. I disconnected without leaving a message.

Thinking back, I realized there was a moment after Ruth wrapped Granny's coverlet around my shoulders when she said something I missed. Maybe she'd started to tell me about the murder and I was lost in whatever blue-and-white-wool haze I'd drifted into. I would give her the benefit of the doubt and find a way to ask her, carefully, in the morning.

In the meantime, me and my big perversity buttons.

Murdered man's house . . . murdered man's bed . . . murdered man's shabby, comfortable chair. It took me several minutes of pacing, not quite to the point that I was wringing my hands and muttering "woe is me," but I finally decided I'd convinced myself I wasn't squeamish

about spending the night with a murdered man's memory.
Maybe.

There were a couple of things I could do, though, guaranteed to ease the loneliness of the evening and keep my
mind from dwelling on the retch, creep, or any other factors of my new dwelling. I pulled Granny's letter from my
purse again and I replayed a message on my phone. I'd
lost track of how many times I'd already played it over the
past few days, but I held the phone to my ear and listened
to Granny's voice again.

*Hello, Dearie. Got your e-mail about the gig in Richmond next week. I was going to e-mail you back but then
I thought I might as well call and chat with whoever's
home on your end. Hello, phone, tell Kath I miss her
and I want to hear all about the collection in Richmond,
especially if she finds anything interesting. And her
birthday present is finished and wrapped and will be in
the mail soon. Late, but soon. Ow! Maggie! Keep a civil
claw in your paw. That's no way to behave just because
I'm talking to Kath and not you. Maggie sends her love,
too. Oh, and I thought you'd like to know, I finally
started my Blue Plum tapestry. It's . . . well, it is what it
is. A bit of a puzzle, but . . . Well, I'll stop crowding your
inbox now. Catch you later, Dearie.*

Typical Granny. Interested in what I was doing and
busy and distracted with her own projects. I'd sent her a
quick e-mail in answer. Got busy myself, packing or preparing or whatever. Could have called her back. Didn't.
The birthday present hadn't arrived before I left home.
Maybe I'd find it at her house, still waiting to be mailed.

After blotting my eyes and nose, I saw the quart of
milk and packet of cocoa still sitting on the floor where
I'd left them. The episode with Pantry Guy seemed like
hours ago but the carton was still cool. I gathered myself
and the fixings and went to make the cocoa I wished I

were sharing with Granny. Heck, I'd even have shared it with snarly Maggie if she'd been there.

Now that I wasn't in vigilante mode, I could see why Deputy Clod had sniffed at my attempt to barricade the pantry door with the kitchen table. It was part of a light-weight tubular metal dinette set. I laid the envelope from Granny in the middle of it, then rummaged through the cupboards and drawers, finding an assortment of mismatched flatware and dishes. I came up with a coffee mug and spoon and gave them a quick rinse. Then I remembered the details Deputy Dunbar had supplied about Emmett Cobb's death—poison in something he drank. I eyed the mug and spoon, thinking about rational versus irrational reactions. I opted for irrational and soaped and scoured them so thoroughly I could have performed surgery with them. Then rinsed them again for old times' sake.

I tipped the packet of cocoa into the mug, stirred in the milk, set it spinning in the microwave, and glanced at the envelope in the middle of the table.

. . . make yourself comfortable, read this letter, and remember, always, I am your loving Granny.

The microwave beeped. I jumped. Then I wrapped my hands around the steaming mug and made myself comfortable in one of the dinette chairs. Somehow this seemed like the kind of moment for a brightly lit room. The envelope waited patiently on the table in front of me as I inhaled warm cocoa vapor. What had Neil Taylor said when he handed the envelope to me? *She was one in a million. Don't let anyone tell you different.* And my unanswered question, why should they?

I hopped up. One more thing to brighten the room and the moment further. I fumbled with the radio sitting on top of the refrigerator. Apparently Em's taste ran to nasal and twang, though, which wasn't quite what I had in mind. I tapped the tuning buttons until sounds of a lilting flute and lively fiddle filled the room. Granny would have liked that. I could see her sweeping Ardis or Maggie into an impromptu hornpipe. I was delaying, and I knew it, though I couldn't have said why.

I sat back down. Tapped my toe to the jig on the radio. Inhaled more of the calming chocolate steam from the mug, then took a long, deep swallow of the dark, velvety stuff. Felt it slide over and smooth the catch in my throat. Finally slit the envelope.

Inside were two sheets of paper the color of pale celery, folded together in thirds. I ran my fingertips over them, feeling the thin plant fibers that gave them their faint texture. The texture was like Braille to my fingertips, bringing to mind with a rush the Christmas a few years back when I gave Granny a box of these handmade papers. Before unfolding the letter, I turned it over, looking for . . . yes, on the back in the lower left corner was a tiny pencil sketch of Maggie washing her paw. Every letter or card or postcard Granny had ever sent me included a drawing of one of her cats. It was Purl before I learned to read her letters myself, Cumber Bund when I started scrawling notes back to her, then Overshot and Raglan. And for the last ten years or so, when we more often exchanged e-mails and phone calls, it was pretty gray Maggie with her white bib and tucker.

I touched a finger to the sketch of Maggie, then opened the letter.

Dearest Kath,

   Are you alone and comfortable? Sipping that nice cup of cocoa? Ah, ah, ah, if I know you as well as I think I do (of course I do), you're sitting bolt upright somewhere pretending you're as comfortable as Maggie

> *sleeping in a puddle of sunshine. But you're*
> *just pretending. Go on now and sit in my*
> *old blue comfy chair. Trust your old*
> *Granny. You'll be glad you did.*

I laughed out loud. Hadn't Ruth said at the cemetery that Granny was always right? Yes, indeed, she was always absolutely right.

But this time she was wrong, too, because sitting in her big, soft blue chair was out of the question. It was locked up tight in the house on Lavender Street. And the house was no longer hers and, so, not mine. But was that true?

I flipped quickly through the letter, looking for a date, and didn't find one. Not on the envelope, either. The paper was from Christmas two or three years ago, though, which gave me somewhat of a time frame. So, when had she written this, and what had happened between then and now? If for some reason or somehow she'd sold or lost the house, why hadn't she updated this letter? And why hadn't she told me? There'd been no hints of trouble or sudden changes in any of our conversations over the last few years.

> *Go on now and sit in my old blue comfy*
> *chair.*

I wished I could. The radio continued to pipe jaunty airs into the kitchen. I left it playing and carried the letter and the cocoa into the parlor, not even close to laughing now.

> *Trust your old Granny. You'll be glad*
> *you did.*

Trust her? Of course I did. Yes, of course I did, despite Dunbar's insinuations about Emmett Cobb's murder and his rude presumption in calling her Crazy Ivy. I nestled into the recliner, half expecting Granny to reach over my shoulder to tuck a pillow behind my back and adjust the shade on the floor lamp.

> *That's my girl. Now, you've always known everything that's mine will be yours—the Weaver's Cat (the business, the building, and the lot it's sitting on) and the house and property on Lavender Street. Maggie, too, and her catnip mice (if she'll let you share). But there's something else that's yours, which I will try to explain without making you think your old Granny is gaga. Are you sitting comfortably?*

Oh for heaven's sake.

> *That nip was a good idea, too, so I hope you added something to the cocoa.*

Out with it, Granny.

> *I'm a bit of what some people might call a witch.*

Oh. My. God. The nip would definitely have been a good idea. I swigged the rest of what I did have without tasting it, felt blindly for the side table, set the mug on it, and gave my head a shake to see if that improved my brain's reception any. I turned back to the letter, attempting to feel competent and collected, but I'm sure my mouth was hanging open.

> *To say, outright, "I am a witch" is putting it too bluntly. Too black and white.*

*There are so many shades of gray in this,
you see, and mauve and lilac and every
other color, for that matter. I don't like
using the word "witch," anyway. I prefer to
think of the situation more in terms of
having a talent. I have a talent which allows
me to help my neighbors out of certain
pickles from time to time. It's a marvelous
gift, Dearie, and I hope you know I don't
use the word "marvelous" lightly.*

*But I'm not going to burden you with
details now. There's time enough for that
later. I've kept notes, over the years, in my
private dye journals. You'll want to find
them and take your time making a proper
study of them. They're locked away in a
safe place in my study at the Cat. Read my
journals and all will be revealed. There,
that's rather exciting, isn't it? I hope it gives
you a chuckle to think of your old Granny
being mysterious and melodramatic. It
makes a change from responsible and
unflappable, a reputation I've cultivated
and tended as carefully as my dye garden.*

*I also hope I needn't tell you that what
I've just told you is a secret and must
remain one. I've never discussed it with
anyone, not at the Weaver's Cat or
anywhere else. There are inklings and
"quiet understandings," shall we say, at the
shop, in town, and around out in the
county, but I'm quite good at leaving them
unacknowledged and going about my
business. Of course, if I'd hung a sign in the
shop window all these years, my reputation
as "Crazy Ivy" would have been colorfast*

and permanent. (Yes, I am aware of the nickname and it has never bothered me. Its origin isn't important, either in the great crazy quilt of life or in my own small patch of it.)

Enough philosophy, though. Here's what I really want to tell you. In addition to my worldly possessions, you also now have my talent. I inherited it from my grandmother. You have inherited it from me. Kath, you are a bit of a witch.

Chapter 6

I needed more than a nip.

Or maybe I *had* added something to my cocoa and I was blotto. That could explain the over-the-rainbow sensation I was swimming in. It would be nice if *something* explained it. Or maybe I'd somehow gotten a dose of the poison that killed Emmett and I was hallucinating before keeling over. Or I was out of my mind with grief over Granny's death. No, unfortunately, I was pretty sure neither nip nor poison nor abject misery was a likely possibility. But that's all I was sure of.

Kath, you are a bit of a witch.

Oh my God. There were a few more lines to the letter but I couldn't bear to read them. I dropped it in the chair and resorted to pacing. And muttering. There was great relief in muttering. She *must* have been going gaga. Senile. Goofy. Whiffy, as she so politely described the mental state of some of her elderly friends. Whatever. This was nuts. And it turned out muttering wasn't much relief after all.

. . . mysterious and melodramatic . . .

Loony, Granny. Try loony and out to lunch.

. . . what I've just told you is a secret and must remain one.

You think?

. . . inklings and "quiet understandings" . . . "Crazy Ivy" . . . it has never bothered me.

I allowed myself a few more pointed mutters, took several deep breaths, slowed my pacing, stopped. I closed my eyes and took several more breaths. This was no time to go crazy myself. I retrieved the letter and sat down to finish reading it. Maybe, just maybe, there was a big "ha-ha, got you" at the end.

> *Finish your cocoa, now. Better yet, have another cup and a larger nip. The main thing, the important thing, is that you shouldn't worry about any of this. In fact, you needn't ever do anything with the talent. You can ignore it and move on with your excellent career. You are like me, though, you know, and you might be surprised how much you enjoy this gift. A bit of advice from your old Granny: Never take surprise or joy lightly. Look for them. Weave them into your life wherever you can.*
>
> *Well, a good night's sleep will give you perspective. Sleep tight, now, and always remember, I am your loving Granny.*

The radio in the other room took a mournful turn, playing some dirgelike piano piece. I couldn't be bothered to get up and either change the channel or turn it off. I sat with my head bowed, fingers laced over the top of my skull, probably keeping my wits from flying off in all directions.

I am your loving Granny.

She was. I knew she was. And if believing she had a "talent" made her happy, whether in the great scheme of things or in her *great crazy quilt of life*, what was wrong with that? Especially if she hadn't advertised the fact. And so what if she believed she'd somehow passed that talent on to me? I thought back to the day she died. I certainly wasn't aware of any sudden jolt running through me. Couldn't pinpoint any zap of power transferred. No flash or frisson of abrupt good fortune. I sat back and sighed, absentmindedly running my fingers over the fibers in the light green paper, stroking it as though it were a cat. It was soothing, somehow. More soothing than pacing and muttering, anyway.

The radio slid from mournful to downright lugubrious. Ridiculously lugubrious. There was even sobbing in the background. Talk about melodramatic. If they were going to keep that up, I'd have to stir myself and turn it off. Thankfully that piece drew to its soggy conclusion and the lively fiddle sprang back into action.

And then someone hiccupped. In the kitchen.

What? I strained to hear over the annoying accordion that had joined the fiddle. Was Dunbar back with a last insult? Or Pantry Guy? Had he been drinking and decided to slip back in the window to finish whatever it was he started? This was too much. By God, I'd scare the hiccups out of whoever it was. I didn't even try to be stealthy. I stomped over to the fireplace, grabbed the poker and shovel from the convenient homeowner's fireplace weapon rack, and started for the kitchen. I was armed, dangerous, and dangerously close to being unhinged. Kath on the warpath in full cast-iron attack mode.

Another hiccup. More sobbing.

I pulled up short, not quite to the kitchen door, not quite sure I could believe my ears. This wasn't sound effects on the radio; it was live. Live sobbing and distinctly female. What on earth? How many people had keys to this place or were wont to wander in through the pantry window? Two other questions, more obvious, escaped me for the moment, maybe due to that surprise thing Granny was so keen on, which seemed to be disrupting the connection between my ears and my brain. In this small space, how had someone gotten in without my noticing or, conversely, how had that someone not realized I was there, too?

I hugged the wall and moved closer to the door, weapons still at the ready. I slid my left eye around the corner and spied . . . a woman sitting at the kitchen table, her head bowed. I saw her and yet I didn't see her. Thinking my vision must be blurry, I rubbed my left eye with a knuckle. I rubbed my right eye, too, for good measure, then peeked all the way around the edge of the door.

The woman was weeping with such abandon at this point that I could have taken a flying leap over to the refrigerator and beaten it like a gong with the poker and she wouldn't have registered my presence. But, still, I was barely able to register hers. If my own eyes had been teary, I'd have understood why I was having trouble focusing on her, but the table, the cabinets, the radio, all the rest of the kitchen appeared crisp and clear. I blinked, tried squinting. Neither did any good. The woman wavered as if I saw her through a film of water or through a raindrop on a windowpane. Details of the hair on her bowed head and the cloth covering her arms and heaving shoulders were distorted. She wept as though alone in the universe, indistinct, colorless, altogether unearthly.

I stepped all the way into the kitchen, poker and shovel forgotten as weapons, now only deadweight in my hands. The word "dead" repeated itself in my mind several times. No, it couldn't be. I didn't believe in ghosts any more than I believed in witches. That otherwise sane adults ever did believe in either had always amazed me. But something well out of my sense of the ordinary was going on before my unbelieving eyes. And as bright as I liked to think I was, it took several more blazing road signs before my rational self took the indicated detour.

The first hint that caught my attention was the appearance of the chair the woman was drooping and dripping in. The parts of the chair that I could see *through* her were as blurry as she was. That made me feel a little dizzy. Or crazy. I couldn't tell which. I put the back of my hand to my forehead. I wasn't feverish, more's the pity.

The second clue that my accustomed beliefs might be on shaky ground came when the woman started moaning. If I'd thought my nerves were nearing the edge earlier over the whole Pantry Guy and Dunbar incident or after reading Granny's letter, those mournful lamentations told me different. Her keening vibrated up and down my spine so that my nerves weren't just teetering on the brink—they were abandoning hope and preparing to dive. Despite that, my feet refused to carry me out of the room.

The moaning didn't last long, thank goodness. The effort seemed to tire the poor thing, and her moans subsided with a few shuddering breaths and another hiccup or two into quieter sobs. I felt as though I'd watched a storm reaching a crescendo and tailing off into a clammy gray drizzle, albeit a drizzle rocking back and forth in a stainless-steel dinette chair.

Then she spoke. At first it was more of a blubber, not easy to understand. I thought she was saying "Ebb, ebb" over and over again. That was logical, my newly reorganized sense of reality told me, because ebb was something her life had obviously already done. But after she blew her nose on her sleeve, with another sound I'd be just as happy never to hear again, her articulation was better.

"Em, Em, my darling, darling Em," she wailed. "I'll never forgive myself. Why oh why, Em? Why did I do it? Why did I kill you?"

"You?" I blurted. And that's when the third sign, more like a flashing neon marquee, smacked me over the head, confirming that my views on paranormal phenomena needed an adjustment.

With a startled yelp, the woman stopped rocking. Her hands flew to her mouth, stifling her hiccups and sobs. She sat hunched and frozen for several moments like a worried wet rabbit. Then slowly, hesitating with each slight movement, she lifted her head enough to peer at me. Her eyes, which should have been red and swollen from her torrential weeping, were as colorless as the rest of her, but less blurry. They struck me as being the oldest eyes I'd ever seen. Ageless. Definitely lifeless.

"You're kidding." Somehow I managed to get that out with only a few stutters. "*You* killed Emmett Cobb?"

Not taking her eyes from mine, she straightened, drawing in a long breath as she did. She seemed to swell along with the intake and held the breath as she continued to hold my eyes. Without thinking, I held my breath, too, wishing she'd give up and let go. That is, until she did let go with a piercing scream, as though I were the apparition who'd scared *her* out of *her* wits. It was a scream that could only be described as bloody murder. Dropping the poker and the shovel, I clapped my hands to my ears and shut my eyes, too, trying to keep that sound out of my head. It went on way too long, then abruptly vanished, leaving behind a silence almost as painful.

My hands stayed clamped to my ears, but I opened my eyes a slit.

She was gone. Vanished with the last shattering notes of the scream. I whirled around. No one behind me. I ran to the back door. It was closed. Locked. I raced from it to the front door, then from window to window. All closed. All locked.

That did it. I'd arrived in town driving like a crazed woman and now it was time to reverse that process. Maybe even go faster. I took the stairs two at a time to grab my still-packed bag, a nanosecond away from hyper-ventilating and needing a respirator. Either this place was haunted or I was as gaga as Granny. *Get me out of here,* every hair standing up on my scalp begged. I snagged the suitcase from beside the bed, spotted Granny's coverlet Ruth had lent me, and snatched it up, too. Throwing it around my shoulders, I started back down, suitcase in hand.

By the time I reached the bottom of the stairs, my breath started to come more easily. By the time I was crossing the kitchen, heading for the door, I'd slowed to a walk. At the back door I stopped and held a corner of the coverlet to my cheek. Something was different; some-thing had changed. I tried to figure out what and dis-carded every possibility other than that rational thought was seeping back, sealing off my panic. I'd been sleep-walking or hallucinating or having some kind of mind-blowing hysterical interlude. No matter. Whatever mental flip I'd experienced was over. Given the stress and grief I was operating under, it was understandable.

. . . a good night's sleep will give you perspective.

Granny was, indeed, always right. Relief, respite, perspective—a good night's sleep should bring some or all of that. I walked back to the bottom of the stairs and eyed the dark at the top. My feet were reluctant to carry me back up there. In fact, they encouraged me to experi-ment with the comforts of a good night's sleep in the backseat of my car. In the end I convinced my feet to com-promise and together we curled up on the sofa, in the par-lor, wrapped in Granny's comforting coverlet.

Chapter 7

It wasn't until sunlight streamed through the eastern window, puddling around my head on the makeshift pillow I'd fashioned from my sweatshirt and all the socks and underwear I'd packed, that I woke up. My coverlet cocoon and the sofa had provided a peaceful refuge. A bit of the bright puddle dripped into my eyes and I opened them ready to laugh at myself and my wild imaginings. I was also hungry enough to eat anything not nailed down, possibly even tuna casserole.

It was only a little after eight. Plenty of time before I had to shower and look presentable for my appointment with Homer Wood to go over Granny's will. I emptied the underwear and socks from my sweatshirt pillow back into my suitcase and pulled on the sweatshirt and the only jeans I'd packed for what was supposed to be a short business trip. I was staring into the open freezer, contemplating a jog to the convenience store versus chipping off a corner of Ruth's casserole and tossing it in the microwave, when someone knocked on the back door. It was testament to the comfortable sofa and Granny's coverlet that I didn't yelp and slam the freezer on my hand.

Ruth stood smiling on the doorstep, looking as though she'd stepped off the page of a vintage clothing Web site, but not because she wore a costume appropriate for the era depicted by the Homeplace. She'd stolen a pair of Katharine Hepburn's high-waisted trousers in a dark chocolate tweed and borrowed someone else's buttery-biscuit-colored twinset. As I'd obviously entered the describing-colors-in-terms-of-food stage of starving, I was delighted to see she also held a bakery bag and two cups nestled in a cardboard drink caddy.

"Coffee and a choice," she said when I opened the door. "I wasn't sure if you have a morning sweet tooth or not so I brought sausage biscuits and cherry almond Danish."

"Perfect choices! From Mel's?" I tried not to embarrass myself by grabbing the bag from her.

"Mel's, of course. It's the only place anyone should ever go for Danish. I left home a little early and stopped by on the way."

"You're an angel."

"No, I'm not." She entrusted me with the booty, going unerringly to a cupboard for plates and a drawer for forks, obviously familiar with the kitchen.

I started to wonder about her denial of angelhood, then opened the bag and fell in love. "I think you better hurry if you want your share."

She chuckled, and doled out the plates and forks, but didn't sit when I did. Instead, her smile flickered and dimmed. "Kath," she finally said, gripping the back of the chair opposite mine. "I am so sorry. Cole Dunbar called me this morning."

"Oh, well, I should have . . ."

"For heaven's sake, what are *you* apologizing for?" She laughed, her eyes looking pained.

"Um." I shrugged a shoulder.

"I started to tell you about Emmett yesterday. About the murder." She stopped, looked down at her hands, shook her head. "I hate saying that word. The whole thing was terrible *beyond* words. Something I'd like to forget."

Me, too, I thought. Along with most of the previous evening. Not to mention Granny's funeral.

"After living in this town as long as I have, you would think I'd know a story like that wasn't going to keep two hours, much less overnight. I should have told you about the situation yesterday. Anyway, I'll understand, completely, if you don't want to stay here after all."

"Ruth—" I wasn't sure what I was going to say, but it didn't matter because she had her piece prepared and shushed me with a flip of her hand.

"Kath, I have to tell you, I was very glad to find you still here. It gave me a real sense that things can return to normal. That they *will* return to normal. But I need you to tell me, on top of everything else you were dealing with yesterday, after hearing about Em, were you able to get any sleep at all?"

"Yes."

She looked both surprised and pleased by that answer. I was surprised by it myself, and gave it a quick fact check to make sure I wasn't just playing the role of Polite Girl by feeding her a line to make her feel better. No, with only a minor adjustment, it looked as though the "yes" could stand.

"Actually, I slept on the sofa. And I won't lie, the night did get off to a rocky start, but after I triple-checked the locks on the doors and windows, yes, I did get a reasonably good night's sleep." I hesitated before continuing, looking around at the kitchen, all parts of which were once again in focus. Quiet and dry, too. But was it "normal"? Probably more normal than the apparitions running amok in my head the night before.

I looked back at Ruth. She'd been waiting through my hesitation, watching my perusal of the kitchen with interest. She didn't strike me as a person who believed in paranormal anything. Good. More power to her. I didn't believe in any of it, either, I told myself firmly. I picked up one of the cups of coffee she'd brought and held it up to her in a toast. "Ruth, if it is indeed all right with you,

I'd like to stay. At least until this mess over Granny's house is straightened out."

"Excellent. And leave the straightening out to Handsome Homer. That's his specialty." That settled, she scooped up the biscuits and Danish and put them in the microwave for a reheat. The microwave did its thing with an efficient hum, then beeped, and Ruth returned the pastries to the table. "Bless Mel's miracles," she said, sitting down across from me. "Let's eat."

Had anyone ever asked me if there was a witch operating somewhere in Blue Plum or its environs, after first scoffing, I would have pointed my finger at Melody Gresham. Mel works pure magic at Mel's on Main, her bakery slash café slash sorcerer's kitchen. Anyone within several blocks of Main Street can close their eyes and easily stumble their way to Mel's by simply following their nose to the headwaters of cinnamon, yeast, and whatever spices dance through the day's tantalizing specials. Back home, surrounded by the flat farmlands of central Illinois, I've dreamed of Mel's paninis piled high with roasted portobellos and Brie and mounds of thick, crisp, homemade potato chips capped with melting blue cheese. She outdid herself with the cherry almond Danish that morning. The sausage biscuits weren't too shabby, either.

"Look, you match." I pointed from my biscuit to Ruth's twinset, pleased that I'd pegged the color.

"Yummy, isn't it?" she said, admiring her sleeve. "For me, looking at yarn on an empty stomach is more dangerous than shopping for food. I bought the wool for this when I skipped lunch one day."

"You knit that? The stitches are so tiny. It's gorgeous."

"I'm good, aren't I?" There was no hint of bragging in her statement and no need for it; the twinset did the bragging for her. "Ivy taught me. Another thing I loved her for. She gave my ADHD fingers a purpose. Apparently I'm a natural." She brushed a crumb from her front and adjusted the drape of the cardigan. "I found the pattern in one of those old boxes up on the third floor at the Cat. Ivy even had mother-of-pearl buttons up there."

"Ivy's Archives. Old wool and notions don't go baaaad," I bleated. "They just move up a floor and wait for the right customer to come along decades later."

Ruth laughed behind her napkin and a mouthful of Danish.

"I told Granny the shop was like reverse archaeology. The older the artifact, the higher up it floated in the stratigraphic layers of the store."

A sip of coffee cleared her throat and then Ruth cocked her head. "What are your plans for the Cat? Sell it?" No beating around the bush for Ruth. When I didn't answer right away, she rushed to reassure me. "I don't mean to pry, Kath, and you certainly don't need to answer my nosy questions. It's just that we are all wondering."

"Me, too. That's the simple answer, anyway. I'm wondering, too. I love the place as much as anyone."

"But."

"Yeah. But."

"We'd hate to lose it. It's hard enough losing Ivy."

I tried to speak but my throat had closed. In fact, with this turn of the conversation, my whole body had drawn in on itself. Shoulders up, arms crossed, one leg twined around the other, chin tucked. It was a perfect demonstration of a new yoga posture I'd call the Stress Pretzel. I made an effort to uncoil and take a deep breath.

"I'm meeting with your husband this morning and then someone at the bank."

"Rachel Meeks?"

"That sounds right."

"Good. Between Homer and Rachel, you're in safe hands. They'll help you sort your thoughts and plans from the purely emotional to the starkly financial. And now it's time for me to hit the office before we throw our gates open to the clamoring public." She pushed back her chair and started clearing the table.

"I'll get that, Ruth. Thanks for stopping by with breakfast. It was a feast and very welcome."

"My pleasure, and my penitence. Again, I'm sorry I didn't tell you about the situation with Emmett myself. When Cole Dunbar called this morning and said he dropped by last night and let it slip, I could have kicked myself."

Dropped by? Let it slip? Ruth had started for the back door when she said that, so she missed my complete and absolute dumbfoundedness, which couldn't have left me anything but pop-eyed. She didn't know why Dunbar "dropped by"? He didn't tell her about the break-in?

"I think it's sweet the way Cole was worried about you," she said, pulling the door open. "I didn't realize you knew him."

That louse. He didn't tell her. Why in blue blazes not?

"It's good to have you here, Kath," she called with a wave over her shoulder. "I'll see you later."

"Sure," I squeaked. "Bye."

Deputy Dirty Rat Louse of a Dunbar. I knew why he hadn't told her about the break-in. He didn't believe it had happened.

Chapter 8

"Mr. Wood will be a few more minutes yet, Ms. Rutledge. I do apologize for the wait. Would you like another magazine? I'd offer you coffee or tea, but Mr. Wood likes the down-home touch of offering refreshments himself, so you'll also have to wait for that and I apologize for that delay as well." Homer Wood's receptionist seemed to enjoy apologizing for him. "I would bring you a glass of water, only we have a man in doing some work on our kitchenette this morning and he found it necessary to turn the water off."

"Thank you, I'm fine, Ms. O'Dell."

"Please do call me Ernestine."

"Ernestine, thank you. Really, I am fine." I leafed through the magazine she'd first handed me to demonstrate how fine I was.

Homer Wood's reception area, in a sizable alcove opposite Ernestine's desk, was a pleasant enough place to wait. I could imagine Handsome Homer's clients shedding their anxieties about laws and infractions as they crossed the plush carpet. Their trepidations about shyster lawyers would slip away as they settled into the palatial leather wing chairs, and confident visions of contracts and estate planning would visit them as they gazed into the highly polished surface of the mahogany coffee table. The deep burgundy walls, the somber framed landscapes, the issues of *Architectural Digest* and *Fine Art Connoisseur* whispered, "Trust me."

Ernestine O'Dell sat behind her orderly desk, smiling in my general direction, hands clasped on the large desk calendar that served as a blotter. She was easily in her late sixties and possibly in her late seventies. Her glasses were so thick I wasn't sure how clearly she saw me. It was tempting to find out by making faces, but the setting and the occasion weren't appropriate.

"You might be wondering," Ernestine said, still smiling, "how Mr. Wood will offer you coffee or tea if we have no water from the tap this morning. He has one of those large bottles of spring water in his office." She measured off the size and shape of an imaginary version of the bottle, her eyes growing larger behind her thick lenses at the thought of the bottle's amazing dimensions. "I told the man who delivers them he should use a hand truck to save his back. I doubt he paid me any mind." She refolded her hands. "Also, I should tell you, though I'm sorry to do so, but due to the water situation, we have no facilities this morning."

"Oh. That's inconvenient."

"Wait until you're my age and you'll really know how inconvenient it is. In the meantime, we can run across the street to the courthouse if necessary."

That was an oddly chummy thought and I returned her smile in case she could see my face from that distance. The chairs in the waiting area were deep and wide enough for two of me. I perched on the edge of one in order to remain politely upright. When Ernestine had ushered me in I'd dithered over taking a chair facing her or choosing one of the others. Sitting in profile with my allotted magazine might have indicated my desire for personal space and privacy, but I liked the twinkle in Ernestine's thick lenses. And the clutter of small talk was more appealing than being stuck alone in my own head anticipating the emotions of hearing Granny's last will and testament read out in lawyerly tones.

"How long will the water be off?"

"I'm sorry." Ernestine smiled. "I don't have that information. The man doing the work is another one of Mr. Wood's good deeds." If eyebrows could supply air quotes, hers did for the words "good deeds."

My own eyebrows rose in question but she either didn't see them or missed them, and I lost my chance to find out what she meant.

"Lord love a duck," she said, slapping her hands on the desktop. "I've only just realized. You're Ivy McClellan's granddaughter."

"Yes, I am."

"Bless your heart and bless hers, too. Oh, my goodness, I was so sorry to hear she passed." Ernestine put a hand to her own heart and I had no trouble believing her sincerity. "But," she said, a bit of the twinkle returning, "as you are Ivy's granddaughter, you won't mind if I do this." She swiveled in her chair, took a knitting bag from a lower drawer, and plopped it on the desk. "Unprofessional, I know, but my first great-grandson is on the way"—she pulled a cloud of soft blue from the bag—"and I have miles to go before he can sleep under this."

"You go right ahead."

"Bless your heart. I wouldn't ordinarily knit on Homer's time, but with Ivy's granddaughter sitting right here in front of me, I think it's the proper thing to do. My tribute to a wonderful woman." Ernestine and I were suddenly old friends. She relaxed into her knitting and started whistling a jaunty version of "My Blue Heaven."

The flicker of her needles and the shimmer of yarn transforming before my eyes mesmerized me and I wondered why in blue heaven's name I let my job hijack my own creative energy. Except that wasn't entirely true. My work at the museum had a perfectly willing accomplice.

Me. True, there was a lot of the analytical and unromantic to my job. Microscopes, test tubes, and fumigation hoods can't help themselves that way, bless their hearts. But the job did take several micrograms of creativity and an unquantifiable spatter of imagination to pick apart and unravel the problems and mysteries presented by antique textiles. The horrid stain I'd found on a fragile eighteenth-century chemise might have been nothing more unpleasant than an accident with red wine, but arriving at that answer and deciding on a next step was the kind of excitement I studied long and hard to be a part of. Chemical analysis? It thrilled me. Wiping out a weevil infestation? It wowed me, if not exactly to the point of making me giddy, at least leaving me satisfied that I'd saved one small corner of the world.

Still, I wasn't Ivy's granddaughter for nothing. My days and energy were spent tending the artifacts of other people's creative efforts with textiles and fibers, some of the artifacts only remnants, dirty and damaged, and most of the people long dead. Watching Ernestine with her billowing blue, my fingers tingled for fibers of their own to manipulate and bring to life.

"Are you a knitter, Kath?"

"On occasion. I'm more of a weaver. I like the mechanics of looms."

"They're not so easy to carry around, though, are they?"

"A tapestry frame, maybe, but no, you're right—not as portable as your needles."

"You take after your grandmother, all right. I can see that," Ernestine said with a nod. "Although Ivy did it all and did it all well, didn't she? Spin, dye, weave, knit, tat, crochet, embroider, sew, you name it. Really, she was an artist. And generous with her talents. What a loss. Goodness, now I've dropped a stitch." She fussed quietly until she recovered her rhythm, then looked up, smiling again. "I was in absolute despair when I heard my granddaughter was expecting this child."

"Oh, I'm sorry."

Ernestine's hands and needles stopped mid-dance. "That didn't come out right, did it?" She shook her head and started knitting again. "What I meant to say is that I was in despair over ever being able to knit a blanket for the little button. I knit one for each of my own four babies and I knit one for each of my ten grandbabies and when my oldest granddaughter found out she's expecting, she said she wanted me to knit one for the beginning of this next generation, too. Thomas Andrew—that's what they're going to call him. Did I tell you that? They already know it's a boy. Isn't it an amazing world we live in today?"

"Why were you in despair?"

"My eyes. I'm blind as an old bat these days. It's no wonder I didn't recognize you when you came in. I expect you look just like your grandmother but I'm sorry to say I couldn't tell you from Adam or that man in the kitchen there."

"So, what did you do? You're knitting so fast now, I can hardly see the needles flying. Is it like riding a bicycle and you just needed confidence to hop back on?"

"Oh, I don't think so. I'd say it's all thanks to Ivy." She beamed and began whistling "What a Wonderful World."

"How do you mean?"

"Hmm?"

"How is it all thanks to Ivy?"

"It's this blessed yarn she sold me. It practically knits itself."

A small warning bell I thought I'd deactivated with my good night's sleep went off somewhere in my analytical, unromantic mind. Yarn that practically knits itself? For a woman blind as a bat? From Granny? No, no, no. This had not and was not going to happen in my life.

"We aren't expecting anyone else for your meeting with Homer, are we?" Ernestine interrupted my agitation. She finished a row and bundled the soft blue cloud back into her knitting bag, then swept the bag back into the drawer. "No, oh my, no. I do not recall these two having an appointment here this morning." She primly folded her hands and returned them to the middle of the blotter in the center of the desk.

From where I perched in my wing chair, I wasn't able to see who was approaching the front door and blotting the sunshine from Ernestine's smile. As it turned out, I didn't need to see them. I recognized those voices.

"Why, Ernie O'Dell."

"As we live and breathe."

"Where's that pretty young Heather who used to be here?"

The Spivey twins. They taunted their way in and planted themselves, hands on hips, in front of Ernestine's desk. They were dressed in identical knife-creased khakis and similar, though not quite matching, embroidered pullovers. Both pullovers were pink, but one was a light rose and the other was electric bubblegum. That didn't help me know which was Shirley and which was Mercy, unless one habitually wore more eye-killing colors than the other. I'd never paid enough attention over my years of sporadic Spivey contact to notice that peculiarity. Maybe Ernestine could clue me in later. If only one or the other had a noticeable scar, maybe a saber slash across one cheek.

"Good morning, Shirley, Mercy. It's nice to see you, as always." Ernestine's reversion to her pleasant but formal manners could not have sounded more puckered if she'd been sucking lemons. "Heather—Ms. Monroe—is taking a leave of absence. Mr. Wood was kind enough to ask me to fill in while she's gone. Unfortunately, if you're hoping to see Mr. Wood, I must inform you that he will be engaged all morning. He also has plans for lunch. I am so sorry."

"We're one of his morning engagements," Light Rose Spivey said.

"Oh, I don't think so." Ernestine moved her clasped hands a fraction to the left and peered at the square with the day's date on the blotter.

"How can you tell? Here, let me see." Electric Bubblegum invited herself over to Ernestine's side of the desk. "Why, Ernie, what a large calendar you have."

"And I don't see you anywhere on it," Ernestine snapped. She splayed her hands over the calendar, protecting her territory. "Mercy Spivey, I will ask you to kindly step back around to the appropriate side of the desk."

Aha, unless Ernestine was mistaken, Mercy was Ms. Electric Bubblegum. But what was her trick for telling them apart if she couldn't see them clearly?

"Shirley," Electric Bubblegum said with a lift of her nose.

"Don't play your games with me, Mercy. I know exactly who you are."

"Check your spelling, then, Ernie, before you jump down someone's throat," Electric Bubblegum said. "What I started to say is this: *Surely* we have a right to be present when our dear late cousin's will is read."

"And to support Katie in her sad bereavement," Shirley added with nauseating treacle.

"Kath," Mercy said, giving the point of her elbow to Shirley's ribs.

Shirley drew in a sharp breath, then pretended to clear her throat. "Such a sad time for all of us. Kath included."

The two had been so intent on crowding in and bullying Ernestine, I wasn't sure they'd seen me sitting in the waiting area. I was fairly well camouflaged in the dark leather chair, wearing my all-purpose and well-traveled black trousers, black silk blouse and a brocade jacket that was such a deep eggplant it might as well have been black, too. It isn't as easy to hide a redhead's hair and complexion against that backdrop but maybe my head appeared pale and floating. Like a ghost. No. No, no, no. I was not, I absolutely was not, thinking along those lines.

"How did you know what time I'd be meeting Mr. Wood this morning?" I asked, making one of the twins, Ms. Light Rose Shirley, jump.

"You told us," Mercy said, smoothly covering her own surprise and slewing around to face me.

"I did?" Darn, I might have. I couldn't remember.

"Yes. Yesterday," Shirley said.

"Yes. You told us yesterday afternoon," Mercy agreed. "Of course, you were upset over not being able to get into Ivy's house at the time, so you might not remember. Stress affects some people that way."

"You didn't even remember to take the casserole we brought you," Shirley said. "By the way, where did you stay last night? We looked for your car at the motel up on the four-lane and didn't see it."

"Not at the B and B, either," Mercy said.

I ignored their nosy question while my nose wrinkled in memory of the casserole Shirley hadn't, in fact, ever handed to me. A memory slip on her part, no doubt, due to the stress of my not accepting their eagerly volunteered help in breaking into the house. For my part, not receiving their wretched casserole had been one of the few bright spots of the day.

Abandoning Ernestine, the twins advanced on me, pink shoulder to pink shoulder. I could almost smell thawing tuna as they came. That imagined aroma was just the prod my memory needed. Maybe they'd been patrolling for my car again and found it parked in the lot behind the courthouse and surmised I'd be visiting Wood, Attorney at Law, this morning. But I definitely had not told them when I was meeting with Homer.

I stood. They stopped.

Ernestine leaned out of her chair precariously to see around them and made some interesting faces and gestures at me. She appeared to be miming removal of the twins from the premises. Her suggestions looked alarmingly aggressive, possibly involving a hatchet or shovel. That made me smile.

"Shirley, Mercy," I said, holding out my hands, "it's so kind of you to come down here this morning." Judging by Shirley and Mercy's response, the smile made my words sound genuine. "You're absolutely right about the stress of yesterday, too. And believe me when I say you don't know the half of it." Oops, that last bit offered too much information. Definitely a mistake, as I saw quickened curiosity blooming in their eyes. I took evasive action by putting my hands on their shoulders. "But now I'm afraid I've gone and wasted your morning, and I'm so sorry." I amped my smile up several watts and gave each pink shoulder a gentle squeeze, at the same time maneuvering the twins so they faced the front door. "You see, my meeting with Mr. Wood is private this morning. I'm sure you understand. It's all this stress, you know. I am so sorry."

I was about to take my hand from Shirley's shoulder to open the door and escort them out when Ernestine appeared at my elbow. The apologetic look she gave them as she held the door was worth memorizing for future personal use. If I'd had my camera with me or my phone out, I would have snapped a picture for reference.

"Do you think they'll try to come back?" I asked, staring after them. Just then, Mercy looked over her shoulder, half turning, and I again smiled and waved, although the gesture might more closely have resembled a shooing motion. "They can't really think they inherited anything, can they? Granny was never close to them."

"Oh, I think they'll stay gone for now," Ernestine said. She turned a key in the lock and gave me a satisfied look. "As for the other, they're just nosy with a pinch of mean. Always have been, always will be. And their brand of mean came, literally, with a pinch when they were children. They'll track you down again before too long, I have no doubt." She gave me a wicked smile. "And I am so sorry."

I laughed, as she knew I would.

"There, that's better. You deserve some small joy at this sad time, bless your heart. Now, Homer's ready to see you, and I believe I'll slip out the back door and over to the courthouse for a necessary break."

"Before you go, Ernestine, I have to know. What's your trick for telling Mercy and Shirley apart?"

"Ah." She tapped her nose. "No one else in this world, not even her sister, would wear the dreadful scent that Mercy Spivey dabs behind her ears."

Chapter 9

Granny certainly knew handsome. Everything about Homer Wood was just that. His posh furnishings, his elegant manners, his lovely tie and beautifully tailored suit, his lean face, long nose, and Paul Newman eyes. He met me at his office door with a warm Georgia drawl. His two large hands enveloped mine and then he ushered me in, one consoling hand transferred to the small of my back, guiding me to a club chair in front of his desk. Then, rather than put the barrier of the desk between us, he took the chair next to mine, crossing his lithe legs and leaning slightly toward me. He was every inch the solicitous solicitor Granny had told me about. If Homer and Ruth weren't the kind of couple who glide across dance floors, sharing candlelit dinners into the wee hours afterward, they were missing a good bet and countless photo ops. I was pretty sure, though, that Homer was aware of handsome, too.

"Before we even start, Ms. Rutledge, let me apologize for making you wait this morning."

"It wasn't a problem."

"Thank you. And may I call you Katherine?"

"No, it's Kath. Just Kath."

"Of course. Your grandmother told me that. That's what we wrote in the will." He tapped his fingers against his brow, shook his head, smiled. "Slow down, Homer," he told himself with a soft chuckle. "Get your facts straight. Kath. Let me tell you how very nice it is to finally meet you. Of course, I'd rather the circumstances were different." He shook his head again, this time with his lips pursed and that stricken look I couldn't quite get used to no matter how often I'd seen it in the eyes of Granny's friends over the past two days. "I can't tell you," he said, reaching over and putting a hand on mine, "how sorry I am that I missed her funeral yesterday. I was unexpectedly called to Nashville and was not able to break away from the meeting to make it back in time. I do hope I knew Ivy well enough, though, to know she wouldn't have minded so terribly much."

"Burial."

"I beg your pardon?"

"It was a burial. Granny didn't want a funeral." He was being kind and gracious. Why was I suddenly nit-picking?

"You're right again, of course, and I see you have your grandmother's eye for detail. She was a very bright woman. A bright light in our community and well loved."

"Except . . . I've heard a few things."

Homer sat back, head cocked. Was he dubious? Surprised? I couldn't tell but decided his raised eyebrows were inviting me to continue.

"Her—her house—" And now why was I suddenly choking? It wasn't tears this time. Anger? Anger with a prickling strand of worry . . .

"It's all right. Take your time, Kath. May I get you a cup of tea or coffee?"

I didn't want either, but I couldn't help looking around for the giant bottle of water that so impressed Ernestine. Homer took my interest as an affirmative.

"Tea, then?"

I nodded. It was easier.

"Good. I'll step into the kitchen and you can have a few minutes to yourself. Then you can tell me what you think you've heard or whatever it is that's concerning you. I'll do what I can to find the answers you need and make things right. I want you to know that I'm here to make things as smooth as possible for you during this sad time of transition."

After he patted my hand, which I could have done without, he filled a carafe from his mega-gallon bottle of spring water and went through to the kitchenette. Before he pulled the door closed, I heard him greet someone who promptly dropped what sounded like a couple of hammers and a bag of nails.

I did some deep breathing and inner admonishing. This was not the time to fall apart or lash out. I needed to concentrate on appreciating Homer's efforts and consideration. But, really, a line like *during this sad time of transition?* Maybe he was lunch buddies with Neil Taylor, the funeral director, and couldn't help absorbing phrases that sounded as though they came straight out of a mortuary science manual for model customer service. This probably wasn't a time to snicker, either. Homer meant well. People usually do during sad times of transition. And if he were able to find answers and make things right, that would be a fine thing.

A list would be a fine thing, too, I thought, and I should have started one sooner. Granny always said any project worth beginning was worth beginning with a detailed list. I was a confirmed acolyte of that philosophy in my professional life and my private life. Arriving listless for my appointment with Homer was a sure indication of stress-related backsliding. It was easy enough to remedy that.

As I rummaged in my purse for a notebook, something bright, white, and lined caught my eye. The corner of a legal pad winked at me from Homer's desk. A legal pad would be larger than anything I had with me, with plenty of surface area, allowing for a better-designed list or even an outline or a diagram. Ooh, with that pad and my favorite mechanical pencil . . . I heard the siren call of having the right office supplies for the right job.

But I couldn't do that. What if Homer's personal notes were on that pad of paper? Or notes from another client's appointment? Or notes scribbled during a conversation with someone who knew something about Emmett Cobb's murder . . . What if my imagination was launching itself into the ozone?

I dug further for my crabbed little spiral-bound, locating it under my cell phone and a rolled-up reusable bag. I pulled the notebook out and kept my eyes from wandering back to the tempting legal pad. My bent and rumpled paper might produce something that looked more like an impromptu grocery list, but it would be an honest effort.

First bullet point on my list, with its attendant mini-bullets: Granny's house on Lavender Street. Who owned it? Were the Spiveys and the uninformative rent-due notice correct and did Angela's husband, Max, now own it? If Max owned it, how did that happen? *Did* he inherit it? From whom? And how had *that* happened? The initial phrasing of that question was more colorful before I marked through parts of it. Next, why were the locks changed? If the place was broken into, did anyone know if anything was missing? Missing. Oh my God.

Second bullet point: Maggie. I couldn't believe I'd forgotten about her again. Where was she? Locating Granny's cat might not be exactly what Homer meant by finding answers, but her disappearance might be a clue to the break-in. If there'd been one.

Third point: Joe Pantry Guy and the break-in at the cottage. It hadn't occurred to me before, but could the break-in at the cottage and the supposed break-in at Granny's be related? Would Homer believe someone broke in last night if the police didn't? Could last night's break-in be related to Emmett Cobb's . . .

Fourth: Emmett Cobb's murder. *Murder*. Ruth didn't like saying the word and I discovered I had trouble writing it. I almost substituted something less permanent-sounding in its place. Then I pictured Cole Dunbar curling his lip at my squeamishness. I underlined "murder" twice. The sub-bullet I added below that really did make me feel squeamish. I scribbled it in anyway. Was Cole Dunbar right? Was Granny a suspect? Why? Then, to show I was an independent and possibly more astutely suspicious person than Cole Dunbar, I wrote down my own favorite suspect: Joe Pantry Guy. I thought about adding Dunbar, too, figuring I could make a case for him poisoning his poker buddy in a fit of pique, but I didn't want to invite bad luck. Or incur the further wrath of a still pretty much unknown quantity of a cop. Which led to the next bullet point.

Fifth: Cole Dunbar. Was he an honest cop?

"I would have asked," Homer said, coming back through from the kitchen, making me jump, "but I pegged you for a black tea drinker." He carried a tray loaded with teapot, cups, creamer—the works—and set it on the desk, eclipsing my view of the legal pad. "It's a knack I have. Choosing the right color tea for the right person and occasion. Ivy, for instance."

"Granny only drank coffee."

"Exactly." Homer laughed. "'Homer,' she told me, 'don't waste your water if you're going to run it through a teabag. I'll have coffee and I'll drink it black.'" His imitation of Granny was fair enough. I smiled, despite the list of unhappy questions glaring in my lap. Homer poured two cups and handed one to me. "Would you like anything in it?"

"No, thanks." I doubted there was a nip of anything on the tray. Too early, anyway.

"I thought not. I'm a honey-and-lemon man, myself." He sat in the chair opposite mine again, content with his tea and his parlor trick. "Now, tell me what you've been hearing and we'll see what I can do to put your mind at ease."

His charm and patter worked, as he must have known they would. I sat back, warmed my hands and breathed steam from the cup, took a sip. "Granny's house on Lavender Street."

"It's yours, of course. Lock, stock, and the rain barrel she keeps in the backyard for her dyeing projects. A very pleasant little property which should have good resale value even in this economic climate."

"But . . ."

"Only if you should choose to sell, of course. It might also bring you a tidy sum as a rental property. As for the property on Main Street, the business, the building, and the lot are yours. I would imagine you'll be looking to sell those as well, and we'll start probate. Are you familiar with that process? It can be lengthy, but with a single heir and an uncontested will . . ."

Words had failed me back at the "but" that he'd bulldozed under and right on past. Fortunately, my left hand took control of the situation, and while it flapped for Homer's attention, my right hand valiantly kept tea from sloshing all over my lap.

Homer skidded to a stop. I related my encounter of yesterday afternoon with the locked door on Lavender Street and the Spiveys with their information bomb about someone named Max supposedly inheriting the house, and Granny owing back rent. Once started, momentum carried me downhill through every bullet point in my hastily assembled list. When I arrived, breathless, at the bottom, I looked up.

Homer sat motionless, completely focused. Then, without a word, he reached over and set his teacup on the tray. He stood, walked around the desk to his own chair—his black, high-backed, throne of a chair—and sat down facing me. He moved the tea tray aside, placed the legal pad in front of him, lining it up with the edge of the desk, unnecessarily smoothed its flat, crisp surface, and took a pen from the inside pocket of his suit coat. He rolled his shoulders, adjusted his cuffs, turned his long nose toward me, giving me the look of an intent raptor. He clicked the pen.

"Go through it all again," he said. "Slowly."

Chapter 10

That authoritative click of Homer's pen woke me from my bad dream. There were no longer any answers he needed to find for me, because there weren't any questions. He needn't work his lawyer magic to make things right, because there were no snags, no wrinkles in my little patch of the world. Granny was gone—that was true and incontrovertible—but otherwise the forecast, thanks to Homer, was for smooth sailing through this time of transition. My life was suddenly almost jolly.

Sadly, it was also delusional. Of course the click of Homer's pen didn't jolt me out of troubled sleep. I was having a bit of a struggle to either feel or appear competent, but I was most definitely wide-awake. I started through my list of questions again.

Homer listened, made notes, and asked for clarification on several points. Did Shirley and Mercy say when the break-in on Lavender Street occurred? Did it look as though there actually had been a break-in? Had I walked around the house? Tried my key in the back door? Did I mention that break-in to Deputy Dunbar? Had I brought the rent notice with me? Did I know who Max was? His last name? The way Homer's left eye narrowed when he asked about Max and looked at the receipt gave me the impression he was pretty sure he already knew who Max was.

Homer apologized, again, for being away when I could have used his help immediately. In fact, he said, he hadn't returned until that morning. He hadn't even seen Ruth yet.

His total concentration calmed me at the same time it disturbed me further. His attention to my concerns made me feel safe, even if I half hoped he would shrug me off with a smile and another pat on the hand. But the fact that he paid such serious attention also confirmed my worries. Far from there being no snags or wrinkles, my little patch of the world was unraveling and possibly motheaten. If that weren't true, then why was Homer using up so many sheets of his legal pad?

I finished reading my list and waited. Homer made a few more notes. He had a light hand and the pen made a soft, expensive sound gliding over the paper. He glanced through his notes again, clicked the pen, and returned it to his inside pocket.

"I really appreciate Ruth coming to my rescue like that yesterday."

"And you're probably wondering why she didn't call me in Nashville and tell me about this situation with Ivy's house."

I lifted one shoulder in what I hoped came across as a nonjudgmental shrug.

"If there had been a dire emergency she would have. No question," Homer said. "But Ruth knows that I don't discuss my clients' business, and understands why, even in a situation such as this. There are circumstances wherein it is difficult to maintain lawyer-client privilege. In a small town—" He spread his hands and paused. "Well"— he refolded his hands and brought them to rest in the middle of the legal pad—"as you might imagine, it's hard to keep anything private in Blue Plum. In the meantime, Ruth took care of the immediate needs of the situation, with her invariable capability, and she left me to gather initial impressions for myself, as I prefer."

"Holmes." That slipped out. Only halfway audible, though, thank goodness.

"I beg your pardon?"

"Sorry. I was thinking how nice it is to be home. I've always thought of Blue Plum as a second hometown. People like Ruth and you, Homer, are part of the reason why."

"Thank you. I'll take that as a compliment."

I nodded, wondering if he were prone to fits of melancholy or if he slipped into a smoking jacket when faced with long hours of difficult cogitation. Or was it Poirot who was so fond of gathering initial impressions?

"To be quite frank," Homer said, abbreviating my digression, "I doubt I could have done anything more substantive for you than Ruth did had I been here yesterday, as late as all this happened. But here we are now, and we will find out what has happened and what is going on and what we can do about any of it."

"So, what are your initial impressions?"

"In this town?" He spread his hands again, this time adding a quick smile that had a flash of sneer attached, unless I imagined it. "I wonder how any of this managed to stay quiet."

"Granny was pretty good at keeping secrets."

"Ivy was a practical woman."

"And keeping secrets is practical? Huh. I never thought of it that way. But the secrets I'm thinking of are more along the lines of surprise parties or hiding a bicycle before a birthday."

"Small things."

"Compared to her not owning her house anymore, yes. Selling her house is a huge secret. And she kept it so secret she didn't even change her will." I was not going to mention, refused even to think about, her other huge "secret." Except, maybe the business about being a witch and the business with the house were part of the same problem. And not because she *was* a witch, but because she *thought* she was a witch.

"That is a curious point," Homer said.

"What is?" Had I said *"witch"* out loud?

"Are you feeling all right?" he asked, looking at me more closely.

"Oh, yes, sorry. It's just all of this . . ." Thank goodness for grief as a handy excuse. "I'm fine." I took a sip of the now cold tea, then put the cup next to his on the tray. He smiled encouragingly. "Okay, I'm wondering two things, coming at this from different directions. First, is the house thing really a secret? The Spiveys knew about it, so maybe other people know and haven't said anything because they assume I know, too."

"A possibility. Ruth didn't know anything about it, though?"

"No."

"I haven't heard anything about it, either. And Ivy did not change her will."

"No. So, looking at this from the flip side, I wonder if it's true? Did she really sell the house? What if she didn't and someone's trying to pull a fast one?"

"A fast what?"

"A fast property grab? I don't know. But this guy, Max, is married to Mercy Spivey's daughter, Angela, and there's never been any love lost between Granny and the Spiveys."

Homer's beak inclined toward me. "Kath, be very careful what you say along those lines, and where, and to whom."

"Libel?"

"Slander."

"Oh, right." I flapped a hand. "I always get those two confused."

"It's serious. I'm serious."

"I am, too. Who's Max—other than Angie's husband?"

Homer's left eye narrowed again, very slightly. Because of the poor manners I'd showed by lapsing into slander? Or at the mention of Max? He didn't answer my question, but brought his pen back out and tapped it on the legal pad. He clicked it open, clicked it shut, open, shut, then made a check mark beside one of his notes. I was tempted to stand up so I could see better and try reading that note upside down. But placing myself more directly in front of that nose and those eyes wasn't a comforting thought. It would be safer to approach obliquely, by swinging around behind him and reading over his shoulder. I gave myself a discreet pinch and told myself to pay attention.

"First, your idea of anyone pulling a fast one"— Homer paused and tapped his pen one more time before continuing—"to gain possession of a small, nondescript, basically insignificant house is unlikely."

"Hmm."

"I don't mean to insult Ivy, you, or the property by that statement."

He did insult us, but maybe he couldn't help himself. I pictured the lovely house he and Ruth must live in. He probably couldn't imagine relaxing in a cozy place like Granny's, or stretching his long legs out in such close quarters. I let the slight pass.

"Second, if Ivy sold the house it will be a matter of public record and should be easy enough to track down. Maybe trickier if Max inherited the property. I'll see what I can do this afternoon." He made another note.

"And Max?"

"I only know one Max. It's very likely there are others in town and around the county."

"Oh, dozens, I'm sure. Who's the one you know?"

"Max Cobb. Emmett Cobb's son." He gave no special

emphasis to the words in either of those two short statements. His voice and face were clear of emotion. He held my eyes with a bland look for a moment, then nodded as though agreeing with me. "Exactly," he said. He flipped his pen in the air, caught it, and pointed it at me. "Exactly."

"Um, exactly what? I didn't say anything." Couldn't say anything was more like it.

"You haven't got a lawyer's face, Kath."

My face had probably screeched "bloody hell" while my mind sat there gulping and inarticulate. "Maybe I'll work on that. Wow. Emmett Cobb who was murdered? Max is that Emmett Cobb's son?"

"We don't know for a fact that he's Emmett Cobb's son."

"Sure we do." I didn't have a lawyer's prissy approach to facts, either. "Even if we don't, we can find out fast enough. Ask Ernestine. I bet she'll know."

"I will."

I started to get up. Homer waved me back into my chair.

"Kath, we need to consider this situation matter-of-factly."

"Okay."

"Without emotion."

"I can do that. But I think I see where Cole Dunbar might have gotten the idea that Granny should be a suspect in Emmett Cobb's murder—if he somehow got hold of her house. But I don't believe, not for one single minute do I believe, that she had anything to do with his death at all."

"Without emotion."

"Oh. Right. Really, I can do that." I peeled my hands from their death grip on the arms of the chair, took several calm, deep breaths, tried to relax my teeth.

"May I tell you what I think we should do?" he asked,

obviously modeling the state of calm to which he wished I'd aspire.

"Sure."

"First, if you don't mind, I'll keep the rent notice for the files."

"Sure."

"Then I will call Sheriff Haynes and find out if there is an official line of inquiry connecting Ivy with Emmett Cobb's murder. I agree with you. I find it hard to believe she had anything to do with his death."

"Not just hard to believe. Impossible."

"Beyond the realm of imagination."

"Thank you."

"You're welcome. Next, let me ask what your plans are for the rest of the day."

"Meet with Rachel Meeks over at the bank. Meet with Ardis and maybe some of the staff at the Weaver's Cat. I'd kind of planned to start going through things at the house, too." The thought of going through Granny's clothes made me sniff, but I pulled myself together for Homer's sake. Maybe, if I asked, Ardis would come over and lend a shoulder and helping hands. Instantly, as the words "helping hands" came to me, an image flashed through my mind. A pair of hands pawing through Granny's chest of drawers, her closet, her desk. Hands helping themselves . . . An involuntary shake of my head cleared the image, as though it had been a gnat buzzing between my eyes and ears. "Do you know Nicki Keplinger?"

"Who?" Homer asked.

I don't know which of us was more surprised by my blurted question. I felt a trickle of sweat on the back of my neck and rushed to explain and cover the confusion the image left behind. "I was just thinking out loud, thinking of asking Ardis Buchanan, over at the shop, if she'd help me go through Granny's things. And Nicki." Nicki who was wearing a jacket she said Granny gave her.

"Of course, and Nicki works at the shop, too, doesn't she? Her name rings a bell. No doubt Ruth has mentioned it. Although, if she used the name Nicki in any sentence also containing the word 'yarn' or 'wool,' I can't vouch for paying close attention. And, please," he said, pointing his pen at me again, "do not ever repeat that to Ruth." He nodded when I dutifully returned his quiet laugh. "It's never an easy task, sorting through a loved one's life. A lot of emotion. A lot of memories."

"A lot of good memories," I said.

"That will help. And I should think any of the women at the shop will be happy to give you a hand. Ruth, too, I'm quite sure."

"Everyone has been very kind. Um, but, what about the break-in, or the supposed break-in? If there really was one, will the police object? Will there be any problems getting into the house?"

"Was there crime scene tape across the door?"

"No. Gosh, that would've been horrifying to come across. Do they really use that stuff? On the other hand, if there was tape, you don't suppose the Spiveys took it down, do you?"

Homer wasn't amused.

"Slander again? Sorry."

"Always remember how small this town is, Kath. Like a family of twelve sharing a two-room apartment. There's no privacy, and a virus spreads like wildfire. Or think of it like a group of seven-year-olds playing that old telephone game. Massive amounts of misunderstanding."

I sighed.

"But a lot of laughs and good times, too. That also is worth remembering. This is a good place. Good people." He made another check mark on his list. "I'll make some calls and we'll get you in the house. Maybe not today, if Max is still in Kentucky, but I don't want you to worry about the house. It's locked. It's safe. How long do you plan to be in town?"

"Two weeks."

"That's fine, then. You have time. The house isn't going anywhere and we will get you in. Now, what is your meeting with Rachel Meeks about?"

I blanked. Had I really had the presence of mind, sometime in the past few days, to make an appointment with Granny's banker? How practical of me. How Granny-like. "I guess I thought it would be a good idea to know exactly where the business stands, where Granny's estate stands, before I try to make any decisions."

Homer nodded his handsome head. "That makes good sense. You have some not inconsequential decisions to make regarding the business, and those decisions will, of course, affect not only the shop's employees but the town as well. You're smart to approach that decision with your eyes open, armed with all the facts."

I found myself nodding along with Homer and feeling businesslike and incredibly wise.

"I'd like to suggest a change in your plans, though," Homer said. "Let me talk to Rachel on your behalf. Have you met her?"

"No. I set this up with her assistant on the phone."

"Ah." He looked down, but not before a smile pulled at his lips. He made half a dozen quick hash marks on his pad. "Allow me to do this small favor for you," he said, looking back up, having recovered his lawyer face. "I'll meet with Rachel. You and I will need to meet again, anyway, and at that point I can give you a summary of what Rachel has to say." He tried not to smile again. "Trust me on this, Kath. It will save you time, if nothing else."

"And that 'if nothing else' will remain unspecified due to problems with slander?"

"Something like that. One more thing before you go. Two, actually. We'll get Ernestine to set up another appointment. But I also want to address what happened at the cottage last night."

"Have there been other reports of strange things happening there?" I had to stop myself from slapping my forehead or rolling my eyes. Of course he wasn't talking about the weepy ghost. Which, this morning, I absolutely was refusing to believe I'd seen.

Homer cocked an eyebrow.

I feigned a tickle in my throat. "Strange men leaving through windows?"

"I'm not aware of earlier break-ins, but I will contact the sheriff's department and obtain copies of any reports, if there are any. But now, your question concerning Cole Dunbar's honesty . . ." He sat back and rested his elbows on the arms of his chair, steepling his fingers and looking at me with that nose and those eyes. It was all I could do to keep from squeaking. I was glad he was on my side and that I wasn't really much of a mouse. "I won't go so far as to say you questioned Deputy Dunbar's honesty," he said, "because I believe you have an honest need to know if he can be trusted."

"Okay, that sounds fair."

"I agree. You understand, of course," he continued, "I can only speak from my own experience and knowledge base. In my profession one quickly learns that honesty is not a permanent quality in anyone. That said, I have no personal knowledge of and have never heard anything to suggest that Deputy Cole Dunbar is anything but honest."

That struck me as a bravura performance of a non-ringing endorsement. I wasn't sure where it left me. Maybe it meant I could trust Cole Dunbar to be as honest as the next man, whoever that man might be. Maybe it meant Cole Dunbar was a man who meant well but sometimes fell short. Whatever it meant, I decided I'd reserve the right to still think of him as a clod and a louse. Homer looked satisfied with his statement, though, and my nod, which he chose to interpret as my acceptance of it. Of course, all his answer really told me was that he was a master at hedging his bets.

"I will tell you this," he continued, still hedging. "Cole is a pretty fair poker player and that takes a certain talent for bluffing." He laughed and shook his head in a we'd-better-keep-an-eye-on-those-rascally-gamblers kind of way, as though that would make me believe he wasn't keeping the door to Dunbar's honesty ajar.

We wrapped up the meeting soon after that. Homer accompanied me as far as Ernestine's desk, stopping to confirm that Max was, indeed, Emmett Cobb's son, and to consult with her over how best to fit me into his hectic schedule the next day. While Ernestine placed a call canceling and rescheduling another client's appointment, Homer and I shook hands, his warm and steady, mine cold and a little overwhelmed. Ernestine, the phone cradled between her shoulder and ear, rolled her chair to the end of her desk, the better to peer around Homer's back. She fluttered a wave to me while informing the client on the other end of the line how sorry she was to be calling.

I scanned my list of questions before shoving it into my shoulder bag. I hadn't made any of Homer's elegant check marks or any further notes, but three words scrawled across the page would have sufficed to sum up the meeting. *Wait and see.*

With a small pang, not unlike the sting of a single swiped claw, I realized we hadn't touched on the question of Maggie's whereabouts. I hadn't really expected Homer to address the issue of a mislaid cat, though. Her plight, if she were in one, was more of a private bullet point on my list. For all I knew, she was living it up in the lap of milk and catnip with one of Granny's cat-loving friends.

But I owed it to Granny, and to Maggie, to find her. Even if she bit me when I did.

It was interesting to learn, I thought as I pulled the heavy glass door shut behind me, that Homer had personal knowledge of Cole Dunbar's poker game. But where did that information get me?

Chapter 11

Midmorning Blue Plum greeted me on Homer's front stoop. The sky was blue and high, with a flotilla of cartoony clouds sailing by. Freed from my meeting at the bank, I stopped on the brick sidewalk for a moment, absorbing the laid-back bustle of downtown. The sun felt good on my cold hands. I held them out palms up, then turned them over like toast to warm their backs as well. It was the sort of morning that could be improved only if it smelled of lilacs or cut grass or the savory and sweet scents of Mel's around the corner on Main Street.

Unfortunately, a rust-spotted green pickup stood idling at the curb in front of me, polluting the air with its exhaust. I went and stood next to the open passenger window and coughed dramatically for the driver's benefit. But the guy behind the wheel was oblivious to everything except the music pumping directly into his bloodstream through his earbuds.

"Moron." Oops. More slander. But only very quiet. I looked around, not quite guiltily. There wasn't anyone near enough to hear or care, though, other than the driver, and he was still plugged in. He was bobbing his head and drumming with his forefingers on the steering wheel, eyes half closed, having his own kind of happy morning.

And except for his engine chugging away and filling my happy morning with carcinogenic particulates, how could I complain? Homer was probably right, though, and I promised myself that I would watch my mouth in the future.

I jaywalked across the street, going around the front of the pickup to avoid the worst of its spewing fumes. If I remembered right, Homer's office, so convenient to the courthouse in case of plumbing emergencies, was in a building built and occupied by the town's first professional photographer. Granny "collected" names and the photographer's had delighted her. From the courthouse lawn I looked back. Yes, there, centered above the second-story windows and below the roofline, was the ornate rectangle of limestone she'd pointed out to me, set into the dark red bricks. Chiseled into the stone were a date, 1872, and the photographer's name: GENTLE BEAN.

"There, now," I could still hear Granny say, "they don't give boys names like Gentle or Pleasant anymore and the world would be a better place if they did."

She loved taking me on what she called "time warp walks" up and down the streets of Blue Plum. "The whole town is a tapestry," she'd tell me as I trailed along. "And it's a far more interesting tapestry than anything I've ever woven or possibly even conceived."

On one memorable walk, when I must have been about seven, she took me into the courthouse and down a hallway past the line of people waiting to renew their car tags, past a courtroom door propped open to catch a breeze on that stifling day, and on down to a door that drew no attention to itself. We waited until no one was in sight, and then she opened the door and shooed us both in. It felt tight and smelled musty in the space behind the door. It was dark and Granny kept a hand on my shoulder until she flicked on the flashlight she'd pulled from a pocket or the air; I didn't know which. We were in a narrow stairwell.

"Up we go," Granny said, and we climbed. We followed Granny's wobbling beam of light, our steps hollow and stirring a layer of dust, and eventually came to another door. I tried turning the knob and couldn't. Granny reached around me, turned it with ease, and we slipped out onto one of the tiny balconies of the courthouse cupola. A pigeon cooed in greeting and moved farther along the railing to make room.

"Just a quick look," Granny said. "Then we'll duck back inside before anyone but the pigeons knows we're here."

I'd never been so high up in Blue Plum. The rooftops and chimneys were a new world to explore. I could have hung over the railing listening to the pigeon and Granny all afternoon.

"See how the streets run?" Granny traced the grid of streets with her finger. "They're the warp and the weft of Blue Plum's tapestry and the buildings and houses are part of the story being told."

"Is the pigeon part of the story?" I was sure the pigeon was watching us, waiting for the right answer.

"All the birds in Blue Plum. All the people and their cats and dogs and their cars and bicycles and gardens and everything else are part of the tapestry's story. One of these years, when I've learned enough and have the right vision, I'll start my own tapestry. It might be up to you to finish it, though, because I probably won't be ready to start it until I'm about a hundred and three. Here, now. Hold my hand going down."

"I'm not little anymore."

"But I'm already old."

She wasn't such an old lady then, but she always got her way, even if getting it involved the misdirection sometimes necessary with children. I took her hand and felt completely responsible for our safe passage back to earth.

Granny always got her way. She was always right. Two statements of fact, basically true. Although, of course, they were exaggerations. She wasn't *always* right. She didn't *always* get her way. But.

"Ma'am?"

I was still standing on the courthouse lawn looking up at Homer's building. Probably slack-jawed and blank as my mind raced ahead without the rest of me. How did always being right and always getting her way fit with Granny no longer owning the house on Lavender Street? Had she wanted to sell it? Otherwise how had Emmett Cobb gotten it from her? If he *had* gotten it from her and if Max inherited it from him. And what was right about someone killing Emmett Cobb? But that couldn't have had anything to do with Granny, even if she'd wanted her house back. And now she'd finally started weaving her Blue Plum tapestry and I wanted to see it.

"Ma'am? Are you all right? Whoa, there. Didn't mean to scare you."

If he hadn't meant to scare me, he shouldn't have snuck up on me from behind, or wherever he'd come from, and tapped me on the shoulder. Banging a couple of garbage can lids together as he'd approached would have been a better plan.

"Can I help you? I couldn't help noticing you've been staring at that building and I wondered if you're nervous. About seeing the lawyer?" He looked familiar, but I couldn't place him. "Old Homer, he ain't half bad, if you need one of them ass . . . one of them rascals."

"Thank you. That's good to know."

"You looked worried or lost or something and I thought I'd do my good deed for the day by asking could I do anything for you."

"Well, I hope all your good deeds are so simple. I'm

fine, just lost in memories. Thank you. It was very nice of you to stop."

"All right, then, you have a good day, now." He nodded, crossed the street, and climbed into the rust-spotted pickup, which was still running.

Son of a gun. The morning-polluting moron was also a knight in rust-spotted armor. I watched as he stuffed the earbuds back in his ears, his head picking up the rhythm. He gave the engine an extra rev to get the motley vehicle moving, lifted an index finger to me in the standard Blue Plum salute, and chugged off. I wondered if either the truck or driving it with earbuds was legal, but supposed it didn't matter. He knew a good ass. . . rascal who could probably get him off.

A glance at the courthouse clock showed ten forty-five. Ardis wasn't expecting me at the Weaver's Cat much before noon. Thanks to Homer's taking the meeting at the bank with Rachel Meeks, I had time to spare. I left the car parked in the lot behind the courthouse and took myself on a time warp walk of my own.

Homer had asked if I'd tried my key in the back door of Granny's house. I hadn't. I'd let emotion, the Spiveys, and the tuna casserole distract me. He also asked if it looked as though there had actually been a break-in. I hadn't noticed anything when I drove up or when I looked for Maggie through the front window. But unless there was an obvious burglarlike mess left behind or a broken window, I wasn't sure I'd be able to tell. I was willing to try, though.

And that's what Deputy Clod Dunbar found me doing some fifteen minutes later.

Chapter 12

"Police. Hands where I can see them. Step away from the window, slowly. Well, wouldn't you know it. It's you."

"Are you the only policeman in Blue Plum?"

"Feels like it lately."

I turned around, hands still where he could see them, in case Deputy Clod felt jumpy as well as put upon. "I was just looking through the windows."

"I could see what you were doing, Ms. Rutledge. Would you please put your hands down? I received a call asking about a break-in. Are you the only person mixed up in burglaries in Blue Plum?"

"Nice. Wait—you mean you're just now getting around to investigating? I don't believe this. Last night you took your sweet time looking around the whole Homeplace before dropping by the scene of the crime, and now you're showing up, what, two, three days later to check out this one? For heaven's sake, I've probably destroyed valuable evidence trying to get in the back door and tramping around looking in the windows."

"As you say."

Darn. I looked at my hands, at the soles of my shoes.

"Nah, you don't need to worry." He lifted his hat and massaged his scalp, then rolled his head from shoulder to shoulder and scrubbed his neck. "You probably didn't destroy anything useful. We investigated when the initial call came in. That'd be three days ago."

"The day after Granny died. It seems more like a week ago. Or just a couple of minutes."

"That's the way it felt when . . ." he started to say, but the rest of his words turned into a yawn. "Pardon me," he said, pulling his voice back out of the gaping depths. "I assure you, it isn't the company." From the smile disappearing into a second yawn, he judged himself either suave or witty. Considering he was armed and appeared dangerously sleep deprived, I didn't roll my eyes. "I read through the report after it was filed," he said. "There wasn't much evidence to go on at the time. And then we had that gully washer yesterday. No, you didn't likely trample anything worthwhile."

"But someone really did break in?"

"That's what Cobb reported, anyway."

"I was kind of hoping it wasn't true." I turned back to the window and cupped my hands to the glass. There wasn't anything obviously amiss. "How did they get in and what did they take? How did Cobb know?"

"He found a few drawers pulled out, a cupboard hanging open. Said it looked like someone was in a hurry or interrupted. No sign of forced entry." Dunbar joined me at the window. His shoes were the size of monster trucks compared to mine. If there had been any evidence left after I waltzed through, his feet took care of obliterating it. "Wouldn't win any prizes for housekeeping, would she?"

"Hey!"

"I'm just saying. Observation only. Not an indictment. But a room like that makes it hard to tell if anything's been disturbed."

"She would know if anything was disturbed."

"No doubt," he said mildly. "Shame she's not here."

That was the closest he'd come to offering sympathy about Granny's death.

We were at the side of the house looking into the third bedroom, which she'd turned into another workroom. Her big floor loom lived in the front room, where there was enough space for it. In here, she kept her treasure, a piece of art. It was a tapestry loom my grandfather made from cherry and walnut with brass for the hardware. Somehow he kept his project a secret from Granny while he cut, smoothed, polished, and assembled the pieces. He gave it to her for their twenty-fifth anniversary, fixing a small brass plaque to the frame that read *MY DEAREST IVY*.

I could see five or six inches woven on the loom and a canvas pinned behind the warp—the cartoon—her painting of the design. From the angle the window gave me I couldn't see clearly, but it had to be her Blue Plum tapestry. What did she say in her phone message? *It's . . . well, it is what it is. A bit of a puzzle.* What did she mean? Something about it bothered her. Maybe Ardis knew. I was dying to get in there and take a good look at it.

The walls of the room were lined with shelves full of books and bins and baskets of wool. Beater combs, heddles, shed sticks, a couple of old raddles, and a spare batten hung from hooks she'd screwed in the ceiling. The dismantled parts to another loom crowded one corner. Someone found it in an attic earlier in the spring and left it on Granny's front porch like a stray cat for her to take in. She called me, excited and sneezing. *Early nineteenth century, Kath. Looks like chestnut! It hasn't been touched in a hundred years and has all the dust to prove it.*

If I could paint a picture of Granny, rather than the light in her blue eyes, the twist of silver hair on her neck, or the tilt of her head as she wondered what I was up to, I'd paint this room. Every inch of it looked like her. Like home. And I was stuck outside, looking in through a window. And if the window were open, I would smell home, too. Lanolin and wool.

"I need to get in there."

"Clutter," Dunbar sniffed, turning from the window. "Well, it might be useful if you looked around and could tell us if anything is missing. If you can tell. Then maybe we'd have a chance of returning it to you. Whatever 'it' is. If we ever find it. Doubtful in cases like this."

"Aren't you Mr. Jolly Optimist. But wait, you said you read the report. You mean you didn't write it? You aren't the one who investigated?"

"One of my colleagues took the call. Contrary to your experience, Ms. Rutledge, I am not the only deputy in Blue Plum. Sometimes I'm allowed to go home and get some sleep. But I am here now. I hoped you might appreciate the personal attention."

"Huh? Why? Don't you trust your colleague to make a proper investigation?"

"Do you always jump to conclusions?"

"It saves time," I said. "Can you get me in?"

"Not without breaking in myself."

"I'm game. Please?"

"No."

He was no fun. I kicked a clod of dirt and enjoyed the symbolism.

"Cobb's due back in town tomorrow," he said. "I can get you in then. In the meantime maybe you . . ."

"Cobb can get me in *then*," I interrupted, not interested in his meantime. "I need to get in *now* because Max bloody Cobb already re-rented it and the new people are sitting like vultures waiting to move in. And I need to pack all this up and clear it out and for God's sake where am I supposed to clear it all out to? It's a lifetime accumulation of, of . . . It's her whole life in there. I cannot, cannot, *cannot* believe this is happening." I closed my eyes and wrapped my arms around my head and wished everything, including Deputy Dolt, would go away.

"Jesus. Are you all right?"

Drat. He was still there. The rest of the world was still there, too, because my phone rang. I yanked it out of my shoulder bag, checking the caller ID as I walked away from Dunbar.

It was salvation in the form of Carol Mumford, my good friend and supervisor at the museum in Illinois. Excellent. With luck, it would be a short consultation, laying out a dilemma that only my preservation skills could solve, winding up with Carol expressing undying gratitude for my clear analysis and precise plan of action. Visions of crinolines in peril danced in my head, followed immediately by a less likely but more entertaining scenario.

"Carol, hi. Please tell me we've just received the pitiful but fascinating remains of a singed milking apron newly excavated from a building site in Chicago, complete with the hoofprints of the cow that trampled it into the muck, which saved it from burning up altogether. And tell me you need all my wits marshaled to preserve the darling apron and earn a great honking endowment for the museum from Mrs. O'Leary's great-great-grandchildren. Really, you don't know how important it is for me to hear something sane like that right now."

By the time I was halfway through my plea, she was laughing so hard she was almost crying. Good. It always made me feel better to make her laugh. She wasn't an easy mark, being the serious, fiscally responsible type she was burdened to be by both her nature and her job. Relieving that burden by making her laugh once a week was a goal I wrote into my private version of my official state-authorized job description.

"Carol, I'm serious. You would not believe what's going on here. I need something, anything, to snap my cognitive skills back together so I can deal with the incredible mess I have on my hands."

It turned out she really was crying. I stopped blathering and listened.

"It's not computing," I finally said.

"I'm so sorry," she said between sobs.

"Say it again without the sound effects."

"You heard me the first time. I know you did. Don't make me say it again. I'm so sorry. And I have to go now. I have to tell Laurie, too. And I know this is going to sound tactless, but with your grandmother dying, at least with the inheritance you've got something to fall back on, so thank God for that. Laurie's got the children and that huge mortgage."

"Right. You're right. Listen, it's not your fault. I know that. I've got to go, too. And, yeah, thank God Granny died. Solves everything." I said the last two sentences aloud, but only after I disconnected. Carol didn't deserve my crass comments. She was miserable enough already. I hadn't said good-bye, but she was crying again and wouldn't have heard.

I turned my phone off. Stared at nothing. A big, fat nothing. There was nothing to go back to. The state's budget crisis, which had been a runaway truck and gaining momentum for several years, had just smashed into the museum and careened through the conservation department, running over jobs left and right. Mine didn't survive.

"Are you all right?" It was Dunbar asking that again.

I might not have a job or my sanity, but this guy and his snarky attitude were becoming a fixture in my life. It didn't seem like a fair trade. He obviously didn't believe in privacy, but maybe that was a cop-at-a-crime-scene kind of thing he couldn't help. I'd walked around the corner of the house to put some distance between us.

He'd circled around the other way and had apparently been standing in front of me.

"It looked like you were hearing bad news," he said.

"It's okay. I'm fine." I was telling myself as much as him. And I would be fine. I knew that. Maybe not that afternoon. Or the next day or the next week or the week after that . . .

"You don't want to talk about it? Sometimes it helps, so maybe we . . ."

"I don't. Thank you, anyway."

"Just that it was an odd way to end a phone call," he said.

"Sorry, what?"

"How exactly was it your grandmother died? I'm not sure I heard the details."

"She had a massive heart attack. Why are you . . . do you . . . oh for Pete's sake, Dunbar. I was using sarcasm and I'd already hung up. The person I was talking to, in my *private* conversation, said it was lucky I'd inherited my grandmother's estate. I would rather have my grandmother."

"You having money problems?"

"No, and you know what? I'm not having this conversation, either. First you hint that Granny killed Emmett Cobb and now you're thinking I killed Granny. No." I pivoted, with a mental raspberry in his direction, then immediately turned back. "But I would like to know why you told Ruth Wood you only just happened to stop by last night. Do you or don't you believe a man was in that pantry?"

"I know how stress and unfamiliar surroundings can affect the mind."

My mouth opened. It snapped shut. I shook my head and started back around the house, back downtown, on my way to the Weaver's Cat, where they might have some of that rosemary chocolate whatever cake left over and I could drown my aggravations and sorrows in four or five slices.

Dunbar caught up with me at the sidewalk. I didn't stop. He matched his steps to mine, hands in his khaki uniform pockets as though he were Andy Taylor out for a stroll in Mayberry. I ignored him.

"So, I was wondering," he said.

I didn't ask what, just kept walking.

"You want to grab a pizza some night?"

That did stop me. "What?"

"A pizza, maybe a beer?"

Clod and me? Raising a pint together? Over a pizza at the local joint? Where did that bizarre idea come from? Was he serious? I stopped laughing when I realized he wasn't laughing with me.

"Oh my God, you are serious, aren't you? Was that your 'meantime' and 'maybe' back there? No, look, I'm sorry I laughed, but I can't, and this is another conversation I'm not going to have. Just, no."

He turned around without another word, although he tipped his hat first, proving he completely understood sarcasm and knew how to use it.

Chapter 13

My life as a weaver's glossary: tension, warped, balanced, unbalanced, beaten, snagged, frayed, snapped . . . I felt like the living, breathing embodiment of all those terms and tribulations as I walked away from that phone call and the undateable Deputy Dunbar and that snug little house. "Living" and "breathing" were the key words, though. I had a place to sleep and a business I could step into, if that's what I wanted to do.

One foot in front of the other, head held high, nose firmly thumbed at anything and everything trying to bring me down. I pushed away thoughts of bad state budgets and doltish sheriff's deputies and let my footsteps echo the mantra running through my head. *I will be fine. I will be fine. I will be fine.*

Granny gave me the foundation of my career when she taught me the rhythm of weaving on the big floor loom in the corner of her living room. It was a huge piece of equipment to a six- or seven-year-old child, and more like a jungle gym. Granny called the loom Olga.

"She's a sturdy, dependable old gal," Granny said, patting the loom the way she might a faithful nag come to nuzzle carrots from her pocket. "We could have an earthquake and she wouldn't walk across the floor like some of these lightweight hobby looms they sell to folks who don't know any better. I've seen more frustration woven on those than whole cloth."

I loved the names of the loom's parts and pieces—batten, beam, heddle, raddle, sley, shuttle, harness, ratchet, reed, temple, castle. What child wouldn't love a contraption that had a castle? Learning to weave on Olga was an acrobatic experience for one so small, but Olga and Granny were patient and steady. And although I felt frayed and unbalanced by the blows of the past few days, Olga and Granny had woven a safety net for me, too. I turned the corner into Main Street telling myself I was glad to be alive and thankful I'd had those two old girls in my life. Thankful for the Weaver's Cat, down at the end of the block, too. One way or another, I would be fine.

I passed the bank, picturing Homer listening handsomely as Rachel Meeks described Granny's finances with the elaborate detail of a medieval tapestry. Mel's on Main was harder to pass but, with a little effort, I convinced myself that if I removed my nose from the window and walked away quietly, I wouldn't shrivel into a pathetic bit of lint. Also that I could stop in later and pick up something tasty for supper.

I approached the Cat with new eyes and questions that hadn't ever been within a blip of my radar: Should I start looking for another conservator's position? Could I be happy slipping behind the sales counter, into Granny's groove? Would I be happy settling into Blue Plum? Did I know what I'd be getting into or have any business at all thinking I could take over?

The string of camel bells hanging inside the Cat's front door jangled as I pushed it open. Ardis, bagging a purchase at the sales counter, looked up and waved.

"How are you today, hon?"

"I'm fine. How are you?"

"You are?" She raised her eyebrows, prompting her customer to turn and see for herself.

"Yes, I am. That's what I keep telling myself and sometime soon I might believe it."

The customer stopped on her way out and put her hand on my arm. "If you want my advice, you'll buy some of the new baby alpaca they just got in. That's what I did. I found out this morning my daughter is moving back home. With her dog and her boyfriend. Though, frankly, I find the dog and the boyfriend completely interchangeable. First thing I did, after I realized it was already too late to call a locksmith because Tina—that's my daughter—was calling from her car while she was sitting in my driveway, first thing I did was run down here to drown my sorrows in chocolate-colored alpaca. Better than drowning myself in alcohol or chocolate-covered cherries is the way I look at it."

I took a deep breath on her behalf. "What are you going to make?"

"Could be I'll knit myself a straitjacket. Probably need it." She took her hand from my arm and patted her bulging bag. Then she plastered a smile on her face, straightened her spine, and marched out the door.

"She'll have that straitjacket done and have herself strapped into it in no time, too," Ardis said. "Ivy's pet name for her was Frenetic Fredda. She knits as fast as she talks."

"And that's a good example of a problem I don't have." I turned back to Ardis, pointing my thumb over my shoulder at the departing Fredda.

"What problem's that?"

"Children moving back home. The beauty of always losing the guy or falling for the wrong one is that you don't usually end up with children to worry about." Something about my tone of voice alarmed Ardis.

"Hon," she said, coming from behind the sales counter, "I think you do need to drown something in alcohol or chocolate." She put her hands on my shoulders and pointed me in the direction of the kitchen. "Alcohol isn't available, but you go on back to the kitchen. There should be plenty of the other left over from yesterday."

"Join me?"

"As soon as Nicki gets back from the bank."

Despite Ardis' gentle shove, I took the long way to the kitchen. I wanted to find that baby alpaca Fredda bought as a substitute for family therapy. Maybe some of that would bolster my *I will be fine* mantra. I also wanted to see what else was new. I hadn't been in the shop, hadn't been back to Blue Plum since Christmas, not even to celebrate Granny's eightieth birthday the previous month.

"No fuss," she'd said when I asked if she wanted a party. "Send me a card and donate some time at a nursing home. Do something nice for the poor old souls spending their last days shivering in your wretched prairie winters. And remind me to tell Ardis she'd better not plan any surprises. Better yet, you tell her. She doesn't always listen to me these days."

She never had liked a fuss, so I hadn't thought anything about her refusal of a birthday bash at the time. But now I did wonder.

I passed rainbows of yarns and roving, finding the alpaca almost by accident as my fingers made their way from skein to skein, my thoughts following other threads. An involuntary "oooh" escaped me when my hand brushed against a raspberry-colored hank, and a barely appropriate "ohhhhh" when I picked it up and held it to my cheek. I'd have felt self-conscious, but I was probably only the latest customer unable to control herself around the stuff.

The shop was rarely a silent place. Fondling and cooing were openly encouraged. Granny called it word of mouth and moan advertising. I returned the raspberry skein to its littermates and stroked a sage green one in the next bin. It was no wonder Fredda ran down here and bought all the chocolate brown she could lay her hands on. It was comfort food in the form of fiber. And if Fredda could knit a straitjacket from it, maybe I could knit myself a cocoon. Or a cave.

"That darker green, up there, would be beautiful with your hair."

A woman appeared at my side. She wasn't looking at the darker shade, though. She stared at the sage green my hand rested on.

"Darker? You think? I kind of like the muted tones of this one." I picked up two sage skeins and posed, holding them to my hair.

"Oh, no, no, no." The woman countered with a deep jade, plucking the two sage skeins from my hands, and replacing them with three of the darker bundles. "Oh, yes. Yes, yes," she said. "That sets off your red beautifully."

She might have been right, and even sincere, but she ruined the effect by turning away immediately, scooping up all but one of the sage skeins, tucking them in her shopping basket, and bolting. Thank goodness I hadn't really intended to buy any of it. She looked wiry and wily enough to wrestle me to the floor, break my arm, and use my carcass as a stepstool.

It was tempting to keep one of the jade skeins with me, to carry it around like a tension-relieving purse dog. Mauling the merchandise for short-term personal gain wasn't a good business practice, though. Reluctantly, I tucked all three back in their bin.

Reluctant. Why had Granny suddenly been reluctant to see me? Because, now that I thought about it, that seemed a better description of her recent attitude—

reluctance. Not adamantly against me coming for a visit, the way she was against a birthday party. She was wily herself, and an "absolutely not" or an "out of the question" would have been immediately suspicious. But at some point she started making excuses and putting me off. Even when I said I'd come for a flying visit and bring her birthday card myself. The excuses weren't earth-shattering. Most of them weren't even memorable.

So what was the problem? She'd sounded like old times every Sunday afternoon on the phone. Busy, feisty, full of plans. Except on the few occasions I mentioned visiting, and then she was suddenly busier, feistier, and full of too many plans to make a visit worth my while or hers. So plausible. Clever, wily Granny.

Or was I being too hard on her, reading more in hind-sight than was actually there? She was eighty, after all. I should ask Ardis and the rest of the staff if they'd noticed a change.

But I was sliding past the real question. Was there a connection between her reluctance or refusal or whatever it was and the fact that her house ended up in Emmett Cobb's hands? Because that's what I was beginning to believe must have happened. And then in Max Cobb's hands because someone killed Emmett?

But, no, not that. I was not going to let my mind go anywhere near thoughts of Granny kil . . . , Granny mur . . . Nope, that was definitely not going to happen. Time to go drown myself in whatever was left over from the wake. I'd kill myself with unnecessary calories before I'd think the unthinkable of Granny. I'd even go ahead and add Deputy Grab-a-Pizza Dunbar to my list of sus-pects. And Max.

The kitchen was empty and quiet. No class of neo-phyte needleworkers learning the ropes or threads of their chosen craft. Too bad. It would have been harder to think in a room full of clicking needles and instructional chatter. Harder to overindulge with everyone staring at me, too. Now I'd have to depend on my small reserve of self-control. Dear, dear. There were several foil-covered plates on the counter. There was also a domed cake server. Under the lid, ah, the rosemary chocolate cake. I could have identified it with my eyes closed. There wasn't much left and I allowed myself the indulgence of cutting a wedge twice the size any reasonable person should eat before lunch. Then I cut the wedge in two and put half on a plate for Ardis.

I was about to check the fridge for leftover watermelon lemonade, when I heard someone moving around in the stockroom just off the kitchen. My first thought was to freeze. My second thought was that I'd turned into a paranoid idiot. The door to the stockroom was ajar, but opened away from me, so I couldn't see in.

"Ardis?" She had probably come back to the kitchen while I was mooning over the alpaca. But she didn't answer, and then I heard her laugh, still out front with customers.

"Nicki? Hello?" My hello was muffled by a forkful of cake. Nice manners, Kath. I swallowed and listened. Something, a box, scraped across the floorboards. Someone from TGIF or one of the teachers must be checking supplies.

"Hello?" I cocked my head as though my ears worked better in that position. From the sounds, someone was busy. I didn't want to interrupt, but I didn't want to startle her if she didn't know I was there. Or it might be someone I hadn't met who would wonder at strangers helping themselves to cake. I should introduce myself.

I took my cake with me, though I should have put it down so I wouldn't forget myself again and take a bite at the wrong moment. Too late. It was irresistible.

I chewed and swallowed and heard a box drop in the stockroom.

"Shit."

I recognized that voice. Darn if I didn't recognize that voice—and its expletive, too. Joe Pantry Guy, murder suspect.

Chapter 14

I'd learned from our last encounter. No wild panic this time. And no need for heroic furniture moving. The doors at the Weaver's Cat all fit squarely in their frames and this particular door, being the stockroom door, had an old-fashioned key for its lock. Of course, leaving that key in the lock only invites trouble. But I was ready to sneak up on Trouble and give him the surprise of his life.

Slowly, silently, I pushed the door closed the few inches it was open. Gently, carefully, I turned the key, removed it, and returned it to the drawer where it belonged. It was a totally calm, controlled reaction to a possibly wrought situation. On my part, anyway.

Steps approached the door from the inside. They weren't exactly stealthy, but it was easy to believe they had sinister overtones. The knob turned. It turned again, forcefully. It rattled.

"What the—?" He rattled it harder, then thumped the door with his hand, maybe even his shoulder, and rattled the knob again. "Well, hell."

I almost shouted something rude at him, but remembered at the last moment where I was. Just in case, though, I took a bite of cake to keep my mouth occupied, then put the plate down and pulled out my phone. I was tempted to ask the 911 operator to send someone other than Dunbar. Then again, this would prove to Doubting Dolt

Dunbar that Joe Pantry Guy was real and appeared to be a career burglar.

The cake and the fantasy of Dunbar's comeuppance distracted me from actually pressing the buttons to make the call and then I heard several clinks on the floor in the stockroom. Tools. Of course. That's how this guy got into places where he didn't belong that didn't leave keys in doors or windows open. And then Ardis came down the hall singing "Dancing Queen."

I tried to wave my hands coherently so she'd interpret the motions as "There's a burglar in the stockroom." But my charades skills were rusty and she missed a nuance or two. Instead of being alarmed, she swept me into a twirl, belting out the finale. As her last notes died, my slightly dizzy fingers found and pressed the nine and a single one, and then we heard a voice calling her name.

"Ardis? That you out there?"

She let me go and looked around. "Ten?"

My mind hiccupped. Ten? What kind of name was that? His last name? Joe Ten? Or did he give me a false name last night? That lying son of a . . . Wait a second. Ardis knew this guy?

"I'm in the stockroom. Door must've swung shut. It's gone and jammed. Feels like it's locked, though." He rattled it to show her.

"You should've called for help."

"Only just realized. Thought I might take it off its hinges."

"Why didn't you?"

"They're out there with you."

"So they are. Well, don't fret, we'll get you out."

"Who's Ten?" I whispered to Ardis.

"Ivy never introduced you? Hold up a sec while I . . ." She went to the drawer where I'd put the key. "We've been on a campaign to convince some of the TGIFs not to leave the key in that lock," she said. "One of them must have chosen the wrong moment to remember." She jiggled the key into the lock, turned it, and swung the door open. "Morning, Ten. May I introduce you to Ivy's granddaughter, Kath?"

"Joe Dunbar." He held out his hand. "It's nice to finally meet you, Kath. Ivy loved talking about you. I'm very sorry for your loss."

I was afraid to open my mouth. For a few reasons. But I had to because, in my bewilderment, I'd pressed the last button and I could hear the 911 operator squawking in my hand. I pointed to the phone, then held a finger up to Ardis and Joe Whoever-or-Whatever-the-Hell-He-Was, indicating I'd be right back. Then I fled to the other end of the room, with my hands cupped around the phone, frantically whispering, "Never mind, never mind, never mind, sorry, false alarm. So sorry." I listened for a moment, then cut in with another "sorry" and disconnected.

"Everything all right?"

Definitely the voice I heard in the pantry last night. Low, calm, and with no hint of the patronizing "little lady" I sometimes detect in tall men's voices. In Deputy Dunbar's voice, for instance. But this guy didn't have the shoulder heft and swagger of the other Dunbar, and maybe that made the difference. If I felt more kindly disposed toward this particular Dunbar, I might describe him as lean or say he had the body of a marathon runner. His forehead would be high and sensitive-looking and his dark beard nicely scruffy. But I didn't feel kindly toward any Dunbar, so Joe was just tall, thin and needed a shave.

He was still waiting for my answer and beginning to look concerned. I smiled, nodded, and dropped my phone into my purse. My nonverbal communication needed to improve, though. Ardis didn't accept my smile as genuine. She rushed over with my half-eaten cake, steered me to a chair at the table, and pushed me into it. If she'd been a man, her voice would have dripped with "little lady," but somehow that would have been okay. Bias on my part, no doubt.

Eating wasn't high on my list of priorities anymore, but occupying my mouth was. Joe hadn't heard my voice clearly this morning and I wanted to keep it that way as long as possible. Or until I found out who he was and what he'd been up to lately. He might know Ardis, and Ardis might think she knew him, but did she know about his hobby of breaking and entering? And how were Dunbar and Dunbar related and why was I unlucky enough to be plagued by two of them?

Ardis offered him the piece of cake I'd cut for her. He earned a small point in his favor by thanking her and declining. He lost the point immediately when she invited him to meet us for lunch over at Mel's and he asked what time.

"Let's make it one. We're spoiling an early lunch, anyway, and if we wait we'll avoid the crowd. Does that suit you, Kath?"

"Sure."

No flash of recognition on Joe's face with that monosyllable from behind my hand. Good. Lunch would be more ticklish. But looking on the bright side, I could inspect him and collect information firsthand. My work with textiles taught me to trust my own tests and analyses over secondary sources or the sentimental lore handed down within families. Not that I wouldn't casually pump Ardis about him, too, but lunch with the thinner half of the Dunbar duo meant I wouldn't have to depend entirely on her rosy opinion of him.

"Did you find everything you need in there?" Ardis asked him.

"Yeah. Think so." He scratched his beard. "Might bring in that bobcat, though."

"Great. They'll love it. Soft as a kitten." Ardis waved good-bye with her fork.

He nodded, sank his hands in the pockets of his worn jeans, and strolled out. Under less shady or peculiar circumstances, I might have found him attractive. Par for the course in my personal book of love.

"I hope you don't mind him joining us," Ardis said.

"With or without the bobcat?" That wasn't really my first question but it was as good a place to start as any.

"Oh, I'm sure he'll just drop that by here. Poor thing."

"Is it sick?"

"Sick? Bless you, no. It's dead. Fur for flies."

"Now I'm completely lost."

"Ten teaches fly-tying. It brings in customers who wouldn't otherwise set foot in here. And not just men. Plenty of women fly-fish who wouldn't dream of picking up a crochet hook. And you should see how silly those fishy people get over the yarns and threads and colors. Especially some of those great big men, in their boots and Trout Unlimited hats, when they see the marabou."

"But the bobcat?"

"It's a pelt. Really just the face. It gives me the willies, and who'd think there'd be enough fur on that little face, anyway? But according to Ten, bobcat is something special for flies. Heaven only knows where he got it from."

"Why do you call him Ten?"

"It's his name," she said. "Short for, anyway."

"Then why did he introduce himself as Joe?"

"He started calling himself Joe years ago, at the start of high school, maybe. Away back, sometime in grade school, he tried calling himself Ox, but that didn't take. Earlier on, he was perfectly happy with Ten. But that's what mean children do to a sensitive child."

"Ten isn't short for Tennessee, I hope. That would be pretty awful."

"Worse. His brother got a better deal, but not by much."

"His brother?"

"Cole."

I knew it.

"Cole, short for Coleridge. Coleridge Blake Dunbar."

"Wow."

"And Tennyson. Tennyson Yeats Dunbar."

"No."

"Mm-hmm. Coleridge at least shortens to Cole and Blake is perfectly acceptable on its own. But Tennyson? Yeats? Their parents taught English literature at the community college."

"And had their heads stuck up their academias. Wow. Names like that might turn anyone to a life of crime."

"You could be right. I always did wonder why Cole went into law enforcement. Near broke his parents' poetic hearts."

Of course, Cole's wasn't the life of crime I meant. So, had the brothers taken the paths of Good Dunbar, Bad Dunbar? Or did Cole turn a blind eye to Joe's activities, making him Bad Dunbar and Joe Worse Dunbar? Somewhere behind my right ear I heard Homer whispering, "Slander." Behind my left ear something else whispered, "Oh, those poor saps, saddled with names like that." That might have been my conscience, but I squashed it.

Ardis finished her cake and took our plates to the sink, then came back and sat opposite me. She folded her hands on the table. "Kath, we need to talk about the business."

"We do." The reality of losing my job came crashing back down on me. But just because that job was gone, why was I suddenly thinking about giving up my career to run the Weaver's Cat? Because that was easiest? Since when did I take the path of least resistance? Since when would I be happy shackled to the daily grind of retail responsibility?

"I'd like to buy it from you."

"What?"

"Don't sound so shocked." She didn't look completely copacetic herself. She gulped before rushing on. "Actually, Nicki and I would go in together." She stopped and fanned herself with her hand. "Sorry. I'm apt to flash when I think about the loan involved."

"But . . ."

"We don't want the place to close and our customers don't, either. We have solid regional business. We're a destination for fiber artists. They plan group shopping trips from as far away as Indiana and Pennsylvania. You probably know all that, but did you know we're building a good presence on the Web, too? Our cyber storefront, Nicki calls it, and it's taking off like Ivy and I never imagined it could."

"But, if I didn't want to sell . . ."

"Forgive me, but we don't think you'll be able to give the business the attention it needs. You'd be an absentee owner with your mind on your own career. And that's as it should be. It's nothing personal. You know I love you almost as much as Ivy did. But we'd like to buy the Cat and we think we can make a go of it on our own."

They didn't want me.

"We've talked to the bank."

Through all my thoughts about safety nets and wondering if I'd be happy living in Blue Plum, leaving test tubes and fumigation hoods behind, I hadn't thought they wouldn't want me. Or need me.

Ardis pushed a folded paper across the table. "It makes me dizzy, but here's what we're offering."

I opened the paper, looked at it, shoved it in my purse. "I need to think."

"Of course you do." She started fanning herself again.

I was feeling a little flashed myself. I needed to get away and think, but first I had to ask the questions I'd been saving. "Ardis, did Granny say anything about a problem with her Blue Plum tapestry? Was something about it bothering her?"

"She finally started it?" That she stopped fanning was answer enough.

"Was she her old self the last few months?"

"How do you mean? Her heart? I told you she was still running up those back stairs. Oh, hon"—she put her hands over mine—"you're not beating yourself up thinking you should have known something was wrong, are you? I don't think even she knew. She was good at keeping secrets, but I don't think that was one of them. Does that help you feel any better?"

"Thank you." It did help and I hadn't realized how much I needed to hear it. But the secrets? "What kind of secrets did she keep?"

"Oh, you knew Ivy. If you told her a secret, did she ever give it away?"

"What about her own secrets?"

"Well, they wouldn't be secrets if I knew them, would they? She didn't let on about starting the tapestry, for one. What's got you worried? It's written all over your face, but I can't read the writing."

"Have you heard any talk, you know, among the TGIF members or anybody, hinting at who killed Emmett Cobb?"

"Of course there was talk. There always is when something like that happens. Not that something like that happens all that often. We didn't solve the crime, though. Not that we couldn't if we put our minds to it, I don't wonder."

"Any favorite suspects?"

"No one I can call to mind," she said.

Good.

"But that can't be what's worrying you. Spit it out."

"Did Granny tell you she sold the house on Lavender Street?"

Ardis reared back as though I'd asked if Granny danced naked on the courthouse steps. "She'd never sell it. Don't be silly."

"Maybe not so silly," I said. "According to Shirley and Mercy . . ."

"Those two!"

"Not just them. Max Cobb, too."

"And he's not much better."

"But he's got the keys and I can't get in."

Ardis stewed on that news, one eye narrowed, lips thinned to an angry slash. "So why didn't you call me?"

Without going into details, I told her that Ruth rescued me. She accepted that with a nod.

"I'm going to tell you a story. One Ivy most likely didn't because it was over and done with and it wasn't her way to carry a grudge. I'm not so good that way. Those two Spiveys came to the first day of a Fair Isle class. This was twelve, fifteen years ago. They sat down in this kitchen with their smiles and their 'heys' and 'you all rights' and they asked who all had heard about Ivy's affair with Homer Wood."

"What?"

"Wasn't true. Wasn't anything more than ridiculous."

"The age difference alone makes it unlikely," I said.

"Ridiculous or unlikely or utter baloney, the moral of the story is the Spiveys are positively poisonous."

"But fascinating, somehow. Like snakes."

"If you say so." She flicked a crumb from her sleeve. "Ivy defanged them properly, anyway. She had a way with people like no one else I've ever known. She got the twins to apologize, in front of the class, and then drop the class. They never did learn to knit Fair Isle." Animated while recounting the Spiveys' comeuppance, Ardis drew in again, looking thoughtful. "That's something I worry about," she said, not looking at me, possibly not talking to me, either. "Ivy's magic."

"Magic?" The word burst out of me, making us both jump. "Sorry, Ardis. I didn't mean to scare you." She'd given *me* a heart attack, though. "What was that you said about Ivy's magic?"

"What we were just talking about, her way with people. Everything she did. I can't help but wonder how much of the Cat's success is because of her and her alone. Look around you. Ivy is everywhere. And now that she's gone?"

"We'll carry on exactly where she left off. It'll be like she never left at all. Hey, Kath. Good to see you again." Nicki bounced through the doorway looking adorable in black leggings and a white and black crocheted granny square tunic. On a larger woman the outfit would invite comparisons to purebred Holsteins. On petite Nicki, with her hair pulled back in a springy ponytail, it made me think of a happy Jack Russell terrier. "Did Ardis tell you our plan?" she asked. "Isn't it exciting? I am so psyched. Sorry, I didn't mean to interrupt, but Thea's here for the Beatrix Potter needlepoint book you found for her, Ardis."

"Oh, land, and where did I put that? It came in the day Ivy . . . It's not behind the counter?"

"Sure didn't see it."

"Think," Ardis muttered. "Where did I . . ."

"That's okay. You know Thea. She won't mind coming back," Nicki said.

"No, I know where it is. Upstairs. A few of the patterns call for Paterna tapestry wool and I was checking if we had the colors she might want. I had it with me and must have left it up there." Ardis sighed and pushed her chair back.

"Don't get up. I'll run get it," Nicki said. "Better yet, I'll take Thea with me and park her next to the Paterna. Let her do a little dreaming and shopping at the same time." She dashed out and I half expected to hear her yip with delight over her ploy.

Which reminded me. "Ardis, do you have Maggie?"

"Didn't anyone tell you?" She started fanning herself again. "You must have been worried sick about her all this time."

"Hey, it's okay, really. I know she hasn't been the first thing on anyone's mind. I think I'm more worried about you, right now."

Ardis stopped fanning and waved my concern away.

"I'm just glad to know where she is. She probably still doesn't like me, though. Do you think, well, would you want to keep her?"

"No, that's just it." It turned out she wasn't waving my concern away. She was swatting at my words of relief so they'd sit, stay, and pay attention. "I don't have Maggie. No one does. No one's been able to find her. We think she disappeared the day Ivy died."

"She's gone?" I said stupidly. True, she'd as soon bite me as look at me, but she was Granny's delight. And now she was gone, too? With that news coming on top of every other jolt of the past days, I might have broken down and cried again. But I didn't. I was beginning to feel empty. Like a husk. Like a ghost. And I might have laughed at that thought, but I couldn't do that, either. Because if Maggie was never found, I was pretty sure I'd be haunted by her unfriendly little mew for the rest of my life.

"Haunted." That turned out to be an apropos word. The ghost came back that evening.

Chapter 15

After hearing about Maggie, I spent the rest of the day avoiding people, skipping lunch at Mel's with Ardis and Joe Whatever-He-Was. What I really wanted to do was mothball myself in a pile of Granny's wool in the house on Lavender Street. Homer didn't call to say he'd learned the whole situation was a hilarious mix-up, though, or that Max Cobb had returned and turned over a set of keys.

So I climbed the stairs to Granny's study in the attic of the Weaver's Cat and I spent the afternoon systematically sifting and sorting her decades of accumulated ephemera—her trove. The activity wasn't exactly cathartic, but for a few hours it restored a sense of equilibrium. And somewhere up there in that comfortable room under the roof with its dormer windows and shelves and cupboards built into the eaves, she'd hidden her private dye journals. Where she recorded in detail the mumbo jumbo she'd worked out for putting the woo-woo in the wool. Dear God.

I didn't find her hiding place and couldn't make up my mind if that was good or bad. Or if I couldn't find it because it and the journals didn't exist. Or if that was because I didn't really want to find either of them.

Granny was a journal keeper, though, and a documenter. She kept recipe notebooks of her batches of dyes and her experiments with materials, attaching samples of the dyestuff and fibers she used. As a child, I'd loved leafing through them, carefully touching the dried plants and bits of colored fleece or cotton or silk. She also jotted and sketched the ideas for needlework projects that burst into her head or popped in and grew there more slowly. I found several dashed-off sketches that might be details for her Blue Plum tapestry—a couple of almost bird's-eye views of buildings, a few small figures, a repeating pattern that might become a border. The sketches could just as easily be the result of her hand and pencil occupying themselves while her mind thought about something else. She undoubtedly had a whole notebook devoted to the tapestry project. I didn't find it, either, but it was probably at the house.

In fact, although I found some of her project and dye notebooks, I didn't find as many as I remembered seeing on other visits. But they were works in progress and reference tools. She used them, carrying them back and forth between this attic room and her dye pots in the kitchen downstairs and home to her own kitchen and back again to this study. She would have known where each notebook was, but would anyone else? Between what Deputy Dunbar called "clutter" in the Lavender Street house and her habit of moving things from place to place, would I know if the person who got into the house took any of them? But that was silly. The garden-variety burglar wouldn't be interested in Granny's notebooks with their bits of fiber and dye garden plants.

I made a stack of the notebooks I did find, then a rough sort of other books and magazines into a satisfying mountain range of piles around me on the floor—a method of organization guaranteed to set Deputy Dunbar's lips in a sneer. Some of the stacks were for Ardis or Nicki or

Debbie, if they wanted them; others I would take with me. I tried very hard to avoid thinking about where I would take them. But there, beyond the book ridge I'd just capped with *The Colour Cauldron: The History and Use of Natural Dyes in Scotland*, Granny's desk waited patiently for me, offering a good place to sit and make plans. Or at least a place to plan to make plans. I sighed, got up, and threaded my way between my lilliputian mountains and molehills.

Grandfather had bought the old oak, two-pedestal teacher's desk at a flea market. He'd refinished it for Granny and hauled it up the three steep flights to the study. It was a piece of furniture I definitely wanted to keep, if anyone dared carry it back down.

I felt as though *I* was daring when I started sliding the desk drawers open. Granny hadn't kept them or the study locked, so there wasn't likely to be anything in the drawers or out in the open for her eyes only. And I'd played at the desk plenty of times as a child, using up her paper with my drawings or sticking my arm as far back as it would go in the kneehole drawer to see what treasures I'd discover at the dark, distant end of it. Even so, the desk struck me as more personal than the bookshelves I'd half emptied.

Then it struck me that I was an idiot. I might find a note or document in a file giving me a clue about what happened with the house. Maybe if I disturbed the desk's contents enough, the name Cobb would jump out at me like a spider and I could hold it up and look it over and then squish it. Or maybe I'd find something that proved Granny wasn't a murderer. It was a good dream, anyway.

What I found were a few more notebooks and her photo files. A quick flip through the photographs didn't turn up a snapshot of someone who wasn't Granny walking into Emmett's cottage carrying a bottle with a skull and crossbones on the label. How disappointing.

There was a rummage of stationery and pocket diaries from previous years in another drawer. My heart quickened at those. The current year was missing, though, probably in her purse at home. And it probably didn't have an entry for the day Emmett died saying, "Did not poison E.C.," anyway.

The kneehole drawer held a nest of pens and colored pencils, a flashlight Granny could have attached to her key chain but hadn't, a couple of small notepads (one with a grocery list that did not include poison), and a doodled-on envelope containing the past month's receipts. The doodles were of the wool cards sitting on the desk, a swan with a nasty squint, and Maggie balancing a candle on her head. There were also a couple of unfiled receipts (neither for anything more dangerous to ingest than Chunky Monkey ice cream), odds and ends of loom hardware and gadgetry, a catnip mouse, and Maggie's rabies tag and the collar she refused to wear. Nothing else, unless it had slid to the back.

Rather than reach my hand all the way in to grope blindly, I pulled the drawer out of the desk. There wasn't anything more to see except for an accumulation of thread tails and miniature dust bunnies. I sat with the drawer on my lap, thinking. This wasn't the kind of desk that had hidden compartments. But Granny wasn't supposed to be the kind of old lady who had hidden talents, either.

I pulled all the drawers out and stacked them on the floor. Then I took the flashlight from the kneehole drawer, got down on the floor, and played the light around the inside surfaces of the desk, craning my neck. Expecting? Not really. Hoping? Only maybe, and hoping for what, I couldn't say. Instructions for finding secret journals? A list of murder suspects jotted after a discussion at a TGIF meeting? A reason for selling the house? Of course I came up empty.

Drat.

So I sat on the floor, in the shadow of the desk and the wall of drawers, and hunted up my own list of suspects—the one I'd started in my crabbed spiral notebook and dropped back in my purse to simmer after my visit with Homer. It was a thin, unsatisfying list with only one name to it. Time to remedy that by giving Joe the burglar company, which I did by adding Max Cobb the inheritor, Mercy and Shirley Spivey the irritating, and Deputy Clod Dunbar the dolt. The Spivey twins were purely gratuitous, but the deputy was looking better and better to me. He'd had access; he'd known Emmett's habits. They gambled and he might have been into Emmett for more than his deputy's salary could handle. And he had a burgling brother. I made my own doodle under the deputy's name—a game of hangman with the words "why not" spelled under the gibbet.

Why not. While I was still on the floor enjoying the idea of adopting those words as my personal philosophy, Nicki bounced up the stairs.

"Are you all right up here, Kath?" she called as she came. "Ardis said you didn't have lunch. Can I bring . . . oh, gee." She stopped in the doorway. "You've sure made a mess. What are you doing down there? Are you looking for something? I can help. I've already been through most of it anyway." She started into the room, friendly and eager.

"No."

She stopped short.

"Why were you in here?"

Now she looked as though I'd slapped her. Drat.

"Nicki, I'm sorry. I didn't mean . . . I'm sorry. I'm just tired and no, I don't need any help." It was an inadequate apology. I stood up, started to do better, but she interrupted.

"I found her, you know. On the floor in her bedroom."

"What?" Oh God, I'd forgotten. "Nicki, I'm so sorry."

"I want you to know she meant a lot to me. I want so much to be like her." She was working hard not to cry. Granny would have been proud of her. I knew I should tell her that.

"The blue jacket you were wearing yesterday—when did Granny give it to you?" Not the kind words I meant to say. My compassion-spreading skills needed help. On the upside, my question helped Nicki get past her crisis.

"Isn't it a dream? I feel so fortunate to have it. It felt so right wearing it for Ivy yesterday. And you left the wake so soon after I got here we hardly had a chance to talk. But I guess you wanted to get away and be alone. And then the house. My gosh. Where did you end up staying?"

"How do you know about the house?" Again I was sharper than she deserved. Why was I angry? Because she babbled and didn't answer my question about the jacket? Because she wanted the Cat?

"Ardis said something about it. About the Spiveys' saying Ivy sold it. What's that all about?"

"I don't know. Granny's lawyer is looking into it."

"Homer?"

"You know him?"

She smiled. "Ivy got a kick out of him. He's been in a time or two looking for Ruth when she gets lost in here."

"She's letting me stay in the caretaker's cottage out at the Homeplace until things are straightened out."

"That's real nice of her . . . Wait, isn't that where that guy was mur—"

"Yeah." I interrupted her, not needing to hear that word again.

"Are you okay with that?"

"As long as I don't think about it."

"Well, you're a braver woman than I am. You know what you should do? Stop by Mel's and get some of her potato soup—comfort food, you know? That's what Ivy would tell you. And maybe get one of Mel's killer brownies, too." She stopped, mouth open. "Eew, I can't believe I said that. Anyway, treat yourself to something decadent and then get a good night's sleep. If you can."

Ardis was in the front room when I trailed down the stairs shortly after Nicki left. She was listening patiently to a woman who was trying to decide between brightly hued, hand-painted yarn and undyed natural brown wool. When the woman phoned her neighbor for her opinion, Ardis stepped away. I thanked her for the time alone and told her not to worry, which didn't ease the pinched lines around her eyes. I tried to save her a few more pinches by not filling in the details of where I was staying. She'd find out soon enough from Nicki. We didn't mention the offer she'd made for the business. I told her I'd be back in the morning, but didn't give her an opening for hugs. My resolve not to cry was reaching its limit.

I checked my phone. No missed calls. No messages. No getting into the house tonight. I thought about driving to one of the hotels out on the highway instead of going back to the cottage. A sterile room, an anonymous bed—they were powerfully tempting. But even though I'd spent the day not putting words to the questions slinking between my more rational thoughts, I didn't think the answers included the words "sterility" and "anonymity." Despite my weird evening and weirder guests, imaginary or not, the cottage was warm and welcoming. Besides, all my stuff was there and by then I didn't have the energy to pack it up and move. And, really, how likely was it for the place to be burgled two nights in a row?

Visiting hours were over when I got back to the Homeplace. The gate was locked. And it was starting to rain. As I fumbled the lock open it started to pour. By the time I swung the gate wide enough to inch the car past, I was drenched. I drove through, slithered back out into the torrent to close and relock the gate, sloshed one more time into the equally drenched driver's seat, and made a note to buy a wetsuit and swim fins in case another deluge like that came through while I remained exiled at the blinkety-blank cottage.

It wasn't until I squelched into the kitchen and stood watching muddy rivulets from my ruined shoes run across the floor that I remembered I hadn't stopped at Mel's to pick up supper. A sound escaped me, something between a strangled mew and a pitiful oath.

That potato soup Nicki recommended would have gone a long way toward warming me and smoothing over being half-drowned. The killer brownie, too, even with its creepy connotations and despite the fact that I'd pretty much eaten nothing but sugary baked goods since arriving in Blue Plum. So, there was no supper. And I'd skipped lunch. I dropped my wet purse on the table. The purse, at least, didn't splash in a puddle of its own. That wasn't consolation enough.

Of course, I wouldn't have gotten any wetter slogging back to the car, repeating the rigmarole with the gate, and driving back to Mel's. Or just to the Quickie Mart. Going back out wasn't appealing, though. I could order pizza and change into dry clothes while I waited for it to show up. Except pizza could come only as far as the locked gate and I'd have to swim out to meet it. There was another option: I could stand there and cry.

It wasn't the rational choice, but crying was the only immediately gratifying one, so I went with that. But I didn't just stand there. I threw myself into a chair at the kitchen table and cried like a great big baby, making a thorough job of it because that's what Granny taught me to do.

If you're going to do a thing, Kath, even if it's awkward or a mistake, do it up right and get the job done properly.

So I did. I buried my sopping head in my sopping sleeves and wept. I mourned for Granny, my job, the house, the shop, the cat—basically the whole foundation of my life and my sanity. I cried until I ran out of tears and sat there snuffling and thinking how stupid it was to run out of them when I needed them most. And that's when I heard the voice.

"Why such a weepy weed tonight?" It was tentative, soft.

I snuffled to myself a few more times, hoping I wouldn't hear it again.

"You should change out of those wet things or you'll catch your death." That suggestion was followed by a sigh.

I sat still, telling myself that I'd sunk so far into misery and was hearing things from so deep inside my myself that I didn't recognize my own inner voice.

"I think you'll have to agree I know what I'm talking about," the voice said. "About death."

No, I was pretty sure that wasn't me. Even in the murkiest depths of my mind, my inner voice was more likely to have a Midwestern twang. This voice had a mountain lilt. So, if the voice wasn't *in* my mind, then I was obviously *out* of my mind. That thought brought a fresh bout of tears. It was pathetic and I knew it, but I couldn't help it and didn't care, and I melted into another puddle of grief for my lost mind.

"Go ahead and cry, then. I'll wait. Lord knows, I have time to wait." Another sigh. "I do wonder why you don't have a television, though."

The non sequitur stopped me. I held my breath, listened more carefully, and heard a muttered "Even a rerun of *Bonanza* would do."

If the voice existed, it was sitting opposite me. I snuffed a last snuffle and picked my head up enough to squint across the table.

It, she, looked back.

"Last night, when you acted like a scared rabbit," she said, "you ran upstairs and grabbed your things and that pretty coverlet. It wasn't until you threw the coverlet around your shoulders that you started acting sensible. Why don't you try that again?"

I didn't answer.

"At least get out of those wet things. Get into something warm and dry. But why not wrap yourself in the coverlet and see what happens?"

It was a reasonable enough suggestion. But I didn't move except to blink hard several times. As last night, though, nothing changed. She was still there, sitting across from me, watery, gray, and slightly out of focus.

"Um . . ."

"Yes?" she asked.

"Um . . ."

"You're repeating yourself. You should learn to be more articulate."

I cleared my throat. "Last night, that was you sitting here crying?"

"Yes. I do that a lot." She blew out another sigh. "Depression is my lot in death. I suffer from it dreadfully. Apparently you're a kindred spirit."

"No! No, I'm not. Not ordinarily." I sat up straight to prove it. Prove it to what or to whom, I wasn't sure, but

I squared my shoulders and wiped a string of wet hair off my forehead in an effort to look less downtrodden and a believable bit livelier.

"Oh, too bad. I thought you were." She slumped dejectedly in her chair.

"You looked like a worried wet rabbit," I said. She turned her bleak eyes on me and I tripped over my tongue to explain. "Last night. You were crying and hunched over."

"Don't make fun."

"I'm not. But you said I acted like a scared rabbit and I thought . . ."

"You'd get back at me? What kind of friend is that? You're not very nice." She covered her face with her hands and started to cry.

"What? No, I didn't. I am."

"You did and you're not." She was boohooing loudly now.

"Oh for Pete's sake."

"And now you're shouting and swearing at me. I hate you. I'm leaving." And she did. First she blew her nose on her sleeve and then, poof, she was gone.

Great. Fine. Now, on top of everything else, I had a silly, depressed ghost on my hands.

No. I was not ready to believe that. I jumped up, knocking my chair over, and for lack of a more original place to direct my words, shouted at the ceiling.

"You don't exist! If I wasn't having such a rotten couple of days I wouldn't hear you! If I'd had a nice hot bowl of potato soup for supper I wouldn't see you, either! You're just a figment of my starvation!" I might as well have added "so there" and stuck out my tongue. I was so incredibly mature.

Sighing better than any figment, I righted the chair. Slung my purse over my shoulder. Turned to leave the room. And heard a voice the size of an olive twig.

"If you take the casserole you brought with you yesterday out of the freezer and put it in a slow oven, it will be warm by the time you shower and change and come back downstairs."

Chapter 16

After showering, pulling on my sweats, and going back downstairs, I discovered I loved tuna casserole. Ruth's version of it, anyway. She added a hint of curry to her mushroom-laden sauce and that did wonders to warm and fill my empty spaces. After my long, strange day, I felt poetic about her casserole and thought I might even ask her for the recipe.

I set the table for two, although as I laid out two forks, two plates, two glasses of water, I wondered how I would explain it to my professional, no-nonsense colleagues. There was no sign of the ghost and I tried hard to convince myself my private jury was still out. But on the off-chance that she did exist somewhere other than in the fog between my ears, setting a place for her seemed like the friendly thing to do. Maybe this had been her house, her kitchen. Maybe there was such a thing as ghost etiquette.

She didn't poof—materialize—in the chair across from me when I sat down. That was okay. If her absence meant she didn't exist, then sitting across from an untouched plate of noodles and tuna only made me feel foolish and that was a healthy step up from feeling unhinged. As I raised my glass of water in a toast to that progress, someone knocked on the kitchen door.

The rain had tapered off, but it was still coming down steadily. It was full dark and the site was closed. Who on earth? For a nanosecond the thought crossed my mind that it might not be someone on earth. Another quick bite of Ruth's casserole took care of that nonsense. In fact, it was probably Ruth stopping by on her way home. As a dedicated employee of a nonprofit, she undoubtedly worked more hours than the site was open to the public.

The knock came again. Definitely not parlor-game, séance-type rapping. I flipped on the outside light and started to turn the knob, but then caution kicked in. I twitched aside the curtain covering the lower half of the door window and looked to see who'd come calling.

Joe Dunbar.

And of course he knew someone was home because I'd just flipped on the flipping light. But did he know *who* was home? I put my eye to the slit between the curtain and the doorframe again. A dark mass blocked my view. He'd stepped closer to the door and was tall enough to see over the curtain. I looked up and met his blue eyes looking down. I jumped. He smiled.

"Hi," he called. "We met at the Cat this morning. Ten Dunbar."

"I thought you said your name was Joe." Did he really think I didn't recognize him as Joe Pantry Guy from the night before? Then again, did I know for an absolute fact that he was? I hadn't seen Pantry Guy and had only heard either of them speak a few dozen words at most. I took a step back to see this Dunbar's face better. He had on a worn-looking broad-brimmed hat. He and the hat looked comfortable together out there getting wet.

"Well, yes, it is Joe," he called through the door. "Strictly speaking it's Ten, though, and I thought . . ." He stopped and scratched an eyebrow.

"Thought what?"

He smiled again. "Thought maybe we'd get off on a better foot than last night if I more formally introduced myself."

"More formally than you breaking in?" I *knew* it was him.

"Well, now, again, strictly speaking, I didn't break in. Say, do you mind if I come in?"

"Why would I possibly think that was a good idea?"

"Because I can explain what I was doing here last night."

"Or you can do that from where you're standing. I can hear you well enough through the door."

"It's really raining out here. And I'm sorry I scared you last night."

"I think I scared you more by calling the cops. Maybe I should call them again," I said.

"I'd appreciate it if you didn't."

A thought occurred to me. "Are you afraid of your brother?"

"No . . ." This time he looked down and scrubbed both his eyebrows. "I'm not afraid of him," he said, looking back at me. "I just don't like complicating his life."

That was an interesting way to put it.

"So what do you think?" he asked. "May I come in?"

"I don't know." He was better dressed for standing in the rain than I'd been. He had on a waterproof jacket in addition to the hat. Ardis had said he was a fisherman. Maybe he had on waders, too, keeping his feet and his long legs dry. But talking through the door was getting tedious. "You broke in here. Maybe you killed Emmett Cobb. Won't you be complicating *my* life if I let you in?"

"Well, see, like I said, technically speaking, I didn't break in. And I didn't much like Emmett, but I didn't kill him. And I really can explain everything, but I'd rather not stand out here shouting it."

"Explaining 'everything' is too vague. Give me one good reason to let you in."

"I have information about your grandmother. I think I know something you need to know."

He'd said the single thing guaranteed to get him in past my better judgment. "Hold on. I'll be right back." I grabbed my phone from my purse and ran to the parlor for my favorite weapon, the poker. Then, armed and curious, I opened the door, hoping I wasn't crazy for doing it.

Joe, or Ten, or He-Who-Seemed-to-Lead-a-Fairly-Complicated-Life-of-His-Own, stepped inside. He looked at the poker and raised his arms until they were shoulder height, showing me his empty hands, fingers spread.

"Are you trying to prove how safe you supposedly are?"

"I'm hoping you won't whack me with that thing," he said, nodding at the poker. "I'll roll over and bare my throat, too, if that'll help."

I lowered the poker a fraction and he relaxed a smaller fraction, slowly lowering his arms. Neither of us made any sudden moves, and after ten or twenty seconds, during which we stood there gauging each other, his eyes left mine and he looked around the room. I kept my eyes on him.

"Your supper smells good," he said. "I'm sorry. I didn't mean to interrupt. Oh, hey, and I didn't realize you had company."

"There's no one here . . ." Except the ghost? I whipped around. The room was empty. I cleared my throat to cover my moment of panic. Then I saw he was looking at the table set for two. With two plates of tuna noodle casserole, no longer steaming.

"But you must be expecting someone any minute."

"Oh, right. Ruth. I invited her. She was so kind to let me stay here. It was the least I could do. In fact, when you knocked, I thought you were her."

He moved closer to the table. I did, too, poker arm tensed.

"I wonder if she was confused, then," he said. "Because she left about an hour ago saying something about skipping supper and going straight to the town board meeting. Isn't this her casserole dish?"

My bad lie was beginning to make me queasy. And annoyed. Why did I feel I owed this guy any explanations about anything? He was supposedly here to tell *me* something about Granny. It was time to start asking *him* questions. "You recognize Ruth's dish?" Not what I'd meant to ask.

"Oh, sure."

"How?" Definitely a fail in Interrogation 101.

"Didn't Ivy ever tell you Blue Plum is the potluck capital of the world? You graze enough potlucks, you recognize the dishes and the cooks behind them. Light green Tupperware salad bowl? Way too much dressing. Ruth's casserole dish? Guaranteed edible. Besides, that smells like her tuna noodle. The curry gives it away. As long as she's not coming, may I?" He indicated the second place setting.

Somehow we'd ended up on either side of the table, me standing behind my chair, he behind the one opposite.

"Um." I'd been saying that a lot lately. Very uncharacteristic.

While I tried to figure out how I suddenly had a guest burglar for dinner, he took off his hat and raincoat, hanging the coat on the back of the second chair on his side of the table and putting the hat on the seat. I held on to my poker.

"How about I warm these in the microwave?" Without waiting for an answering "um" from me, he whisked the two cold plates off the table.

Conversation lapsed further while the microwave

zapped first one, then the other plate. He returned them to the table and pulled his chair out and started to sit. I didn't. He noticed and hesitated.

I nodded at his plate. "Go ahead."

"You sure?" Again, without waiting for an answer, articulate or otherwise, he sat and dug in.

I stayed on my feet, weighing the poker in my hand and my options. I still had my phone in the other hand. I was also still hungry, not having finished what was on my plate, and his gusto only made the food look better. The longer I stood, the slower his rate of fork to mouth became, though, until he put his fork down and dabbed his lips with his napkin.

"Not joining me?"

"Not sure. I have a few questions."

He took a sip of water. Raised his eyebrows.

"First, what were you looking for last night? Second, did you really come out here tonight to tell me something about my grandmother or was that a convenient excuse for getting in without breaking in? Although, come to think of it, why would you tell me if you were planning to break in again? And fourth, or third, or whatever, if you do have something to tell me about Granny, what is it?"

"Hey, look, I really am sorry I scared you last night." He started to push his chair back. I raised the poker. He stopped, raised his open hands. "Do you have to hold that thing like you plan to use it as soon as my back is turned?"

"Yeah. Sorry if that bothers you, but burglars in the house seem to have that effect on me."

He started to smile. I narrowed my eyes and he stopped.

"Okay. Hm. Okay." He brought his hands together in a double fist, head slightly bowed. He bounced one knuckle of the fists against his lips, his eyes moving from left to right and back again. He appeared to be wrestling with something. But what? Bad news? How best to break that bad news to a woman standing over him with a poker? A lie of his own?

His left eye twitched and he straightened his fingers, resting their tips against his chin. With his lean, bearded face he reminded me of a monk in a painting by someone like El Greco. I half expected him to close his eyes and start chanting or say amen.

"Okay." He shook himself and ran his hands through his hair, head still bent. "I kind of got lost in your questions, but I think maybe they can all be covered with one answer." He sat up and looked at me. "It might come as a shock."

"Shock and I are best friends lately. Give it a shot."

"Okay. I was looking for evidence because I think Emmett was blackmailing your grandmother."

Even with his warning, his catchall answer begged for me to drop everything and stare at him. If I'd lost track of the poker and let it fall crashing to the table, it would have been understandable. Through tremendous effort I kept it cocked and ready.

"I expected more of a reaction," he said, studying my face.

"I've been getting some practice. I'll give you a 'wow' on that, though. It deserves it." I thought back over the last day or so: secret dye journals, ghosts, burglars. Now blackmail? Why not? *Why not* was going to be a useful philosophy for as long as I stuck around Blue Plum—I could see that—and without thinking, I began working through Joe's contribution to my weird new life out loud.

"Blackmail isn't the first possibility that jumps into my head, but first possibilities don't seem to matter much these days. And it might explain how Emmett got the house without anyone else being aware. But what could he possibly know that was worth blackmailing Granny for?" My tongue skidded to a halt before "secret dye

journals" slipped out. Oh, surely not. Surely Emmett
Cobb hadn't tripped over or somehow fathomed Granny's notion that she had a "talent."

"Blackmailed her over *what* is definitely the question," Joe agreed. He puzzled over that, brow furrowed,
swirling his fork through the bit of golden sauce left on
his plate.

Granny said she did her best thinking while throwing
a shuttle and thumping a beater bar. The rhythm orga-
nized her thoughts; the warp and weft gave her a scaf-
fold to build on. I watched Joe thinking with his fork, not
offering my answer to the blackmail question. Instead, I
wondered how easily he might form his own answer,
given access to whatever evidence he was looking for.
And how would his answer, correct or not, create its own
cascade of problems? I pictured Granny watching helplessly as her tightly woven fabric unraveled.

Joe rested the fork, cocking his head and looking at
his plate. For a second, the fork looked like a brush in his
hand. Then he licked it. On the plate he'd painted a delicate curry-sauce fish leaping toward the rim, chased by
a swan with wings and neck outstretched. Joe doodled
swans. Granny doodled swans. Mean swans. There was
more to this story than he was telling. Cobb. A male
swan was a cob.

"But, yeah," he said, pushing the plate away. "I was
thinking the same thing. About Ivy's house. Whoa, watch
it." He snatched my water glass out of the way before I
swiped it off the table with the poker I was suddenly paying no attention to.

"You knew about the house?"

"Why don't you put that thing down?"

"I'm not sure I want to." I did want to. It was heavy.
"If I put it down, how do I know I can trust you?"

"Plenty of people do. Ardis, Ruth. Ivy did."

"She did? But you broke in here."

"One time. I came in, uninvited, one time. And I didn't break anything to do it."

"You're a burglar."

"I didn't take anything, either."

I didn't bother pointing out he hadn't had time before I surprised him.

He held his hands out, placating, pacifying. Playacting? "I was trying to help. I really was. And, just so you know, it wasn't me who got into Ivy's house."

"You know about that, too?"

"And Maggie. She must've gotten out when whoever it was got in. I've looked around the neighborhood, asked around town, but haven't found her. I'm sorry. She's a sweetheart. So, can we have a truce? And will you put that thing down before you crack Ruth's casserole dish?"

He cared enough to look for Maggie? I looked at the poker and compromised by tucking it under my arm like a swagger stick. I was still armed, but the tableware could thank me for being less dangerous.

"Can you get me into Granny's house?"

"Absolutely not." He obviously expected me to believe that. The lowered brow, the set jaw, the thinned, unsmiling lips were working hard to convince both of us. But the slight blush playing over his ears betrayed the possibility that I now had a burglar up my sleeve. A burglar with a soft spot for lost cats.

"It probably doesn't matter, anyway. Max should be back with the keys tomorrow. Thanks for looking for Maggie. So, what kind of evidence were you looking for out here? Wouldn't looking at Granny's make more sense? And why didn't you go to the police if you're so sure Emmett was a blackmailer? Did Granny ask you not to? Did she ask you to get the evidence back for her?"

"We didn't discuss it."

"You didn't? Then what's your stake in this and why *didn't* you go to the police?"

He didn't answer, instead chewing his lip and studying a cuticle. I needed to stop asking multiple and multipart questions so I'd know if he was floundering somewhere in my stream-of-consciousness grilling or was just refusing to answer. I decided to help him out.

"You didn't go to the police," I said, feeling my way along that thought carefully, "because he was blackmailing you, too." I tensed for a reaction.

He didn't blink, but asked, "You don't think that's kind of a leap?"

"It was more of a leap to consider blackmail to begin with, and no, I'd say it might take a blackmail victim to know one. Birds of a feather. Granny drew pictures of swans, too."

He didn't answer. The sauce fish and swan on his plate hadn't held their lines. He scraped the fork through what was left of them.

"Okay, well, I think I'd also say that's the real reason you were out here looking around." I continued, feeling my way slowly. "You were looking for a record of some kind that Emmett kept. That he probably kept hidden. Otherwise someone—the police, for instance—would have already found it. And you might be sorry if they found it. You weren't looking just because you think he was blackmailing Granny; you were looking to protect yourself. Because blackmail, and whatever Emmett had on you—those are the kinds of things that would make life complicated for your brother. I'm just thinking aloud here, but don't you think that might be right?" Hidden dye journals, hidden blackmail records—they made sense to my overloaded, overstressed brain.

He again didn't say anything and we stared at each other, seemingly at a stalemate. Although I couldn't think what consensus or goal he hoped we'd reach. Watching him, I also couldn't tell if he thought we'd made any progress toward it.

"I'll give you my phone number," he finally said. "It's a good idea for you to have it."

"Why?"

"Ruth asked me to give it to you. You know, in case something happens. Blocked drain. Roof leak." He took a pen from a pocket, reached across and jotted the number on my paper napkin. "Place is pretty solid, though," he said, looking around. "I doubt you'll have any trouble."

"What are we talking about now?"

"Oh, sorry, I thought Ruth told you. She hired me today as a temp until they find someone permanent for Em's place. Feeding the animals, mowing and whatnot. Lock up at the end of the day. General handyman. You know. Look after the place."

"You have keys?"

"She handed me a whole raft of them, yeah."

"You have a key to this house?"

"No doubt."

"You can let yourself in."

"Well, yeah, I guess . . ."

"I think I need you to leave now."

Chapter 17

He had keys to the cottage?

I needed to think and I couldn't do it with him and his bonny, burglarous eyes sitting there looking at me. Finishing my supper in peace, without feeling the need to clutch a poker, would be nice, too. Despite my request, he didn't leave immediately, and that left me unsure of my next move. How did one eject a seemingly friendly burglar if one wasn't entirely willing to connect a cast-iron poker with his flesh?

"Um." My new word for all occasions.

"I'll only be a tick." He got up, no longer looking worried by me and my weapon. He tucked his chair under the table and took his dish to the sink, being, apparently, a neat and domestic burglar. Which was better than being a feral one, I guessed. I must have snorted. He caught my eye and smiled.

"I'm not smiling."

"Sorry, my mistake." He continued to smile, retrieving his jacket and hat from where he'd left them on the chair. He put the jacket on and glanced out the window over the sink. "Rain's letting up. Downpour like that buggers up the fishing for a few days, though."

I wondered why it was buggered up, but didn't ask. Under other circumstances it's possible I would enjoy getting-to-know-you type small talk with a nonthreatening, passably good-looking, artistic, fishing burglar. But right now I was more interested in getting the burglar out of the house.

He set his hat on his head, opened the door, and looked back at me. "Good night, Kath. Get some sleep. Get your mind wrapped around things. Then give me a call, okay? I'll leave you to finish your supper in peace without the poker getting in your way."

I almost smiled again, almost nodded. He did nod, tugged his hat low on his forehead, and pulled the door shut behind him.

And I immediately thought of twenty-five questions I should have asked and one I wanted answered then and there. I fumbled the door open, still holding both the poker and the phone.

"Wait, er, Joe," I called into the dark. Not loudly enough, though. Where had he gotten to so fast? I couldn't see him or hear him. Then I heard a vehicle start at the side of the house. I hesitated, but stepped back inside and closed the door, watching around the edge of the curtain as he drove past in a pickup. "Why did Granny trust you?" I asked his taillights. Her trust said something important. Ardis trusted him, too. I'd seen that with my own eyes. And Ruth.

Unless friendly Joe had bamboozled them all with those blue eyes. Because being blackmailed over secrets worth searching for, even after the blackmailer was murdered, was a better reason than a spot of burglary for fixing him as my number one suspect. And was brother Clod really unaware of all this or had he known who I surprised in the pantry? Was he covering for Joe? Or were they working together to pin Emmett's murder on Granny? That couldn't happen.

I let the curtain fall and used my handy four-in-one

poker to reach an itchy spot in the middle of my back. It probably left a streak of soot down the spine of my sweat-shirt, but it felt good. It was also beginning to feel like an extension of my arm. I laid it and my phone on the counter, covered a yawn, then turned the dead bolt and slotted the security chain. The chain looked stout. No weak links. Firmly mounted to the doorframe and the frame looked solid. I tugged the chain. No give, no wiggle in the hardware. Good.

Of course, anyone really wanting to get in could break the window, reach inside, slide the chain, turn the bolt, and twist the knob. Or heave an object through any window and climb in. Or let himself in with his officially sanctioned keys whenever I wasn't home.

Not that I had anything with me worth burgling. My laptop. That was easily fixed; I'd carry it with me. With the laptop for a shield and the poker as my sword, I'd be the model for a modern heraldry poster—Kath Rutledge rampant, ready to repel all boarders, including burglars and their brothers. But it wasn't my stuff Joe wanted to snoop through.

I glanced around the kitchen. What did he think he'd find here to prove that Emmett was a blackmailer? Max would have taken all the personal property, including papers and records. Obvious records, anyway, even if they weren't labeled OTHER PEOPLE'S SECRETS OR INCRIMINATING INCOME—IRS, KEEP OUT.

Or was Max pleasantly surprised to discover the business he'd inherited? Had that occurred to Joe? The thought of Max improving or expanding Emmett's empire sent a chill down my spine. I was glad—questions were paralyzing me and the shiver got me moving again.

The most urgent question: Where was Granny's letter? What did I do with it when the ghos . . . when things got weird the night before? I was reading it in the sitting room and left it—dropped it?—when the boohooing began. If Joe let himself in he wouldn't find anything more interesting in my suitcase than my plaid bikini. But Granny's letter was not for snooping eyes. Whether or not Emmett Cobb was holding her eccentric *being-somewhat-of-a-witch* idea ransom, Granny trusted me to keep it a secret, even from trusted friends. I ran to the sitting room.

It was there, on the seat of the recliner, where I'd left it when I grabbed my fireplace weaponry. I picked it up, trying to remember more deliberate movements than letting the pages fall from my hands.

"Did I refold it?" Asking the question out loud didn't jar the memory loose.

"Does it even matter?" A familiar heavy sigh gusted from the kitchen, followed by a muttered "Of course it doesn't matter. Nothing matters."

I moved back toward the kitchen, wary but not bothering to arm myself this time.

"Creeping around isn't necessary. Lord knows, you can't scare me. Though I'd appreciate it if next time your gentleman caller didn't hang his jacket on me."

I pictured Joe's rain-soaked jacket dropping over the poor gray cloud. Surely it hadn't made her any wetter. I apologized anyway. "I'm so sorry. Were you sitting here the whole time?"

"I only wish I could say I had somewhere else to be."

"Oh . . ." I closed my mouth before another "um" escaped. Groping for conversation with a ghost was so new to me. I turned the letter over in my hands, trying to think, my fingertips following the strands of fiber in the paper, a familiar and soothing action. "Um." Rats. I tried again. "Did—did you refold this letter?"

"As I say, I only wish."

She grew taller in the chair, expanding, unfurling.

I stepped back, alarmed. Then I realized she'd been sitting hunched, with her arms wrapped around herself. She straightened one arm and swept it across the table, through the water glasses and Ruth's casserole. I cringed, but everything remained upright and in place. She demonstrated again, this time with both arms, moving them faster over the table until they were a blur. Nothing quivered. She slumped.

"Who are you?" I felt blindly for the chair opposite her and sat down as heavily as she sighed.

"So you finally admit I exist."

I did, but still fell short of saying so out loud. "Why didn't I see you when Joe was here?" I waved a shaky hand at her and the chair. "With the jacket and the hat, I mean. Oh, wait, gosh, that didn't hurt you, did it?"

"Nothing can hurt me now."

"Oh."

"I was only having fun with you when I said that, though. He didn't hang his jacket on me."

"Oh."

"I might be dead, but I mind my manners. I wouldn't dream of eavesdropping when you're entertaining a gentleman caller."

My lips started to go round again, but I managed to keep them from opening. "Oh" would be my new "um" if I didn't try harder. "That was nice of you. What were you doing, or, where were you if you weren't . . ."

"I was waxing melancholic. I do that. It's one of the few things I can do. That and mind my manners."

I thought back over the evening. Had there been any hint of weeping or wailing? Joe hadn't cocked an ear, and I didn't remember any background noises. "Well, thank you, I guess, for being so polite. Were you doing your waxing in the sitting room?"

"No." She followed that with a tremulous whimper.

"No. I was upstairs." Her voice rose several notes, as though floating up those stairs again, and then she began shuddering and sobbing and I missed what she said next.

She was so utterly pathetic and I'd known so much of that kind of sorrow over the past days that I wanted to comfort her. But how? Hugging wasn't an option, so I went with the old standby.

"There, there."

The crying did stop, but the look she gave me was scathing. "I confide intimate details of my evening, then weep with abandon, and 'There, there' is the best you can do?"

She puffed in and out, looking more and more distressed. It was contagious, too. I felt as though my hands should be fluttering like large moths. Instead, I clasped them in front of me on the table, hoping my white knuckles didn't give away my lack of composure. "Please, try telling me again. I couldn't quite catch what you said through the tears."

"And I cry because it is so sad." She shuddered and looked as though she was beginning to enjoy herself. "I'll repeat what I said. Are you ready?"

I nodded.

She drew in her breath and started crying again but kept the tears to a minimum, so she was more or less intelligible. "I was lying on the bed I shared with my darling Em for the first and last time the night I killed him."

She sat back, flickering between looking tragic and artfully droopy, obviously eager for me to be appalled at great length. It was easy enough to stare, and not wanting to disappoint her again, I gasped. She seemed happy with the improved reaction, and that gave me time to think. This thing, this ghostly woman who couldn't knock over a glass of water, couldn't have spiked a glass with poison to kill Emmett Cobb. But she was so emotional that I approached the subject carefully.

"That must have been awful . . ."

"Seeing the horror on his face when he at last beheld my presence?"

"Oh . . ."

"Hearing his mortal scream? Seeing him clutch his heart in the throes of death before my very eyes?" She clutched the area where her own heart would be if she still had one and threw herself back in the chair.

"Yes, well . . ."

"Helplessly watching as he thrashed . . ."

"Yes, thank you, I'm getting the picture very nicely," I said over her, taking the chance that she'd accuse me of shouting at her again.

"Are you squeamish?"

"I guess I am. Sorry. Look, you seem to be okay talking about this, about Em's death."

"Oh, I am. It's very sad, isn't it? My evenings are so empty now, the days so quiet without the constant muted murmur of his television."

"'His television'?"

"Television is a brilliant invention, don't you think?"

"Oh, brilliant, sure. Would you be willing to hear another theory about his death?"

"Isn't that a melancholy phrase, though?" She billowed in and out, ignoring my question. "It was a constant, muted murmur, but all is silent now. It's sad, so sad, it's a sad, sad situation."

"Wait, isn't that last bit a line from a song by someone? By Elton John?"

"Is it? I'm sure I wouldn't know."

"You might, though. Maybe it was one of your favorite songs when you were . . ."

"When I wasn't dead? I doubt it, and I don't want to think about that. It makes me anxious. We were talking about my guilty role in killing Em. How I murdered my darling."

And that didn't make her anxious? I wondered what it was about her previous life she didn't want to think about. But maybe anxiety over their lost lives and being enthralled by other deaths was typical for ghosts. Having no experience believing in them, much less talking to them, I had no idea. This one was happily caught up in it, anyway, sitting across from me, rocking and moaning. The moaning sounded almost like humming, but if that's what it was, I couldn't identify the tune. Not Elton John, anyway.

Rocking and humming seemed to relax her and I hesitated to interrupt. But she was also growing dimmer, the chair becoming more distinct through her.

"Wouldn't it make you feel better to know you didn't kill Em?"

"Better?" Still rocking, she considered that. "Feel better? But that isn't the real question, is it? The real question is can I feel anything at all?"

"You just said you feel sad."

"Oh, I do, I do. And I feel cold."

She stretched a wisp of gray arm across the table toward me. I pulled back, but she was faster and as her hand passed over (through?) mine I felt a bone-deep chill. I rubbed my hands together and blew on them and suddenly couldn't think of anything else but how nice it would be to warm them around a mug of something. Without thinking, I hopped up.

"Where are you going?"

"To make cocoa. Would you like some?" It slipped out without thinking. The curse of being brought up to be polite. "Sorry. That was probably insensitive, wasn't it?"

"Why? Because it's agony to watch you enjoy swallowing and know I'll never again taste the sweetness of food or drink? First you torture me with a plate of tuna casserole and now a cup of cocoa?"

I sat back down and warmed my hands in my armpits.

She smiled, enjoying herself again. "Now, let's get back to your original question."

"I'm pretty sure I've forgotten what that is by now." I was also getting annoyed with her, but made an effort to stifle that uncharitable sentiment. Maybe she couldn't help being irritating. She certainly couldn't help being dead.

"I was bemoaning the fact that I killed my darling Em and you were entertaining the notion that I might feel better if I didn't think myself responsible. But I don't think I could possibly believe I wasn't."

"Will you listen to an alternate theory, anyway?"

"If you must, but please understand that Em's death was tragic. Tragic. I doubt I shall ever get over it. But, please, do go ahead. Don't let my feelings stop you."

It was my turn to sigh. I tried to keep it low-key, though. "The police say he was poisoned."

"Poisoned by my sudden appearance."

"No, poisoned by real, tangible poison."

"Poisoned by my too ghastly appearance as I cuddled up to him in our love nest."

"No, really, you're getting carried away with that idea. I don't know what kind of poison it was, but it was in something he ate or drank. Actual poison was put into something someone gave him and that's not something you could have done, is it? Not unless you really can move objects."

She stopped rocking and wavering and became more opaque. Her hollow eyes stared at me and I had to look at the table to steady my nerves.

"Is this true?" she asked, her voice low now, and without a single pneumatic breath or tremble.

"According to the police, yes."

"I didn't kill darling Em?"

"I don't see how you could have."

"Prove it."

"What?"

"Prove it wasn't me."

"I just did. Think it through logically. If someone put the poison into something Em swallowed and if you can't move anything, if you can't physically pick something up and put it into something else, then you couldn't have poisoned him."

She swelled. "Then who did?"

"I—I don't know," I said, edging my chair back.

"You should find out."

"I'm not sure—"

"How can I rest peacefully until you find out? How can I possibly believe I had no hand in Em's death if you don't hunt down his murderer and deliver him to justice?"

"I don't think it's really that easy—"

"Must I moan and wail through all the days and nights to come, down through the ages?"

"Well, I don't know. Must you?"

"I might." She swelled and billowed, growing grayer and more alarming.

"And I can just as easily pack up and move to a motel," I said, scrambling to stand behind my chair, as if standing made me that much bigger and braver and would save me.

"You'd abandon me?"

"I don't know how to look for a murderer."

"You'd run out on me in my hour of need?"

"Your hour of need? For a skunk of an old man who blackmailed a sweet little old lady?"

"Love is never simple, is it? I've watched enough hours of Dr. Phil and Dr. Ruth to know that much. And I never miss Oprah. She's almost a doctor, too." She sat up straighter and began to sound more alive. "This is rather exciting now that I think about it." Her wispy hands came together in a soundless clap. "I also adore *Law & Order* and *CSI* and *Andy Griffith*, all those cop shows, so I know exactly how you need to go about this. Start by investigating that little old lady you mentioned. It should be dead easy to prove she killed darling Em."

Chapter 18

I spent a second night in that house. Despite the ghost. Mostly because it was pouring again, and I couldn't bear to schlep my suitcase out into the waterlogged dark to find a motel.

It might have been a sleepless night. I didn't have earplugs to muffle the deluge drumming on the tin roof or Ms. Histrionic's wails. She turned them on as soon as I refused to cooperate with her plan to pin Emmett Cobb's murder on Granny. Her level of melodrama increased from barely tolerable to nearly excruciating the longer I tried. Luckily, a cunning plan occurred to me.

Ignoring Her Dolefulness, I fetched my laptop, opened it on the kitchen table, plugged it in, and powered up. Next, I reset the screen saver so it would display photographs from one of my picture files in a continuous random slide show without reverting to a blank screen. Then I started an MP3 I'd downloaded of a Sharyn McCrumb mystery. I didn't say anything, didn't tell the ghost what I was doing. She'd moved to the counter beside the sink and appeared to be cradling herself in the dish drainer, moping in a gray heap, with her back to me.

The slide show—shots I'd taken over the years of the Smokies, Blue Plum, the Weaver's Cat, and Granny— didn't exactly coordinate with McCrumb's *The Ballad of Frankie Silver*, but the narration and the pictures complemented each other fairly well. If I'd had Internet access, I could have let the poor thing console herself with her beloved TV shows. Instead, maybe McCrumb's story or the photographs would capture her attention so she wouldn't follow me upstairs and haunt me in my sleep.

I tiptoed out, leaving Ms. Mope to discover the magic of computer entertainment on her own. Holding my breath, creeping up the stairs, furtively brushing my teeth, slipping into bed and under Granny's coverlet, I thanked Sharyn McCrumb for providing twelve hours and fifty-six minutes of auditory distraction for a depressed, television-addicted ghost. And I thanked the programmer who invented the screen-saver slide show. And Granny for the coverlet. And Ruth for sharing it. And tried not to think of Emmett Cobb's horrible death by poison in that very bed. It wasn't easy. But the exhaustion of several days with too little sleep swept over me and carried me off.

Homer called the next morning before either the sun or I was up. Well before McCrumb's story was due to conclude in the kitchen, too, and I wondered if sometime during the night the ghost lost interest in the laptop's charms. But she didn't shimmer into view at the end of the bed when the phone startled me awake, and a quick check of the room didn't reveal a damp lump snoring nearby. Maybe my idea for overnight ghost care had worked. Good. When she was out of sight, I felt much less out of my mind.

It was too early for an ordinary phone call, so I braced myself when Homer's somber lawyer's voice greeted me. But it was good news and I sat up, rejuvenated and ready to tackle the day, after he delivered it.

Max Cobb was back. He'd rolled into town in the wee hours and he'd agreed to drop by Homer's office with a set of keys that would finally let me into Granny's house.

Homer sounded pleased with himself about the negotiated delivery time. Max had said he'd drop the keys off shortly after noon, a time that Homer summarily dismissed. With only a little persuasion, Max swallowed a gigantic yawn and promised to put the keys in Ernestine's hand no later than eight thirty. I didn't ask Homer how he knew Max was home. Or what his persuasion techniques consisted of.

"Thank you, Homer."

"Don't thank me until we see if he follows through. And I haven't gained a stay of execution yet."

"I beg your pardon?"

"The new renters scheduled to move in at the first of the month. Wednesday."

"Hoo boy."

"Concisely stated. I'm hoping to negotiate for a delay at least until that weekend. That will give you a week, a more civilized period of time in which to remove Ivy's belongings. In the meantime I have the name of someone who can arrange help for the heavy furniture. He's not a professional mover, but he'll be efficient and he also owns an acre or so of those metal storage buildings. Unless you've already made arrangements to move everything back to Illinois?"

"No, the 'hoo boy' pretty much summed up the whole picture. Clear thinking stopped a couple of days ago."

"That's not surprising given the circumstances."

"A few more days to empty and clean the house would be terrific, if you can get it."

"I wish I could guarantee it. Ernestine will give you that fellow's name and number. And I'll have her call you when the keys arrive. I expect Mr. Cobb will show up on time, but there's no need for you to be there or to waste your time waiting at the house if he doesn't. And if he doesn't make his appearance by eight thirty, I will personally describe for him the special place in purgatory reserved for obstructionists when I do see him."

I thanked Homer again and disconnected, picturing his raptor eyes skewering a tardy, blustering Max Cobb. For Max's sake, I hoped he showed up full of cooperation with a jangling set of keys no later than eight twenty-nine. Seeing him squirm, other than in my mind's eye, wasn't appealing and I was glad Homer didn't expect me to be there to witness it. But having the raptor on my side, ready to strike, gave me a reason to hop out of bed and make ambitious plans for the day.

Those plans did not include a ghost. Not her badgering, or her whining, or her theories about homicidal old ladies.

I pulled on my jeans and semigrungy sweatshirt. No need to doll myself up for a day of sorting, packing, and cleaning. Mouse-quiet, I crept to the top of the stairs and listened.

Only a mumble of narration came from the kitchen. I stifled a giggle when I pictured what I must look like sneaking around. I felt like a teenager slipping out of the house and almost went to check for a drainpipe to shinny down. Instead, shoes in one hand, purse slung over my shoulder, I eased down the stairs and along the wall until I could see what was going on in the kitchen.

It wasn't easy to tell. The sun was just creeping in as I was creeping out and the ghost wasn't much more than a ripple in that soft light. She blurred a chair and the end of the table opposite the computer. Her elbows were distinguishable, though, and they appeared to be planted on the table. Using them as a starting point, I was able to make out her hands propping her chin up. She sat, leaning forward, staring at the laptop, enrapt. A ghost hypnotized by gadgetry.

Except for the photographs sliding on and off the

screen, and for the odd effect of the air undulating where she took up space, nothing moved. McCrumb's words were the only sound. No whiff of moldering, ghostly wool or linen tickled my nose—just a trace of tuna casserole.

I crossed the room undetected, invisible as a ghost myself. Rattling the door chain would make me feel like Marley, but I resisted the temptation and muffled the chain and the click of the dead bolt with my hand.

I did wonder about leaving the laptop, open and inviting. But the likelihood of Joe Look-At-Me-I've-Got-Keys waltzing in and grabbing it when he knew I knew whatever it was I thought I knew about him was pretty slim. Or so it seemed after a night's sleep. Besides, I couldn't take the laptop with me. My ghost was using it.

Before pulling the door shut, I glanced over my shoulder. A picture of Granny standing behind the counter at the Weaver's Cat disappeared as I watched. Just the way she had. There one minute, then gone. I closed and locked the door and fumbled in a pocket for a tissue.

Breakfast at Mel's was first on the agenda. But because I tended to thumb my nose at agendas, even my own, I took a detour and drove down Lavender Street first. I stopped the car and sat looking at Granny's house, drawing peace of mind from the lines of the roof, the porch, the windows, the front door she told me a million times not to slam. I almost got out so I could wait on the porch swing for Ernestine's call telling me the keys were in hand. Then my stomach growled and I decided fortifying myself with substantial calories was a better use of my time.

Walking into Mel's on Main is like walking into a fog of bacon, coffee, and yeast. That morning hints of onion soup and overtones of berry pie also drifted past. The memory of killer brownies lingered, too, but my nose returned to the bacon and coffee and I followed them to the counter.

Mel herself stood behind the counter, a pencil behind each ear and two more sticking out of her apron's bib pocket. The apron was an intense mustard color, her spiked hair even more so. The last time I'd seen her, apron and hair were violet. She looked up from taking a camera-slung couple's order and spotted me.

"You couldn't stop by sooner? Get over here." She grabbed me in a hug across the counter, putting a hand on the back of my neck and pulling my ear close to her lips. "I'm sorry about Ivy, but I don't do funerals," she whispered, "or burials. It's rude, but that's tough." She let me go and lifted her chin. Tough. That was how Mel wanted the world to see her.

"It's good to see you, too, Mel."

"Get back in line."

"Yes, ma'am." I snapped a salute and retreated.

"Sorry," Mel said to the touristy couple. "She's from up north. Indinois or Ohiowa or some such outlandish place. Gets impatient and tries to jump." She made a shooing motion at me. "None of your sass, missy. Right to the back of the line."

The couple and I were the only ones *in* line, so that confused them. Mel gave them complimentary doughnuts and they sat down looking unsure but pleased with their good fortune.

"What'll it be?" Mel asked me.

I bit my tongue against asking for the brownie I'd missed the night before. "Spinach omelet wrap and coffee, please. And can you slip some bacon in the wrap?"

"For you? Anything. For here?"

"To go."

"You have someplace you need to be this early?"

I'd decided to risk spilling breakfast on myself eating in the car outside Homer's office. That way I'd be on the spot when Ernestine called. I looked at Mel's Rosie the Riveter clock. Seven forty-five. Maybe I'd been overeager. But this way I'd catch sight of Max if the fear of Homer prompted him to show up early and drop the keys through the mail slot. I wanted to see Max Cobb, wanted to see what a man looks like who'd turn an old lady's possessions out in the cold and who willingly married into the Spivey family. But in thinking that through, I didn't answer Mel fast enough.

She tsked and turned to the order hatch. "Popeye omelet, sharp cheddar, side of sausage, side of rye, coffee black, for here." Turning back to me, she said, "In honor of Ivy. That's what she liked and here's where she liked it. In fact, it's slow, so I'll join you." She untied her apron and hung it on a peg below the hatch. "Double that last order," she called through the hatch. "Couple of large mango juices, too."

She led us to a round table in one of the front windows, maneuvering so she faced the window and the door. "The better to see who's coming in," she said.

Mel's was in an old, narrow hardware store, abandoned for a dozen years after the owner died. Tough Mel, medium height and roughly my age, moved home to Blue Plum and bought the building with money from her divorce. Her brother pulled down the shelving, exposing the brick walls. She refinished the chestnut floors and designed the kitchen. He repainted the pressed-tin ceiling. They hung enlargements of black-and-white photographs their newspaperman grandfather took of Main Street in the forties and fifties. Then her brother joined the Marines and Mel started cooking.

"How's business, Mel?"

"Hopping."

We looked around at the generally hopeless café. Quiet munching went on at a few tables. Others showed evidence of recent occupation. Mel shrugged.

"Tourists don't get up early. My early-morning bread and butter's over there." She nodded toward the back where half a dozen old men sat talking over empty plates. "This is their clubhouse. Gives them a reason to get up and out in the morning."

One of the men raised his cup to Mel.

"You need more coffee, Carl?"

"Wouldn't mind."

"You know where it is. Go on, now, and stir yourself. Don't make me come over there."

The other men laughed as Carl rose, laughing too, and limped over to the pot.

"Wouldn't do to baby him," Mel said watching his slow progress. "He's eighty-eight. Fetching coffee is cheaper than physical therapy and nagging him reminds him of his late wife. So"—she turned to me again—"where were you taking my good hot breakfast? The Cat's not open until ten. My informants say you're staying at the Homeplace. Danish travels that far, omelets not so much." She cocked her head. "And I hear through the Spivey vine that there's trouble over Ivy's house. Don't pretend you're shocked. I'm nosy and good at eavesdropping."

She talked a lot. I'd forgotten.

"Come on, spill. You know I won't pump it back *into* the Spivey vine. Heard in confidence, it stays with me. Overheard in passing, or loitering with intent, it's fair game for sending on down the line. Hold up, though— here's our Ivy McClellan Memorial Breakfast."

While our plates were set down and we lifted glasses of too-sweet mango juice in Granny's memory, I decided it couldn't hurt to fill Mel in—leaving out words like "blackmail" and "ghost." In return, maybe she'd dredge up something useful she'd overheard. She ate and listened with characteristic intensity. When I finished laying out the snarled strands of the story, I drained my coffee, wishing Granny had gone in for cream and sugar. Mel immediately refilled my cup from an insulated carafe, a luxury she apparently didn't believe in offering the gimpy old men. She batted my hand when I reached for sugar.

"No, ma'am. If God or Ivy intended coffee to be sweet or milky they'd have made it that way. Today we're drinking it for her, so suck it up."

"If I drink another cup of this, will you tell me what you've heard?"

"Deal," she said. "What do you want to know?"

"What have you heard about the house, through the Spivey vine or otherwise? What have you heard or what do you know about Max? And what have you heard or what do you know about his father?"

"You mean his father's murder?"

"Or about Emmett himself."

"Kind of surreal, you know?" she said. "Hearing the word 'murder' in Blue Plum? Like a pinch of hocus-pocus comes with it and if you say it too often old Em's ghost will pop up and yell boo. Hey, are you all right?"

"Coffee, wrong way," I croaked from behind my napkin. "His ghost?" That still didn't come out well, so I hid behind my napkin for another cough and to let my vocal cords recompose themselves. "Sorry. Are people saying that? About ghosts?"

"Only a few of the Gothier teenage boys into the whole woo-woo thing. They were in here one afternoon scaring cheerleaders they'd like to date. Why? What hooey have you been hearing?"

"About ghosts? Nothing. 'Hooey' is a good word for it, all right." I meant to laugh, although the actual sound was more like a strangled bleat.

Mel's eyebrows rose, but not in reaction to my sound effects. She was looking past me, out the window. "Okay, promise me you won't panic."

"About what?"

"Spivey One and Spivey Two just parked across the street."

I shrank in my chair, regretting our front-window table.

"It's okay. They aren't getting out. But I'll nutshell what I've heard just in case. About the house? Not a whisper. The little you told me is more than the Spiveys know."

"Even with Max married to Angie?"

"Could be Max and Angie don't know much about it, either, so there's nothing to tell."

"Or Max knows something but hasn't told Angie."

"You're a suspicious so-and-so." Mel cocked her head. "But that could be. Max is less under the Spivey thumb than you'd expect considering the pervasiveness of that thumb and the weedy proportions of Max. From what I hear, he's more like a splinter in the thumb."

"Interesting. I didn't want to like him, but that makes me wonder."

"I'd reserve judgment," Mel said. "He reminds me of my ex. That's not a recommendation of his intelligence or allegiance."

"Lucky Angie."

"So. The murder."

"Please. What are people saying? What do you think?"

"I think it's bizarre. Emmett Cobb? Someone felt strongly enough to kill that dried-up speck of a man? Why?"

"He didn't have any enemies?"

"Only the way a mangy possum does. But you throw a shoe at it. You don't poison it. There was a lot of shock and shriek when it happened. You know the kind of thing: 'We'll all be killed in our beds!'" She waved her hands and goggled her eyes in mock terror. "And there's still some of that because no one's been arrested. But to be honest, maybe brutally honest—" She shrugged. "Okay, to be cynical—most people don't care."

"What do you mean?"

"They don't care that Em is dead. They were het up because someone was murdered, but not because it was Emmett Cobb."

That was an interesting and sad commentary. I thought back to Deputy Clod's sorrow over losing a poker partner. Maybe he was one of the few who mourned Emmett Cobb. He and my poor lovelorn ghost. Maybe I could fix the two of them up. Mel interrupted before the image jelled.

"Something's happening in the Spiveymobile."

The twins had backed their car into the parking space across the street, so they were facing the café with a clear, if not ringside, view of our table. Mel was right. There was a hitch in their shoulder-to-shoulder solidarity in the front seat of the Buick.

"What are they fighting over?"

"Binoculars."

Chapter 19

"Do you think they read lips?" I asked that from behind my coffee mug.

"Let's find out." Mel mouthed something toward the Spiveys.

"Wait, don't leave the sound out altogether. Even if they read lips, I don't. What are you saying?"

Mel held her napkin to her mouth. "Something guaranteed to get a rise out of them. Watch."

"No, Mel, nothing rude."

She ignored me and waved her napkin at the twins. She mouthed something, wiggled her eyebrows, and pointed at me. "No," she said then, clearly disappointed. "They do not read lips."

"Well, thank God. I don't need those two on the warpath against me."

"Warpath, nothing. If they read lips they'd be out of that car, and in here pulling up chairs, only stopping to hug your neck first. I told them you'd buy them breakfast. But hold on, something else is happening."

"Something else" was Deputy Dunbar arriving, light bar flashing. He pulled to the curb in front of Mel's, stopping in a no-parking zone. His siren, which had been silent, came on for one *whoo-whoop* that sounded like a nose-thumb to all parking regulations. He doused the lights, climbed out, adjusted his gun belt, and came toward the café.

"Why do I think this doesn't look good?" I asked.

"Why do I think the Spiveys were expecting it?"

My mouth was still hanging open at Mel's question when Dunbar stalked through the door and over to our table. It snapped shut at his question.

"Ms. Rutledge, will you please come with me?"

"Morning to you, too, Cole," Mel said.

"Ms. Rutledge?"

"How about a friendly cup of coffee first?" Mel got to her feet and stood in front of Clod. Unfortunately, with her spiked mustard hair, she looked less than friendly and more like an agitated canary.

Clod looked over the top of her bristling spikes to where I hadn't stirred from the table. "Ms. Rutledge?"

"Coffee's on me." Mel took a step closer to Clod, her smile not in sync with the fists on her hips.

Clod closed his eyes and said something under his breath that even non–lip readers could decipher. Chairs scraped as the old men rearranged their seats so they wouldn't miss anything. The touristy couple reached for their cameras. I looked at the Buick across the street. No flash of binoculars. The car was empty.

Clod sidestepped Mel. "Ms. Rutledge, last time I'll ask."

"Why?" Mel, my wild mustard forward guard, kept pace with Clod, moving sideways in a belligerent *pas de deux*. "She has a right to know what this is all about."

"She, Mel. Not you. Put your protest sign away and stand down."

"It's okay, Mel." I stood and put a hand on her shoulder, feeling the tension there and wondering if I'd have to stop her from flying at Clod. Or if I'd try. "I'm sure it's something routine. Maybe about the break-in at Granny's house?"

Clod didn't say or mutter anything to confirm or deny that.

I took a steadying breath and told myself to be polite and cooperative. Also not to slip and call him Clod to his face.

He was reaching for my elbow, no doubt to assist me so I wouldn't trip and hurt myself, and I was planning how to remove my elbow from his grasp, when, simultaneously, my phone rang and the bell over Mel's door jingled. The latter was triggered by the Spivey twins. They stepped inside, smiling, not at all self-conscious that every pair of eyes in the café avidly turned to them. They nodded to the table of old men.

My phone continued to trill inside my purse and everyone, including Clod and the Spiveys, suspended their next moves while I dug for it. I'd been expecting Ernestine's call and stupidly had not had the phone easily to hand. It quit ringing by the time I finally dug it out of the depths. I clamped my lips shut before anything audible or readable escaped them.

"No doubt, if that was Ernie, she'll call back," one twin said.

"Or leave a message," said the other.

"I'd have to say that kind of news warrants a call more than a message, though," the first said.

"It surely does," the other said with a nod.

It was impossible to tell which font of wisdom was Mercy and which Shirley. A whiff of Mercy's horrible perfume muscled its way past the coffee and bacon, but I couldn't pinpoint which irritating twin provided the source. The red sweeping up the back of Clod's neck made me think they irritated him, too.

"Or you could save time and call *her*," the first Spivey said.

They smiled and said nothing more, obviously waiting for someone to ask what they were talking about.

Clod seemed to know, though, and he made another move to take my elbow. I slipped his grasp and punched Homer's number into my phone. Clod's attempt was further stymied by three bodies bulling their way between us. Mel, I was happy to have close by. The Spiveys, I wasn't so sure of.

"We thought you might need backup," Spivey One said.

"Our civic duty," said Spivey Two, near enough now that I could identify her as Mercy.

"I don't need your help, thank you," Clod snarled.

"We don't mean you, Cole Dunbar," Mercy snapped.

"Hush, now," Shirley said, "while Kath makes the call she's allowed before you arrest her."

Ernestine answered on the first ring.

"Help!"

Chapter 20

Handsome Homer rescued me. He swooped into the café and out again, me safely under his wing. Ernestine choreographed our flight from her desk at the office, dispatching Homer and staying on the phone with me until we were on our way. The only clue to her excitement was the staccato of her knitting needles in the background.

To my surprise, Clod held the door for us when we left. Mel did her part by thwarting the Spiveys' attempt to follow. Not surprisingly, Clod did follow.

"Deputy Dunbar, thank you for joining us," Homer said when we reached the office and Clod was still with us. Homer sounded genuinely gracious about the intrusion. Another reason he made a good lawyer. I couldn't have used the same words without sounding sarcastic, or maybe jabbing Clod in the solar plexus.

Homer ushered us past Ernestine's desk into the inner office. Ernestine gave me a thumbs-up before Homer closed the door. The knitting needles had disappeared.

"I believe they meant well," Homer said, holding a chair for me.

"We're talking about the civic-minded Spiveys?" There was that lapse into sarcasm I'd worried about.

"They're the ones called me in the first place," Clod said at the same time.

Clod and I looked at each other. Did I appear as non-plussed as he at finding ourselves, if not in harmony, at least picking out the same tune? Homer walked around behind his desk. Clod took that as an invitation and dropped into the chair next to mine. Homer remained standing.

"Why did they call you?" Homer asked.

"You don't know?"

Homer removed a speck of lint from his lapel. "You tell us."

Clod, appearing his usual exhausted self, got back to his feet. It was a good move, erasing the advantage Homer established by not sitting in the first place. They were both imposing men. But where Homer had the sleek, sharp, raptor thing going for him, Clod was a tired battering ram. I stayed in my chair, out of their way.

"Someone broke into the house on Lavender Street," Clod said.

"Again?" That had me hopping out of my chair, but when both men looked at me, I melted back into it with a "sorry."

As soon as the apology was out of my mouth, I wanted to kick myself for being a coward. But the interplay between the raptor and the battering ram was more interesting than my self-improvement problems, so I sat back and watched. At first I saw their moves as a tango, so smooth and subtle I'd miss the slide from wariness to warning to menace if I blinked. Then I remembered Homer saying Clod was good at poker and realized that was what they were playing.

Homer said nothing. He lifted his nose and turned his eyes to a point not directly on Clod. Still he said nothing, but his left eyebrow made it clear he had questions and expected answers. Clod waited, equally silent, chin tucked, expression mulish. The tips of Homer's fingers rested on his desk. Clod's hands were on his hips, one hip cocked. It was as neat a power struggle as I'd ever seen. And a waste of time. I stood up.

"Deputy Dunbar, if you have information about my grandmother's house, I want to hear it."

They actually looked put out at my interruption. They turned toward me, mouths opening. But to do what? Answer my question? Advise me not to speak? Whine that I wasn't playing the game right? I didn't wait to find out. I held up a shushing finger, daring their mouths to go further.

"I also want to know why the Spiveys think you're about to arrest me. And I want you to sit down. Both of you."

I waited until they sat, Homer with a light laugh, Clod harrumphing, before I sat back down. Despite my jeans and grungy sweatshirt, I crossed my legs, put my elbows on the arms of the chair, fingers tented, and glared. I felt like a conflict mediator. Or a middle school guidance counselor.

"Well, Kath, Cole, we're all friends," Homer said with another light laugh.

"But"—I cut in before he wrested control from me—"I want answers to my questions. And I might have more after that."

"Yet I would caution you, Kath," Homer continued.

"No need for cautions," Clod said. "Shorty's over there checking out the house. I'm just asking questions."

"Who's Shorty?"

"Proof I'm not the only deputy, Ms. Rutledge."

"Okay. Good," I said. "Go ahead, then. Oh, no, wait. Max Cobb owns the place. Why aren't you asking him questions?"

"Your grandmother lived there. I knew where to find you. We will get to him. May I continue?"

"I'm not stopping you."

"We received a call at seven forty-two this morning

reporting a broken window and possible burglary at one-oh-three Lavender Street."

"Broken window? With all that rain we had last night? Which one? I didn't see it when I was over there this morning."

"Kath." Homer shook his head at me.

"But what's going on in this town?" I looked from one to the other. Neither offered an answer, poker faces back in place. I wasn't letting them play, though. I stabbed my shushing finger, now a skewer, at Clod.

"You think it was me, don't you? All because of yesterday when you found me looking in the windows and I happened to mention I was game to break in."

I had to hand it to Homer. If I'd been a lawyer like him with a client like me, I'd have thrown my hands in the air and jumped out the nearest high window. Homer didn't even roll his eyes or massage his forehead to ease the headache I must have given him. Clod sat patiently, too, and surprised me by having the grace not to smile or pick feathers from between his teeth.

"Do you have evidence suggesting my client is responsible for either the broken window or the alleged break-in?" Homer asked.

"No."

"Do you have any evidence implicating Ivy McClellan in the death of Emmett Cobb?"

There was a pause, the intent of which could be interpreted in several ways; then, once again, a single word: "No."

"Yet suggestions have been made."

Low rumbles came from Clod. Homer raised a hand. The rumbles subsided.

"Let's move on, then," Homer said. "But I will ask that, considering my client's recent bereavement and events concerning the property in question, you excuse her for being overwrought."

"Sure. And I will be happy to finish answering your client's questions if she will let me and if she will then answer mine," Clod said.

"I will listen to your answers but retain the right to react to them in such manner as any normal human being would upon hearing them."

A quick smile flashed across Clod's face. Just as quickly, it disappeared, leaving behind a long-suffering pinch to his lips. "Keep the reactions to a minimum if you can, Ms. Rutledge. It's going to be a long day."

"I'll do my best. But if you don't have any evidence against me, why *do* Shirley and Mercy think you're going to arrest me? Oh." It took me a nanosecond to realize I already knew the answer. "Because they are, after all, Shirley and Mercy. But then why were you bullying me back there at Mel's? You *acted* like you were about to arrest me."

"I was merely asking you to accompany me to elicit information concerning the break-in while at the same time attempting to keep the situation under control by not alerting everyone in the café and thus the town, if not the state or the entire western hemisphere, to the details of the investigation."

"Pfffft. Oh, sorry. That was a human reaction. It's just I seem to remember flashing lights and a whoop of siren before you made your unobtrusive entrance at Mel's. But, go on. What information do you think I can give you?"

"Do you have any idea who would want to break into your grandmother's house? What that person might be looking for?"

His brother crossed my mind. Joe the Domestic Burglar who did dishes and fretted over the technicalities of word choice. And spent his spare time looking for evidence of blackmail.

"You're having another human reaction there," Clod said. "You're thinking about someone. Who?"

"Think carefully before you speak, Kath," Homer said. "Remember slander."

I nodded and thought carefully. The scientist in me likes being clear and exact, likes being careful. Gets an immeasurable kick out of studying a textile front and back, inside out and all the way down to the least wisp of its fibers. Hairs, fibers, they're all the same to me and splitting either one is good fun. I shrugged and gave Clod my best sheepish smile.

"Sorry, beyond easy pickings from an unoccupied house, I couldn't tell you what anyone would be looking for." Wouldn't discuss blackmail with him, anyway, in case it strengthened his hand or gave him an ace. Maybe mention it to Homer. Later. "The sooner I can get into the house, the sooner I might be able to tell you if anything is missing. As far as who? Again, sorry. I don't know anyone who would break in." Someone who would find a way to slip in, maybe. But break a window? I couldn't say that. Not for certain. Did Clod believe me? I couldn't say that for certain, either.

"That's all right, Ms. Rutledge," he said. "Asking you is routine procedure. Relatives, anyone standing to gain something, people with a bone to pick, they're all good starting points for this type of investigation."

"As long as they are only starting points, Deputy," Homer said. "For my client's benefit, will you fill us in on the statistics involving residential burglaries?"

Dunbar shifted in his chair and his face shifted back to mulish. "You know statistics can be skewed to say almost anything." He might as well have called them mule shit.

"But how often do crimes of opportunity go unsolved?"

"You know the answer to that."

They were playing with each other again, batting their ball of statistics and innuendo back and forth, and it wasn't getting me anywhere. Like into Granny's house. I glanced at my watch.

"Oh, hey, it's after eight thirty. Where's Max with the keys?"

"Excellent question," Homer said. His fingertips again rested on the desk, his long fingers curved. They looked ready to pounce or snatch and I half expected his tongue to flick across his lips. "Fortunately for him, under the circumstances, we might have to cut him some slack." He turned to Clod. "I assume you've contacted him about the break-in?"

"We attempted to contact him by phone. He didn't answer. Shorty will keep trying. If nothing else, he'll run on out to Cobb's place when he finishes up at the scene. You expected him here, though? You been having problems with him?"

Clod looked from Homer to me. I was about to jump in with an explosive "yes," but a cue from Homer kept me in check.

"He's been out of town," Homer said. "There have been some questions about ownership and occupancy of the house on Lavender Street. He agreed to turn a set of keys over to me no later than eight thirty this morning. Mr. Cobb is now officially late."

"Could be Shorty got hold of him and he's over at the house now," Clod said.

"If he's at the house, I can get the keys from him there, can't I? Or if he isn't there, you can let me in, can't you, Deputy?" I hopped up.

"Not so fast, Kath," Homer said. "From this point on we want a record of every transaction pertaining to the Lavender Street property. I want those keys delivered and signed for and I don't want you setting foot in the house without that safeguard."

"But this will be official police business. I'll be going

in, accompanied by Deputy Dunbar, to check for damages and to see what's missing."

"Hold on," Dunbar said.

"Why?"

"No, I mean hold on; Shorty's calling." He must have known Shorty's vibration because his phone wasn't ringing.

He pulled the phone from a shirt pocket and lifted his eyebrows to Homer. Homer nodded toward the kitchenette. Clod stepped through and closed the door. Homer stared after him, leaning toward the door as though he could hear the conversation if he were intent enough.

"I need to get in the house, Homer. It's not just a matter of checking to see what might be missing. At this point I think it's a matter of my sanity."

Homer blinked and turned to me. He didn't tell me I was being overly dramatic. Didn't chuckle or tell me to sit down and be patient.

"I need to get in."

He bowed his head and the fingertips of his right hand came up to rest on his forehead. "I am so sorry about Ivy, Kath."

The unexpected emotion in his voice rocked me. I didn't say anything, though. I was feeling completely selfish and didn't feel like comforting yet another person for my own grievous loss. Homer, head still bowed, didn't seem to notice my lack of manners. We remained like that until Deputy Clod came back into the room.

At the sound of Clod's hand on the doorknob, Homer straightened. He was in charge of the situation again, adjusting his cuffs to prove it. Clod came back with more spring in his step than when he'd left. He looked energized, annoyed, and something else. Happy? More like excited. If Homer was the raptor with eyes not missing a flinch, Clod was now a hound on the scent.

"Something's come up. I'll be in contact, Homer,

Ms. Rutledge." His newfound energy carried him toward the door to the outer office.

"Wait! What about getting into the house? By now it's way past eight thirty and Max still isn't here." I looked at Clod, then Homer. "Is he at the house? Can't we do something? Like hold him in contempt?"

Clod turned at the door. If eyes with bags under them can snap and flash, his did. "Max Cobb is dead."

Homer swore. I was less delicate.

"Did he have the keys on him?"

Chapter 21

"Did I say that?" I clapped a hand to my mouth, then took it away. "I can't believe I just asked that. Granny would die if she heard me being so crass." Another regrettable statement. With both hands to my flaming cheeks, I dropped into one of Homer's chairs, shaking my head.

"Don't beat yourself up, Ms. Rutledge. It's the shock." It was the kindest thing Clod could have said.

"What happened?" Homer asked.

"Investigation's ongoing. We'll release more information when we have it." Clod hesitated. "Shorty says it looks like he might've tripped. Fell down the basement steps. Wife's taking it hard."

Poor Angie. A lot of funerals in the space of a few weeks. First her father-in-law, a weasel of a man for whom she might or might not have felt any affection, then her mother's cousin however many times removed, now her husband.

"Does Angie inherit the house?" I couldn't seem to help myself. But once on the road to completely crass, I might as well continue blundering forward. "Sorry, but with Max dead, I need to know where that leaves the house, the keys, and me. Last I heard, Angie didn't have keys to the new locks. So did Max have them on him when he fell? Does Shorty have them now?"

"Ms. Rutledge, I understand your wish to get into the house," Clod said.

"It's more than my wish. You need me to see if anything's missing and I've got a deadline for packing and clearing everything out for the new tenants."

"I also appreciate your sense of urgency."

"Unless Max's death invalidates the new lease?" I looked at Homer.

"Unlikely if Angie inherits," he said. "But his death might be good enough reason to gain us more time." He made several quick notes, then looked up. "We might be able to slow things down for you, Kath."

"Things are slowed down for today, anyway," Clod said. "At least for the morning or until we complete the investigation. Accidental death on top of a break-in? Gets complicated, but we'll get you over there to go through the place with an officer just as soon as we can." He was through the door and tipping his hat to Ernestine before I processed what he'd said.

"Wait, where?"

I looked at Homer. He was busy scribbling more notes. Hadn't heard my question. I jumped up and followed Clod through Ernestine's office. Caught his sleeve as he started through the front door.

"Deputy, where? Whose basement stairs did he fall down?"

Clod looked at my hand holding his sleeve. I let it go and rubbed my fingers on my own sleeve to relieve the prickle running through them. Clod glanced behind me, then up and down the street. He stepped back in, stepped closer to me. I started to back up, but his answer was so low I stopped so I could hear him.

"Strictly speaking, Ms. Rutledge, they were his stairs. Shorty found him at the bottom of the basement stairs at that dad-blamed house on Lavender Street. And that makes two deaths, both involving Cobbs, and both involving your grandmother."

"You're joking, right? You just told Homer you have no evidence showing Granny had anything to do with Emmett's death. And have you forgotten the small detail that she preceded Max in death by several days? What do you think happened? Her ghost suddenly appeared and pushed him down the stairs?" I immediately wished I hadn't thought of that.

"I think it's less complicated than a ghost story, Ms. Rutledge."

"Just don't rush to simplify it to the point where you're jumping to conclusions, Deputy. I've heard about how you don't like complications in your life."

His eyes narrowed and he leaned in closer. "Who've you been talking to?"

This time I did back up. Backed up but didn't cringe. "Are you threatening me?"

"We'll be talking." From the look on his face, there were a few more words straining behind his teeth, begging him to let them out. But he kept his lips clamped, turned on his heel, and stalked off down the street.

Swell. I'd pissed off the police. Again. And on top of pissing him off, I'd tipped him off that I knew there were undercurrents involving his questionable brother. And that meant I'd probably complicated Joe's life, which added a dose of guilt to my stew. Guilt I resented feeling because, honestly, who feels guilty about throwing suspicion on a burglar? Pffft. Human reactions. I could live without them.

The only saving grace of that confrontation was that we'd kept our voices low, so maybe I hadn't embarrassed myself in front of Homer. Although, if he overheard Clod impugning Granny . . . I turned to see if he'd caught any of our exchange and almost jumped out of my skin. Ernestine stood at my elbow.

She jerked her head toward Homer's office. "Mr. Carlin showed up to finish the kitchenette. Mr. Wood is checking on his progress and possibly offering to hammer or drill something. It slows things down but he can't help himself. I closed the door so they wouldn't disturb you and Cole. Homer asked me to give you this." She handed me a slip of paper. "Our Mr. Carlin also does storage units and furniture moving."

"Oh, good. Homer mentioned that. Thank you. Are you still without water?"

"The water is back on and I'm grateful for that. I am sorry to report the stove is disconnected, so coffee and tea are not being offered this morning. But I won't ask you to share our problems. Your own are burdensome enough."

"I think I just created another one." I couldn't help staring down the street, toward the corner Clod turned, in case he reversed course. Maybe Ernestine would save me with the door-locking trick she'd used on the Spiveys. She peered toward the corner through her thick lenses, then at me. No telling how much she saw in either place.

"Cole Dunbar is an unhappy man," she said. "That makes him prickly. I'll never forget the time I suggested he take up crochet to ease the stress he wears like a hair shirt. Since then I've found it best to ignore him if at all possible." She patted my arm and headed back to her desk.

"It might be better to avoid him altogether."

"If at all possible, yes. Now, may I offer you some advice?"

"I'd be honored."

"Don't go through Ivy's house alone."

"I'm pretty sure a deputy or somebody will follow me around so I can tell them if anything's missing."

She held a finger to her lips and indicated Homer's

office with a jerk of her head. "Is he back yet?" she whispered.

I sidled to the door, listened, then nudged it open and looked around the edge. I heard the mumble of Homer's and another voice from the kitchenette. That door was closed. "Coast is clear."

She beckoned me back to her desk. "A witness is a powerful weapon," she said. "I know this from personal experience. Have someone else with you when you go. Someone you can trust."

It was good advice, delivered with solemn furrows between her eyebrows. I nodded and thanked her. She smiled, erasing the furrows, and winked, the wink made more conspiratorial by the magnification of her lenses.

The mumble of voices from the kitchenette clarified and we heard Homer offer a parting commiseration over the joys of plumbing in old buildings. I glanced at Ernestine. She smoothed the blotter in the middle of her desk and went back to peering at her computer screen and pecking at the keyboard. An odd little old duck, Ms. Ernestine O'Dell.

There was something else I'd meant to ask Homer. I dithered, in limbo, between Ernestine's desk and his office, trying to remember what. Something not for Clod's ears. About the house. Granny's sunny house disappearing into this dismally bad dream. Funny that when a situation looked blackest it could surprise you by getting even blacker. Black. That was it. I knocked on Homer's door.

He looked up from his sheaf of notes. "Kath, I thought you'd left. Come in. Shut the door." Ever polite, he stood and gestured to a chair.

I shook my head. "Just one quick thing."

"If only that were true. Unfortunately, I think we'll find that it's many more things before we're finished. May I?" He indicated his own chair.

"Please."

"We'll get through it all, though. I promise."

"Well, and actually it's two more things." I took a steadying breath, then jumped into the first. "Deputy Dunbar just told me Max fell down Granny's basement stairs. That's where he died."

He didn't swear again, but his rational lawyer's reaction turned out to be more satisfying. He picked up his pen and clicked it open, Handsome Homer ready for note-taking action.

"Interesting that Dunbar didn't mention that pertinent fact when he told us Max was dead," he said.

"He implied it. It just took me a minute to catch on."

"He should have spelled it out. What's the second thing?"

"This one has a Part A and, depending on the answer to that, maybe a Part B."

"Ah, what did I tell you? Things are multiplying even as we speak." He made three quick hash marks on the notepad. "Good enough. What's Part A?"

"Were you able to track the sale of the house?"

"Not yet. There are irregularities that will take more time to sort out. That means more waiting, and I'm sorry. I know that isn't easy." He acknowledged the annoyance factor with a frown, but recovered quickly. "Does that answer suffice or is there still a Part B?"

Did I want to lob Part B on his desk? Yes but no. If it meant regaining the house, yes. If it helped solve Emmett Cobb's murder, yes. But if it turned Granny over to the police as a suspect? If it led anyone to discover her "secret talent"? Absolutely not. If I sounded like a crackpot reaching for straws? No answer. While those considerations knotted themselves in my head, another question occurred to me.

"Is it possible to slander a dead man? This is Part Not-Quite-B."

"The law says no. You cannot slander or defame the dead."

"Okay. Good." On to Part B. B for blurt it out. "Black-mail."

"I beg your pardon?"

Maybe he thought I sneezed and there was still time to back down. I didn't back down. "What if Granny didn't sell the house? What if Emmett Cobb was black-mailing her?"

Homer's only reaction was a lawyerly stroking of his left temple with a single fingertip. "Let's back up to Not-Quite-B. Is it possible to slander a dead man? The law says no. But what does the dead man's family say? They cry bloody slander and defamation from the hollows to the heavens and some of them never forget. And that's something you should never forget."

"Oh."

"Do you have proof that Emmett was blackmailing Ivy?"

"No, and I realize blackmail is a little out there. I'm just exploring possibilities." I wanted to emulate his nonplussed calm, but sliding out the door, right then, would have made me happy. Homer was still giving blackmail his polite consideration, though.

"I'll agree that idea is out there, but out there or not, I suggest you don't mention blackmail to anyone else. You don't need the hard feelings or hostility of Emmett's kith and kin heaped on top of everything else you're dealing with. And I wouldn't mention blackmail to Deputy Dunbar. You haven't, have you?"

"No. Zipped lips."

"Exactly right. Keep them zipped. Do you know, or have an idea, what Emmett could hold over Ivy?"

I shook my head. His eyebrows and lips shifted upward in a minuscule "I see" gesture.

"And, out of curiosity, what made you think of black-mail?"

It was tempting to stutter something about reading too many mysteries. Then maybe he would forget I'd brought it up and the well-bred doubt playing around his eyes would disappear. But I wanted those hawk eyes looking at the idea of blackmail from every angle, no matter how unsubstantiated it was, so I stuttered out a truer answer. "I heard about it from, uh, from another possible victim."

He offered a quick "ah" and clicked his pen closed. "Heard in confidence, I take it?"

Had it been in confidence? I couldn't remember Joe asking or me promising. And yet . . .

"Well," Homer said when I'd missed my chance to nod yes convincingly, "I won't dismiss blackmail, but I want you to leave it with me. I'm in a better—a safer—position to explore. Although, if you'll pardon a small joke, it will be on the 'out there' burner rather than the front."

I dutifully smiled.

"Feel free to call me with anything you hear or learn, Kath. We need to keep each other up to speed on the situation with the house and now this unfortunate situation with Max Cobb. I'll see that we receive frequent updates from the sheriff's office. Thank you for your input. I appreciate it and I appreciate working with someone as open as you are."

I wished I'd kept Part B to myself. He hadn't laughed at it. He was too professional, too polite. But as I turned to leave, I was pretty sure I saw the ghost of a smile flit and die on his face.

Ernestine fluttered a good-bye and I left the building wondering how Homer would react if I were completely open with him. Would his lawyer face slip if he read Granny's letter? How would he handle an introduction to my new friend, Ms. Ghost? Hoo boy. I shook myself to dispel thoughts of ghosts and ghosts of smiles. Thinking about Ernestine's advice would be a better use of my time.

It made sense to have someone else along when I went through the house, someone I could count on to take my side. Whatever my side was. Maybe even keep me out of trouble. Clod's crappy attitude toward Granny cut two ways; I didn't trust him, either. So, who in Blue Plum *could* I trust? Who did I know well enough? Ardis. Possibly Mel. Debbie, Nicki, Ruth? Not really. Homer made the most sense, being the loyal and upright lawyer. But his time would cost the earth, if he even had the time.

And I couldn't help wondering, if witnesses were so important, why hadn't Ernestine wanted Homer to hear her giving me that good piece of advice?

Chapter 22

It was still barely past nine, still quiet time in a Blue Plum morning. The touristy couple from Mel's was across the street on the courthouse lawn. She was taking pictures of him as he tried to look dastardly in the reconstructed pillory. But they were the only people out and about who lacked an obvious business purpose.

Toward the end of the block, the same scabby truck I'd seen the day before was parked at the curb, unless more than one rusted green pickup chucka-chuck-chugged its polluting way around town. This time it wasn't running, my nose and lungs were happy to note, and a pair of legs in faded jeans leaned over the side, rooting around in the bed. As I passed, the jeans' occupant struck gold.

"Hah! I *knew* it was here somewhere." He straightened, exultant, with a huge pipe wrench in his fist. I skipped sideways to avoid it. "Whoa, sorry there. Big sucker, ain't it? Old plumbing's no match for one of these babies."

"No kidding."

"I saw you yesterday, didn't I? Standing over by the courthouse?"

"Oh, you're Mr. Carlin who's working on Homer's kitchenette?"

"'Aaron' does me just fine. So you took my advice

and went to see old Homer? That's good. He'll take care of you. He's helped me out of a jam or two. Yeah, one or two or three." He scratched the back of his head with the wrench. "Say, if you ever need odd jobs done, give me a holler. No job's too odd. That'd be on my card if I had one. But ask Homer. He'll put in a good word for me."

"He already has. I might call you for a moving and storage job, if you have time."

"Give me a holler when you're ready and we'll talk. I'd better get on back now. Nice meeting you." He slung the wrench over his shoulder and whistled off down the street.

I liked the looks of that wrench. If I carried one like that around I could ward off burglars, their brothers, or any number of Spiveys. But when had I become so weapon-happy? Probably when people started breaking into the pleasant bubble I called my life. So grow up, Kath. Real life gets broken and messy.

I turned the corner into Main Street. Actually, I poked my head around the corner first. Acting like a grown-up was one thing. Self-preservation was another. The Spiveys could be lying in wait for me anywhere along my route to the Cat. I didn't see them or the Buick, though, and caught no telltale whiff of Mercy. They'd probably heard the news about Max and gone to comfort Angela. Poor Angela.

The Closed sign hung on the Cat's door. The lights were on, though, and I saw Ardis dusting the shelves of pattern books on the far wall of the front room. She looked up when I knocked on the window and waved to her.

"I thought you'd be over at the house first thing," she said as she unlocked and opened the door.

"Snafu, Ardis, with an emphasis on the *fu*."

"Come on in, then, before we attract shoppers. They're like vampires if they catch you before opening time. Suck the life right out of the day if you let them get started this early."

I slipped in and she relocked the door.

"You can help me with my mess while you tell me about yours. We had an MMIA yesterday." She dipped behind the counter and came up with a box full of embroidery floss, all shades and colors, tumbled together like a fruit salad. There were easily several hundred hanks.

"What's an MMIA? A new embroidery class?"

"Mother missing in action. She left her delightful children in the parlor with the floss while she browsed the knitting patterns upstairs. I came this close to wrapping the angora she finally bought around her neck."

I took a wad of hanks from the box, shook each one out, and started laying them on the counter in a rough sort by color. "This is good, Ardis. I'm practicing making order out of chaos. It gives me hope."

"You're the goddess of harmony and I'm Diana. While I kill the last of the dust bunnies, tell me about the snafu and what you want me to do."

"Am I that obvious?"

"Honey, look at you. You're no bigger than Ivy was, and even if you were, you're only one person. I'll tell you what she knew the whole time we knew each other: I'm here."

As simple as that. Trust.

"And I'm a multitasking marvel. I can dust and listen at the same time."

"Will Debbie or Nicki be in today?

"Nicki's off. Debbie comes in at eleven."

"If it works out, can you leave the Cat for a few hours this afternoon?"

"I expect so. If she isn't busy, Nicki won't mind filling in. In a pinch one of the TGIFs can give Debbie a hand. I'd hire some of them if it wouldn't cut into the time they spend spending money in here. Why? What do you need?"

I told her about the new renters moving into Granny's house and she cruised around the room, bobbing up and down, flicking her dustrag from shelf to shelf. Then I told her about the two break-ins. Her pace increased with each added detail, the dustrag developing a lethal snap. Only the final detail of Max at the bottom of the basement stairs brought her to a stop.

"Oh my word. Max Cobb. He and my oldest were in school together. And now he's dead from tripping down the stairs? Doesn't seem possible. Then, again, it doesn't surprise me much. The Cobbs always were an unlucky family and not the most graceful, either. Graceless and unlucky. What an epitaph."

"Mel said Emmett is unmourned, too."

"Probably true enough. Not much to him. Not a lot to any of them. Max was the last Cobb I know of and I'm not sure even Angie will mourn him for long. And isn't that a sad note?" She went back to her dusting circuit, but moving slower, her dustrag more thoughtful. "What else? You haven't given me the why yet."

"I need a witness." I told her about Clod's animosity and Ernestine's advice, heeding Homer's injunction against mentioning blackmail.

"Is one enough?" Ardis asked. "I can get half a dozen TGIFs to Ivy's house within minutes. We can station ourselves, one in each room, and whether it's Cole Dunbar or some other suspicious son of a beat cop following you around, we won't let him get away with anything that even smacks of disrespect for Ivy or you. What do you think?"

Overkill came to mind, but I didn't like to dampen her enthusiasm. "Clod probably won't go for that many unsupervised people at his crime scene."

"Who?"

"Cole." I skipped past an explanation for the slip and she followed along with only a slightly confused look on her face. "You know when I can use TGIF help? When I get the go-ahead to pack. It's a lot to ask, though."

"Honey, all you have to do is ask. Is it going back to Illinois with you?"

I shook my head. "No room." I didn't add "no job" or "soon no home." "Storage for now."

Ardis flicked her dustrag a few desultory times more. "I do hate to think of Ivy gone from that house. And why on earth did she sell it?" She tucked her rag in the dirty-rag bag behind the counter and looked at me, searching my face. "Have you found out anything?"

I shook my head.

"And why didn't she tell anyone?" She was probing for an entry point.

I shook my head again, tried to keep the word "black-mail" as far from my tongue as possible.

"I mean, good Lord. Emmett Cobb?" Slowly, as though approaching a wary animal, she came a few steps closer. "Why, in all the whole wide world, would Ivy up and sell her house to Emmett Cobb?"

My phone rang. I was actually glad to hear Clod Dunbar's voice.

Chapter 23

Our guided tour of the crime scene started in Granny's backyard, Deputy Clod Dunbar presiding. We drove the few blocks there.

"Otherwise it could take us half an hour to go half a block, depending on who we run into," Ardis said. "It's why Debbie or Nicki go to the bank instead of me. I know my strengths. Walking past a good chin-wag isn't one of them."

She and I made similar shocked noises when we saw the broken window for the first time. For some reason, that it was one of Granny's bedroom windows made it worse.

Dunbar apparently saw the occasion as a teachable moment and started in on a personal-safety lecture about the role overgrown foundation plantings and decorative shrubs play in providing cover for people looking for opportunities to break windows to gain entry. He hardly had a chance to get going, though, before Ardis lopped him off.

"How do we know Max didn't do this?"

"Why would Max break into his own house?" Dunbar asked.

"Heaven only knows. A better question is why does he even own the house?"

"Let's take it on good faith that Max Cobb had keys and a legal homeowner's right to be in the house, Ms. Buchanan. We assume he was here checking on his property, either after noticing the broken window or after receiving word of the break-in."

"Are the police allowed to take things on good faith?" Ardis asked. "Or to assume anything? And did Max hear about the broken window before the police did? Or did he just get here faster than they did?" Ardis was definitely on my side in this equation.

"Ms. Buchanan—," Clod started.

"Yes?" she cut in, chin up, challenging.

"Shall we go inside and get on with this?"

"Oh my goodness, I've only just thought." She caught at Clod's arm, suddenly less sure of herself. "He isn't still in there at the bottom of the stairs, is he?"

"No, Ms. Buchanan. You won't have to step over Max. He left shortly before I called Ms. Rutledge and she so kindly invited you to accompany us."

"She invited me along after receiving insightful legal counsel." Ardis let go of his arm and wiped her hands together as though brushing off her momentary panic.

Clod held his tongue and held the door for us. I smiled to show him I appreciated his appreciation of my kindness. But I hadn't been prepared for finally setting foot inside the house. Stepping over the threshold was too much for even the sham smile I'd produced to irk Clod. At least at the Weaver's Cat there had been the background hum of customers and the crowd of fibers. There, I could almost believe Granny was in the next room or on the next floor up or down. There was bustle and breath and pulse in the Cat. Here, I was home, but there was no homecoming.

The house was closed up, turned in on itself, silent. Ardis felt it, too, and we both stopped just inside the back door, in the kitchen. It still smelled like Granny's kitchen, like her house, but stale and fading, even with the broken window in the bedroom. And it was beginning to smell of dust. Disturbed dust, at that. A succession of people who didn't belong had snuck in or tramped through in the past however many hours.

"Look at the mud." Ardis tsked. "Didn't anyone wipe their feet?"

"Person who broke in did," Clod said. "No useful finger- or footprints anywhere. Max wiped his, too; otherwise Shorty would've found him sooner."

We looked at the basement door in the corner of the room. It was shut, thank goodness. No yawning dark hole to face. No dank basement miasma drifting up the stairs. Drifting up . . . It suddenly occurred to me to wonder about the nature of ghosts. Why did the ghost in the cottage exist, if "exist" was the right word for it? Why was she there, in that particular place? And if she existed, then was Granny's ghost somewhere? I found myself turning in a wild circle, trying to catch a glimpse of something, anything, a blur, a watery outline. Why hadn't I thought of this before? Was Granny here?

"Ms. Rutledge?"

Or Max? I blinked and blinked again, looking for a ripple interrupting the breathless air.

"Kath, honey?"

Nothing. There was nothing. I'd only made myself dizzy and bumped against Ardis. She put her arm around my shoulders and held me still. Solid Ardis. She was there and didn't ask what my dervish was all about, just held me still. Until we heard a cough from Clod, who was standing behind us in the doorway.

"Ms. Rutledge, is something wrong? Is something missing from this room that you expected to see?"

"No." I put my hands to my spinning head and blinked

again, this time to bring Granny's kitchen back into focus. I didn't look at Clod because I didn't want to see if he believed me. "No. So, how do we do this?"

"Walk through each room. Tell me if you think anything has been disturbed or if anything is missing. Take your time, but don't turn it into a nostalgia tour."

"You'll take notes?" I asked.

"Yes," Ardis and Clod both answered.

Ardis gave Clod a look and pulled a large notebook from her purse. "I am the permanent recording secretary for TGIF," she told him. "I am taking minutes of this meeting for Kath's benefit. And don't you roll your eyes at me, Cole Dunbar."

"No, ma'am."

While they sized each other up in the middle of the room, I went to the cabinets nearest the door and opened Granny's junk drawer. Pencils, rubber bands, jar lids, nails. In the cupboard above, several dozen mugs waited quietly for a coffee morning, sitting on the shelves she'd lined with tartan wrapping paper.

"How will I possibly know if anything's missing?"

"To coin a phrase, don't sweat the small stuff. Think about electronics, portable stuff with big price tags, jewelry."

"Look for blank spaces where something was?" Ardis suggested.

"Unless your burglar was clever and shifted things to fill in the gaps. I'm not saying that's what happened here. I'm just saying look carefully but don't get caught up in counting the pencils in that drawer or her shoes in the closet."

"Aw, her shoes." I didn't want to open her closet and see her shoes in a row on the floor, her shirts and pants hanging above, and her bathrobe on its hook on the door, all of them wondering when she'd come home.

"Come on, hon, you can do this," Ardis said. "We'll break down later, when we start packing it up. For now, pretend Ivy asked you to find something for her."

I nodded and opened her maple cabinets and drawers, running the contents past memories and mental snapshots. It was clear pretty quickly that the burglar hadn't been interested in mismatched Franciscan ware or much-used Pyrex and pots and pans. "But her cookbooks."

"What about them?" Clod asked.

"I don't know. They look too even?" I slid a booklike accordion recipe file out from between a couple of church cookbooks with comb bindings. "She used the recipes in here most often." I pictured Granny's hand flipping through the clippings and handwritten cards and almost smelled her peanut butter oatmeal chocolate chip cookies. "But the shelf's crowded, so she'd leave the file out about an inch. That made it easier to get hold of. And she didn't put it between these two, either. They're flimsy and fall over." I scooted the church cookbooks over and put the file back between *Mastering the Art of French Cooking* and *The Best of Craig Claiborne* where it belonged. "She said Julia and Craig liked to gossip over the fence and exchange recipes with her."

Clod muttered something that sounded like "Nancy Drew meets Crazy Ivy," but I chose to ignore it.

"Did she keep cash between the pages of books?"

"No. Not unless she started to recently."

"Okay, well, unless she used her mattress and *The Joy of Cooking* instead of the bank, a box of old recipes out of place in a bookcase full of cookbooks is the kind of small stuff you don't need to sweat. Who's to say she didn't rearrange the books herself or push her file in when she was dusting? If she ever dusted. Hey!"

Ardis had smacked his shoulder with a metal spatula she took from a crock on the counter. "No aspersions, Cole Dunbar. You cast another and I'll crack your skull."

Unexpectedly, he laughed. "Aye-aye, Captain Buchanan. Anything else in here, Ms. Rutledge?"

I opened the refrigerator and stood looking in, willing Granny or her ghost to fuss at me for hanging on the door and letting all the cold out. It looked so normal. She'd probably meant to eat the leftover soup for supper. Cream of tomato and half a grilled cheese sandwich, a Granny specialty. I must have made a noise.

"Don't tell me the lettuce has been rearranged," Clod said in mock horror. He moved out of the way before Ardis got him with the spatula again.

"She's out of cat food." I picked up the carton of milk and sloshed it. "But she's almost out of milk, too." I closed the fridge and slid open the freezer drawer. Her secret vice smiled up at me. Chunky Monkey. But she usually kept the cartons hidden under less-tempting fare. "She must've used up the goldenrod we cut last summer." I caught the blank look on Clod's face. "She had bags of it and last time I was here she was using it to hide the ice cream from herself." His face was still blank. "She dyed with it." His face switched from blank to unnerving and I realized my mistake. "For dyeing wool, Deputy Dunbar. Not to commit suicide or kill Emmett Cobb."

"So is it somehow important that she used up the goldenrod but not the ice cream, and failed to do her shopping?"

I shrugged.

"Then let's move on."

"We don't have to go in the basement, do we?" Ardis asked, following close behind and bringing the spatula.

"We'll save that for last," Clod said. "Maybe by then you'll have gotten tired and gone home."

"Not a chance. If nothing else, I can work out how many boxes Kath will need for packing."

"Boxes! Where will I get boxes for all this?"

"Liquor store, grocery store, buy them from the U-Haul. Focus, please, Ms. Rutledge. Dining room. Is anything missing? Did she have valuable silver?"

She had the walnut table and sideboard that were passed down to her and Grandfather when they set up housekeeping. She had yellowed wallpaper with peonies so ancient they should have wilted and dropped their faded pink petals decades before. She had pictures hanging over the peonies. Family photographs, photographs of women from around the world weaving. She had a small inkle loom sitting on the sideboard, the narrow band she'd been weaving on it half finished. She had a painting of Grandfather sitting at his rolltop desk. And she had so many books my knees threatened to buckle at the thought of packing them.

"Did she keep a tea set or anything in here?" Clod tapped the sideboard.

"No, her cameras and boxes of old pictures and slides." I opened the right-hand door, releasing the familiar smells of old wood, old polish, old celluloid, and old dust. "Someone else looked through here, though."

"How do you know?"

"The left-hand door. The hinges have been missing forever and the door falls out unless you wedge it in place. There, see?" I pointed to a square of paper, folded and creased, just visible under the sideboard. "That fell out when someone pulled the door open. And the door would have come off altogether." I demonstrated, catching the door before it hit the hardwood floor, but noticing, with an inner smirk of satisfaction, that Clod flinched. "Whoever opened it set the door back in place like this. And it looks fine, but it'll fall out the next time someone bumps into it or the humidity changes. Unless I do this." I wedged the paper between the door and the frame.

"That might've been Shorty," Clod said.

"Would he remove a memory card from one of her

cameras?" I held up Granny's little Elph and pointed at the empty card slot and its sprung cover. Then I picked up the new SLR she'd bought herself in honor of Ansel Adams' hundred and tenth birthday and turned it until I found its card slot. The cover was closed, but when I checked, that slot was empty, too.

"No, he wouldn't," Clod said. "They're missing?"

"They're not here, anyway."

"Maybe she took them out to download the pictures," he said.

"But then the cameras would be sitting next to the computer."

"Maybe." He wasn't convinced. "They're nice cameras, though. That one looks expensive." He nodded at the SLR. "Why not take them? Why just the memory cards?"

"Because they're not obvious?"

"They're not worth much, either."

"That depends on what someone thinks is on them," I said.

"And what would that be?"

"I don't know. But she documented her work. Usually from beginning to end."

"And why would that be worth stealing?"

I shook my head. I couldn't imagine. Or didn't want to imagine? I didn't want to follow that thread, anyway, so I asked my own question. "How much small stuff adds up to something big enough to sweat?"

"Rearranged cookbooks, Ms. Rutledge? Possibly missing memory cards? Not enough milk for breakfast?" He wasn't impressed and I couldn't blame him.

Ardis was unimpressed for another reason. "Where's all the fingerprint powder? For a crime scene this seems awfully neat and tame."

"Except for the body in the basement," I said.

She looked at the floor and shifted her feet uneasily.

"But the body wasn't part of the crime scene, Ardis, and I don't think they expect to catch the bad guy, anyway, so they probably didn't waste their powder."

"Or Shorty cleaned up after himself," Clod said with a prissy sniff. "You might still find some in the bedroom at the entry point, if you're itching to see some. But you're right." His sniff turned to a snort of frustration or maybe disgust. "You heard Homer's question. How many crimes of opportunity are ever solved? Not many, and solving any of them takes as much luck as it takes anything else."

"So why are you here, then? Why bother going through the house again after Shorty's been through it? If you're not interested in the small stuff?"

"I'm not *not* interested." He stopped and muttered something to himself. Maybe something rude, judging by the clenching of his left fist.

"Are you left-handed?"

He looked at his fist, then at me. "What's that got to do with anything? You got a problem with that?"

"No, just a point of interest. I know several families where oldest children are left-handed and you're an oldest child, aren't you?"

He narrowed his eyes. I pressed on.

"Is Shorty left-handed?"

Deflected from whatever thought lay behind the narrowed eyes, he looked at his hands, having to think about that part of his answer. "No, he's not." The rest of his answer rolled out without any trouble. "And you know, as a point of interest, this isn't all that interesting. Can we move on?"

I stayed put. "Did you open the left-hand door in the sideboard?"

"No. Why? Oh, I get it. You think because the left-hand door was opened, the burglar is left-handed. That's a fine theory. Another one is that the burglar opened both doors to see inside better and it doesn't matter if he was left- or right-handed."

Rats. He was right.

"Not a bad theory, though." He said that without a hint of gloat, but he clearly did not know when he was far enough ahead so he could quit. "Not bad, as far as amateur theories go, anyway. Just see if you can't tone down your inner Nancy Drew, and we'll be fine and this thing will go faster. Trust me on that. A whole lot faster."

"Or, if you're in such a flipping hurry, we can skip it altogether." I closed my eyes and scrubbed my forehead with my fingertips. "Sorry"

"That's all right, Ms. Rutledge. No doubt you're feeling overwrought again. But believe me when I say I do understand the effects of stress."

He didn't understand the effects of condescension, but the bit of steam I'd just blown off helped and I was able to acknowledge his words with only minor jaw clenching.

"And you already know why we're here," he said, "and why we're not going to skip it. But let me see if I can clarify it for you."

Let me try not to groan. He cocked his left hand on his hip and held his right hand out, ready to illustrate his clarification. I'd seen that posture before, adopted by male colleagues and administrators. It was a clear warning of an impending "male-pattern lecture."

"This isn't your normal break-in," Clod said. "The smashed window is something a kid might do. But this wasn't kids out for the fun of messing up an empty house. Likewise, this wasn't someone looking for a quick grab, because none of the things we'd expect to be missing, like expensive cameras, are missing. But there might be other things missing, little things that only you would know about, and knowing what they are might tell us something.

Knowing what they are could help us answer the bigger question of who did this."

"In other words, small stuff adding up. So"—I gave him an overly large smile he could interpret as he liked—"as you said several minutes ago, let's move on."

He repaid my smile with a sour look. "Small stuff, yes, Ms. Rutledge, but not rearranged cookbooks and a lack of cat food."

I wondered about his lack of imagination. Was it a prerequisite for police work in Blue Plum? Or was it something that kept him from advancing in the ranks or joining a less-provincial police force? I turned my back on Clod, angry at myself for thinking of Blue Plum in such a poor light. Olga, Granny's massive antique floor loom, waited in the next room and I went to see my old friend.

"Olga's known a lot of weavers," Ardis said. "I bet she thought Ivy was something special, though."

"Olga?" Clod asked.

"The loom."

I heard him snort but kept a rein on my temper and my back to him, pretending to concentrate on the contents of the room. How would he react if I told him I knew about the other amateur theory floating around, the one involving his brother and blackmail? Would he dismiss it the way he dismissed someone taking the memory cards from Granny's cameras or pawing through her books? Could I even tell if someone had pawed through all her books? Why would anyone do that? Who would have the time?

There were books everywhere, in every room. Books on weaving, spinning, dyeing, dye plants, wildflowers, ethnic art, fossils, birds. There were favorite mysteries, Grandfather's woodworking books, back issues of fiber art and needlework magazines, books about travel to places she'd never been. I ran my finger along the shelves of the bookcases standing beside and behind Olga. These were mostly books on the history and natural history of Tennessee and maps and guides to hiking trails in the southern Appalachians. Granny loved everything about this part of the world.

My finger followed along in the trail someone else's finger had made in the faint layer of new dust on the shelves. But whose finger and looking for what?

Chapter 24

"Has someone been slithering around looking for Granny's secrets?" I asked a book I pulled from the shelf. "But who would know she had them?" At least two people—Joe, who claimed he wasn't the kind of burglar who broke in to get in, and Emmett, the alleged black-mailer who left his estate to Max. Which brought me to Max—the guy who left me a dunning letter that said Granny had owed him and now I did. I'd given the letter to Homer, so I couldn't refer to it, but the wording, at least in my memory, was sounding less laid-back and more cryp-tic. Tending toward menacing. If he'd gotten in touch with me, had he planned to collect what Granny owed and then tell me I owed more to keep her secret? But if Max already had the secrets Emmett collected, then who broke in? Who searched Granny's recipes? Who took the memory cards? Or was I getting paranoid? I, the newly haunted, wasn't necessarily the best person to judge that, unfortunately.

Ardis pushed her way behind Olga, a good squeeze for both of them, and over to stand beside me. "What are you mumbling about over here?" she whispered.

"Spies."

She raised her eyebrows and made a surreptitious ges-ture toward Clod, still behind us. I returned a barely per-ceptible shrug and a noncommittal sound. She nodded.

"Leave it to me," she whispered. Then she looked over her shoulder, over the top of Olga toward Clod, and spoke at normal volume. "I can't imagine you have room for Olga in your apartment, unless you plan to sling a hammock between her beams and get rid of your bed. What are your plans? Sell her?"

"No, Ardis," I said, looking over my own shoulder, as though sizing up Olga. "I'll put Olga and the other looms in storage with all the rest of Granny's things. How many trucks do you think it will take?" My contribution to the subterfuge was clunky compared to Ardis' performance, but she was kind about it when she swiveled back to face the bookcase with me.

"That's good, honey. He won't be able to help himself. Calculating truck loads ought to distract him for at least a minute or two. Now, what's this about spies?"

"I think someone's looking for something Granny wrote down or recorded in some way. Information, maybe."

"About what?"

"I'm not sure," I lied. And now I wasn't sure I should have said anything, even to her.

Ardis studied my face and nodded. "You need more practice at that, but I understand. Spies and lies. They go together like bad peas in a pod. You tell me when you're ready or when you can."

"What are you two whispering about over there?" Clod asked.

"Storage for the looms," I called.

"There you are—that's better," Ardis whispered. "Now, watch this." She turned her head and turned up the volume again. "And we were discussing the pain of shingles. It's quite singular and can be mortifying, depending on where you find them. If you're interested, please feel free to join us."

"Please feel free to join me in finishing what we came to do," Clod said.

"He's right, Ardis." I moved back around Olga into the middle of the room. "You're right, Deputy. You warned me about turning this into a nostalgia tour and I didn't realize how hard it would be not to. I appreciate your patience and I'll make a better effort to move along more quickly."

He looked gratified and not the least bit suspicious, another indication that he lacked imagination. He could hardly miss the change in Ardis. She might be the better liar, but her face was suddenly alight with the possibilities of spies and unspoken clues. Maybe Clod thought that was the shingles, though. Or maybe his starched poker face had a few tricks up its own sleeve.

"I don't think anything's missing from this room."

"No TV?" Clod asked.

I looked around at the general lack of space for a TV. His eyes followed mine, taking in the kilim on the floor (worn), the bookcases (no two alike), the comfortable chairs (covered with cat fur) facing each other from either side of the front window the Spiveys had suggested they jimmy two days before. Clod's mind was probably busy assigning a different range of adjectives to the furnishings, a range that didn't include "cozy" or "well-loved." My mind was busy picturing Shirley and Mercy heaving a brick through Granny's bedroom window and hoisting each other through. The image didn't quite work, neither of the twins looking hoistable or boostable. But as in so many situations in life, it was the thought that counted and I added that thought to the others I was collecting about sneak thieves, spies, and lies.

"There should be a small TV in the bedroom," I said.

"We saw that. You mentioned a laptop?"

"She usually kept it on the desk in the other loom

room." I started down the short hallway, faltered at Granny's bedroom door, but moved past it with a hand blinkering my eyes. I wasn't ready to look at the broken window from the inside yet.

"Do you know someone who can board up that window?" Clod asked. "By rights, the landlord should take care of it, but under the circumstances..."

A new Perry Mason title: *The Sad and Sadly Annoying Circumstance of the Clumsy Dead Landlord.* "Yeah, I think so." Another job for Mr. No-Job's-Too-Odd Carlin.

"Joe could do it for you in two shakes," Ardis said. "He'd be happy to, I don't doubt."

I didn't doubt it for a minute. And help himself to a look around inside, too. Maybe for the second or third time.

"Ten's up a creek," Clod said. "Unavailable."

This was interesting news. "Without a paddle?" I flipped over my shoulder. "Why? What's he done?"

Clod waited until we were in the weaving room before answering. During the interval I felt his eyes removing a portion of the back of my skull and filleting my brain to find out what I knew about his brother's activities, how I came to know it, and why I might be interested. Unless that feeling was just the prickling of my imagination as it danced closer to the edge of trouble.

"As a fishing guide, Ms. Rutledge," Clod said. "It's one of his sidelines. 'Up a creek' is one of his jokes."

"A joke. Of course. Very funny, too." I started to laugh, but stopped because I'd just seen the tapestry loom. A few warp threads dangled from the beam. That was all. "The tapestry and cartoon. They're gone?" I looked at Clod, pointed at the empty loom. "We saw them here yesterday. Granny's tapestry and the canvas behind it."

"Oh, yeah. I thought something looked different."

"Something looked different? Something? The tapestry wasn't just *something*. Deputy, I don't care what you think of me or of what I'm about to say, but one way or another I should have gotten in here before now. Before this rotten, stinking thief stole Granny's tapestry. When you and I were standing outside that window yesterday, and we saw the tapestry then, we should have gotten in here. We had the chance and we should have taken it. Granny was planning that piece her whole life. Dreaming it and designing it and storing up in her head every minuscule element she saw and wanted to weave into it. Her whole life. It was going to be her masterpiece, even if she never talked about it like that. It was going to be all her love for Blue Plum poured out and woven in. And she didn't get a chance to finish it. But part of it was here. Here, and now it's gone, and I'll never get to see the finished piece and I might not even get to see that small beginning of it ever again. *I* should've broken a window and climbed in."

Clod didn't blink. "Did you break the window?"

I didn't answer or I might have called him an idiot. Lips clamped, I glanced around the rest of the room, then crossed to the desk and went through the motions of looking through it. I was pretty sure I'd figured out what else would be missing, though, and I didn't need a close inspection of the desk drawers or the baskets and bins and shelves of wool and spare loom parts, or the books and books and books, to verify it. There was no way to know exactly which of the dozens of sketchbooks and notebooks Granny wrote in over the years were missing. It was enough to know someone was after something she knew. And that was a scary thought raising scary questions. What information was someone after? Which secrets? Which ones had they found?

"So this tapestry was, like, a personal kind of thing?"

Clod asked, interrupting my personal fright show. "But not finished. Not valuable."

I slammed a drawer. "Personal, yeah. Not valuable, no." It was hard to think my own thoughts while helping this guy work through his.

"Ivy is a nationally known and respected fiber artist, Cole," Ardis said. Bless her for trying to educate the Philistines. "Her pieces sell for very good money."

"How do you know she hadn't finished it, then, if you never got a good look at it? It looked like she had six inches or so, from what I remember. Maybe it was a table runner."

"The cartoon," Ardis said. "Ivy always worked from one. It was there, Kath? How big?"

"Full width of the loom. Same in height."

"Forty-eight inches, then, and what you saw woven was just the beginning," Ardis told Clod. "When it was finished, it would have been the same size as the painted canvas. The tapestry would have been a woven version of the painting."

"So, who'd want just a scrap of it?"

"They're probably both in a Dumpster," I said. I didn't believe it, but I knew he would.

"Petty vandalism." He nodded his head, satisfied to fall back on something he understood. "Anyway, the laptop isn't missing. It's on the desk there," he said, pointing out the obvious.

But not the memory cards for the cameras. The thumb drive Granny used to back up the laptop's files was missing, too. I didn't bother to tell him.

"Weird couple of break-ins," he said, continuing to nod. "They don't add up. Weird." He eyed the cones of wool and cotton and silk on the shelves surrounding us as though daring them to do anything to top his quota of weirdness. He reached up and tapped a raddle hanging from a hook in the ceiling and set it swinging. "All in all, though, I'd say you got off pretty easy. Considering what could have happened. Could've been a huge mess in here. Books in piles, upholstery slashed, stuff ruined in various nasty ways." For a minute, he looked as though he smelled one of those nasty ways. "And the whole weirdness of it kind of fits, too. You know?"

"I beg your pardon?"

"Well, don't get me wrong—no one likes a burglary, but a couple of minor break-ins? Where you haven't got much more going on than a busted window and a piece of some unfinished arts and crafts project missing? You see what I mean, don't you? There's usually some point to it all, even if it's a stupid one or a vicious one. But what was the point here? It's weird. And that fits with your grandmother's nickname. Crazy Ivy."

That was when I punched him.

Chapter 25

"Sorry, sorry." There I was apologizing again. "I didn't mean to hit him so hard."

"I'll just run to get more ice for her hand," Ardis said. "Back in half a tick."

Apparently I broke Clod's nose. Ernestine told us when she called from Dr. Keene's office. She'd arrived with Homer, whom I'd called while Clod was doubled over and incoherent, and she insisted on driving Clod to Dr. Keene's herself. Either he was a great big baby or a broken nose hurts more than I realized, because he'd sat in the passenger seat of his patrol car with a wad of paper towels pressed to his face and handed her the keys. I was surprised she could see over the steering wheel, much less see the trees well enough not to hit one or two backing down the driveway.

After they left, on Clod's muffled and mumbled instructions to Homer, we'd made a quick tour of the rest of the house. The residual adrenaline coursing through me, and especially through my sore hand, did wonders for my powers of concentration. Granny hadn't owned or worn much jewelry; none of it was missing. The contents of the closet and chest of drawers looked rumpled; so did Granny, most days. Homer used the bath mat to blot the puddle of rain below the broken window. The spare room—my room when I stayed—was just that, spare, except for more books. Ardis let us go into the basement on our own.

Homer gave me another jolt of adrenaline by almost tripping on one of the uneven steps on the way down. He caught himself, though, blaming his own inattention, and admired the shelves of canned peaches and beets when he reached the bottom safely. I offered him a jar of each but he politely declined. I didn't tell him what was missing from the corner near the utility sink.

Now he sat in one of Granny's comfy chairs in the living room, looking at me. I sat in the chair facing him, cradling my hand and looking at the pattern in the rug on the floor, picturing Ernestine loose on the streets of Blue Plum in a patrol car. I wondered if she'd be tempted to turn on the siren. I wondered if she had a valid driver's license. Crowding my head with those thoughts was preferable to thinking about what kind of trouble I was in for biffing a sheriff's deputy on the nose. And "biff," as a word, was far preferable to the stark, cold, and legally more accurate term "assault."

"I was provoked." He hadn't asked, but something about his eyes and his beaky nose compelled me to explain my action against Clod.

"And possibly out of your mind." Unfortunately, it didn't sound as though he was suggesting that as a defensible excuse.

"I was provoked."

"You should have your hand looked at."

I looked at it, slowly spread the fingers, curled them in, spread them. What an amazing little weapon.

"I meant you should have Dr. Keene look at it."

"It's okay. A little sore." It really was only a little sore, which surprised me, considering the damage I'd done. I'd hit Clod from the side, though, with more of a glancing smack than a full frontal fist-slam into anything solid like a cheekbone or his stupid, mulish jaw. But who knew a nose would break so easily? Or with such a sickening, wet crunch? "I was provoked." The words sounded wobblier each time I said them.

"He's an irritating man," Ardis said, bustling back into the room. She handed me a bag of frozen peas. "There was only the one tray of cubes. The peas are more like an ice pack, anyway. Homer, I want you to know that I was about to kick Cole Dunbar, myself, if Kath hadn't saved me the trouble of crossing the room to get at him. He was being deliberately rude. He is an irritating man. And I want to testify to that in open court."

"Deputy Dunbar won't be pressing charges," Homer said, getting up and brushing at the cat fur that left the chair with him.

"Why ever not? She popped him a good one." Ardis demonstrated on an imaginary deputy with a right and a left and another right and some quick footwork between jabs.

"Good Lord, how many times did you hit him?" Homer looked up from his battle with Maggie's fur.

I held up one finger.

"I think we're all right, then. Ms. Buchanan, your civic-mindedness is admirable and duly noted and Kath is lucky to have such a good friend. Do you hear that, Kath? You are lucky." He waited until I nodded. "You're also lucky that Cole Dunbar has anger-management issues of his own. I've had the opportunity to smooth things over for him on one or two occasions and I feel confident he'll see this as an opportunity to reciprocate the favor." He swiped a few more times at the fur on his dark trousers but recognized it for the lost cause it was and gave up. Maggie had never been so clingy in real life.

"Granny has a lint brush here somewhere," I said. Anger-management issues? Me?

"That would be useful, but only if it's no bother."

"She keeps it in her bureau, although I don't remember seeing it."

"I'll look," Ardis said. "You hold on to your bag of peas."

"Try the top drawer, right-hand side." I looked at my right hand again, opening and closing the fingers.

"One more thing, Kath," Homer said.

"I don't think I have anger-management issues." I made my hand into a hard fist, winced, and put it back on the bag of defrosting peas, then looked up at Homer.

"Perhaps not," he said mildly. He might even have looked bemused, if it's possible for a hawk or an eagle to look bemused. "Nonetheless, I think you should avoid further contact with Deputy Dunbar, if possible. Agreed?"

"Definitely." That might have come out fraught with more issues than I expected. I put the fingers of my non-aching left hand to my lips for a moment and recomposed myself before speaking again. "Thank you for coming, Homer. I'm sorry to be taking up so much of your time. That's twice you've had to fly to my rescue this morning."

"So far. No, now it's my turn to apologize. That was a poor joke at your expense. I'm happy to come to your rescue. That's what a good lawyer does. And the good client pays the good lawyer for his time, so it all works out. But even apart from the fee, I'm happy to do it. You add an unquantifiable level of *je ne sais quoi* to my day."

"If you're so short of entertainment, maybe I should be charging you." He didn't take me up on the offer, so I took a chance on further entertaining him with one of my blackmail questions. "Homer, if there's proof that Emmett got hold of the house illegally, does it revert to Granny's estate?"

"If there's proof, yes, a good chance. You agreed to

leave this exploration to me, but have you found something?"

"More like a lack of something. Odd things missing from the house."

He looked at me, his head tipped a fraction to one side, as though he were sizing up that piece of information and wondering whether to swallow it. "You didn't tell me there was anything missing when we walked through the bedrooms and basement."

"No." I went ahead and told him about the missing memory cards and thumb drive. Told him about the tapestry and cartoon, the possibly missing notebooks. Didn't give him a laugh by telling him there wasn't any cat food in the house.

"You told Dunbar?"

"He doesn't think it amounts to much. But, he doesn't think Granny amounted to much, either."

"And therein lies the problem between you two. I think I might take a swing at a policeman who maligned my grandmother, too. Did Dunbar explain to you how hard it is to trace small items? In fact, I'm sure he did, though perhaps not so delicately. He probably also pointed out that, without knowing Ivy's habits exactly, you can't be sure they're missing. She might have a special place she keeps them and you'll find them tomorrow or next month. And, then, I hesitate to belittle your concerns by using the word 'inconsequential,' but do you know what might be on the devices that would make them worth taking?"

"No."

"It's a shame about the unfinished tapestry and the— the cartoon, is it? I understand their personal value. Do you know why anyone would find either worth stealing?"

"No."

"You're guessing there's proof of something on or in

one of these items—is that right? But it certainly wasn't
Emmett who took the tapestry. You said you saw it here
yesterday."

"I kind of wondered if Max was taking over where
Emmett left off."

"If that's your worry, then you're safe. Max is gone."

"But if there's someone else?"

"Well, again, not to belittle your ideas, but you do see
that you're getting further and further fetched, as it were,
don't you?"

No, I didn't. But Homer obviously did and if that was
his attitude toward something that might prove important, then I definitely wasn't telling him what was missing from the corner near the utility sink in the basement.

"Far-fetched or not, though, Kath, you need to leave
this with me for two very good reasons. One, my judgment is not infallible. Two, someone murdered Emmett
Cobb. That unknown person is dangerous. Now, may I
assume that, even in the heat of your moment of glory
with Deputy Dunbar, you remembered the agreement
about zipped lips from our earlier conversation?"

"Yes. Of course. I hit him, but . . ."

"Kath, you broke his nose."

"Yeah. I did." I swallowed. "But I'm not totally hopeless. I didn't say anything about blackmail."

Ardis returned, just then, from her hunt for the lint
brush. "Blackmail?" She looked from my face to Homer's, then zeroed back in on mine. "I couldn't find the
brush, but blackmail is much more interesting. So, tell
me, who, what, when, where, why, and how?"

Oops.

Chapter 26

If someone put together an illustrated encyclopedia of facial expressions, Ardis could be the model for "agog." Homer's version of "there is nothing to discuss" was a winner, too. "Oops," though, was all mine.

We left the house together, Homer politely stonewalling Ardis and Ardis angling for a chink in his masonry. I tuned them both out, reluctantly turning the lock button on the inside doorknob and pulling the door shut behind us.

The keys were still AWOL, either with Max or with his effects. I thought about waiting around the corner until the coast was clear and then climbing back in through the broken window. Maybe no one else would see a twice-burglarized house as a place of safety. But I could see myself scrambling through the window, seeking the shelter of my bolt-hole. I would burrow into my bed in the spare room, pull Granny-made quilts over me like so many deep leaves, and fall asleep until danger slunk past.

I wasn't so deep into that daydream, though, that I didn't appreciate the pattern of my recent emotions. Shout or cry; arm myself or run away; punch the nearest nose or crawl into a hole. Vulnerable yins engulfed me, pulling me under in one direction. Violent yangs caught me in their jaws and dragged me in another. "Balanced" wouldn't be the best word to describe my mental state, but something in my wild mood swings stirred my creative juices.

Instead of burrowing or hiding, I should re-channel my emotions and design the weaving pattern I so clearly saw. It would be a variation of Tennessee Trouble, where the geometrics represented wings and hidey-holes intertwined with fireplace pokers and running chain saws. I'd call it Fight or Flight and use it in a border around my own version of a Blue Plum tapestry. In Granny's honor.

Homer interrupted my design plans with a dose of practicality. "Aaron Carlin will be around to board up the window." I hadn't even noticed him pull his phone out. "Did Ernestine give you his number?"

"Yes."

"Hold up there," Ardis said. "Do you know him, Kath?" She didn't give me a chance to say I'd almost met his wrench. "Because I do, as who doesn't who ever reads the paper? He's one of the Smokin' Smoky Carlins from down by Newport—am I right? Wonderful, upstanding citizens, all of them." She turned to me. "They like to set fires in the national forest."

"He was acquitted, Ms. Buchanan," Homer said.

"Uh-huh."

"Found innocent of all charges. What's more, I believe he actually was innocent, and that isn't always the case."

"And now he's working for you," Ardis said.

"It's a fair trade. People should be convicted for the crimes they commit, not because they can't pay a good lawyer."

"And you are an excellent lawyer, Homer. I'm sure you're a great comfort to the family." I hadn't seen them side by side before. Solid Ardis was a hair taller than the raptor. She looked very much as though she'd like to pat him on the head, but she didn't. "I'm sorry I couldn't find the lint brush for you," she told him. "You should stop by the Western Auto and pick up a roll of masking tape. Makes a good substitute in a pinch."

Homer looked down the length of his trousers and took a few more swipes at the sides of his knees. "I think I conquered the worst of it. A little cat fur goes a long way, but it isn't the end of the world and I have other clients waiting. Kath, a word before I go? You'll excuse us, Ms. Buchanan?"

Homer and I walked to the end of the front walk, where he repeated his instructions not to communicate with Deputy Dunbar and not to let the word "blackmail" pass my lips, not even to Ardis. Especially not to Ardis. The house keys, he once again promised to track down. In the meantime he had a suggestion.

"I sense yours is a sunny personality and that these last few days have done their damnedest to drench you and bring you down."

I wanted to ask him how that sense fit in with his other sense about my anger-management issues, but he wasn't finished being solicitous.

"Don't spend the rest of the day alone with your anxieties and frustrations. In fact, I'll call Ruth and see if she has luncheon plans." He was quick on the draw and already had his phone in one hand, the other hand up to stop my protest. Ruth didn't answer, though. He left a message asking her to call me later if she was free, and told her he'd be home at the usual time. "I'm sorry that won't work out," he said.

"Thanks, anyway, Homer. I'll be fine. I'll go to the Cat."

"The Cat? Oh, the shop. That's the perfect solution. Ardis can drive you there and you can indulge in some 'me' time, as they say. Make a pot of herbal tea. Spend time being creative with all those wonderful, er, strings."

"Fibers."

"Fibers, yes—a much better word. Create, relax, chat with those wonderful ladies, and you should be able to face the next few days refreshed and revived."

I smiled and nodded. His idea that creativity erased frustration and anxiety and produced tranquillity showed an interesting lack of insight into the creative process. But I thanked him and didn't quite promise anything. I held out my hand on its bed of thawing peas and that gallant man took them together in both of his, shook them gently, and wished me an uneventful remainder of the day. When he turned to walk away I saw he still had enough cat fur on the back of his coat and trousers to make a whole new cat.

"Not his usual look," Ardis said, coming up beside me, "but it makes him more human, don't you think?"

We watched him get in his car. She waved good-bye, then hit me with the opening salvo of her third degree.

"Blackmail? Please do tell Dr. Buchanan everything."

"I've been advised not even to breathe that word."

"Why not? It's a perfectly good word. Full of that other thing. You know, intrigue. Let's find a substitute for 'blackmail,' then. I do that a lot these days, anyway, when I can't think of a word. So, tell me all about the shakedown."

"Walk toward my car and open the passenger door for me. Homer thinks you're taking me to the Cat and I get the feeling he won't pull away until he sees we're leaving."

Homer's sleek sedan was parked on the street. My nondescript rental was in the drive. When we reached it, Ardis made a show of rooting in my purse for the keys, pulling them out, dropping them, then unlocking the passenger door and opening it.

"Founding member of the Blue Plum Repertory

Theater," she said as she handed me in and pretended to fuss with the seat belt. "You should have seen me as Aunt Eller in *Oklahoma!* Would you like me to sing? Never mind, there he goes. Don't get out yet. I'll close the door, in case he looks in his mirror."

In her exuberance, she slammed the door, then started around the front of the car. I looked out the back and watched Homer head down the street. Ardis waved again as he turned the corner. Then she came back, laughing, and I climbed out.

"Most fun I've had in years. What's next?"

"Can you read and take a few more notes while I drive, or will you get carsick?"

She thumped her midsection. "Iron Stomach Buchanan."

"Good. I'll drop you back at the Cat and fill you in on the way."

"You're sure you can drive with your hand?"

I tossed her the bag of peas. She caught it and held it by one corner while I gingerly ran my fingers through a few agility tests. "As long as I don't have to punch anyone else, I think I'll be fine. What do we do with the peas now?"

"I have a recipe for green pea hummus from the *Bugle*. So, how does this sound for supper tonight? The hummus, toasted pitas, goat cheese, fruit salad, and you're invited. Daddy won't know who you are, but he'll enjoy meeting you over and over. In the meantime, I'll put the peas in the fridge at the Cat."

"Can I let you know later? I might have a subsequent engagement."

"Working on the case?"

I wasn't sure how to answer her. Partly because I wasn't sure I wasn't out of my mind. Again. But seeing and hearing ghosts was one kind of crazy, a loony kind. This other thing, playing detective, if that's what I was planning to do, was maybe just an ill-advised, imprudent kind of crazy. And because I was handling the loony so well, it seemed logical to think the ill-advised should be a piece of cake. Unless I made myself even crazier thinking about it.

"Hon?" Ardis waved the bag of peas to get my attention. "You're working on the case tonight?"

"Can I get back to you on that, too?"

"Mysterious doings *and* blackmail *and* more notes? Very exciting. Drive slow so I get everything down."

We did go slow, taking the scenic route, thanks to distracted driving. Given the size and simplicity of Blue Plum, we should have been able to point the car in the right direction and let it take itself. Or maybe we did and that's why we went around the corner at Hillside and Maple twice from two directions. I was too busy trying to keep straight what I had and hadn't told Homer and Clod and what I would and wouldn't tell Ardis. It was enough to send anyone around the wrong bend. Ardis, taking notes, wouldn't have known, or cared, if I'd peeled off and headed for Timbuktu.

We still arrived at the Cat too soon to suit her. She urged me to keep going, saying it might be her only chance to live her fantasy of being in a buddy road trip movie. I convinced her we shouldn't take the chance that Homer would see us and ground us, or the chance that Ernestine was on her way back from Dr. Keane's and *wouldn't* see us and would put us out of commission altogether by plowing into us with the patrol car and a really cranky deputy.

I pulled into the alley behind the Cat and parked. To placate Ardis, I told her she could pretend we were on a stakeout. She told me in that case I owed her a doughnut.

"Not one of those namby-pamby things filled with air, either. A good old-fashioned cake doughnut. Chocolate.

With chocolate icing. Nuts on top for protein. Mel has the best. So," she said, scanning her notes, "I won't ask why you didn't tell Cole or Homer everything you think is missing. And I won't ask if you told *me* everything that's missing. I will be your loyal recording secretary and leave questions of legality or sanity to bother your conscience, not mine."

I hadn't told her everything. It felt right to keep some of it quiet. Safer. Safer for whom, I wasn't sure. But she'd turned colors suitable for embroidering a tropical sunset when I told her Emmett and Granny's respective roles in the shakedown. That couldn't be healthy for someone who liked doughnuts as much as she did. I did tell her I was going to fetch my laptop from the cottage, telling her I was used to thinking with electronic organization. She offered me use of the office computer, but using my own was part of keeping things quiet. Safe.

"Keep your phone with you, then, and keep it on," she said, handing me her notebook. "Something's afoot and I'm not sure it's a game. Don't be gone long. Oh my, I've just thought of something I've always wanted to do. Wait there." She closed the passenger door and came around the front of the car. I lowered the window to ask what she was doing, but she answered before I got the words out.

"Iconic cop show stuff," she said. Then she squared her shoulders, saluted, and slapped the car top twice. When I looked in the rearview mirror, she was grinning like an electrified cat.

The ghost flitted through my mind as I left town. Flitted, nothing. She swooped in and took over my latest attempt at rational thought. One minute I was making plans to uncover a blackmailer and the next I was wondering how she'd been spending her time since her audiobook ended. Waxing melancholic in the bedroom? Lying in wait for me behind the kitchen door? I made a quick mental list of things I'd rather avoid. Thinking about her went on it. Also sheriff's deputies and herbal tea.

My phone started ringing halfway to the cottage. I didn't answer and added distracted driving to my avoidance list. It stopped ringing. Then started again. And after that, again. By the time I turned in at the Homeplace, an entire swarm of annoying phone tweedles had invaded the car, converting the space from compact to claustrophobic, and finding a new ringtone was more important to me than finding a new job.

I parked, closed my eyes, and breathed slowly, practicing phone anger-management skills, glad I didn't keep knitting needles in the car. Homer might see them as a symbol of tranquillity. I might stab the phone with them when it rang again. Which it did. I massaged the back of my neck, counted to ten. The phone quit. I looked at the display.

All the missed calls were from a single number. A Blue Plum number. No surprise I didn't recognize it. The phone rang again. Same number. I breathed out one more time and answered. The caller barged into my ear without waiting for a hello from my end. It was one of the Spiveys.

"Thank God you finally answered. I told Shirley if we didn't give up trying, you'd eventually give up and answer."

So it was Mercy. "Wha—," I started to say.

"Don't interrupt. No time for chat. This is urgent. Max is dead."

"I heard. I'm sorry. Please tell Angie—"

"What did you hear?"

"He tripped and fell down the steps."

"Then it's not the kind of dead you're thinking."

"What other kind is there?" I asked.

"He was pushed. He's the murdered kind of dead."

"What?"

"And we need your help. You're our alibi."

Chapter 27

Thank God I'd done my slow breathing before answering the phone. I wasn't sure I had any breath left after Mercy's call. They'd been busy.

They'd taken it upon themselves to find out where I was staying, asking around town the day before until someone told them, as I hadn't the good manners (Mercy's words) to tell them myself. When I asked who told them, she said she didn't remember. She didn't lie any better than I ever did.

Not wanting to miss any exciting developments in my life (my words), they drove out early that morning, parked at the Quickie Mart, and waited until I drove past on my way into town. Not being the suspicious sort, I didn't notice them following. That's how they knew I stopped at the house first, and why they were fighting over the binoculars while I ate breakfast at Mel's.

They also followed me when Homer and I, trailed by Clod, went to Homer's office. When Clod left Homer's they argued over whether to follow him or wait and see where I went. They stuck with me. They saw me speak to Aaron Carlin. They recognized him and were shocked (Mercy's word) that I knew him.

They broke off following me and rushed to Angie's side when she heard Max was dead. Now they were panicking because Angie was told there were questions about how Max got that way.

"It hasn't been verified he was murdered?"

"As good as," Mercy said. "And we need you to back us up about where we were and what we were doing this morning."

There was the sound of a scuffle on the other end and errant beeps as of a misplaced hand pressing keys. Then Shirley came on.

"We'll be right up there on the list of suspects because we didn't like him. Mercy especially didn't like him."

There was a muffled "ouch" and Mercy came back on the line.

"Don't pay any attention to Shirley. I loved him like the son I never wished I had. So, what'll it take?"

"Take for what?"

"To give us an alibi. Someone might have seen us at the house this morning and turned us in."

"But *I* didn't see you," I said. "How do I know you were there?"

"How else did we know *you* were there?" Mercy asked.

"Sorry, it doesn't work that way."

"Okay, put it this way. If we hadn't followed you to the house, then followed you to Mel's and seen you were staying for breakfast, and then if we hadn't gone back to see if we could get in the back door of the house, you know, trying to help in case you hadn't thought of that, if we hadn't done that and found the broken window, then how could we report the break-in? And then if we hadn't gone back to Mel's and seen you were still eating your eggs and sausage, how could we know to call Cole Dunbar and tell them where to find you? It's simple."

Sounds of renewed scuffling reached me from the Spivey end of the line.

"She put that badly." Shirley had the phone again. "What she meant to say was, basically, we were with you all morning, so we couldn't have been with Max, killing him."

"What she said was, *basically*, you two reported the break-in and made it sound as though I did it and then told Deputy Dunbar where to come pick me up for questioning."

"I told her it would sound like that."

"I'm hanging up now." And I did, to what sounded like wails and the gnashing of teeth, although that might be an exaggerated memory. I got out of the car and was about to turn the phone off, despite my promise to keep it on, when it rang again. I started to toss it in the lavender bush when I looked at the display and was glad I had at least a few anger-management skills under my belt. This call was from the Cat.

"Kath?" Honeysuckle and good sense on the line.

"What's up, Ardis?"

"I've been giving it some thought and I believe what you need is one of those people."

That was vague enough to sound either ominous or helpful.

"Have you got a minute and I'll explain?"

"Oh, good, sure." I unlocked and opened the kitchen door, peeking around it first, to see if the ghost was there. No shimmer met my eye. All was quiet. The slide show on the laptop continued flicking through its photos but the McCrumb novel was long over.

"The way I see it," Ardis was saying, "there are two kinds of detectives. There are the Columbos and Miss Marples, who are extremely competent and work solo, and there are the Sherlock Holmeses and Nero Wolfs, equally competent, but who have their Nigel Bruces and Archie Goodwins. Did I get that right?"

"Right enough. I know what you mean."

"Hon, you need your Nigel. Someone to aid you in your investigation. Someone trustworthy who will stand guard when necessary. Who can keep you out of trouble or get you out of trouble. Preferably the former."

"That's funny." I put my purse down on the table, shut down the computer. "Ernestine said the same kind of thing earlier this morning."

"Ernestine's blind but she's not batty. She wouldn't be any good to you, though. Not enough muscle to her. I'm solid enough and I'd do it like a shot, but with the Cat and Daddy, my discretionary time is limited. This morning was a hoot, and I can operate Brainstorm Central here at the shop for you. But you need one of those people."

"A sidekick?"

"Bingo."

I went to the sink and got a glass of water.

"And I know who it could be. What about Joe Dunbar?"

Granny would have been appalled at the way I spit water all over the kitchen floor.

"Kath? You all right?"

"Sorry, I thought you said Shirley or Mercy." *Shirley or Mercy* didn't sound remotely like *Joe Dunbar*, but I was about as likely to ask the twins to tag along with me as the Fastidious Burglar of Blue Plum. "I'll think about it, Ardis. Thanks."

I hung up and mopped up. I also turned the phone off. Homer or Ardis might not approve, but I'd be at the Cat soon enough and could turn it back on there. In the meantime I'd avoid something else on my list. Spiveys.

A sidekick wasn't a bad idea but it wasn't going to work. Everyone I knew was too busy, too upright, not upright enough, or dead. I started humming "All by Myself," but I couldn't remember the tune beyond those three schmaltzy words so I quit and sniffled to myself instead.

For some reason I didn't want to fathom, I was stuck

with a ghost. And for some other reason I couldn't possibly fathom, it couldn't be the ghost who would make this mess bearable. If I had the ghost of my choice, it would be Granny. Her ghost could probably even make all this entertaining. But the ghost I got stuck with was a depressed ditz. I didn't even know who she was. Or who she'd been. Poor thing. And she was erratic. Where the heck had she disappeared to?

I looked around, blinking, as if the problem was only that she was more out of focus than usual. It wasn't. She wasn't there. I sighed, packed up the laptop, picked up my purse, and let myself out again.

I caught sight of Ruth in the distance, surrounded by a group of schoolkids. Small rivulets of children were dribbling away in other directions, as though the group had sprung a leak. Ruth raised something over her head—a pitchfork—and waved it. Like magic, the group coalesced and followed her toward a log barn. I should ask her to show me around the farm sometime. As a professional courtesy, she'd probably show me behind the scenes, too. Who knew, maybe she had spare payroll idling in a corner of the coffers and needed a full-time textile preservationist on staff. Ha. Ha.

As I passed the Quickie Mart on my way back to town, I checked for spying Spiveys. Unless they'd traded the Buick for a Farmers' Co-op truck, they weren't in sight. I turned the radio on, not sure what it was tuned to. Nerve-grating static. I started to reach for the tuner but put both hands back on the wheel for a tricky couple of curves, glad I was paying attention when a pickup coming toward me swung wide. Then the radio caught a signal from a talk show.

"Have you seen the movie *Blithe Spirit*?" the radio personality asked.

Except the voice was coming from somewhere behind my right ear instead of the car's speaker.

"Oh my God." *I* swung wide in the next curve.

"I only ask because the characters in the movie, one of whom is a ghost, also take a drive into town. Is that what we're doing? Driving into town? Watch out for that squirrel. Oh dear, too late, and not enough left for stew."

Considering the poor squirrel's fate, I took a chance I shouldn't have and shot a look over my shoulder. Her watery, unblinking face was right there, hovering inches behind me, watching the road ahead. "You're haunting my car? You can't do that. This is a rental!" I slowed and looked for the first good place to pull over. A driver coming up from behind honked and whipped around us. "What are you doing here?"

"I overheard you on the phone with someone named Ardis. I've never heard that name. It sounds like a bad perfume."

"I'll be sure to tell her."

"How rude. Please don't. Do you always hold the wheel so tightly that your hands shake?"

A clapboard church came up on the right. I slowed even further, pulled into its parking lot, and stopped.

"Where are we?" she asked.

I could see her in the rearview mirror moving between the two side windows in the backseat. Her motion reminded me of a seal shooting from one side of a water tank to the other, back and forth, back and forth, around and around. She was making me seasick. "Could you please move up here into the passenger seat and be still?"

"But you're the driver."

"What difference does that make?"

"I don't know. As far as I know, this is my first ride in a car." She shimmered into the front seat, taking up less room than I'd expected.

"As far as you know?"

"And that isn't very far. It's sad, but my memories are as slippery as grease on a griddle."

I was afraid she'd start crying again, as she seemed so fond of doing. Then I wondered if that would fog up the inside of the windows. I lowered mine partway in case. There were no sniffles or sobs, though. She continued staring all around—at the trees, the grass, the sky—and turning to watch when vehicles whisked past us and disappeared around the next bend.

"Who are you?" I'd asked her that the day before, but we'd gotten sidetracked into her graphic rendition of Emmett's death and she hadn't answered. She didn't answer this time, either. She was too caught up in everything she saw out the window. She drank it all in as though her senses were starved. And they would be, I guessed. She was, after all, dead. But had she also been asleep?

"When was the last time you were out of the house?" I asked.

"No idea. Look, a redbird." There was nothing wrong with her distance or color vision. She pointed out a male cardinal calling from one of the oaks in the churchyard, then followed its bobbing flight as it flew to another tree.

"How long have you been *in* the house?"

She snorted.

"What's that supposed to mean?"

"Ashes to ashes, dust to dust. You might as well ask a dust mote your questions."

"You really don't know? Have you ever left it since you, um, arrived?" Arrived? There was a good euphemism. Why hadn't it occurred to me before that she must have died in the cottage? But did ghosts only haunt the places where they died? Obviously not, because here she was in the car, glued to the window, fascinated by a grackle strutting across the grass, as though she'd been locked away in solitary confinement for decades. Or dead to the world. "Don't you ever look out the windows at the cottage?"

"Emmett mostly kept the curtains drawn. Besides, he

had his television. Your setup back there on the kitchen table was clever, with the screen and the pretty pictures and the woman telling the story, but television is so much more. It can go all day and all night. It's practically eternal. At least, it was until Em died and strangers took his things away and left me alone as if I'd died all over again. But you're still asking me silly questions. You're also staring at me. You're tactless."

"How do you know I'm staring? You have your back to me." She was right, though. I was staring. As for my questions, I decided to keep going. "You said Em saw you the night he died."

"And you said I only scared the bloody blue bejeebers out of him but I didn't scare him to death."

"I didn't put it quite like that but, yes, someone else killed him. Did he ever see you before that night? Did he know you were in the house?" She turned her hollow eyes on me and I started to flounder. "I don't mean to be rude, it's just . . ." She didn't billow or turn grayer or groan so I barged ahead. "It's just I'm trying to figure a few things out and I'd like you to help me."

She shifted around so that her whole foggy shape faced me and then she wriggled as though getting more comfortable in the seat. Once settled, she closed her eyes slowly and opened them again the way a cat does. "I think I'll make a good detective, if I do say so myself."

It wasn't exactly a *sequitur* sort of remark, but the whole situation—me, in a rental car, in the parking lot of Plum Valley Baptist Church, chatting with a smug-looking ghost—was so far beyond odd that I let the remark pass. "So, may I ask you a few more questions?"

"Only if you promise to play the good cop."

That remark really should have given me pause. I should have asked for an explanation. But I was being mindful of her feelings, and her tendency to moan and billow, so I didn't. "I'll try to be considerate."

"Then I'll try to answer," she said.

"Thank you."

"You're welcome."

We were being so civilized, the ghost and I. I pinched myself. We were both still there in the car.

"I'm waiting," she said.

I repeated my earlier question. "Did Em know you were there?"

"Until the night he died, he was oblivious." She shrugged. "Men."

"Why do you think he saw you that night?"

"There's juniper in gin, isn't there?" she asked. "I think it had something to do with that."

"He drank gin that night?"

"He drank a *lot* of gin that night. I never knew him to touch a drop of alcohol before then."

"Never?"

"My dear old mother used to rant about the evils of demon rum. I only wish she could have warned darling Em about the devil in a fifth of gin."

"But isn't gin an acquired taste?"

"Now that I think back," she said, "from the way he tipped the bottle, Em and that taste were more like long-lost friends and they were mighty happy getting reacquainted."

"So I wonder what prompted the binge."

"Finding the bottle in the middle of the kitchen table might've done it," she said. "It was there when he got home and he looked at it the way I wished he'd look at me. And then he said to it, in his manly, gruff way, 'Well, aren't you a pretty thing,' and down the hatch it went. Men are such weak creatures."

Alcoholic men, anyway. While she sniffled, I wondered who knew that Emmett fell into that sad category. And if the police found the bottle and had it tested for poison. Or if they hadn't because the person who left it came and took it away again. Too bad Clod was off-limits. He might know, although he might not give me a straight answer. Did I dare ask Homer to find out for me? But how would I explain where the questions or information came from? Left field? Elysian Fields?

"Would you like to know who left the bottle for Em?"

I was so dense. I didn't need to ask Homer or Clod. Talk about a fly on the wall; every detective should have a ghost hanging around the ceiling. "Fantastic," I said. "Yes."

"So would I."

I was rude and stared at her again.

"Your eyes are blue," she said, "like mine."

I turned away and started the car.

"Oh, good, we're going to town now? I can't wait to see it."

I turned the car off again. "There are a few things I need to know first. Maybe Em didn't see you, but did anyone else? Did anyone stop by to see him and see you, too?"

"No one ever said hello to me, if that's what you mean. Sometimes there's a turn of the head or a twitch of the eyes, but after a few seconds they stop looking or trying to hear. Some people sweat, but between you and me, a clammy, dripping brow isn't attractive and when I see one I leave the room."

"Why can *I* see you?"

"How should I know? I'm not an expert. I'm just dead. Why are we still sitting here?"

"Just one or two more questions. Please." There were more like a thousand and two, but she was beginning to bounce in an ominous way. Driving while distracted by Ardis was dangerous enough; driving while haunted by a volatile ghost would be suicidal. She still hadn't answered my primary question, so I rephrased it and tried it again. "Who were you when you were alive?"

"You don't have to go all past tense on me," she said. "I still *am*, as far as I can see." Suddenly her face was inches from mine. "Boo! There, see? I still am as far as you can see, too." She settled back into the passenger seat and crossed her arms. I should have told her that looking superior and petulant were both rude. "I might be null," she huffed, "but I'm not void. Anyway, you haven't told me who you are."

"I guess I haven't. Okay, I'm Kath." I automatically held out my hand. "Kath Rutledge."

We both looked at my hand sticking out there between us. I quickly pretended to assess my manicure needs, but before I could oh-so-nonchalantly pull the hand back from where it didn't belong, she reached over and slid her fingers across my palm. It felt like a trickle of ice water or a particularly cold dog nose. I swallowed, smiled, and congratulated myself for not yanking my hand back and rubbing it on my pant leg.

"And you?" I asked.

She swayed a bit. "Geneva?" She didn't say it with any confidence, more as if she had to drag it out of a dark corner and dust it off.

"That's a nice name."

She shrugged a shoulder.

"Geneva what?"

She swayed faster and went into her humming-cum-moaning routine, which in the confines of the car was even eerier than it had been in the kitchen. Or maybe that showed I had insensitivity-management issues to deal with, too.

"That's okay. It's okay," I said. "Geneva is a fine name. Geneva's great. Let's go with that and not worry about the rest. Okay?"

"Okay, let's go." Her recovery was remarkably fast.

"Uh, no. Not yet. One last thing. What are you doing here? I mean here, today, now, in the car? And what exactly are you planning to do when we get to town?" My imagination provided a whole spectrum of answers, heavily weighted to the "horrible" end. If my head had been screwed on right, that question would have been the first one I asked. What was I thinking, taking a ghost into Blue Plum?

"Oh," she, Geneva, said. "I thought you guessed. I'm what that person on the telephone, Aramis, said you needed. I'm your side trick."

"Her name is Ardis. The word is 'sidekick.'"

"Yes. That's me. And I get to play the bad cop."

Chapter 28

You can't strangle a ghost.

I didn't actually try because despite what Homer thought, I didn't ordinarily have violent reactions in moments of anger or frustration. Besides, I knew it wouldn't work. I did lower all the car windows, though, with the idea she might blow straight out of one. But, apparently, once a self-satisfied ghost is sitting in the front seat of your car, it's impossible to get her to go until she wants to. And that wasn't until I'd parked the car in the lot across from the Weaver's Cat. At that point *I* felt like moaning but I didn't want to draw attention to myself. To us. Whatever.

We'd argued over the bad-cop, good-cop thing all the way into town. I threatened to drive back to the cottage and not take her anywhere. If she'd been a two-year-old, I would have. But I didn't want to be stuck out there anymore than she did. I had questions to ask and prying to do. It was time I figured out what Granny knew, who knew she knew it, and who knew to look for it in her house. And maybe it was time to figure out who killed Emmett Cobb. I'd already broken Clod's nose; maybe I should break his case for him, too.

"How is this going to work?" I asked her, Geneva, before getting out of the car. "Are you going to float along next to me or what?"

"Don't be surly. That's my role."

"Don't start again. It makes no sense. If no one else can see or hear you, you can't be the bad cop." I threw my hands in the air. "I'm arguing with a ghost." I let my hands drop back into my lap, then raised them to run my fingers through my hair, no doubt making it extremely attractive. "I must sound like a lunatic. And if people are looking, they'll see me talking to myself, and they'll *know* I'm a lunatic. Oh my gosh. I just thought of something. What if we run into someone who's been drinking daiquiris for lunch?"

"I think you're getting upset over nothing," she said.

"Why?"

"Daiquiris are made with rum, not gin."

"How do you even know that? And you know what I mean. What if someone sees you?"

"When was the last time you heard of anyone believing in, much less seeing, ghosts?"

Apart from being tired of arguing with her, I couldn't on that point. I got out of the car and stood with the door open, expecting her to glide out after me. Instead, she wafted through the passenger door and wavered there above the pavement, taking in the sights and sounds of downtown Blue Plum.

"It's changed," she said.

"You remember being here?"

"I think I must."

"Will you be okay crossing the street?"

"We'll find out, though I have a suggestion."

"What?"

"You probably shouldn't talk to me. You do look like a lunatic." She laughed and did an imitation of Mary Tyler Moore twirling and tossing her hat in Minneapolis.

She was having fun while I was adding nervous breakdowns to my list of things to avoid. I grabbed my laptop and purse and stalked across the street to the Weaver's Cat, not looking around to see who'd seen me talking to no one and not bothering to see if Geneva made it safely or came with me at all. She did, though.

"Oh, my stars," she said when she saw the window displays. "What is this place?" She moved along the porch, flickering from window to window. Without waiting for me to open the door, she flickered right through the glass into the shop.

And blessed silence descended. Except for a tour bus idling up the street, a dog barking—the usual hubbub of downtown Blue Plum—no more prattle filled my ears. Her mouth was moving, but it was no different from seeing and not hearing Ardis on the other side of the glass. It surprised me for some reason, but maybe because it made her more human. Or maybe it gave me the respite I needed to refocus on what I planned to do. This traveling with an unearthly sidekick was going to be tricky business. I enjoyed the quiet for another moment, then followed her inside.

"Why didn't you tell me about this place?" Geneva asked when she heard the bell on the door and saw me walk in. "I'm in heaven." She'd draped herself, like an animate cobweb, around a bolt of batik quilting fabric. "Does this bring out the blue in my eyes?"

That was not a pair of baby blues looking at me.

"Kath, there you are!" Nicki called from the sales counter. "Homer Wood's been calling wondering where you are and why you aren't answering your phone. Ardis told him you were crawling around in the unfinished part of the attic and probably didn't get reception up there. But if that's where you were, then why did you just come in the front door?"

Prattle. Straight onto my avoidance list. Although prattle falling from my own lips, just then, would have helped. I couldn't think of a plausible reason or lie. I needn't have worried.

"Were you out at your car?" Nicki asked. "I guess you were. I see you've brought your laptop in."

Geneva left the window, gliding to a mannequin nearer the counter. She rose up behind it and her face appeared above its shoulder like a second head. The chartreuse sweater set the mannequin wore did nothing for her coloring.

"Oh, now, there. Do you see a fly?" Nicki asked. "I thought I saw one buzzing around in the window when you came in and then . . ." She pulled a swatter from behind the counter and peered at the mannequin. "But isn't that always the way? As soon as you find the swatter you can't find the fly. Do you see it?"

I shook my head. Geneva snickered.

"You're awfully quiet. Are you feeling all right?" Nicki stopped peering at the mannequin and peered at me. "What were you doing in the attic, anyway?"

"That's a good question. I've been wondering what I'm doing almost everywhere I go these last few days."

"Aw, it's the stress, don't you think, dearie? It's all right if I call you dearie, isn't it?"

"I guess, if you want to sound like an old lady."

"I just thought you'd like to hear it again, you know, because that's what Ivy called you, isn't it? And I thought you might miss it. Oh, now . . ." She bounded over and gave me a quick, hard hug, no doubt mistaking the look on my face as "gosh, that's so sweet." As she pulled away I saw an angry scratch on the back of her hand.

"That has to hurt. Have you put anything on it?"

"I told her to wait and let Joe trim those roses," Debbie said, appearing from the back. "It's what we pay him for. Those things are like tigers out for blood when they get hold of you."

"Well, he can finish them," Nicki said. "I've learned my lesson."

"At least you wore jeans," Debbie said. "Are those yours? They look like Ivy's."

"They look good, too, don't they?" Nicki turned in several circles admiring her jean-clad legs and rear. "Ivy gave them to me."

"Oh, hey, before you go, Ardis is looking for the price sheet for the new Blue Ridge. Will you find it for her?"

"Will do. And, Kath, you'd better call Homer. He's probably wondering if you got lost up there in the rafters. And he asked about knitting groups and when I told him about Friday Fast and Furious he asked me to be sure and tell you that it starts at three o'clock in TGIF's workroom. Wasn't that sweet of him? And before I forget, if things work out, and you get the house back, will you rent it to me? I love that little place and I'd feel just like Ivy living there. Promise me you'll think about it, okay? Well, I'm off. See you in the morning. Bye now!"

"Does she wake up like that," I asked, watching her go, "or does she work up to it with triple shots of espresso?"

"Her nickname was Bunny when she was a kid, if that tells you anything."

At that, Nicki popped her head back around the corner. "I almost forgot, Kath. The Spiveys are looking for you."

"Where?"

"Behind you." That was Shirley. Or Mercy.

Chapter 29

"Your phone is off again," one or the other Spivey said. "Better check it for low batt."

They were indistinguishable in matching black sweat suits, possibly their idea of appropriate mourning attire honoring Max. A wavering to their left caught my eye— Geneva floating closer. The twins blinked in her direction, then looked back at me.

My face must have reflected my (a) dislike, (b) distrust, (c) anger-management issues, or (d) all three. I was happy going with all three. Debbie was happy going away altogether. She gave me a cowardly wave and disappeared around the corner, on her way to warn Ardis of the Spivey blight, no doubt.

"We snuck down the alley and slipped in the back door," one twin said.

"Like a couple of shadows. The cops never saw us."

"Were they looking for you?" I asked.

"Let's move away from the windows," they answered.

Looking furtive, they relocated to a corner out of view of passersby. Geneva floated after, settling in a basket of purple wool. The three of them presented a strange picture and, in a surreal fashion moment, I saw that deep purple was a better color for ghosts than chartreuse. All three of them looked at me expectantly. I joined them, not in the friendliest of moods and asking myself hard questions. Why was I letting myself be sucked into these Spivey dramatics? Why weren't there any customers to interrupt us?

"We think we can help you," the twin closest to Geneva said.

"How?"

"I knew she'd like the idea, Shirl," the other twin, Mercy, said, hearing my incredulity as acceptance.

"Tell her about the boxes," Shirley said.

"Stacked in Angie's garage," said Mercy. "What Max cleared out of Emmett's place. No telling what all is in them."

"But we can look," Shirley said. "Because now they belong to Angie."

I felt like groping for a chair to sit down. Access to Emmett's things? The answer to how he got the house might be sitting in Angie's garage? This was huge. From their twin smirks, Shirley and Mercy knew it, too.

"Okay. Why are you telling me this? Oh, no, wait. Not the alibi again. Trust me. You don't want me trying to lie for you."

"Forget the alibi," Mercy said. "We'll lay low and keep to the shadows, but we aren't afraid of Cole Dunbar anymore. This is bigger than he is. This is about sticking together. About family. Ivy could be a tetchy old lady, but she was kin and so are you. Besides, if you can break Cole's nose, we don't need an alibi."

I didn't see how that last part made sense. But who was I to question sense? I didn't see anyone else in the room watching a ghost twine around and between the Spiveys as she inspected every inch of their identical-ness.

"You know about the nose?" I asked.

"He came by to ask Angie more questions," Shirley said. "The bandage cheered us right up."

"And that's how we know the boxes are full of Emmett's things. We hid out in the garage until Cole was gone," Mercy said. "He left Angie in tears. That's when we decided to join forces and came to find you."

Geneva glided around behind me and I felt a brush of cold on my neck. "I like them," she said in my ear. "This is better than television and twins are good luck. Unless they're bad luck. I don't really remember. Anyway, is the tetchy old lady they're talking about the same one we're trying to prove killed darling Em?"

"*They're* your sidekicks?" Ardis asked when I told her about my pact with the twins.

"Independent operatives is a better description."

"Goons is a more accurate description. Since when do you trust those two?"

I explained the logic of trusting Shirley and Mercy's bottomless pit of nosiness. "Add that to their cockeyed family loyalty and I think it's worth a shot. If they can find something in those boxes, the whole nightmare of who owns the house could be over."

"But not the nightmare of who broke in," Ardis said. "Twice. That person, those people, are still out there and . . . What's the matter?"

"It's nothing." It wasn't exactly nothing. I hadn't told her about Max being murdered yet. She should know, but I didn't want to say anything until I found out for certain. "I forgot to call Homer. Be right back."

There were customers milling and although Ardis and I had kept our conversation quiet I didn't want to take a chance on this call being overheard. I went into the small office, back behind the sales counter, and closed the door. Ernestine answered and put me through to Homer immediately. When I asked him if it was true about Max being pushed, his answer was characteristically to the point.

"Where did you hear that?"

"The Spiveys. Oh." When would I learn? "So it isn't true. Sorry . . ."

He cut in. "There are questions. Apparently the truth awaits an autopsy."

"But how can they tell? You almost tripped down the stairs yourself."

"Inconsistencies with bruising, lividity, primary and secondary skull fractures. I'm not entirely sure of the vocabulary or the reasoning." He paused. I tried to swallow. "Are you still there?"

"That's horrible."

"It is."

"Homer, I'm sorry I didn't call back sooner."

"No apology needed. I told you to forget your problems for the afternoon. You were doing that. Now this adds to them."

"It does? I mean, I know I sound callous, because it is horrible, but why would Max being murdered add to my problems?"

"It will mean there's an extremely dangerous person out there interested in the Cobb family. We don't know who. We don't know why. But you've suggested a reason and if that reason proves to be true, then you've stirred up trouble. You have already agreed to keep quiet about that reason. But I want to make this crystal clear. Be very careful who you speak to and what you say from here on out."

"I'm not a threat to anyone." I wondered if he would consider encouraging the Spiveys to search Emmett's boxes as stirring up trouble. Or playing good-cop, bad-cop with a ghost.

"I would rather you didn't argue with me on this. Suffice to say, someone is feeling threatened."

"If Max was murdered."

"If—yes." I pictured him nodding his concession to that qualifier and thought I heard the click of his pen.

"Will you call me if you hear anything one way or another?"

"Kath, I want you to keep safe. And quiet."

"I hope ignorance isn't your idea of safety."

I left the office annoyed at myself for being short with the person who was trying to protect me, but I was not a little spooked by Homer's intensity. Then I saw Geneva hovering behind the counter watching Ardis ring up a sale of self-striping sock yarn. "Spooked" didn't begin to cover what was going on in my life. Geneva was fascinated by the electronic cash register and if she'd been corporeal, Ardis would have stepped on her. The only notice Ardis took was to shiver and take a shawl from under the counter.

"Someone walking on my grave," she said, wrapping the shawl around her shoulders. Geneva made a rude noise and Ardis drew the shawl tighter. "What's the word from Homer?" she asked when the sock-yarn customer left.

I broke the news about the questions surrounding Max's death. She closed her eyes and said something I couldn't hear. Maybe a prayer. Then I repeated Homer's warnings and instructions. She thought about both, then came up with a more proactive plan.

"A sidekick might not be enough. What you really need is one of those other things. Not just a couple of goons. A whole group."

"A gang?" I asked. "That sounds scary."

"No, you know what I mean," she said. "With horses and shotguns."

That was even scarier.

"A posse," Geneva said.

"A posse?" I repeated for the ghost-deprived.

"Exactly," said Ardis.

"Like Marshal Dillon," Geneva said. "Darling Em loved Marshal Dillon's television show. If you have a posse, may I have a Colt single-action army revolver with a seven-and-a-half-inch barrel like Matt's?"

"Hush," I told Geneva, pretending to sneeze.

"Bless you," Ardis said.

"Why do I need a posse?"

"Information," Ardis said. "You need it and you need it fast and the more eyes and ears you have out there, the more likely you are to find it."

"Except I'm not sure what 'it' is. And if Homer's right . . ."

"Kath, honey, I'm a great believer in clichés and what Homer doesn't know won't hurt him. The Friday Fast and Furious subset of TGIF meets this afternoon. It's one of the study groups, one of the smaller ones. Debbie will be there and you'll know the others. Ask them for help. They'll do it for Ivy, and I'd trust any of them. And remember, there's safety in numbers. Oh, and hon? You still owe me a doughnut. I'll take it anytime."

Geneva stayed behind at the shop. I figured that was safe enough. If the worst she could do was make someone long for a wool sweater, she couldn't cause too much trouble. And it was just as well she didn't prattle along beside me. My walk to and from Mel's was about as distracted as my drive with Ardis earlier. My thoughts went around and around about information. Gathering it. Analyzing, using, misusing it. Encoding it. Hiding it. Killing for it.

I bought three doughnuts, including one for Geneva. Thoughtless. Distracted. Mel was away from the shop; otherwise her banter and sharp comments might have brought me out of my fog. I paid, almost forgot the bag, stopped outside the door to remember where I was going.

Information. Ardis recorded it in the notebook she gave me. The Spiveys were looking for it in Emmett's boxes. Joe Dunbar was after it the other night in what he thought was Emmett's empty cottage. Someone wanted it badly enough to break into Granny's house—and I was convinced it was information the sneak thief was after, not a television or an expensive camera.

I needed time to analyze the information I had, including the information I hadn't shared with anyone else. And I needed more of both—more time and more information.

"Hon," Ardis said when I got back, "information is power and access to information is more power."

"Access this," I said, dropping the doughnut bag on the counter.

"When do we saddle up the horses?" Geneva asked. I ignored her.

Access. While Ardis waited on customers and Geneva pouted, I thought about access. Seemed like a whole lot of access was going on in Blue Plum. Access to secrets. Access to houses. Access to a bottle of gin. And Ardis was right. Deputizing a group of people who knew Granny, who knew Blue Plum, knew how to gossip—the Friday Fast and Furious knitters of TGIF—that would give me access to more information. Information that might help fill in the gaps in the picture I was weaving. But if I wanted to ensure a complete picture, a complete, full-color, three-dimensional picture, then gaining physical access to a few places could be helpful, too. And for that I might need . . .

"Hey, Ardis." Joe Dunbar stood in the hall doorway. "Can I get in the shed?"

. . . a burglar.

"I forgot to put the key back, didn't I?" Ardis said. "Here it is. Hold up, though, Joe, before you start on the roses." She turned from him to me. "It's entirely up to you who you deputize. But things might be getting rough and you already put one Dunbar out of commission. I think you're going to need this one."

"And guns," Geneva said.

Chapter 30

I left one doughnut for Ardis and took the other two and Joe up the back stairs to Granny's study. Geneva came, too, doing her doleful hum. When I opened the door, revealing the controlled chaos I'd left the place in, Joe stopped short.

"I call it organizing," I said to his raised eyebrow. "Come on in."

He stayed at the door. "What did Ardis mean, you put one Dunbar out of commission?"

"Doughnut?" I held one up. It didn't lure him any farther into the room. "The other things she mentioned, about deputizing and things getting rough—they didn't pique your interest any?"

"That one stuck out."

Geneva floated past him, her hum taking on the flavor of the theme song from *Bonanza*. He didn't blink. "Why don't you tell him about the guns and horses?" she said.

My recap of developments didn't include guns and horses and elicited only minor reactions from Joe. The least understated was a bowed head for Max. Clod's nose didn't even get a wince. I told him my ideas about information and access, the need for more of both, about the Spiveys and the TGIF posse.

"No."

"No, what? I haven't asked you anything except about a doughnut."

"You're leading up to it, though. Look, I'm happy to pool information. That makes sense. But 'access'? Like I said last night, absolutely not." And just like that, he turned and left.

I hardly had time for an overstated reaction to his refusal and exit when he was back for another parting shot.

"And Emmett's boxes? They're a dead end. I've already looked."

"Spurned," Geneva said with swooning pathos.

Once again, only after Joe was gone did I think of what I really wanted to or should have asked. Like, if he and Granny were such friends, why hadn't she mentioned him? Where had he planned to look for evidence at the cottage? Why shouldn't he be the primary suspect for the house burglary? For all of it? And why didn't I turn him in myself?

"I like this room," Geneva said. "I enjoy hidden nooks and crannies. They're ideal for waxing melancholic."

"Good. You explore and wax. I need to make plans." As I should have done before approaching Joe. Rushing and poor planning put the banana peel under many a promising analysis or project.

"I feel I should tell you something," Geneva said.

"What?" I powered up my laptop.

"It's very sad, but since I passed over, I frighten animals. Even the least of the mice and beetles."

"Yeah?" I opened a new document; I didn't want to know where she met mice and beetles.

"Here is the saddest part. The horses, no doubt, will bolt."

"Geneva, there are no horses. There won't be any bolting."

"No horses? What about guns?"

"No. Please be quiet."

I checked the time. An hour, still, before Friday Fast and Furious met. More than an hour since lunchtime arrived and left unheeded. That was something I could fix immediately. I ate the two doughnuts, then set about keying in and organizing the data I had, highlighting the gaps, planning how to fill them.

The basic information and questions were scary enough: Granny sold/gave her house to Emmett Cobb; someone poisoned Emmett with a bottle of gin; Cole Dunbar suspected Granny; Joe Dunbar was sure Emmett blackmailed Granny, which gave Granny a grand motive for Cole to chew over; blackmail—was Emmett blackmailing other people? Joe? Cole? Did Max Cobb inherit a blackmail business as well as the house? Did he kill his father to get the business? Now Max was dead—if he was murdered, did that mean he didn't kill Emmett? Were there two murderers?

At the end of the hour, some of my notes scared me, especially the last question that suddenly occurred to me: Cole Dunbar was fixated on a connection between murdered Cobbs and Granny's house, which I'd repeatedly told him I needed to get into. Would he try to pin Max's murder on me?

And none of that touched on the break-ins. I made a quick list of the small things missing from the house: tapestry, tapestry cartoon, tapestry notebook, other notebooks/journals (maybe—who knew?), camera memory cards, thumb drive, cat. I hesitated, then added birthday present to the list. I refused to label any of the things inconsequential. And if someone had only taken Maggie for safekeeping, why didn't anyone else know?

And where were all my suspects? Shouldn't there be more than the Dunbar duo? Not if they were guilty. But the guilt of either Dunbar felt like a bigger if than the if about Max being murdered. Because Granny trusted Joe and Homer said Clod was as honest as the next man. Too bad Max was gone. I had no reservations about suspecting him. What it finally came down to was the fact that I didn't know enough to know who else to suspect. And that's where I hoped Friday Fast and Furious would help. But could I ask them to help with something so potentially dangerous? I shook my head and shrugged. Why not?

By the time I'd made myself feel sick with questions and worries, Geneva had disappeared. I went to the door to make sure no one was within earshot, then called her. She didn't answer. That made me uneasy.

The clicking needles of Friday Fast and Furious reached my ears before the low mumble of their voices. It was barely past three, but as I approached the TGIF workroom, their industry sounded serious enough to be mistaken for a sweatshop. Half a dozen furious knitters sat in a circle of eight chairs. They didn't seem surprised to see me and there was nary a bobble in their speed when I joined them. I was surprised, though, to see one of them—Joe Dunbar, Mr. Suspect. How awkward.

"Hey, Kath." Debbie smiled and patted the chair next to hers. "Ardis gave us a heads-up."

"No slackers," Mel said. "Where are your needles?"

"I have extras." Ernestine held out needles and a ball of pastel green. "We're knitting hats for preemies. Our goal is one thousand by New Year's Eve. I'm happy to report we're on target."

Ruth waved. Her yarn was rosy pink. Mel's matched her mustard hair. Joe's was sky blue. The sixth member was the loud librarian, Thea. She held up a tiny red and white striped hat.

"Part of my early literacy outreach," she said. "*The Cat in the Hat.*"

Ernestine handed me the needles and yarn. "Cast on seventy-two."

"But we know you didn't just wander in looking for a quick knit," Mel said. "Ardis said you need our help."

I looked at Joe. He shrugged in his minimal way. He kept the rhythm of his knitting but the other needles paused as if for a bated and choreographed breath.

"It's going to be asking a lot," I said, "and it might sound kind of unbelievable."

Thea nodded. "Truth is stranger than fiction."

"Spill it, sister," Mel said.

"Okay. I think Emmett Cobb was blackmailing people. I'd like your help to find proof."

The needles started clicking again.

"Blackmail is nasty," Ernestine said with some relish. "We'll need to ask any questions delicately."

"And we'll need to keep it quiet," said Ruth. "That won't be easy and will put some of us in difficult positions. I'm not really sure we can do anything. Or if we should."

"And I'm not one hundred percent certain it's true," I said.

"Close enough," Joe said.

The women, needles flying, darted glances around the circle at one another. Joe knit steadily and studied the floor.

"If he found people worth blackmailing, no question we can find them, too," Mel said. "But it'll take time, and snooping around like that might make us no better than Emmett."

"No. So let's turn the problem over and study its reverse," I said. "We won't look for his victims. We'll look for his patterns."

"I love it," Debbie said. "Sample, sample, sample. Ivy's weaving mantra. We look at Emmett like a tricky design problem and we work out the solution by constructing samples. What if, what if, what if."

"We'll need information," Mel said.

I held up my thumb drive. "Files galore." I looked at Joe again. "They're, um, uncensored."

"Only makes sense," he said. "You'll give us access?"

"Yes. Absolutely."

He snorted, almost smiled. Ruth showed the only reluctance. She might have been the only one with sense. They all listened to my summary of the data on hand. They nodded when I pointed out the gaps. Only Ruth asked a question.

"You realize you might stir up a murderer? And it might be someone we know?"

"Every murderer is probably somebody's old friend," Thea said. "That's not me. That's Agatha Christie, queen of mystery."

I made eye contact with each of the others. All nodded.

I made arrangements to copy the files onto flash drives and distribute them. Ernestine insisted I take the needles and yarn so I could finish the hat. Mel mouthed "no slackers." Ruth caught my eye and I waited for her outside the workroom.

"I can't be part of this," she said when we were alone in the hall. "For the sake of Homer's position. I hope you understand."

"I do. Can I ask you not to tell him, though?"

She hesitated before answering, and I liked her for that. "I won't unless I see a need to. And, Kath? Be very careful."

"Yes. Absolutely."

I couldn't find Geneva. She didn't answer when I went back to Granny's study and called, didn't shimmer into sight when I stood listening. I looked around the store, didn't know what else to do. I finally left, wondering if taking a ghost to town had been like letting loose an unknown virus. When I got to my car, Joe was leaning against it, sans knitting.

"Well, aren't you the mysterious man of many talents? A regular Renaissance burglar."

"Funny, Ivy never mentioned your rapier sarcasm."

"It's my secret weapon. She rarely saw it. Did you want something?"

"Couple of things," he said. "Why don't I copy the files? Save you time and trouble."

"I don't know." It suddenly felt as though we were negotiating something. A trade? A truce? "What else?"

"I want to search the cottage. With your permission."

"With my permission. And with my help."

Chapter 31

We agreed he'd come over at six. With a pizza.

"You have the files backed up in case there's a problem?" he asked.

"Yes, and for another kind of backup, I'm going to let Ardis know you're coming over."

"Good idea," he said, without any sign he was insulted by that precaution.

I handed him the flash drive and hoped Ardis' and Granny's trust in him was merited. I drove back to the cottage wondering if a ghost could be trusted at all.

Bees buzzed in the lavender by the doorstep. The lavender's spice brushed my nose as I passed. I unlocked the door and stepped into hell.

The smell hit me first. Vomit. And worse. I should have run back out, would have, but I saw Nicki lying half in, half out of the pantry. In a pool of bloody vomit. I added my own vomit to the floor, then went to her. Knelt beside her. No pulse. No breath. Cold, cold, cold. But she must be alive, because out of the corner of my eye her leg moved. Slithered. Rattled? Not her leg. What . . . oh dear God.

The world shrank to the size of a snake. The world didn't have to shrink far. It was a big snake. A big, provoked, diamond-patterned snake and, as close as we were—me kneeling and it coiling, me shaking and it rattling, me staring into its black, black, unblinking, bottomless eyes—things didn't look good for us ending up buddies.

The strike was like lightning. The bite like fire. My scream would have been endless, but a gray cloud descended, surrounding me, driving the snake away.

"Even the meanest snakes can't abide me. It's very sad," Geneva said.

I started to cry.

"It's not that sad. *I* don't much care for *them*."

She hummed "Shall We Gather at the River?" and I wondered how long before I slipped under those waters and didn't have to listen to her anymore.

"Oh, but I have good news. Perhaps I should have mentioned it first. Em and I watched a television documentary about surviving wilderness medical emergencies, so I know exactly what to do for snakebite. For some species, unfortunately, that isn't much. I wish I remembered which ones. But the important thing is to remain calm. So you close your eyes and think peaceful thoughts while I keep all the snakes away."

"All?"

"Three or four, it's hard to say. Close your eyes. Don't worry. I'm here."

I did close my eyes, but only so I wouldn't see three or four snakes sizing me up.

"You're dying more neatly than Em did or this poor girl must have."

Oh my God, how had I forgotten Nicki? Lying right there in her own . . . "Talk to me about something nice? Please?"

"I'll tell you about Em. He was darling, though he really wasn't much to look at. He had ginger hair and it stuck up here and there in funny places because of cowlicks. And he had a bald spot right on top. And I imagine his breath was fairly awful on account of his teeth. But if you ignored his teeth, he had the sweetest smile, and he never said a harsh word to me." She sighed at the happy memory of a rancid blackmailer who never knew she existed.

"Where did you go this afternoon? How did you get home?"

"I went to look for the horses in case you'd lied. But you were right and that made me sad, so I sat by myself in the backseat of your car. I didn't feel like talking on the drive home. You're not dying very fast, are you? How do you feel?"

Not so bad. I opened my eyes a crack. I was huddled against the shelves just inside the pantry. Nicki lay beside me. I closed my eyes again. "Where are the snakes?"

"The far corner. They'll stay."

I gulped air and opened my eyes again, turning them and my hands, by slow degrees, to assess the damage to my hip where the snake had struck, peeling my jeans open, inching them down to investigate the horror, the swelling, the blackening flesh, the . . . lifesaving, snake-bitten phone in my pocket? Surprisingly, it still worked.

Both Dunbars arrived about six. Clod first, in response to my 911 call, looking wary and with a seriously overdone bandage on his nose. Then Joe, wild-eyed, with a spinach-mushroom pizza, seconds behind the ambulance.

Nicki didn't need the EMTs. Neither did I, but for a different reason. I had a bruise where the snake slammed into the phone, but that was all. There were a lot of questions. For Clod, the broken window in the pantry and the cloth bag under Nicki's body answered two. I couldn't help with many others and when I told him I didn't agree with his answers, he turned my new philosophy against me.

"Why not? Window's broken, she's here, snakes are

here, cloth bag is an approved way to carry snakes, snakes bite. Simple."

Simple didn't explain *why*. I didn't have the energy to argue. Nobody was happy about the snakes.

I closed my eyes when the EMTs pulled the zipper on the long black bag and carried the bag out. When I opened them again, Joe stood at the pantry door, eyeing the snakes.

"You really think she brought them with her in that bag?" he asked. "Weird the way they stay in the corner. Maybe I can scoop them up with a shovel. Put them in a box or something."

"I can get them with my gun," Clod said.

"You are not shooting snakes in this house," I said.

"I know what we do," said Joe. "Ruth told me Homer has one of the Smoky Carlins working for him. They're snake handlers."

Clod's answer was a sneer. Then he shrugged. "Sure. Better him than me. Hell of a thing to happen is all I can say."

Clod took the pizza, which neither Joe nor I had the stomach for, and he left to search Nicki's apartment. Joe, one eye on the snakes still huddling in the far corner of the pantry, quietly cleaned the floor where Nicki had lain and I'd added my own contribution. I sat at the kitchen table, arms wrapped around my knees, which I'd pulled to my chest. No way were my feet touching the floor, ever, until Geneva could tell me all the snakes were gone. I wasn't sure I trusted anyone else to know.

"You all right?" Joe asked.

I felt as though I'd been beaten by sticks for days on end. "I didn't know there were snake handlers around here."

"A few congregations. Mostly in the mountains." He came and sat opposite me, propping his forehead on the heels of his hands. "What was she doing? What in God's name was she thinking?"

"Was she searching for something Emmett left? That's what you were going to do."

"With snakes? I don't know. Doesn't feel right."

Nothing about any of it felt right. "We need to call Ardis and Debbie and Mel and the rest. Call off the posse."

"Why?" His surprise surprised me.

"Killer snakes? What if Nicki didn't bring them? What if she just found them? Ruth warned us we might stir up a murderer. I can't put anyone else's life at risk. Who knows what might be next?"

"Hold on," he said. "Slow down. Nicki was dead at least an hour before you found her. The EMTs were talking about it. You didn't hear that?"

"I was trying not to and I'm not sure I want to hear it now, either."

"Hey, shhh, now, shhh. It's going to be okay. Carlin will be here soon. He'll catch the snakes. I'll get that window boarded up. It's going to be okay. But I need to tell you what the EMTs said. It isn't nice to hear, but it's important. She didn't die right away. And probably not from the bite. Not from the venom in the way you'd think. Although a bite in the face like that . . . anyway, they think she had an allergic reaction. That she died of anaphylactic shock. And if she hadn't been alone and hadn't panicked, she might've survived that, too, because most people do survive snakebites. But what all this means is that she was bitten and in extremis at least an hour before you talked to anybody at the meeting. She probably came here soon after she left the Cat. So this has nothing to do with the posse. Nothing to do with Em's blackmail."

"But then what *does* it have anything to do with? What was she doing?"

"Scaring you? Warning you? She knew you were over at the house this morning with Ardis and Cole."

"But why? Nicki and snakes? They don't go together. And warning me about what?"

"That would be the danger in unfinished or cryptic messages," he said.

"That and innocent bystanders ending up dead."

"But was Nicki either innocent or a bystander?"

Clod had the answer to that when he called from her apartment.

Chapter 32

"I believe we've solved ourselves a crime wave." That drawled gloat was Clod's way of saying hello on the phone. "Your Ms. Keplinger's been a busy little body," he said, being his usual offensive self. He also didn't bother to listen for reactions or questions that might come from my end. "As soon as Carlin's been by for the snakes, I'd like you to come on over here and take a look. I just might have found your tapestry for you. Oh, and hey, ask Carlin if he wrangles cats in his spare time. She's got a mean one. I'd like to shoot *it*."

When Carlin did show, I was disappointed. He brought more cloth bags. I wanted something made out of six-inch steel with an industrial padlock.

"Don't that beat all," he said when he saw the snakes behaving themselves in the corner of the pantry. "Next time take a broom and sweep them into something like a garbage can. That's all you need."

"I thought about scooping them with a shovel," Joe said.

"That would work, too. No need to call me, really. Look at them sitting there so meek and mild. What's the matter, fellers?" he crooned to the snakes. "Did you get yourselves spooked by all the big bad commotion? Look at you. I can just come on in there and pick you up."

"Please don't," I said.

"I'll go get the catching stick, then," he said.

"Why didn't he bring that in to begin with?" I whispered to Joe when Carlin went back to his truck.

"Because I think he *can* just pick them up," Joe said.

Even with the stick, I couldn't bear to watch and went into the parlor. Geneva, relieved of her guard duty, floated in after me.

"There were only three snakes, not four," she said, "and that man stroked the biggest one on the back of its head. I would rather have a kitten. Did you know your life is almost as exciting as reruns of *Hawaii Five-0*? What shall we do next?"

"I have to go to Nicki's. Can you stay here, keep an eye on the place?"

"Shhh," she said.

"What?"

"Shhh. Your gentleman friend is standing behind you wondering to whom you are speaking."

I turned around, no doubt looking as off-kilter as I'd sounded, but figuring it didn't matter. It was that kind of evening.

"Carlin's gone," Joe said. "Strange guy. Put the snakes in the bags, put the bags in a foam cooler, and carried them out like he'd stopped by the Quickie Mart for a twelve-pack and ice."

I wondered how long it would be before the idea of setting foot inside the Quickie Mart quit giving me the yips.

"I called Ardis," he said.

"Oh God. Thank you. Poor Ardis."

"Yeah. There wasn't any easy way to put it. Um, did you want me to stay here while you go to Nicki's?"

"Hm? Oh. No." I didn't explain, but when he said maybe he should drive, I let him.

———

Nicki lived in a nondescript block of apartments set down in a vacant lot between two graceful Victorian houses. Her unit was on the first floor, on the back side, looking out on a gravel parking lot edged in weeds.

"Did you know she had a cat?" I asked as we got out of the truck.

"No."

Clod opened the front door before we knocked and it was obvious as soon as we stepped inside that we didn't know much about Nicki at all. The door opened directly into the living room. It took a gentle prod from Joe to make my feet carry me beyond the sill. It took another gloat from Clod before I quit gaping.

"Case closed and tied with a bow," he said.

Every inch of the room was dedicated to the art and life of Ivy McClellan. Every item in it. Photographs of Granny papered the walls. Granny at the Cat, at the grocery store, weeding the garden, drinking coffee and laughing at Mel's. Shots that could only have been taken without Granny's knowledge through her own windows. There were a tapestry loom, dyestuff, wool, yarns. Spare loom parts and bundles of goldenrod hanging from the ceiling. A cheap, machine-manufactured kilim on the floor. Shelves of books. And notebooks. It wasn't a mirror image of Granny's weaving room. More like a distillation of its essence.

"Freaking obsessed," Clod said.

"Obsessed, maybe," I said, "but it looks like more than that, too. Like infatuation. Adoration, even."

"Even beyond that," Joe said. He was flipping through a couple of the notebooks, comparing entries between them. "I think she was trying to *be* Ivy."

"And that, Ms. Rutledge," Clod said, "even you have to admit is plain crazy."

I didn't argue.

Many of the notebooks were Granny's, taken from the house, maybe from the attic study at the Cat, as well. I took the two Joe had, under the pretense of comparing them myself, and then gathered the rest. The secret dye journals were almost certainly still safely hidden at the Cat. Granny was careful and cagey and Nicki probably hadn't looked for them because she hadn't known they existed. But she'd been looking for *some* part of Granny. Piecing her together. Did she think by taking, absorbing, re-creating, she could become Granny? Was she collecting mementos or was she collecting talismans because she was aware of "inklings and quiet understandings"? Where had her obsession come from? And was it horrible of me to be relieved that she was gone?

"Deputy Dunbar, may I take my grandmother's notebooks with me?"

He agreed and also let me roll the tapestry and the cartoon. I wanted to pore over every detail of her painting, to see Blue Plum as she loved it and planned to weave it, but I needed to do it in privacy. In that quick search, I didn't find the memory cards or flash drive. But Joe found Granny's birthday card to me. I turned it over and found her sketch of Maggie balancing a birthday candle on her head.

"I wonder what the present was. She said she was sending it, but then . . . I thought I'd find it at the house."

"A blue jacket she made to match your eyes," Joe said. "Sorry, I read the card before I realized it was yours. Do you think Nicki took the jacket, too?"

I knew she had and I meant to get it back. But I also suddenly knew she'd taken something else. "Where's the cat?"

Maggie, Granny's sweet kitty, took a swipe at Clod, either because he'd locked her in the bathroom or on general principle. She purred and rubbed against Joe's legs. We took her back to the cottage, along with the missing lint brush, the cat food, and the cat pan that usually sat beside the utility sink in Granny's basement. Maggie tolerated the drive, curled on the seat next to Joe. But after he boarded up the window in the pantry, rubbed her white chin one more time, and left, she was one unhappy cat. She vocalized every nuance of her opinion of me, letting me know it hadn't changed, wasn't likely to, and that she thought even less of Geneva.

"I thought I wanted a kitten, but that cat isn't any friendlier than the snakes," Geneva said, as Maggie yowled. "Did it belong to the tetchy old lady who killed my darling Em?"

"Yes, and please don't say that again. That tetchy old lady was my grandmother and she did not kill Em, who may have been yours, but who was not darling."

"Then who did?"

Good question. Unfortunately, the threads of it were so tangled in my head by then I couldn't think them straight. Nicki pretty obviously broke into Granny's house and had no qualms about helping herself to memories, literally and figuratively. But murder? Would she kill? Maybe Joe was wrong and Emmett *had* blackmailed her. But Max? Had he surprised her at the house, so she killed him? Or did he try his inherited blackmail on her and she hit back? But why break in here? To take whatever I had of Granny's in my suitcase? After seeing her apartment, maybe I could believe that, but snakes? Where would she get snakes like that? And why? But, if she didn't bring them, who did?

"Who killed him?" Geneva asked again.

I didn't know. Didn't know if I could, in good conscience, ask the posse for help sorting out this mess or if I should disband it.

"Who murdered my darling?"

"I don't know," I snapped.

"You're as tetchy as an old lady yourself."

"And you're a tetchy ghost. Would you like to look at this with me?" I unrolled the tapestry cartoon and laid it on the kitchen table.

"Not if you're going to be that way."

"What way?" I looked up, looked around, didn't see her. "Oh, fine. Go off and pout or wax or whatever. That only proves my point." I smoothed the canvas, traced a line along the edges of the triangles making up the border. "You should come see this, though. It's something beautiful and good to counteract all the horrors." But she didn't answer and I had the painting to myself. That suited me and I stood at the table, head bowed, in communion with Granny's memory and her vision of Blue Plum.

The triangles of the border were mountain ridges, shading from green to blue to deep purple and back again. And within that sheltering border of mountains, Blue Plum lay before me, spread out like a picture map, with Main Street running through the center from side to side and tree-lined secondary streets carrying me the rest of the way around town. Individual buildings were recognizable and I felt I could walk past the library and post office. I stopped to look at the courthouse. A train chugged down the tracks a few blocks beyond Main. I wandered into the town park and along the creek and then I realized there was another whole level of detail to peer at. It was ten thirty by the courthouse clock. The door of the Weaver's Cat stood open. And there were tiny vehicles and people. A fisherman in the creek. A woman walking a dog past the bank. A tourist in the pillory on the courthouse lawn. A woman handing something to a thin splinter of a man in front of Granny's house.

If I'd had a magnifying glass, if I could have tumbled

straight into that picture to see for myself, I knew that man's ginger hair would be standing up in funny tufts because of cowlicks and that he had a bald spot. And the paper Granny was handing him would have one word written on it. "Deed."

Chapter 33

On some level of sleep-deprived consciousness, I knew it was ironic that I was being haunted that night, but not by the ghost. By Granny's tapestry. By the tapestry I'd thought would bring me a sense of peace, would fill the hole in my heart. But the tiny figures in the cartoon wove their way through my troubled sleep. One figure in particular insinuated himself into every fitful and waking moment. That thin splinter of a man taking something from Granny. Not that there would have been much sleep, anyway. Maggie yowled the whole night long. When I finally did fall into an exhausted sleep, she bit my toes.

I called Joe in the morning and he came to take Maggie home with him. She leapt into his arms, purring. He rubbed her ears and glanced at the rerolled canvas on the kitchen table. When I didn't offer to show it to him, his eyebrows rose slightly but he didn't say anything. I told him I was calling the posse together for a meeting at the Cat at two for those who could make it. He said he might or might not, but he'd like to stop back by the cottage later for the search we'd never gotten around to. I agreed. Why not? How could it hurt, at this point? Maggie looked at me over his shoulder as he carried her to his truck. Thumbing her nose, I was pretty sure.

It turned into a morning of phone calls. Not surprising. And not surprising that Ardis was first.

"I am opening the shop this morning, like a normal day," she said, as though reciting a declaration. "And I am going to get through it. If I have to do it sleepwalking or with strong drink or with a stick of dynamite tied to my tail." She could have added that she would not falter and would not fail, but she was beginning to tear up. Before she fell apart or disconnected, I told her I'd be in to help.

After her call I made a pot of coffee to bolster my stamina. The Spiveys checked in before the first cup took effect.

"Terrible shame about Nicki," the Spivey on the line said. "We were glad to hear you weren't bit, too."

"Oh. Thank you."

"Shocking."

"It was horrible."

"Mm. Shocking," the Spivey repeated.

I nodded, which of course she couldn't hear.

"Thought you'd like to know we've found a few things in Emmett's boxes."

"You have? Anything we can use?"

"Oh, wait, there's Shirley yelling something. I better see what. I'll get back to you."

For a Spivey interaction, the call was oddly encouraging, if for no other reason than because it was so short. Ruth didn't call and I pictured her avoiding the phone so she wouldn't have to say she told me so. Homer did call.

"Kath, I am so sorry for all you went through yesterday. I've communicated with Deputy Dunbar and I agree with him that we need to look at recent events philosophically."

"Really? He said that?"

Homer coughed discreetly, no doubt communicating to me something about slander or manners. "The human condition is such that we crave answers, Kath. You hear in the news every day about people yearning for closure. But I don't think we need to spend time searching for the reasons this sad woman's life derailed so disastrously. There won't be a trial for her in a court of law, so we will let the dead bury the dead. It's enough to know she was responsible."

"Wait, for all of it? They say she killed Emmett and Max?"

"The authorities are satisfied she did."

"On the basis of what?" The tangled threads I'd tried to follow the night before weren't any less confusing this morning, but that only made me more certain that *no one* could be sure Nicki had killed anyone. "Homer, there are too many questions left. Surely you see that."

I heard the click of his pen. "I'm listening."

"The burglaries, yes. She derailed, sure. But not snakes. Not poison. Not killing. If you want to look at this philosophically, Nicki was obsessed with Granny, with creating something. Except for a couple of broken windows, she wasn't out to destroy anything."

"Go on."

"Okay, something more tangible? Less philosophical? The broken window at Granny's. That happened before the rain. You know that; you mopped up the water. But you also talked to Max in the morning, after the rain. Nicki must have been long gone before Max showed up at Granny's. And then the snakes. Where would she even get great huge rattlesnakes?" I shuddered. "And why?"

"So you think someone else brought the snakes? That still leaves us with why."

"Um." I'd been pacing. Now I sat. All this talk of snakes made me bring my feet up in the chair with me. "And with who. What if it was the guy who came and got them? Aaron Carlin. He made those snakes seem like pets."

"You saw him?"

"Yeah, and apparently his people are snake handlers, so he'd know where to get snakes. Plus, he's got some kind of record, right? But that still leaves us with why."

"It does and I'm going to suggest an answer. You might not like it but, as your lawyer, as your friend, I need to impress this upon you. I think the snakes were a warning that you should forget blackmail, forget murder, stop asking questions."

"But . . ."

"Kath, you've raised legitimate questions and I think you might be right. This isn't over. I want you to take the warning seriously and I'll speak to Deputy Dunbar.'

"No! No, Homer—what if he's involved?"

For several seconds all I heard was the clicking of his pen. "Well, I can't fault you now for not taking this seriously. All right, I'll go directly to Sheriff Haynes."

I didn't feel a whole lot better after hanging up.

"Why are you so glum? I'm the one who's dead." Geneva coalesced across from me at the kitchen table, damp and depleted.

"I'm arguing with my better judgment, trying to convince it I can't let a slithery warning keep me from finding out what happened. What about you? I thought you had some fun yesterday. You went to town. You enjoyed the shop. If I'd really been bitten by that snake, you would have saved my life by keeping me calm. And you almost got your wish to have a cat."

"My existence is a dreary pattern of yesterdays and that cat was a banshee."

"Well, the banshee's been banished and patterns can be altered."

"You have a pattern. You are up, then you are down, then you are up, and then you go down. Your dramas are exhausting." Said the Sarah Bernhardt of the spirit world.

"That's just my yo-yo life right now. I'm usually fairly content." It was nice to stop and remember that was true. Or it had been. When I had the job I loved. When I had the grandmother I loved. "Okay," I said, standing up and hoping that would reverse the downward yo the morning was traveling. "Phooey to better judgment. We've got patterns to explore and new pieces to examine. I'm spending the day at the Weaver's Cat. You, Ms. Sidekick, are welcome to come with me. Or mope here if you're too exhausted to help with the investigation."

"What's the point? Em is dead. I heard you say the police think Nicki poisoned him. I am in mourning." She put her head down on her wispy arms.

"Geneva? Honey? Listen to me. There is a point and it has to do with patterns. The point is, Nicki killing Em doesn't fit."

Ardis unlocked the Cat's door for us. Rather, for me. Geneva trailed behind as my personal, invisible rain cloud. I hadn't been sure she'd come with me and on the way into town she'd been uncommunicative except for a dismal moan or two. The shop drew her, though. Something about it agreed with her and she seemed to stretch and breathe more easily once we were there. Odd to say of a creature who didn't have any more need of breath than a limp dishrag.

"Do you know that today is Saturday?" Ardis asked. "I don't work on Saturdays. Debbie and Nicki work on Saturdays, and when Debbie came in and asked where Nicki is, I realized my mind is such a mess I hadn't even thought to call her and tell her what happened. Who am I kidding that I can pretend everything is normal? But Debbie's in the kitchen pulling herself together and we'll make this into a normal day if we have to beat it with sticks."

Geneva had draped herself over the chartreuse sweater

set again. They really did nothing for each other. But she perked up when Ardis mentioned beating with sticks and drifted closer.

"I'll give you the morning to pretend everything is normal," I told Ardis. "You and Debbie and I will play shopkeepers and live out a lovely fantasy that nothing has changed. It'll be good for us."

"Like a vacation from madness."

"And we need one. Oh, sister, do we need one. But let's close the shop this afternoon, in memory of Nicki."

She got weepy at that point but nodded.

"And for another reason. I'm assembling the posse and I need you and Debbie there."

She straightened her spine. "We will be."

"And me?" Geneva asked.

"Yes." Oops. I glanced at Ardis, but she took the extra affirmative in stride.

"Yes!" she repeated, pumping her fist. "Mild-mannered shopkeepers this morning. The posse rides this afternoon. We are here. We are strong. Time to open the door to our clamoring public. Get the lights, will you?"

Geneva followed me over to the light switches. "Warn her about the horses," she whispered. "She's large and excitable and I'd hate to see who she'll beat with sticks if you disappoint her the way you disappointed me."

The pattern of a small town reacting to tragedy is vivid with shock and sorrow. We should have known that would overwhelm the soothing morning we hoped for. News of Nicki's death, although not the details, spread and TGIF members and others stopped in to share their disbelief and offer comfort and memories. Geneva enjoyed the tears.

Platitudes and bromides were foremost, as might be expected, but a few snippets I overheard helped me begin to understand the pattern of Nicki's life. The most illuminating came from three women who staked out the comfy chairs nearest the counter and brought their work with them.

"I remember a skinny little girl, always following behind, trying to be like the big kids," the first said. She gave her drop spindle a twirl and let it fall, drawing out a fine thread of wool.

"Like a little moth fluttering around the brightest lights she could find," the second said as she measured the shawl she was knitting against her arm. "And she got burned a time or two."

"Bless her heart," the third said, glancing up from her cutwork. "Looking for someone or something to fill the holes that pitiful excuse of a family left."

Debbie caught me listening in. "They only come in on Saturdays," she whispered. "Ivy called them the Three Fates."

"What holes did her family leave?"

"More than holes, really," Debbie said. "The family pretty much disintegrated. Dad in and out of the picture. Mom with a string of boyfriends. Grandmother an alcoholic. They're all still around, but they never gave her what she needed. Nicki told me she finally found herself when she took a fiber arts class at the community college and met Ivy."

Halfway through the morning I received another interrupted report from the Spiveys. This time it was Shirley.

"Emmett Cobb was a boring man," she said, "but we're making progress. Mercy was a tad miffed when you hung up on her earlier. I told her what we've found is important enough we should try calling you again because no doubt you're distracted in your grief, the way Angie is now that she'll have to go out and join the workforce."

"Oh, well, I'm sorry to hear about Angie and I would like to hear what you've found."

"Can you hold a sec? Another call coming in."

I did hold and finally disconnected because she didn't come back. I decided that later I would run by Angie's. It would be better to see for myself what they'd found, anyway. Ardis saw me with my phone.

"Have you alerted the rest of the posse?" she asked quietly.

"Not yet."

"You call Ernestine and Joe. I'll call Mel and Thea. What time?"

"I did talk to Joe and told him two."

"Something else to think about, hon. Do we expand or stick to the original group? There's a lot of talent and ardor to draw on. And loyalty."

"I think we need to keep it small, keep it close."

"Keep it safe." Ardis said.

By one o'clock we were emotionally exhausted. Debbie locked the front door and we ate a quick lunch in the kitchen before heading up to the TGIF workroom.

"High noon would have been more appropriate than two o'clock," Geneva said on the way up the stairs. "You should have asked my advice."

I chose my words so they'd mean something to her *and* Ardis and Debbie. "Meeting first, showdown later." Big words and I hoped not foolish.

Chapter 34

Ardis, Ernestine, Debbie, Mel, and Thea sat facing me. Geneva insisted on standing next to me as loyal sidekick. Or hovering next to me. Whatever she did, her presence at my side didn't give me the sense of support she seemed to think it should. Joe hadn't showed up. He had delivered the flash drives to everyone, but the situation had changed, and that changed the data of some of the questions we needed to answer.

"You're on, hon," Ardis said.

"Wait." Debbie went across the hall and came back pushing a large whiteboard on wheels. "There—now we're an incident room." She handed me a marker and eraser and sat back down.

"Don't blow it," Geneva stage-whispered.

I abandoned the notebook I'd planned to use for my visual aids. Breathed in, breathed out, faced the inspiring expanse of the board, and wrote four words: *pattern, construction, connection, access.* "This is what I've been thinking about since, um, since the incident last night. We're looking for patterns and we're constructing a picture. We're looking for how the patterns and the pieces of the picture are connected, the way the separate sections of a tapestry are sometimes joined together."

They nodded.

"And we're looking at access. How did Emmett gain access to people's secrets? Who had access to poison? And access to the cottage so the poisoned bottle of gin could be left where Emmett would find it? Who had access to the information that Max Cobb was back in town? Who had access to snakes? The police believe all of that is down to Nicki. That it's over. I don't. Her pattern of collecting, amassing, obsessing doesn't fit."

"Why not?" Thea asked. "Devil's advocate, but Emmett was collecting secrets. So how is that different?"

"You're right. Nicki's pattern is similar to Emmett's. They were both collecting. Creating something. Nicki was creating something extremely weird, to the point that Joe thinks she was trying to *be* Granny, not just enshrine her. But she *was* creating. The murderer's pattern is one of destruction."

"But, oh, this is awful to think, but what if Nicki didn't really find Ivy when she died?" Debbie asked. "What if she killed her?"

I stared at Debbie. Her question was a complete sucker punch and left me almost gagging. Nicki kill Granny? Why hadn't I thought of that?

"No." Ardis came around the table and put a steadying hand on my shoulder. "No. Definitely not part of the pattern. Nicki did find Ivy. She would not have killed her. She couldn't have killed her. Nicki was in the shop with me the entire morning. Ivy was at home. She got up out of bed and dropped to the floor and no, the attack was not induced by digitalis or any other means. Her old heart plain gave out. No one killed Ivy. Trust me." She stayed there with her hand on my shoulder.

"This is all worth talking through, though," I said, when I was breathing normally again. "Debbie's question is exactly the kind of thing we need to look at. But first I want to show you something else. I'm going to rearrange these words and add one more." I erased them, then rewrote them in a column, this time with *construction* and *connection* sharing a line:

> *Pattern*
> *Access*
> *Construction, connection*
> *Trust*

"P.A.C.T. Corny, huh? But each of us needs to be clear on this. Whatever secrets we dig up, whatever personal information we discover, none of it goes any further than this group unless it has to go to the police. Agreed? If not, now's the time to leave the group, same as Ruth did yesterday, and no hard feelings."

They sat there, calm and serious, eyes on me and not gauging one another's intent. Each of them nodded. Except Geneva. She'd draped herself over a corner of the whiteboard looking like a bored teenager.

"Guns would be more exciting," she said. "Trust me."

She yawned ostentatiously, then drifted out of the room. I had to remind myself not to roll my eyes or tsk. Instead, I held up the rolled canvas.

"This is the design for the tapestry I told you Granny was working on. The one missing from the house."

"Nicki took it?" Ardis asked.

"Mm-hmm. Maybe she planned to weave it herself. I don't know. Anyway, if you had a chance to read the files on your flash drive, you know what this is and what it meant to Granny. What you don't know is what she told me in a message she left on my phone a couple of days before she died. She said, 'It is what it is, a bit of a puzzle.' I thought she meant she was having trouble with the design. That it wasn't turning out the way she planned. Now I think she meant that it is literally a puzzle. Take a look." I unrolled it on the table.

"Oh law," Ardis said. "I might cry. I surely might."

"No time for tears," Ernestine said. "I've brought my magnifying loupe. Let's see what we've got."

"You want to give a hint what we're looking for?" Mel asked.

"No. I want to see if you see the same thing I did. It's what kept me awake last night." I watched as they examined the painting inch by inch. Mel laughed when she found the little purple Mel on Main Street. Ardis touched the open door of the Weaver's Cat.

"Oh my." Ernestine looked up. "Perhaps I have an unfair advantage with my loupe." She took the hands-free magnifier from around her neck and passed it to Thea. "Did you count him six times?"

"Eight."

"Nine," Ardis said. "In case you missed one, he's hiding near the culvert in the creek. Nine nasty Emmett Cobbs in the Blue Plum tapestry. It sounds like a vile children's rhyme."

"I like the one in the pillory," Mel said. "Serves him right. Kind of elaborate, though, isn't it? Ivy was always straight up. Why not just turn him in to the cops instead of turning him into a tapestry?"

"Or leave a simple, written record?" I asked. "I wondered the same thing. But remember, she hadn't told anyone anything so far. Not Ardis, not me, not her lawyer. We might never know why she didn't."

"But we do know she didn't expect to die when she did," Debbie said. "And she could always go back and take Emmett out of the tapestry later, if things changed."

"Or not put him in," I said. "This is only the cartoon and she'd only woven the lower border. We don't know that she really planned to weave him in. But I think maybe she did. I think she didn't say anything because she didn't know who to say it to and she was worried about other victims. Or other repercussions."

"It's a beautiful painting," Ernestine said. "And quite wicked, too."

"Okay, I've changed my mind. This is exactly like Ivy," Mel said. "Because the more you look, the more you see, and the richer the story she's telling. It's Blue Plum in all its grime and glory. Look, there's a Dumpster. Hah! And those are Emmett's legs sticking out of it, like he's Dumpster diving."

"He was," Ardis said. "You can bet he was, like a rat sneaking through people's garbage. And do you see him there, at the post office? A year or so ago he was in the habit of stopping by here each morning for a bit of a gossip and before he'd leave he'd offer to drop the mail by the post office for us."

"Only maybe he took the mail home for a look-see first," Debbie said.

I felt a chill down my left arm, and not just from the perfidious activities of Emmett. I glanced over. Geneva was back and staring at the cartoon, as absorbed as we were.

"This is the evil blackmail edition of *Where's Waldo?*" Thea said, ever the librarian.

"It's a Tennessee stack cake," Mel said. "Layer upon layer upon layer and each one hiding a secret filling."

"It's full of hiding places for the darling little Em," Geneva said. "Like the secret hiding places he had at our house."

"What?"

"Secret hiding places. At our house."

"Are you kidding? Why didn't you tell me?" I asked. Well, shouted.

Chapter 35

My shout was followed by silence. But only from the living humans in the room. The dead one took vociferous offense. It was all I could do not to cringe and cover my ears. Pretending to cough or sneeze wasn't going to cover this slipup. It was barely possible Mel thought my "Are you kidding? Why didn't you tell me?" was directed at her remark about stack cake. Except I'd been looking at Geneva, to my left, and the only thing visible in that direction was a dressmaker's dummy standing in the corner.

"Don't shout at me!" Geneva said, trying in vain to stamp her foot. "You frightened the tar out of me!"

"Hon?" Ardis asked. More questions than "Hon?" lurked behind her worried eyes. Behind all their eyes. It was a *tableau vivant* of concerned friends.

Except for Geneva, who continued to flounce and huff. "How rude! Why, if you were Opie Taylor, I'd take you over my knee."

I took refuge in squeezing my eyes shut and offering a blanket apology and mostly accurate excuse. "Sorry. I'm sorry. It's the lack of sleep. I'm just going a little crazy with all of this."

"Well," Geneva said. "Hmph."

Ardis touched my cheek. "Honey, you go on home. Take a nap. One of us will bring the cartoon by later."

The others murmured agreement and made kind, shooing motions. Interestingly, Geneva picked up on their concern and she started crooning a lullaby. It was a little eerie. Still, her soft alto was an improvement over her shrill scolding. She followed me back down the stairs, but before we were out of earshot I heard Ardis say, not as quietly as she thought, "More like Ivy every day. Uncanny, isn't it?"

On the way home Geneva continued to croon her lullaby about murk gathering and shadows creeping. It suited my mood so I didn't ask her to stop.

Back in the cottage, I went to the parlor and sat on the sofa.

"Come sit down," I said, patting the place next to me. She floated over and tucked herself in at the opposite end. I scooched around and tucked my feet up, too, so we were facing each other like a couple of gal pals. I wanted this to be as friendly as possible so that I wouldn't alarm her again.

"What about your nap?" she asked.

"I don't really need a nap. I'm sorry I shouted. I wasn't angry. I just had a eureka moment, is all, and got overexcited. Tell me about Emmett's hiding places."

"What's so important about them? The man who packed Em's belongings and took them away found most of the places."

"Oh." I tried not to sound too disappointed. "Did you ever see what Em hid in them?"

"Mostly money. In books. Behind pictures. Under the mattress. Darling Em was a traditionalist that way."

"Do you know who the man was who found the money?"

"No. He favored Em, with ginger hair, but he did not introduce himself to me."

Max, probably. I wondered how much he found squirreled away. By then I was almost certain he knew where the money had come from.

"Wait, you said he only found most of the hiding places?"

"He missed my favorite one, but all Em put in it was boring papers. No money." She unfurled herself and floated over to the newel post at the bottom of the staircase. "It's hollow. The cap comes off."

It didn't come off easily. A push-button, spring-loaded, release latch would have been convenient. Or a crowbar. I couldn't get a good grip on it and gave up tugging. Thought of options. Ruth would have tools somewhere at the site. Ardis had tools at the Cat. Snake Man Carlin had tools in his truck. Joe was coming by later and he undoubtedly had a full array of sneaky tools. Ah, but so did I.

I smiled at my homeowner's combination fireplace weapon and tool rack. I patted my friend the poker, and picked up its soul mate, the shovel. The shovel's edge fit perfectly into the slim space between the post and the cap and with a little levering action did the trick.

Down inside the long, hollow space was a cloth-wrapped bundle.

Then I made a difficult decision. I didn't pull the bundle out. I called the posse and invited them for supper.

Thea brought Ernestine, I was glad to see. Ardis, Debbie, and Mel arrived separately. Joe hadn't said when he'd be over. When I called the others, I called him, too, but had to leave a message. It was cryptic, but considering what might be in the bundle, that seemed safest. He still hadn't showed by the time we finished eating.

Geneva and I had anticipated their gaggle of questions.

"How could you stand to wait?"

"How did you ever think to look in there?"

"How did you get the top off?"

"How do you know Emmett put it in?"

"How about a tad bit more chili?"

Our prearranged answers satisfied them: I waited because I wanted a photographic record and witnesses for removing and opening the bundle. To make the waiting easier, I made a pot of chili, putting my squeamishness to the test by running to the Quickie Mart for the fixings. I looked in the newel because I'd heard stories about people finding house plans in them and seeing this one prompted my favorite question—what if? I demonstrated my pry-shovel for them, earning delighted "oh mys" from Debbie and Ernestine. I couldn't be sure the bundle was Emmett's, but I could bet. Ardis and Mel had seconds on the chili.

While Ardis stood ready with my camera, I reached my hand into the hollow post. Felt cloth. Flashed back to cloth bags and snakes and yanked my hand back out so fast . . .

"Big baby," Geneva said. "Hush. There aren't any snakes."

"Did I scream?"

"We all did," Mel said. "Need a steadier hand?"

"No, I'm okay." I reached in and pulled out a pillowcase containing, and folded around, something the size and heft of several copies of the *Blue Plum Bugle*. Nothing inside wriggled. I held the bundle out, sitting on my palms, to give perspective. The camera made its soft click and whir. The women were silent. I looked at Geneva floating back and forth behind Mel and Thea.

"Storm coming," she said. "Thunder in the distance."

They cleared the kitchen table. I put the bundle in the center. We all stared at it.

"So, here we are," Mel said. "Six weird sisters."

Seven, if she counted the really weird sister who couldn't seem to settle and kept floating back and forth between the table and the window.

"And it's starting to rain," said Thea. "So open it and let's get this over with before the night turns nasty."

I unrolled the pillowcase and drew out a curled stack of a dozen or so manila envelopes on top of a flexible black plastic binder. I flattened the stack on the table and we saw a name printed in neat half-inch letters in the middle of the top envelope. *Joe Dunbar.*

"Oh, now," Debbie said and stopped, her hand to her mouth.

"Do they all have names?" Ardis asked.

"If they do, I'm not sure all of us need to know them," Debbie said.

"Second thoughts are okay," I said. "Debbie, would you rather leave? I meant what I said this afternoon. No hard feelings. I dragged you into this without warning and without knowing where we'd end up."

"No, I'll stay. I'm just saying, if these are all blackmail victims, there might be more names we recognize. And we don't need to know, the next time we see one of them, that she had some private sorrow or shame that Emmett Cobb found out and was mean enough to hold over her head. Or his."

Ardis took over. "All right, here's what we'll do. Everyone sit. Kath, you look at the names on the envelopes. If Ivy's name is on one, you open it. That'll settle the blackmail question right there. We'll decide the next step after that. Simple."

"Simple." I sat down at the head of the table and pulled the stack toward me. "But I'm going to take pictures of each envelope. I want a complete record. I'll destroy the record when I know this is settled." I propped the envelopes on my knees, leaning the stack of them against the table like an easel. I took two pictures of the envelope with Joe's name, briefly wondered where he was, then flipped that one toward me. I was glad not to recognize the next name.

Geneva came and hovered over my shoulder. "Em loved these envelopes," she said. "Sometimes he'd sit and smile and stroke them the way I would stroke a kitten if I had one and if it didn't scream like a banshee."

It was hard to ignore the ick factor of the first part of that remark. I continued flipping through the envelopes and taking two pictures of each. Most of the names meant nothing to me. Flip, click, click. Flip, click, click. The seventh name was a Baptist preacher from out in the county. The name after that was a photographer for the *Bugle*. Then nothing, nothing, nothing, and then *Ivy McClellan*.

"What?" Mel asked.

"I thought I was prepared for it." I pressed my lips together, didn't lift my eyes from that envelope.

"Kath, honey, take your time," Ardis said. "Open it and read it and don't think you have to tell anyone else what's in it. But if it is blackmail, we need to call Homer and tell him to come out here. Tonight. So we can prove to him this is real."

"Ardis is right," Ernestine said, and the others agreed.

I nodded, made myself take two pictures of Granny's envelope. Then I tucked it under my arm, not wanting to let it go, while I quickly photographed and flipped the rest. Until I got to the last envelope.

"Or maybe he already knows it's real." I put the last envelope faceup on the table, Homer's name in the center. "Now what?"

Chapter 36

"Follow the plan. Open Ivy's envelope," Ardis said. "If it isn't blackmail, if it isn't any of our business, we burn the lot and go home."

"And if it is blackmail, do I call Homer and ask him why he told me it couldn't be blackmail? Why he told me not to mention blackmail to Cole Dunbar? Why I shouldn't even breathe the word?"

"He obviously has something to lose, too," Mel said. "Maybe you should cut him some slack."

"That's just it," I said. "How much does he have to lose? Someone killed Emmett and then Max and maybe didn't mean to kill me, but did end up killing Nicki. Someone with so much to lose that committing murder was a better deal."

"It could be any one of those others," Thea said.

"Maybe."

"Here comes good luck," Geneva said, from the window. "It's the twins, blowing in on the gale."

"Oh good God almighty! Hide the envelopes and don't tell them what we're doing," I said.

The others stared at me. As well they should. They hadn't heard Geneva.

"Er, um, it's the Spiveys," I explained. "You know how sometimes you can recognize the sound of someone's car?" I held up a finger as though listening, then nodded.

On cue, someone knocked and thunder clapped. "That'll be them now. I'll just get the door if one of you wouldn't mind hiding the envelopes."

"We saw the cars, so we knew you were home," Shirley said.

"Filthy night for a party," said Mercy. "What's the occasion?"

"We're planning Nicki's memorial service," Ernestine said. "It's so good of you to come out on a night like this to contribute toward the catering and musicians. How much shall I put you down for, seventy-five or one hundred?"

The twins had been shaking water from their coats, onto the floor, preparatory to settling in among us. When they heard Ernestine's question they stopped in mid-shake and put their coats back on.

"We just stopped in passing to make sure Kath is all right after her ordeal yesterday," Shirley said.

Mercy leaned in too close for olfactory comfort. "And to tell you we've found irregularities in certain bank statements."

"Emmett's?"

"Not now," she whispered, nodding sideways toward the group at the table at the same time Shirley whispered, "Max's."

"But did you at least bring them? May I see them?"

"They're somewhere safe," Shirley whispered, rubbing the spot on her ribs that Mercy's elbow had found.

"You came all this way. In this weather. But you didn't bring them."

"Rain's coming down harder, too," Mercy said, "so we'd best run along and hope the creeks don't rise."

I wanted to shake them by their scruffs until they told me what was in Max's bank statements and where they were, but Shirley got the door open, Mercy slipped my grasp, rain and wind blew in, and the twins escaped.

"Spiveys," Ernestine spat after I'd slammed the door.

"What was that all about?" Mel asked.

"Independent corroboration," I said. "Irritating and incomplete, but promising. If I ever get to see it. It sounds like it might be proof that Max figured out what Emmett was up to and started making his own demands."

"They're up to something," Ardis said. "I don't know what and I can't hold back any longer. I told you so."

"You did. But they would have snooped through Emmett's boxes, anyway. This way at least we know where Emmett's boxes are and that the twins have expanded their snooping to Max's papers and they've found something useful."

"Unless they're lying," Ardis said.

"True."

"Or unless they plan to use the information for themselves somehow."

"Also true. And if they're playing games with whatever they've found, there's no telling how soon it'll blow up in their faces or turn around and bite them, or us, because they're not good at secrets and not exactly subtle. But we're several steps ahead of Shirley and Mercy, and we have seven good heads to their crackpot two."

"You can't count," Thea said. "We have six."

"I'll leave the counting to you, then, but ladies, the clock is ticking."

"And the lightning is getting closer," Geneva said from the window. There was a flash and she glowed eerily before the thunder crashed.

Ernestine stood up, blinking toward the window. "I would like to make a suggestion, then, as to how we should proceed. There is no more time for squeamishness. We'll adjourn to the parlor, where the sofa might be kinder to my old bones. Kath, you look through Ivy's envelope. Mel, Thea, Debbie, you examine the binder. Ardis and I will open Homer's envelope. And Kath, you keep the rest of the envelopes safe with you."

Mel scraped her chair back and stood up. "Let's do it."

Ernestine and Ardis took the sofa. Mel, Debbie, and Thea squeezed into the window seat. After a few settling murmurs, they started reading. I sat on the edge of the old recliner, as though it were a high diving board I was afraid to jump off. Déjà vu. I'd felt the same nerves, in this same chair, before reading Granny's letter. The words on the front of that envelope came back to me . . . *Make yourself comfortable, read this letter, and remember, always, I am your loving Granny.* I made myself sit back, breathe deeply, and remember her love.

The contents of Emmett's envelope were straightforward enough. So was my opinion of him after reading through them. He slithered on his belly like a reptile. He'd snooped and pried until he was convinced Granny had a sideline in hexing her neighbors. He offered no proof of ill will or of a hex succeeding. But he collected "evidence" consisting of rumors, no doubt the inklings and quiet understandings Granny had mentioned. He had photographs of plants in her garden and pages he somehow got hold of from one of her dye journals. These were some of her dye recipes using foxglove and aconite, both of which are poisonous, and both of which she grew. He was especially shrill in noting that, historically, aconite was used by witches in their "flying ointments." What baloney. Except she did say in her letter, *I'm a bit of what some people might call a witch.* Oh, Granny, you silly old thing.

But surely she hadn't worried that Emmett could destroy her business or her life in Blue Plum with talk of flying ointments. She was wiser than that, even if there were people who believed every tabloid report of devil worship or an Elvis sighting. So why had she caved when he demanded her house? Why hadn't she hooted with laughter? Or, if he thought she knew how to hex someone, why wasn't he afraid she'd hex *him*? Or why, if he wanted the house, had he agreed to let her live there as long as she wanted? In fact, there was no mention of the rent Max claimed was past due—just that the house became Emmett's upon her death or when she chose to leave it. What kind of blackmail demand was that? Were they both crazy?

"Damn," Mel said, looking up from the binder. "Who knew Emmett was such a . . ."

"Bastard?" I interrupted.

"Bloody genius," Thea said.

"Well, and a bastard, too," Mel agreed, "but the whole blackmail scheme was about creating a retirement plan."

"I beg your pardon?"

"It's all here. He wasn't shy about putting down the details. Says he lost his pension from the Westman plant when the plant and the pension fund went belly-up and Social Security wasn't going to let him live as comfortably as he wanted. That's why he was working at the Homeplace and living here, making ends meet for the time being. But he was also looking ahead to a time when he couldn't work, and he came up with this scheme to create his own enhanced Social Security by inviting certain community members to make private contributions."

"That's what he called it, an invitation to contribute?"

"Yeah. He makes it sound almost friendly. Says Ivy practically insisted he take her house, telling him, 'Cash is fine but you can't beat a mortgage-free roof over your head.'"

"They were both crazy," I said faintly. "But that's exactly what she would do. A cockeyed blackmailer and a cockeyed act of charity. Are the, um, the secrets, whatever he blackmailed people for, listed in the binder?"

"No, this is more or less a narrative and record of contributions," Mel said. "If all you read is the binder, you'd have no idea he was threatening anyone. He kept the secrets and corroborating evidence in the envelopes. And, although this is him telling it, it doesn't sound as though he was even particularly greedy. Fifty dollars a month from some, a hundred from others."

"Until he tapped Homer," Ardis said. "That's when he made his mistake."

"You're sure?" I asked.

"Oh, yeah," Thea said. "Emmett's stupid started showing when he hit on Homer. Homer's contributions were twice as much as the other contributions combined and Emmett said they'd make the difference between getting by in Blue Plum and living high in Hilton Head."

Rain drummed on the cottage's tin roof and I heard Geneva singing her murk-and-gloom lullaby in the kitchen. It might have been a cozy evening in with friends.

"Homer's secret is worth killing for?" I asked.

"Homer isn't even Homer," Ardis said. "He's Dewey Tarwid. He's from Pikeville, Kentucky. Here's a picture Emmett took of Dewey Junior, who works at a gas station in Pikeville and has a child of his own. Homer's daddy died in jail. Homer barely graduated high school."

"Max got back from Kentucky the morning he was killed," I said.

"Checking out Emmett's story for himself?" Debbie asked.

"Sounds like," Thea said.

"But law school?" I asked. "The accent?"

"Dewey shook off the dust of Pikeville and never looked back," Ardis said. "Took himself to Atlanta, worked days, applied himself nights, made his way through law school, and the first thing he did after graduating was legally change his name. Only thing is, he never divorced his first wife."

"Do you think Ruth knows?" Mel asked.

"No and that's what made it an even better secret," Ardis said. "She thinks she married Homer Leroy Wood, Esquire. A regular Jimmy Carter or Atticus Finch."

"So we have to hurt her in order to finish this?" Thea asked.

"Homer," Mel said. "Homer hurt her. And he killed Emmett to keep his secret. And Max to plug the new hole. And, wait, did he kill Nicki, too?"

"That was an accident," I said. "Homer was right. The snakes were a warning to me so I'd forget blackmail, forget murder, and stop asking questions. Nicki was in the wrong place and completely unlucky."

"Sweet Jesus," Mel said. "Call the cops, Kath."

"But don't bother the 911 operator, dear," Ernestine said. "I have Cole Dunbar's personal number."

Chapter 37

Clod, of course, was overjoyed to hear from me. I was calm and polite and explained clearly and objectively what we'd decided it was safe to tell him—that we'd stumbled across important evidence in Emmett Cobb's murder and it was essential that he hop in his car and drive through the storm to see it for himself. We'd decided not to say we knew *who* killed Emmett. Just in case. The "just in case" covered a number of worries ranging from legal to paranoid. I thought I put it all rather well. But Clod was still having trouble getting past the nose thing, even though we'd interacted without further damage just the evening before. Ernestine heard the way it was going and took the phone from me.

"Cole Dunbar. This is Ms. O'Dell. You come on over here. Yes, now. Thank you, dear." She handed the phone back to me. "He was in my Sunday school class for more years than he'd like to remember, bless his heart."

"I think we should put everything but the binder and Homer's envelope back in the newel post," Ardis said. "In case Cole wants to search the place or search us. He won't think to look there."

"He wanted to know where we were stumbling around when we stumbled across the evidence, though," I said. "What should we tell him?"

"Under the window seat," Geneva said. "Emmett kept jigsaw puzzles there."

"Really? He did jigsaw puzzles?"

Strange looks from the others. Dang. I kept forgetting my friend wasn't their friend.

"Ha-ha," I laughed lamely. "I mean, can you imagine a jigsaw-puzzle-doing blackmailer? Anyway, he kept puzzles in the window seat. We can say we found the binder and envelope there."

We slipped the other envelopes back into the newel. The cap went on more easily than it had come off, taking only a few good thumps from Mel's and Thea's fists.

"I'll burn them or shred them tomorrow," I said.

"But don't you wonder what's in Joe's envelope?" Thea asked.

"No," Ardis said. "Lead us not into temptation. Shred them, then burn the shreds." She gave the cap a final thump.

"And to deliver us from evil," Geneva called from the kitchen, "here comes Emmett's card friend."

This time I remembered to wait for the knock before going to open the door. Then I hurried to let Clod in out of a renewed onslaught of rain and wind. Except it wasn't Clod on the doorstep. It was Homer.

"Now *that's* what I call a gun," Geneva said.

Chapter 38

"Cole didn't say there were so many busybodies involved," Homer said when he had the six of us standing at gunpoint in front of the fireplace. He looked less like a hawk then, and more like a vulture or a carrion crow. "This is more awkward than shooting only one or two, but never mind. We'll make do. No, Kath, keep your hands where I can see them. It's too late for the 911 call you should have made instead of calling Cole. That decision was good luck for me and stupid of you. He and I were playing our Saturday night poker game and I overheard the gist of your call. He told me the rest. Then he received a call about downed wires, which trumped yours, and here I am. It's somewhat ironic, too, as we used to play our games here with the idiot Emmett."

"Oh, you're in a fine mess, now," Geneva said. She floated back and forth behind Homer. "And he called darling Em an idiot. How rude."

I almost said, "Shhh," but changed my mind. "You thought Emmett was an idiot, Dewey? Really?"

"Blithering. And you're no better. I want you all to know, you can thank Kath for the predicament you're in. I told her to have no further contact with Cole Dunbar. She didn't listen. I told her not to involve herself, not to mention blackmail to anyone else. Now you'll all pay the price because she did not listen. And that poor young woman. Was her name Nicki? That was unnecessary, Kath. The snakes were a warning for you. If you had listened, if you had been smart and listened to me, your friend Nicki would still be alive."

"But, Dewey, getting back to Emmett, how stupid was he if he found out you're a complete fraud?"

"Kath, what are you doing?" Ardis whispered.

I wasn't sure, but Geneva became more agitated every time Homer maligned Emmett.

"He called himself a reformed alcoholic," Homer said, "but he wasn't reformed enough to resist the doctored bottle of gin I left for him. How smart was that? He was weak and he was stupid. He could have poured that bottle down the drain."

Geneva billowed behind him. If the others could have seen her they would have been impressed and trembly in the knees instead of looking at me like I might be crazy.

"So it's Emmett's fault he died that horrible way? Gasping, eyes bugging out, retching, vomiting, right up there in his own bed? You killed Emmett, but it's his fault? Dang, Dewey, I thought darling Em was your friend."

"Emmett Cobb was shit."

Geneva looked like a thunderhead. Lightning flashed, making her glow.

"Sorry, Dewey, I didn't hear you over the thunder."

"He was stinking mule shit."

I waited two heartbeats. "But still better than you, right?"

"Emmett Cobb was . . ."

He might have howled the rest of that sentiment, but I didn't hear anything beyond my pounding heart. Geneva heard him, though, and she'd heard enough. Lightning struck again, thunder crashed, and she, a pulsing tornado green, surrounded Homer. He couldn't see her to know what was happening, but he must have felt her intense chill. Confused, he took his eyes from me for just an instant too long. I grabbed the poker, swung it wide and connected with the side of his head like the wrath of God and Hammerin' Hank Aaron.

The gun went off as he fell and shot a hole in the newel post.

Chapter 39

It wasn't completely hunky-dory after that.

Clod arrived about the same time as the ambulance. The others clamored to tell him what they had heard and seen happen. They weren't entirely sure why Homer had suddenly lost his concentration, but they were willing to believe I'd done something clever. They repeated Homer's confession and his intent to kill us. Ardis and Ernestine gave Clod the envelope and the binder. Joe wandered in at some point with a nod to his brother. Mel and Thea asked if I'd join their softball team. I stood by feeling sick and watching without contributing. None of that was really unexpected. Debbie's reaction surprised me, though.

"You deliberately egged him on," she said, jabbing her finger at me, then turning to Clod. "She used us as bait. It's a wonder he didn't shoot us all where we stood. It was unforgivable behavior. She should be arrested for endangerment."

"Good for you, Ms. Rutledge," Clod said, "making friends left and right."

Mel purposely stepped on Clod's foot as she and Thea gathered Debbie, her purse, and her coat, and took her home. There was an awkward silence after they left. Ardis filled it.

"Darling Em?"

I shrugged. "Bit of ad-lib. Deputy Dunbar, do you have any more questions? If not, and if you all don't mind, I'd like to call it a night."

Dunbar was looking through the binder. That created another awkward moment when Ardis, Ernestine, and I looked at one another, simultaneously realizing there was a hole in our story and one of the characters in that hole was standing there with us. We looked at Joe. He caught the uneasy vibe showing plainly on our faces.

"What've you got there, Cole?" he asked.

"Record Emmett kept." Clod turned pages, nodded, didn't look up. "Makes interesting reading. All these names. People he was taking money from. Had himself a regular industry. But you didn't find any other envelopes? Just the one with Homer's name on it?" He looked up then. Glanced at Joe. Looked at us. We shook our heads. "Well, I'm guessing old Emmett was smart enough to get rid of any other information he collected after he dug up Homer's dirt. Probably burned it in the fireplace there. That's what I'd do." He closed the binder and tucked it and the envelope under his arm. "So, no, Ms. Rutledge, there might be more questions later, in a day or two, but I believe that's all for now. Ms. O'Dell, do you need a ride home?"

They left together. Before I shut the door I heard Ernestine asking Clod if he'd like her to drive. Thunder rumbling and echoing between the mountains kept me from hearing his response. I'd hoped Ardis and Joe would follow them out the door, but they'd invited themselves into the parlor. Ardis was laying wood for a fire. Joe admired the bullet hole in the newel post.

"No time like the present," Ardis said.

"You're right." I picked up the shovel. Joe backed away. I sighed. "I'm really not a violent or angry person," I said to no one in particular. No one commented. And then I wondered. Where was Geneva? Not in the parlor. I handed the shovel to Joe and went back to the kitchen. Then up the stairs at a trot. Nowhere.

"Kath, honey?" Ardis called.

"It's nothing," I said, going back down. "I thought I heard something." I hadn't. I just wanted to. "Let's burn the envelopes. Then I'm going to bed." I took the shovel back from Joe, pried the cap off the newel, and pulled out the envelopes. "Would you like this one?" I held out the envelope with his name. He didn't move to take it. "We didn't open it."

"Burn them all," he said.

Envelopes full of papers, like books, take longer to burn than people tend to imagine. But I made myself be patient as we fed them, one at a time, into the flames. Ardis pulled a chair over. Joe and I sat on the floor. We were silent at first, staring into the flames. Then the steady rain and the crackling fire worked their magic, lighting our dark spaces, drawing us in.

"I thought you might join us this afternoon, Ten," Ardis said.

"Sorry to miss the excitement. I was curious about Carlin and the snakes and I went to find him. Wasn't easy. Carlins know how to disappear."

"Curious about what?" I asked.

"Turns out the snakes were his. Carlin's been working off his debt to Homer and Homer said the snakes would make them even. Carlin swears he had no idea what Homer planned. He seemed awfully friendly with them last night, though, and that got me wondering. After he left here he took off for some land he's got down by Newport. Says his dream is to be a forest ranger. I don't know if there's much chance of that."

I fed another envelope into the fire, thought about dreams and lives going up in smoke. "Do you think Ruth had any idea about Homer?"

"I don't see how," Ardis said.

"I can't imagine what she's going through right now," I said.

"She's going to need good friends to stick by her."

"We can do that," Joe said.

"What are we going to do with the Cat, now, Kath?" Ardis asked. "It's not really we, though, is it? I've been putting off thinking about it, but the reality is I can't swing a loan by myself. So what are *you* going to do with the Cat?"

"Be a shame to lose it," Joe said.

"It's a shame to put her on the spot like this, too." Ardis stood up, breaking the spell of the flames. "Forget I asked, honey. It's getting late and we're all tired. We'll both have time to think and talk before you go back to Illinois."

Joe waited until I put the last envelope on the fire, and then he got up, too. I was glad Ardis had saved me from laying my own dream out in front of them. She hadn't wanted me as an absentee owner of the Cat. I wasn't sure yet if she would accept the idea of me as owner in residence.

"What are you looking at, Ten? Did we leave one behind?" she asked.

I spread the last of the fire out with the poker, then looked around. Joe was peering into the newel post.

"It's not an envelope, but something's still down there at the bottom. The bullet hole's letting in a smidge of light." He reached his long arm in, looking up at the ceiling as he fished. For a second, it looked as though something up in the corner of the room caught his eye, but when I turned to see what, nothing was there. He brought his arm out and handed me a folded square of paper. "Maybe it fell out of one of the envelopes?"

"Maybe." But it looked older. It was a heavyweight paper and not brittle. I unfolded it and read aloud:

Finished this house this day for this family
My dear wife and our dear children
Elihu Bowman
29th April 1853

"Cool," Joe said. "May I?"

I hardly noticed him take the paper from my fingers. "Bowman?" I said, and listened. Then I turned around and listened again. "Geneva Bowman?"

"No, it says Elihu," Joe said. "And where do you suppose he came from? I thought all this property was owned by Holstons. Since time immemorial. What do you think Ruth will make of this?"

"Tell you what," Ardis said. "Let's not shake her or anyone else up too much more right now, especially not tonight. Sound good?" She was looking at me. That might have been mild concern drawing her eyebrows together.

"Sounds good," I said. "Joe, you're the new caretaker. Do you want to hold on to the note or put it back in the newel?"

"I'm only here temporarily. The newel's done it well enough for the last hundred and sixty years."

He refolded the paper, laid it back in the bottom of the post, and put the cap back on. I followed them to the door, thinking about hiding places. There was a hiding place at the Weaver's Cat I still needed to find.

"You open at one tomorrow, Ardis?" I asked. "I'll be in and we'll talk."

"Kath, oh, Kath," she said, swallowing me in a honeysuckle hug, then letting me go. "Good Lord, we've had a few of them, but tomorrow is another day."

"Yep," Joe said, "and probably a good one to go fishing."

"This rain won't bugger it up?" I asked. We listened to more thunder moving in.

"It's always buggered up somewhere," he said. "Then you just go somewhere else."

He opened the door to another flurry of wind. As they dashed out, heads lowered against the pelting rain, a blur of half-drowned fur streaked in.

"Gah!"

The blur skittered across the kitchen and disappeared around the corner. I looked after Ardis and Joe. Gone. I looked toward the living room. Only a muddy streak across the floor proved what I'd seen. Rain was blowing in, but I left the door open. One or the other of us was going to need an escape hatch. Ready to scream again, I followed the muddy trail, sorry the poker was once again holstered with the other fireplace tools.

In the chair Ardis had left near the fireplace, sat a bedraggled, mud-spattered ginger cat, fastidiously licking a front paw as though that simple act was the obvious and complete solution to everything that troubled the world. The cat looked up when a floorboard under my foot squeaked.

"Meow," it said calmly, clearly meaning, "Oh, hey, how are you?"

"Do you think it's a good idea for you to be in here?" It did.

Chapter 40

I still didn't know who he was, but he was curled up beside me in bed the next morning. Purring. He was purring, that is. I was lying there listening to him, amazed, and dozily following the threads dangling in my head. I wondered how Ruth was holding up . . . if I wanted to make the huge transition and move to Blue Plum . . . if I could sit down at Granny's tapestry loom and weave her Blue Plum tapestry myself . . . if Angie would be gracious about losing the house . . . what Shirley and Mercy would say when they found out I didn't need whatever they'd found . . . if Ernestine needed a new job and if she'd like to work at the Weaver's Cat . . . how Maggie was getting along with Joe . . . who this cat belonged to . . . why it liked me . . . if it had fleas . . . if Geneva's last name was Bowman and where she was. She hadn't come back. I didn't wonder how Homer was because I didn't care.

"Meow?"

"There isn't much. Do you like tuna noodle casserole for breakfast?"

It turned out we both did.

"Who's this?" Ardis unlocked the door for us before the Weaver's Cat opened.

"Meow."

"I don't know," I said. "That's all he'll tell me. He's kind of like a dog, though. He follows me everywhere."

"He's got a bald patch. Does he have mange? And why does some of his fur stick up like that?"

"Cowlicks?"

The cat jumped up on the counter and purred for Ardis.

"Where did he come from?"

"Out of the storm. Joe says there aren't any ginger cats at the Homeplace."

"Oh, you talked to Joe, did you?" She had a glint of speculation in her eye.

I scritched the cat's head and ignored the glint. "I'll ask around, take him to the vet, see if he's microchipped."

"Will you take him back to Illinois?" Her voice was even and her face impassive, but the effort it was taking for her to appear calm, while only just approaching the subject of the shop's future, was obvious in her rigid hands.

I brushed a bit of orange fur from the sleeve of my beautiful indigo jacket, put my hands over hers, took a deep breath, and leapt. "Ardis, I lost my job and I want to move here and run the Cat with you. Do you think that will work? Will you teach me what I need to know? Do you think we should offer Ernestine a job because she won't be working for Homer anymore? If the cat behaves, can it come to work with me the way some of Granny's used to?"

She answered yes to all my questions with tears running down her face. The cat and I left her alone to pull herself together before it was time to open the doors to customers, and we climbed the stairs to Granny's space under the eaves.

"Are you any good at finding hiding places?" I asked. "By the way, what's your name?"

"Meow."

"That answer is no help. What are you looking at?"

The cat jumped onto the window seat and sat as though facing someone who might offer to rub his chin.

"He is an unusual cat, so he needs an unusual name," a voice said. And as I watched, Geneva appeared.

"I was afraid you were gone. Are you okay?"

"Why? What did you imagine could happen to me beyond being dead?" she asked.

"Um, I'm not sure. But I wanted to thank you. You saved our lives."

"I'm glad being dead is good for something."

"Where were you?"

"Around. I needed to be alone," she said.

"Mourning Em?"

"Mourning my idea of Em. He wasn't a good man, was he?" She sniffled.

"He didn't kill anyone, though."

"No. But I'm glad I have someplace else to go because I cannot bear to stay in that tainted house any longer."

"Oh?"

"Yes. I could hardly bear waiting until we got in your rental car and came back here."

"Here?"

"Yes. Larry and I will be very happy here."

"Larry?"

"I named the cat Larry," she said.

"And who says you get to name him and since when is Larry an unusual enough name for an unusual cat?"

"Do you know any other cats named Larry?"

"I'm not calling him Larry."

"You could try."

"No."

"Once?" she coaxed.

"No."

"But, still, I can stay here, can't I?"

I looked at her, nestled comfortably in the window

seat next to the unusual cat who tolerated both of us. The cat made happy eyes as it watched us arguing. I sat down in Granny's chair and put my feet up on her desk, as she'd done so many times. I looked around the snug room, wondering where I'd look first for her private dye journals and what I'd do with them if I found them and what Ardis would say if she heard the question I was about to answer.

"Geneva, we can all stay."

Rosemary Watermelon Lemonade

This lemonade is gorgeous and absolutely delicious!

INGREDIENTS

> 2 cups water
> ¾ cup white sugar
> 1 sprig rosemary leaves, chopped
> 2 cups lemon juice
> 12 cups cubed, seeded watermelon

Bring the water and sugar to a boil in a small saucepan over high heat. Stir in the rosemary and set aside to steep for 1 hour.

Strain the rosemary syrup into a blender. Add a third of the lemon juice and a third of the watermelon. Cover, and puree until smooth. Pour into a pitcher.

Puree another third of the lemon juice and watermelon. Add to the pitcher and repeat with the last of the lemon juice and watermelon.

Stir the lemonade before serving. Hold your glass to the light and marvel at the beautiful color.

Rosemary Olive Oil Cake with Dark Chocolate

Preheat oven to 350° F.

Line a 9½-inch springform pan with parchment paper.

INGREDIENTS

¾ cup whole wheat flour
1½ cups all-purpose flour
¾ cup sugar
1½ teaspoons baking powder
½ teaspoon salt
3 eggs
1 cup olive oil
¾ cup milk (2% or reconstituted nonfat dry milk is fine)
1½ tablespoons fresh rosemary, finely chopped
5 ounces semisweet, bittersweet, or a combination of the two chocolates, chopped into ½-inch chunks
1½ tablespoons sugar to sprinkle on top for crispy crunch

Mix the first five ingredients in a large bowl and set aside.

In another large bowl, beat the eggs. Add the olive oil, milk, and rosemary and beat again.

Fold the wet ingredients into the dry, gently mixing until just combined. Stir in two thirds of the chopped chocolate, reserving the other third for the next step.

Pour the batter into the prepared pan. Sprinkle the remaining chocolate and the 1½ tablespoons sugar over the top.

Bake 40 minutes or until a toothpick inserted in the center comes out clean. At this point the cake will be pale.

Run the cake, still in the pan, under the broiler to caramelize the sugar—browning the crown and giving the cake a nice top-crunch. Watch the cake carefully while it's under the broiler.

Eat warm, cooled, or cold. The cake will keep—leftovers? Ha!—wrapped in plastic.

Thea's Red and White
Baby/Toddler Hat

Designed by Kate Winkler. Designs from Dove Cottage.
Designed for Molly MacRae's Last Wool and Testament.
19" finished circumference at bottom

MATERIALS

Worsted-weight yarn, 100 yards each of two colors
16" circular and double-pointed needles, US 8 (5mm)
or size needed for gauge
Stitch marker
Tapestry needle
Gauge: 20 st = 4 inches in stockinette.

Using circular needle and Color A, cast on 97 stitches.
Being careful that the stitches are not twisting around
the needle, knit the FIRST stitch you cast on, then pass
the LAST stitch you cast on over it. Place marker on
needle to mark the beginning of the round. You have 96
stitches.
　　Work K1 P1 ribbing for 1.5 inches.

Change to Color B.
　　Round 1: K
　　Round 2: K into the stitch of Color A below the first
stitch on the needle*; K normally to end of round.
　　Rounds 3-8: K
*This will make the stripe line up without a "jog."

Change to Color A.
　　Round 9: K

Round 10: K into the stitch of Color B below the first stitch on the needle; K normally to end of round.

Rounds 11–16: K

Repeat these 16 rounds once more. Your hat should be about 5.5–6 inches from the cast on edge. Continuing with color stripes, shape top, changing to double-pointed needles when necessary.

Decrease Rounds:

Round 1: *K10, K2tog, repeat from * around—88 stitches.

Round 2: K around.

Round 3: *K9, K2tog, repeat from * around—80 stitches.

Round 4: K around.

Round 5: *K8, K2tog, repeat from * around—72 stitches.

Round 6: K around.

Round 7: *K7, K2tog, repeat from * around—64 stitches.

Round 8: K around.

CHANGE COLOR AS BEFORE

Round 9: *K6, K2tog, repeat from * around—56 stitches.

Round 10: K around.

Round 11: *K5, K2tog, repeat from * around—48 stitches.

Round 12: K around.

Round 13: *K4, K2tog, repeat from * around—40 stitches.

Round 14: K around.

Round 15: *K3, K2tog, repeat from * around—32 stitches.

Round 16: K around.

DO NOT CHANGE COLOR

Round 17: *K2, K2tog, repeat from * around—24 stitches.

Round 18: K around.

Round 19: *K1, K2tog, repeat from * around—16 stitches.

Round 20: *K2tog around—8 stitches.

Break yarn and thread through remaining stitches with tapestry needle. Draw up snugly and fasten off on inside. Weave in all ends.

If you like, top the hat with a pom-pom or tassel using either color or both.

Read on for a sneak peek of

Molly MacRae's next
Haunted Yarn Shop mystery,

coming from Obsidian in summer 2013.

"Where are the lambs?" Ernestine asked when she and I caught up to the rest of the group at the pasture fence. "Did Kath and I dawdle too long? Have they already run off to play?"

"Oh, sorry, Ernestine," I said. She was spry for being nearly round and almost eighty, but I'd been sure I was doing her a favor by walking slowly down the farm lane with her. As it turned out, she'd been the one waiting for me because I couldn't help stopping to take pictures along the way. She kindly hadn't complained, but now I felt bad because we'd expected to see Debbie's new lambs frisking in the field. "Did we miss them?"

"No, they're with their mamas," Debbie said, "at the far end, over there under that beech tree." She pointed across the hillocky field.

Not knowing much about lambs or their mamas, I wasn't surprised they weren't hanging around at the fence waiting for us. Debbie seemed puzzled though, and it was her farm and they were her sheep, so I mimicked her scrunched nose and stared across the field where she pointed. I could just make them out standing in a white huddle under a huge tree.

Ernestine put her cheek to Debbie's extended arm, using it and Debbie's index finger as a sight and squinting toward the sheep, her thick lenses flashing in the sun. Her head barely reached Debbie's shoulder. Concentrating and leaning into her squint the way she did, and dressed in a gray sweater and slacks, she looked like an ancient mole trying to bring the world into better focus. She wasn't as blind as a mole, but she probably didn't see the tree, much less the sheep, at that distance.

Thea and Bonnie, the other two women with us, had already gotten tired of straining to see the sheep. Thea, in jeans and a Windbreaker, climbed up and sat on the fence. Bonnie was checking her phone for messages.

"I don't get it," Debbie said. "Usually they'll come see if I've brought treats. And the lambs are always curious. But I don't think they've even noticed us."

The five of us, all members of the needle arts group Thank Goodness It's Fiber (TGIF), had met up that morning at Debbie Keith's farm, Cloud Hollow. Thea and Ernestine had been smart and carpooled with Bonnie, letting her navigate the half dozen winding miles up the Little Buck river valley from Blue Plum, our small town in east Tennessee. I'd driven out alone, arriving last and feeling as though I'd made it despite rather than because of Debbie's directions, which included the near-fatal phrase "and you can't miss it."

We'd all been looking forward to spending the morning in Debbie's studio. She was going to teach us her techniques for dyeing yarn and wool roving by "painting" them. Unfortunately, in her flurry of preparations, Debbie had locked the key to the studio inside it. She'd called her neighbor across the river, who kept an extra set of keys for her. The neighbor said she'd drop the keys off on her way to town, and we'd decided to make the most of our wait by walking down the farm lane to visit the new lambs. But, as we saw, the lambs and their mamas were otherwise occupied.

"Can't you call them?" Thea asked. "Whistle for them or something?"

"Not at this distance," Debbie said. "I'm not loud enough. And that's not really how sheep work, anyway."

"See, Bonnie?" Thea said. "I told you—that's what Bill is for."

"I know what a sheepdog is for," Bonnie said. "But dogs in general don't like me, except to bite, so I don't like them back. And I make it a point to never give them the chance to bite in the first place. No offense intended, I hope you know, Debbie, but I am much obliged to you for putting what's-his-name in the house."

Debbie, still looking at the distant flock, waved off Bonnie's thanks.

I was pretty sure I heard a muttered "Wuss" from Thea, but Bonnie, farther down the fence and engrossed in her phone again, didn't catch it.

Bonnie pocketed her phone with a disgusted noise. "The morning's turning out to be a complete bust, though," she said. Ernestine tried to shush her but Bonnie continued grousing more loudly than seemed polite. "Driving the whole blessed way out here and trying to find this place was bad enough, but now we're standing around in wet grass and accomplishing absolutely nothing."

"But isn't it a beautiful morning for getting nothing done?" Ernestine asked.

No one could argue with that. It was the kind of gorgeous spring day in the foothills of the Blue Ridge Mountains that looked like the inspiration for an Easter card. The world smelled of fresh breezes. Also of the wild onions I was standing on. I stepped back from the fence and took a picture of the grassy lane we were in and another where the lane disappeared around the next hill. Then I snapped a few candids of the other women.

Thea, sitting on the top fence rail, was a tempting target. Her orange Windbreaker was stretched across her broad back, making her look like a giant pumpkin perched on the fence, her brown head making the stem. I skipped that picture, though. Thea was our town librarian and defied all stereotypes associated with that position except two—she was single and she had more than two cats. But she was far from being hushed and, in fact, called herself the "beautiful, black, loud librarian," and I knew she'd be loudly unappreciative of a picture taken of the particular view I had in my lens.

Ernestine and Bonnie stood farther down along the fence, with Ernestine distracting Bonnie's grumbles by asking about her winter in Florida. Ernestine's white hair became a dandelion nimbus as she turned her wrinkled face toward the sun, eyes closed behind her thick glasses. She was retired after holding a number of jobs, most recently as receptionist for my late grandmother's lawyer. She had a dry sense of humor and although her eyesight was failing, she saw the good in people and frequently apologized for their shortcomings.

I'd met Bonnie for the first time that morning. The only things I knew about her were what I'd just been hearing—she'd returned from Florida the week before, she was a gung ho spring, summer, and fall member of TGIF, and she didn't like dogs. She also seemed to be expecting a phone call or expecting someone to answer a call she was trying to put through. And she wasn't exactly patient. At a passing glance, she looked to be on the good side of fifty. But after studying her face and hair in my viewfinder, I suspected she was closer to the upper end of sixty and had a hairdresser and possibly a plastic surgeon under orders to fight for every year they could gain.

Debbie stood at the fence, a hand shading her eyes, staring across the field toward her sheep. With her blond braid down her back she could have been a Norse maiden scanning the horizon for sails. My grandmother liked to say Debbie looked as though she'd stepped out of one of Carl Larsson's nineteenth-century Swedish watercolors.

Debbie worked part-time at the Weaver's Cat, the yarn shop in Blue Plum that had been Granny's pride and passion up until her death six weeks earlier. The shop was mine now, which made Debbie my employee but, truthfully, she and the shop's longtime manager were still "teaching me the stitches" of owning and running the business, as they liked to say.

At the shop, Debbie tended toward long skirts and embroidered tops, hence Granny's Carl Larsson comment, but that morning she was wearing farm-sensible jeans, a navy blue fisherman's sweater that brought out the blue of her eyes, and a great pair of red tartan rubber boots that I coveted. She had four or five inches on me, though, and was strong enough, so I'd heard, to toss a bale of hay or hold a sheep between her knees for shearing, so I didn't plan to try to wrestle the boots off her feet.

Framing each face in my camera, I realized we were a nice range of ages. Debbie was in her early thirties, I'd turned thirty-nine the month before, Thea was an honest mid-forties, Bonnie could cover both fifties and sixties for us, and Ernestine capped us out with her nearly eighty years. I snapped another picture of Ernestine smiling at Bonnie, who was showing her the size of something by holding her hands out and looking from one hand to the other, maybe telling Ernestine a Florida fish story. Thea turned and I was able to get a picture of her pretty face in profile.

"I know what the sheep are doing," Thea said. "It's Monday-morning book group. They're reading *Three Bags Full* and making plans. You need a smart brown sheep out there to be the ringleader. I'll let you name her Thea."

"I've been thinking about trying a few Icelandic sheep," Debbie said. "The color variations are really nice and they're supposed to be unusually intelligent."

"Well, there you go," Thea said. "Get yourself a set of

twins and call the other one Queen Latifah. I'm sure we'll both be fine with that."

Debbie nodded and said, "Mm," but didn't look as though she'd really heard Thea. "Hey, Kath, have you got a zoom on that camera?"

"Oh, yeah, probably. Good idea." The camera was new to me, one of several I'd inherited from Granny, and I hadn't played around with all the features yet. I fiddled with the adjustments, held the camera up, and fiddled some more before finding the beech tree and the sheep in the lens. "Okay, got them."

"What do you see?" Debbie asked.

"Sheep. And . . . something? Nope—they shifted for a second but now they're not budging. They're standing with their backs to us."

"Well, I think I want to go out there and see what's going on with those girls," Debbie said, still staring across the field. "That's so unlike them. Anyone want to come with me?"

"Sure." I looked at the others. They might have come prepared for playing with pots of dye, but Debbie, Thea, and I were the only ones wearing anything on our feet suitable for crossing a wet pasture.

"Come on, Thea. We'll go with her," I said.

"Sorry, no." Thea shook her head. "Mud, maybe, but these shoes don't do ewe poo."

"You two go on and round them up," Bonnie said. "We'll stay here holding up the fence and cheering you on."

The others laughed and Debbie and I climbed over and started across the meadow. The sun felt as yellow as the patches of buttercups and warmed every delicate shade of green in the fields and woods around us. A flock of clouds meandered high above in the soft blue sky. The mud and the ewe poo were mostly avoidable. But through the camera's zoom I'd caught a glimpse of something under the beech tree that wasn't right. From the behavior of the sheep, Debbie knew something was up, too, but from her own behavior I didn't think she had any idea what. She was a fast walker, and I skipped to catch her.

"Debbie, I need to tell you—"

"Look at them, would you?" she said. "It's like they're standing in a prayer circle. They don't look scared, though. I hope one of them isn't hurt." She walked faster.

"It isn't a sheep."

"Sorry, what?" She didn't slow down.

I grabbed at her arm. "It looked like a person."

Debbie turned her head, nose wrinkled. "What?"

"Well, I'm probably wrong. I got only a quick look when a couple of the sheep moved and it was hard to tell. Wow." We'd gone about three quarters of the distance from the fence to the sheep under the tree and not only was the size of the tree more amazing the closer we got, but the sheep—my goodness. I'd been picturing a flock of Mary's little lambs—petite things prancing and nibbling grass, maybe, but certainly not what I was seeing, which was more along the lines of a herd of St. Bernards. I couldn't help but repeat myself. "Wow. You know, I thought sheep were shorter than that."

"They're Cotswolds."

"That makes them big?"

"Yup, Cotswolds are big," Debbie said. "The older ewes weigh a hundred eighty, a hundred ninety pounds. If your boots don't have steel toes, try not to get stepped on."

I wondered how I'd avoid that if the whole flock turned and suddenly came at me. Did sheep do that?

A couple of the lambs heard us and finally decided we were more interesting than whatever the herd was still engrossed with. They galloped toward us, very cute with their spindly legs and wagging tails even if they were taller than I'd expected. Debbie stopped and greeted them by name. I was brave and went a bit closer to see over the backs of the mamas. And immediately wished I hadn't.

"Debbie?"

She was down on one knee making goo-goo noises to her babies.

"Debbie? Hey, Deb. Debbie! These sheep need you." That brought her head up. "And we need the sheriff." It was probably too late for an ambulance.

I hadn't known how sad sheeps' eyes could look. Debbie's flock stood like woolly mourners around two bodies at the base of the beech tree. Debbie, good shepherdess that she was, checked first to see if any of the animals were hurt. Then, when she was sure they were uninjured, she reacted.

"Ohmygodohmygodohmygodohmygod." She stared at the dead man, who looked as though he'd been cradling the dead woman in his arms. "Ohmygod. What's he *doing* here?"

"You know him?"

She nodded, unable to speak, and started to shoo the sheep out of the way.

I stopped her. "Leave them, if they'll stay. They make a good screen so the others back at the fence can't see."

She looked back toward the road, wide-eyed. "Oh my god."

"Do you have your phone? Can you call 911? Debbie!"

She whimpered but pulled her phone out. Then she stopped and stared again. "Are you sure they're dead?"

How could they not be? The woman, young and pretty and fallen sideways from the man's arms, had two wet, red blossoms in the middle of her chest. The man, not much older, his head fallen forward, had strands of blood drying at the corner of his mouth and his nose and a terrible hole in his right temple. A gun lay on the ground near his right hand.

"Make the call, Debbie, and stay here. I'll see if there's anything, any—"

I pushed between two of the sheep and knelt beside the bodies in the hope of finding a pulse. I reached toward the woman, stopped, then made myself touch her wrist and push aside the blond hair to feel the side of her neck. Cold. Cold. She was gone. He was gone, too.

But when my hand fell away from him it brushed against his sweater and an immediate twist of love and unbearable sorrow jolted me. I looked at my hand as though it should somehow be glowing. Of course, it wasn't. Tentatively, I laid the tips of my fingers on his sleeve again. How could they feel what they were feeling? I moved my fingertips to the woman's pullover and a rush of terror knocked me back on my heels.

I worked hard to swallow a scream, control my breathing. Worked to explain away the transferred emotions. It was delayed shock. It was my overactive imagination. It was the incongruence of finding violent death in this field of buttercups and new lambs. It was not, could not be, what my beloved and possibly delusional grandmother had written in the letter she'd left for me to read after her death. It wasn't any kind of special talent or ability or anything to do with hidden secrets. It wasn't.

"They're coming."

I looked up. Debbie pointed at her phone. I stood up, rubbed both hands on my jeans, scrubbing all sensation from my fingertips—pushing the memories of love, sorrow, and fear into what I hoped was an unreachable corner of my mind. "What did they say we should do?"

Debbie stood staring, arms hanging at her sides. She'd let her phone slip from her hand. I picked it up. "Are we supposed to stay here? Debbie?" I looked at the phone.

She'd shut it off. I looked at her. She was shutting off, too. "Okay, come on. Let's go back to the road." I started to take her by the elbow but pulled my hand back before I touched her. "Come on."

She started walking with me, but turned to look back at the tree and stumbled.

That time I did grab her elbow and was relieved when I didn't feel anything more than her trembling arm. We stood for a moment, and I continued holding on to her but I was afraid I was losing her.

"Debbie, did you warn the dispatcher about the sheep?"

"What?"

"About how big they are and about how the sheriff's people need to be careful to not let them step on their toes?"

Debbie shook her head as though she didn't quite believe how foolish the words coming out of a city girl's mouth could be. She didn't answer me, though, and looked back toward the tree again.

"Or what if the sheep are startled by the uniforms or the shiny badges and charge at the cops? Because, you know, those sheep really are big." I didn't need to see Debbie's face that time to know I did sound completely idiotic, but at least I'd prodded her mind in another direction.

"They'll be fine."

"The sheep, too?"

She made an impatient noise.

"Well, good. So come on, we can go back to the road and the sheep will be okay and the police will be okay. But are *you* going to be okay? The guy—was he a friend? Who is he?"

She turned and started across the field toward the road again. The sheep, their vigil disturbed, followed us in single file.

"I know both of them," she said. "His name is Will.

That's Will Embree." Tears ran down her cheeks but her voice was steady. "And, Kath, this is so awful. That's Shannon Goforth."

I shook my head. "I'm sorry. I don't think I know who either of them is."

"You must have heard of Will Embree. Or, I don't know, maybe you haven't. There was some stuff happening at Victory Paper a couple of years ago that he got mixed up in and blamed for. There were protests and he was one of the protesters and it got real ugly."

I remembered reading about it. Ugly was right. And deadly. Granny had sent me the articles from the *Blue Plum Bugle*, but it made the national news, too. Victory Paper International ran a pulp and wood product mill on the Little Buck, farther up in the mountains above Blue Plum, near the North Carolina border. The company had been accused, numerous times over the years, of causing massive fish kills in the river. The company always denied responsibility, pointing to reports from its own and from state and national inspectors. It had also denied responsibility for the odiferous brown foam that floated down the river from time to time. There wasn't anything unusual, as far as I could remember, about the back and forth of accusations and denials. The concerns for the river were reasonable and the corporate response typical.

What I'd enjoyed reading about in the *Bugle* articles were the odd and odiferous misfortunes that befell Victory Paper. One misfortune involved graffiti depicting dead fish—hundreds of bloated, belly-up fish painted on the outside walls and windows of the mill, and on just about anything else within range of a can of paint, including dozens of fish on each of the company vehicles. The artwork had taken a lot of time and a whole lot of paint. In a festive touch, the empty spray-paint cans had been hung like ornaments from a tree inside the security fence surrounding the plant. The pictures in the *Bugle* were great.

The odiferous misfortune involved a quantity of brown organic matter of unspecified but hinted-at origins. It was left on company doorsteps. Once or twice a week. For months.

But then there'd been another fish kill and local environmental groups staged a couple of raucous protests at the mill, surrounding it on all sides, with people up in trees and on the river in canoes and kayaks, and *in* the river, too, in wetsuits and fishing waders. It was the kind of thing I'd like to have witnessed and maybe taken part in. Had Granny been younger, I think she would have been one of the first up a tree or in the water.

"Some guy died, right?"

Debbie nodded.

"He drowned, didn't he? But they decided it wasn't an accident." And the guy the authorities were sure did it had taken off into the mountains and no one had seen him in the two years since. It was a sad story for everyone involved. "I'd forgotten all about that."

"Will didn't kill anyone," Debbie said, her face tight.

"Wait—you mean that's him? That's *the* Will Embree back there? Good Lord. What's he doing here?" I realized I'd echoed Debbie's words from when she first saw him. Except her words had sounded different somehow. "That guy didn't look like someone who's been hiding out in the national forest for two years." He didn't. He was clean-shaven with trimmed hair. His jeans were worn and his sweater pilled and faded, but he had on new-looking running shoes. He looked more like a poor graduate student than a mountain man on the run. And when had I noticed all those details? "How did you recognize him?"

She didn't answer, and slowed our already-slow pace, then stopped. "We're going to have to tell the others, and

I don't think I can. No, I know I can't. I can't. No. Oh-mygodohmygod." Her voice had started low and urgent but ended in that string of rising babble. Before it reached hysteria, I squeezed the elbow I was still holding. Maybe too hard, but squeezing it was less obvious than a slap on her cheek and just as effective. She closed her mouth and yanked her arm away.

"Sorry, Debbie. But it's going to be okay. You don't have to say anything. I'll tell the others there's been an accident and we're waiting for the police. That's all they need to know and they'll be okay. And then the workshop will be good for everyone—don't you think? It'll be color therapy. Are you still up for it? What colors have you got for us? Aw, and look at that." I pointed at the sheep. "The lambs are following us to school. So come on." I took her elbow again and urged her toward the fence and the other women.

I was practically babbling by then. Of course, we weren't going to continue with the workshop. And if Debbie had set out pots of red dye for us, she'd probably have thrown up when she'd looked at them. But I hoped my yammer would act as a dampener to drown out her thoughts. It didn't, though.

"You don't understand." She pulled away from me. "That's Shannon Goforth back there." Again she said the name as though it should mean something to me. "Bonnie Goforth's daughter."

"Bonnie Goforth's daughter," I repeated, shaking my head, still clueless.

A couple of the older lambs pranced past us and up closer to the fence. Thea hung over the top rail with a handful of grass. Ernestine reached between the rails with her handful. Bonnie had climbed right over and into the pasture. And then the name clanged into place.

"*Bonnie's* daughter? Oh my God."

Amanda Lee

The Embroidery Mysteries

The Quick and the Thread

When Marcy Singer opens an embroidery specialty shop in quaint Tallulah Falls, Oregon, everyone in town seems willing to raise a glass—or a needle—to support the newly-opened Seven Year Stitch.

Then Marcy finds the shop's previous tenant dead in the storeroom, a message scratched with a tapestry needle on the wall beside him. Now Marcy's shop has become a crime scene, and she's the prime suspect. She'll have to find the killer before someone puts a final stitch in her.

<u>Also available in the series:</u>

Stitch Me Deadly
Thread Reckoning
The Long Stitch Goodnight

**Available wherever books are sold or at
penguin.com**
facebook.com/TheCrimeSceneBooks

Juliet Blackwell

In a Witch's Wardrobe
A Witchcraft Mystery

Lily Ivory is living her dream of owning a vintage
clothing store—and practicing magic on the side.
But when she encounters a sinister sleeping spell,
Lily comes face-to-face with a nightmarish evil…

"Extraordinarily entertaining."
—*Suspense Magazine*

Also available in the series

Hexes and Hemlines
A Cast Off Coven
Secondhand Spirits

**Available wherever books are sold or at
penguin.com**

facebook.com/TheCrimeSceneBooks

Coming soon

Melissa Bourbon

Deadly Patterns

A Magical Dressmaking Mystery

Bliss, Texas, is gearing up for its annual Winter Wonderland spectacular and Harlow is planning the main event: a holiday fashion show being held at an old Victorian mansion. But when someone is found dead on the mansion's grounds, it's up to Harlow to catch the killer—before she becomes a suspect herself.

**"Harlow Jane Cassidy is a
tailor-made amateur sleuth."
—Wendy Lyn Watson**

<u>Also available in the series</u>
A Fitting End
Pleating for Mercy

Available wherever books are sold or at
penguin.com

facebook.com/TheCrimeSceneBooks

OM0081